# The Darkest Sin

D. V. Bishop is the pseudonym of award-winning writer David Bishop. His love for the city of Florence and the Renaissance period meant there could be only one setting for his crime fiction. The first book in the Cesare Aldo series, *City of Vengeance*, won the Pitch Perfect competition at the Bloody Scotland crime writing festival and the NZ Booklovers Award for Best Adult Fiction Book. It was also shortlisted for the Wilbur Smith Adventure Writing Prize. Bishop was awarded a Robert Louis Stevenson Fellowship while writing that novel. He teaches creative writing at Edinburgh Napier University.

'A great insight into Renaissance Florence. What I love about these books is the seamless weaving of factual history with a great story' — Abir Mukherjee

'Bishop builds the suspense well, masterfully connecting the disparate strands of the story . . . Given the quality of the first two novels about Cesare Aldo, this series could become essential reading for fans of the historical novel' — *Crime Fiction Lover*

'Impressive' — *Literary Review*

'History, mystery and the eternal mystique of Renaissance Florence in perfect harmony!' — *Lancashire Evening Post*

'Cross-dressing, torture, oodles of violence – this pungent example of historical noir has the lot' — *The Times*

'A complex, intriguing plot which weaves its way through the treacherous streets of sixteenth century Florence, encountering danger at every dark corner' — Sarah Maine

'In Cesare Aldo, Bishop has created a character with the cunning, bravery and balls of steel to take on the twisty, toxic politics of the Medicis with panache. I can't wait for his next outing' — Alison Belsham

'This atmospheric murder mystery is packed with political intrigue and questionable morality. Secrets and conspiracies abound, danger is ever present and tension rises within the complex plotting' — *Choice*

# The Darkest Sin

D. V. BISHOP

PAN BOOKS

First published 2022 by Macmillan

This paperback edition first published 2023 by Pan Books
an imprint of Pan Macmillan
The Smithson, 6 Briset Street, London EC1M 5NR
*EU representative:* Macmillan Publishers Ireland Ltd, 1st Floor,
The Liffey Trust Centre, 117–126 Sheriff Street Upper,
Dublin 1, D01 YC43
Associated companies throughout the world
www.panmacmillan.com

ISBN 978-1-5290-3884-2

5 7 9 8 6 4

A CIP catalogue record for this book is available from the British Library.

Map artwork by Hemesh Alles

Typeset by Palimpsest Book Production Limited, Falkirk, Stirlingshire
Printed and bound by CPI Group (UK) Ltd, Croydon, CR0 4YY

MIX
Paper | Supporting
responsible forestry
FSC® C116313

Visit **www.panmacmillan.com** to read more about all our books
and to buy them. You will also find features, author interviews and
news of any author events, and you can sign up for e-newsletters
so that you're always first to hear about our new releases.

*For Ruth Bishop,*
*20.2.1938–26.10.1988*

*Most people, on beginning a task which looks fine at first,*
*cannot see the poison that is hidden in it.*

Niccolò Machiavelli, *The Prince*
translated by W. K. Marriott (1908)

# SENIOR NUNS OF
# SANTA MARIA MAGDALENA

**THE ABBESS**
*Leader of the convent*

**THE PRIORESS**
*Deputy to the Abbess*

**SUOR GIULIA**
*Apothecary, maker of remedies*

**SUOR FIAMETTA**
*Sacrist, keeper of vestments &
books*

**SUOR CATARINA**
*Teacher of boarders & visiting
girls*

**SUOR SIMONA**
*Infirmarian, the convent healer*

**SUOR ANDRIANA**
*Draper, runs the laundry*

**SUOR BENEDICTA**
*Listening nun for the visitors'
parlour*

**SUOR PAULINA**
*Almoner, dispenses alms to the
needy*

**SUOR VIOLANTE**
*Younger sibling of the prioress*

# NOVICES OF
# SANTA MARIA MAGDALENA

*Maria Vincenzia*
*Maria Celestia*
*Maria Teodora*

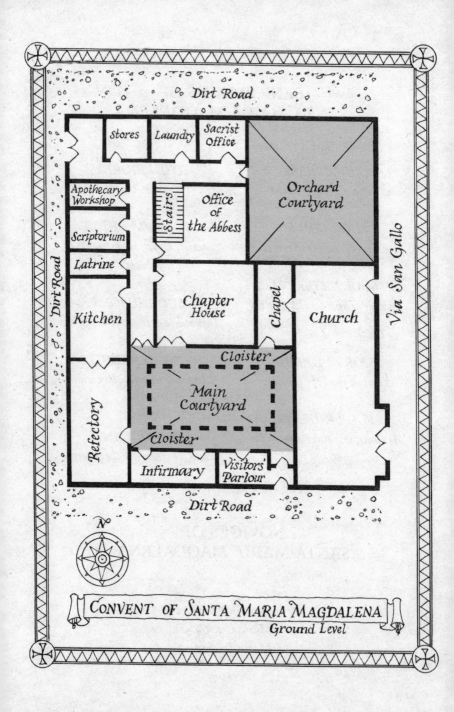

Dirt Road

Stores | Laundry | Sacrist Office

Apothecary Workshop

Scriptorium

Latrine

Stairs

Office of the Abbess

Orchard Courtyard

Kitchen

Chapter House

Chapel

Church

Via San Gallo

Dirt Road

Cloister

Main Courtyard

Refectory

Cloister

Infirmary | Visitors' Parlour

Dirt Road

N

CONVENT OF SANTA MARIA MAGDALENA
Ground Level

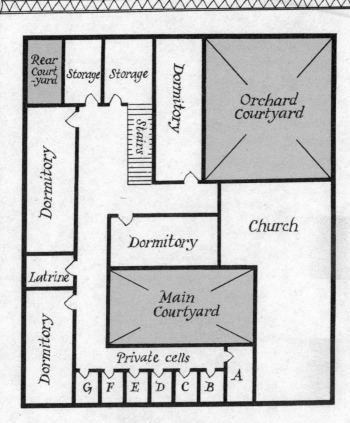

A   The Abbess
B   Suor Paulina, the Almoner
C   Suor Andriana, the Draper
D   Suor Giulia, the Apothecary
E   Suor Fiametta, the Sacrist
F   Suor Benedicta
G   Suor Violante

CONVENT OF SANTA MARIA MAGDALENA
Upper Level

### Statement by Cesare Aldo,
### officer of the Otto di Guardia e Balia:

I was at the visitors' parlour of Santa Maria Magdalena on a personal matter when I heard a scream from inside the convent. It was shrill, the sound of shock and horror. Another voice cried out: 'Murder! Murder!' The internal door of the parlour was opened as a nun ran past, her face stricken. 'Blood, there's so much blood—' Her words stopped, I do not know why.

I persuaded a young woman staying at the convent to let me into the main courtyard. I was familiar with the interior, having come to Santa Maria Magdalena on court business the previous day, Palm Sunday. Nuns were gathering at the north-west corner of the cloister. Several were comforting a novice who had blood on both her hands. She was trembling, her face ashen. I later learned she had made the initial discovery.

The novice directed me inside, saying what she found was on the left.

I went through the doors, passing entrances for the convent kitchen and a latrina. The third door on the left was ajar, the smell of fresh blood strong in the air, but the floor around the entrance was clean. I pushed the door open. Inside was the scriptorium where nuns copy and illuminate holy texts. Unlit candles stood on each desk next to brushes and pots of ink. A single lantern hung from the ceiling, its light revealing the bloody mess below.

I was not surprised that the novice had screamed.

*A body was sprawled across the stones, naked and bathed in blood. More blood spread out from the corpse, pooling across the floor. I cannot recall having ever seen so much around a single body. There were numerous stab wounds, at least a dozen to the chest and torso, but it was the face that had suffered most. This had been a frenzied attack, a work of hatred.*

*One more thing about the naked corpse discovered inside the convent caught the eye.*

*It was male.*

## Chapter One

### Sunday, March 25th 1537

*L*iving in a *bordello* spared Cesare Aldo from religion most Sundays. While most of Florence went to church, Signora Tessa Robustelli and her women stayed in bed recovering from the night before. Once Mass was concluded, men would soon return to the humble building at Piazza della Passera, south of the Arno. But this was Palm Sunday, the first day of Holy Week. Special Masses were taking place across the city to celebrate one of the most important times in the Church year, with many parishes holding processions to mark the day Jesus entered Jerusalem. If there was one thing Robustelli could not resist, it was a procession.

'Clodia! Elena! Matilde!' she shouted as Aldo came downstairs. 'We haven't got all morning!' The buxom *matrona* was wearing her finest brocade gown, a blue shawl draped across her bosom in a rare show of modesty. 'I'd like to see the procession this year!'

'Coming, signora!' playful voices chorused above, between giggles.

Robustelli eyed Aldo's plain tunic and hose. 'I take it you're not joining us.' She pointed to the stiletto tucked in his left boot, its hilt visible beside his calf. 'Father Anselmo doesn't approve of his flock bringing blades to church.'

3

'Father Anselmo approves of very little,' Aldo replied, 'but I doubt anyone will bring a blade to Mass.' Carrying weapons had been banned in Florence since Cosimo de' Medici replaced his murdered cousin Alessandro as the city's leader in January. Cosimo had not yet seen eighteen summers, but he was no fool. He remained vulnerable until his election as leader was confirmed by the Holy Roman Emperor, Charles V. An edict restricting weapons within the city certainly lessened the likelihood of an armed uprising by those eager to see Florence return to being a republic. Only those enforcing the law, Cosimo's own guard and the city militia were allowed to carry weapons. Being an officer of the Otto di Guardia e Balia, the most feared criminal court in Florence, meant Aldo could retain his trusty stiletto. He was grateful for that. The blade had saved his life more than once.

'Are you coming or not?' Robustelli asked.

'Not today. I'm due at the Podestà.'

The *matrona* nodded, her attention shifting to a young woman bouncing down the stairs. 'No, Clodia, that won't do. Go and cover yourself properly.'

'Why?' Clodia pouted. Her nipples pressed against the thin lace of her flimsy top, demanding attention. 'I'm proud of my body. Why do I have to hide it?'

'Because we're going to church,' Robustelli replied, 'not an orgy.'

Leaving them to argue, Aldo stepped out of the *bordello*. It was not yet mid-morning, but the sun was already touching the stones of Piazza della Passera. The days were getting longer, and warmer too. Aldo breathed in, savouring the aroma of bread baking in some nearby oven. It had been a hard winter, but spring had come early this year, bringing fresh life to the city. It was a pleasure to be alive.

Aldo strode away, heading east. Warmer days meant less pain from his unreliable left knee, so it had no need of remedies or salves.

But he still cut north into via dei Giudei, the narrow street where most of Florence's small Jewish community lived. A door stood open among the houses on the left, beckoning him into the home of Doctor Saul Orvieto. How easy it would be to go inside. Aldo missed Saul, his warm hazel eyes, the ease of their friendship. But they had parted on bad terms, sundered by duty and bloodshed.

Better to keep walking. Safer for both of them.

At the end of via dei Giudei Aldo turned east again, striding towards Ponte Vecchio. This approach to the bridge was usually crowded with the stalls selling fish, vegetables and fruit. After a long, barren winter the produce was inviting again, no more frost-bitten brassica or wizened citrus. But this was Sunday, the Lord's Day, when most shops and stalls were shut. Palm Sunday processions elsewhere helped to make Aldo's progress brisk.

Aldo marched up the steady rise of Ponte Vecchio, pausing at the bridge's highest point where a gap between buildings allowed a view of the river. The water was mottled with *merda*, dyes and other liquids that drained into it from workshops. Florentines threw almost anything into the Arno. Even corpses went in the water sometimes, victims consigned to the river by those eager to banish the proof of their crimes. If a killer was lucky, or the current strong enough, a body could float miles downriver before eventually washing ashore. But most got caught on the weirs between bridges, giving river rats a chance to feast on the rotting flesh until the remains were pulled out. Aldo turned away from the Arno with a shiver.

After leaving the bridge he cut a ragged path north-east, careful to avoid larger piazze where processions were gathering before Mass. He reached the Palazzo del Podestà early, the forbidding brick fortress looming ahead of him, its stone bell-tower pointing at the sky. In a city full of beautiful buildings, the Podestà was an ugly brute, all sharp edges and glowering menace. That outward appearance matched its inner workings as home to the Otto. Little of beauty occurred within these walls. The few windows facing out were too high to offer any respite in the bleak stone. The fortress had stood for hundreds of years, and doubtless would remain for hundreds more. From here laws were enforced and those found guilty of breaking them faced judgement from the Otto's magistrates.

Inside the Podestà was an imposing courtyard, a wide stone staircase running up one wall to the *loggia* that led to the court's administrative area. A cold breeze chilled Aldo even as he paused next to the one wall touched by the sun. It was always cold inside the Podestà, regardless of the month. But Aldo's unease stemmed from the men he saw at the top of the stairs: Bindi and Ruggerio. No good ever came of them sharing words.

Massimo Bindi was *segretario* to the Otto. In theory that made him simply the court's administrator, a bureaucratic functionary whose sole purpose was to assist the magistrates. But the Florentine practice of replacing the entire bench every few months meant the *segretario* was the court's most powerful constant, able to wield considerable influence over rulings. Magistrates came and went but the bloated Bindi remained. Every day Aldo had to report to Bindi, and every day it darkened his mood.

The *segretario* was a self-serving creature who clutched his power in a clammy fist, but the man opposite him was far more dangerous. Girolamo Ruggerio was a silk merchant, among the leaders of that powerful guild, and a leading figure within the Company of Santa Maria, a confraternity with considerable influence in the Church. More than that, Ruggerio was a cunning creature capable of having anyone he deemed a threat destroyed. A few months before, Ruggerio learned a young lover had written of their trysts in a diary. The youth was beaten to death on Ruggerio's orders. When an investigation by the Otto came close to identifying Ruggerio, he made the men who had killed for him confess. They did so without hesitation, yet kept his secret safe. Such was the power Ruggerio wielded. Blood never touched his hands – he was too clever for that.

Aldo watched the *segretario* bow low, not easy with a belly so rotund. Ruggerio had no direct authority at the Otto, yet Bindi could not help giving way. It was sickening, but not a surprise. Ruggerio swept down the wide stone stairs, the morning sun glinting off his smooth and hairless scalp. Satisfaction twisted his thin lips into a smirk, while silk robes billowed around him, the rich blue fabric adorned with fine golden embroidery. Aldo gave a small nod as Ruggerio approached. 'Signor.'

The merchant paused two steps from the bottom to look down on Aldo. 'Have we met?' Ruggerio asked. They had, but still the merchant forced Aldo to introduce himself. Everything was a joust with Ruggerio, a *stratagemma*.

'In January, when I helped find those responsible for the murder of a youth called Corsini. Two of your guards confessed to killing him,' Aldo said.

Ruggerio nodded, as if it were a distant memory, long forgotten. 'Ahh, yes. One died soon after in a prison brawl, while the other was left with the mind of an *idiota*.'

Aldo had been part of that brawl, the only one to escape with his life and wits still intact. No doubt Ruggerio knew that too. 'Le Stinche is a dangerous place. Full of criminals.'

'Quite.' The merchant studied Aldo a moment longer before descending the final two steps. 'I believe the *segretario* had a matter for your attention. I hope you will pursue it with the same vigour and fortitude as you do other matters.' Ruggerio strolled away, leaving Aldo to ponder the threat behind that farewell. A shout from above demanded his attention.

'Come to my *officio*,' Bindi called, gesturing him up the stairs. Aldo grimaced. How little it took to sour a beautiful spring day.

Ponte a Signa had been Carlo Strocchi's whole world when he was a boy. It didn't matter that a much bigger town was just across the Arno, over the same bridge that gave Ponte a Signa its name. And he didn't care about the boats coming downriver from Florence, taking cargo west towards Pisa. Strocchi hadn't been interested in either city then, not when everyone he cared for was in the small village nestling by a bend in the river.

True, Ponte a Signa was little more than a huddle of simple houses and dirt roads, but that was enough. There were several large palazzi up in the hills, owned by merchants who only came in the scorching summer months to escape the city. The rest of the year their grand houses stood empty, villagers trudging up the hill to clean empty rooms or tend the unappreciated gardens. To Strocchi, the palazzi seemed to sneer at those below, judging them. His friends often claimed it was possible to see all the way to Florence from the palazzi – Strocchi hadn't cared. Ponte a Signa was enough for him.

That changed the week his papa died, collapsing in the garden behind their humble home. Father Coluccio gave Papa the last rites, and he slipped away that night. Strocchi had seen only seventeen summers; now he was the man of the house. But he had no talent for farming, and no siblings to help tend their rented field. Three years of hard work brought only diminishing returns. The land couldn't support Mama and him, not the way it had when Papa was alive. Strocchi admitted defeat after a spring flood took their meagre crop. Reluctantly, he left home, walking to Florence in search of work, promising to send coin whenever he could.

That was a year ago. Now Strocchi was coming home for his first visit. But as the constable got close, he almost didn't recognize Ponte a Signa. It looked so small. A few drab buildings clustered beside the Arno, the houses crumbling and neglected, dirt roads overgrown by weeds. This was where he'd had so many adventures as a boy. It had been a happy place for the most part, a community of friendly folk who smiled when they met.

Now the village looked wizened, broken. Desolate. Not at all how Strocchi had described it to his travelling companion. They had ridden from Florence on a hired horse, before entrusting the animal to the local ostler and walking into the village.

People in doorways glared at the new arrivals. Was that due to suspicion, or envy? Strocchi looked down at his clothes, at the new tunic he had bought before leaving Florence, eager to show he'd made a success of himself. The sin of pride coloured his cheeks. *Sancto Spirito*, what kind of welcome should he expect from Mama? He had been a good son, sending home all the coin he could spare, along with letters he struggled to write. Hopefully, Mama had taken those to Father Coluccio to read for her. Hopefully.

Strocchi rounded a corner and his mood lifted. The early spring flowers Mama grew every year were blossoming outside the house, their colours a joy to soften the hardest heart. The front door stood open, welcoming all. He could hear Mama humming inside, no doubt making a hearty Sunday stew, brought to life with torn shreds of basil and a generous splash of olive oil. Yes, there was the familiar smell, making his mouth water.

He was home.

'It's just like you described,' his travelling companion said.

Strocchi nodded, the smile returning to his face. 'Yes, it is.' They strolled on side by side, until Strocchi stopped a few paces short of the door. 'Would you mind if I went in first? I haven't seen Mama for so long, and—'

'Of course. I'll wait out here. Call me when you're ready.'

'Thank you.' Strocchi took a deep breath and ventured in. He paused at the doorway, letting his eyes adjust to the darker interior. Should he knock? No, that was foolish. This was still his home, even if he'd been away for a year. 'Mama? Mama, it's me – Carlo.'

'Carlo?' The sound of her voice was so warm, so welcoming. Strocchi hadn't realized how much he had missed her. It was an urgent tug at his chest, a pull so strong his eyes were brimming and his chin trembling a little.

'Yes, Mama,' was all he could say.

She appeared from the kitchen, wiping both hands on her apron, those sharp blue eyes staring at him. Then she flung out her arms and they were hugging and sobbing and laughing, all at the same time. Mama took his face in her hands and kissed him, tears of joy spilling down her rosy cheeks. 'My *bambino* is home! My boy, my boy, come back at last! Oh, how I've missed you, Carlo. Things haven't been the same since you left. Why didn't you send word you were coming? I would've made your favourite, if I had known.'

She stepped back, looking him up and down. 'Don't they feed you in the city? You're nothing but bones, *bambino*. What have you been eating?' Mama reached forward, rubbing the material of his new tunic between thumb and fingers. 'Spending all your coin on clothes. Since when did you become fond of such finery?'

Carlo laughed. He had been gone a year, was now a constable for a powerful court in Florence, and yet nothing had changed. He still couldn't get a word in.

'What's so funny?' she demanded, a playful twinkle in her eyes.

'I suppose you think your old mama is not good enough for you now?'

'No, Mama.'

'Quite right,' she said, grabbing hold of his hands. 'Come into the kitchen and tell me all about the city. Now that you're back, I want to hear everything—'

'Mama, wait.' Strocchi stopped her before she could go any further. 'I sent coin, and letters by messenger. They swore on the Bible each one reached you. Didn't you get them?'

She nodded. 'Yes, yes. I put the coin in a pot, up on the high shelf in the kitchen, you know the one. It's waiting there for you, all of it.'

'No, the coin was for you, Mama. To help you.'

She frowned. 'Why would I need help? I have all I need, now my *bambino* is home.'

'Well, did you take my letters to Father Coluccio?'

'The first few, yes. But I didn't like to bother him.'

More likely she was embarrassed at having to ask the parish priest to read them for her. As if Father Coluccio didn't do that for other villagers already. Strocchi had feared she wouldn't ask for the priest's help. It meant she hadn't heard what was in the latest letter. Strocchi guided her to a chair. 'Mama, please, sit. There's something important I need to tell you.'

'I don't need to sit—'

'Please, Mama.'

She huffed and puffed, but did as he asked. Strocchi gathered his courage. 'I've come back to visit for a day or two, but I'm not staying. I'll be going back to Florence soon.'

'Oh.' Mama's face fell. She had no time for guile or falsehood, never had, so she made no attempt to hide her disappointment. 'Well, at least you're here now. That's something.'

'Yes. And there's something else.'

Mama's gaze slipped past Strocchi to the doorway. Someone was standing there, framed in the bright morning sunshine. 'Can we help you?'

Strocchi went to the doorway, taking the visitor's hand, guiding them inside. 'Mama, I want you to meet someone. This is Tomasia.'

The young woman bowed her head a little, showing the proper respect. 'Signora Strocchi, it is an honour to be in your home. Carlo has told me so much about you.'

'Has he? I'm sorry, my dear, but I know nothing about you.'

Strocchi gave Tomasia's hand a squeeze. 'She hasn't heard about our news.'

'Oh.'

Mama folded her arms. 'Carlo, who is this stranger?'

He hesitated before replying, struggling to find the right words. 'Tomasia is . . . my wife.'

Mama Strocchi fainted dead away.

## Chapter Two

*B*indi waddled across his *officio* to the imposing desk, squeezing himself into the sturdy, high-backed chair behind it. A pox on men like Ruggerio who treated the Otto as if it were something to be used when it suited their purpose, then cast aside afterwards. The court worked in the service of the city and its people, not as an investigating militia for wealthy individuals. Yet that was what the merchant expected.

Ruggerio had been far from coy about the consequences if his request was not met. One of the current magistrates was among Ruggerio's guild brethren, while another was a junior member of the same confraternity as Ruggerio. If either of them should suggest that the Otto replace its *segretario*, Bindi's position would be in considerable peril. If both sought his dismissal, he would never find another post in Florence.

To be humiliated with such a threat was bad enough; to have it happen here, inside the Podestà, that was almost beyond forbearance. But Bindi would bear it, because he must. Men such as Ruggerio rose to power by accumulating influence over others. When they fell from grace, their descent came far faster – and was far more satisfying for those they had trodden underfoot. Bindi's father had not been much of a man, but one of his sayings stayed with the *segretario*: watch the Arno long enough, and you will see the body of your enemy float by. So it would be with Ruggerio, and Bindi intended being there so he could witness that. The sooner, the better.

There was a knock at the door. Bindi waited his usual three breaths before replying: 'Come!' Aldo entered, closing the door after himself before approaching the desk.

'You wished to see me, *segretario*?'

Bindi found Aldo irksome. There was little to fault in the officer's work or conduct. He was quick of wit, a shrewd judge of what motivated people, and had proven himself able to solve matters few others serving the Otto could untangle. The lines beneath Aldo's eyes and the greying hair at his temples were evidence of his many summers. Still Aldo kept himself lithe of body and swift of hand, when many his age had become bloated or drunken, slaves to their baser instincts. Yet there was something about Aldo that Bindi could not abide:

The *segretario* never knew what Aldo was thinking.

Aldo stood silent and still in front of the desk, his features giving no clue as to what was occupying him. It was an apt ability for an officer of the court, enabling Aldo to pass unnoticed almost anywhere. But that same skill unsettled the *segretario*, as if he was being judged by the steady gaze of those ice-blue eyes. Bindi longed to slap the casual assurance from Aldo's face. Perhaps the task set by Ruggerio would achieve that instead.

'What can you tell me about the convent of Santa Maria Magdalena?' Bindi asked.

Aldo frowned, hesitating before he replied. 'I . . . Very little, *segretario*.'

Bindi savoured the moment. It was not often that Aldo lacked an answer.

'I do know it's in the northern quarter,' Aldo continued, 'near via San Gallo. There are a dozen convents in that area, but Santa Maria Magdalena is among the newer ones.'

Bindi ground his teeth together. 'Anything else?'

'Some convents benefit from the charity of a confraternity. In the case of Santa Maria Magdalena, I believe it shares an allegiance with the Company of Santa Maria.'

The *segretario* forced a smile. 'I thought you could tell me very little?'

Aldo gave a slight shrug. 'My last statement was speculation, but a reasonable deduction from your question and Signor Ruggerio's visit.'

'You're correct,' Bindi conceded. 'The Company of Santa Maria makes charitable gifts to the convent, but certain members of that confraternity are concerned. There has been a report of male intruders scaling the convent's walls the night before last. The confraternity fears for the safety of the godly women within the convent, and wishes to see them protected.'

'That sounds like a task for a constable,' Aldo said. 'If these reports are correct, the night watch could be directed to make regular patrols past the convent walls.'

'Are you telling me how to do my job?' Bindi asked, letting steel into his voice.

'Of course not, *segretario*—'

'Perhaps you have ambitions to replace me one day?'

Aldo shook his head, falling silent.

A wise choice.

Bindi leaned back, forming his fingers into a steeple. 'Go to Santa Maria Magdalena, and find out if these intruders made it inside. Strictly speaking, convents are not within the Otto's jurisdiction, but the confraternity wishes to be reassured that all is well. Besides, Signor Ruggerio asked for you by name.'

The shadow that fell across Aldo's face was quite delicious.

'Did Signor Ruggerio reveal the source of this report about intruders?' Aldo asked. 'It would be helpful to have a direct account of what happened.'

Bindi smiled. 'I'm sure you can reasonably deduce that yourself.'

Aldo nodded, for once not bothering to hide his anger. 'Was there anything else?'

Bindi shook his head, letting Aldo get all the way to the *officio* door before speaking. 'Actually, there was one other matter. Have you learned anything further about Cerchi?'

'No *segretario*,' Aldo replied. 'A few citizens claimed to have seen him since he disappeared in January, but none could offer any proof. They probably heard he was missing, and hoped there might be a reward. Our patrols have found no trace of him within Florence, and none of the city gates have a record of Cerchi leaving. But he might have slipped out without being noticed by any of the guards.'

Meo Cerchi had been absent from the Podestà since disappearing a few days after the feast of the Epiphany. Like Aldo, Cerchi was an officer of the Otto, but the two shared few other similarities. Cerchi was a blunt weapon, blessed with animal cunning and brutality, but not much more. He and Aldo were frequent adversaries, driven apart by their differences in attitude and approach. Bindi had deliberately chosen Aldo to lead the search, knowing he would not lack the motivation to find and humiliate Cerchi. But even the Otto's best investigator had been unable to solve this mystery.

'Is that what you think happened?' Bindi asked. 'Cerchi left the city?'

Aldo remained impassive. 'If he was still in Florence, we would have found him by now. If he had died here, I would have expected his body to be uncovered. Bearing all of that in mind, I do not believe Cerchi is still in the city.'

The *segretario* recognized the sense of this. 'Very well. Go and visit this convent. Bring back a full report. No doubt Ruggerio will also want to hear what you have found, but tell me everything you discover first. Understood?'

Strocchi got his mama into a chair while Tomasia fetched a damp cloth and a cup of wine from the kitchen. This was what he had hoped to avoid. Sending word ahead should have given Mama time to become used to the idea. But this – this was not part of his plan.

Mama's eyelids fluttered open. 'Carlo? Is that you?'

'Yes, Mama.'

'I must have been asleep. I had the strangest dream –' She stopped, noticing Tomasia standing beside him. 'Who is this?'

'My name is Tomasia Strocchi. Carlo and I were wed just before Lent.'

Strocchi held his breath, fearful of Mama's response. To his surprise, she smiled.

'My dear, it's a pleasure to meet you!' Mama rose, pulling Tomasia into an embrace. 'Let me look at you. Let me see the young woman who has won my *bambino*'s heart!' She stepped back, taking in Tomasia.

Strocchi looked at his wife, trying to see her as Mama would. Tomasia was two summers older than he was, with dark hair down to her shoulders. She was a handsome woman, with an oval face and an olive complexion. Tomasia had known more than her share of hardship, and that left a watchfulness in her eyes. But when she smiled, as she was doing now, her face blossomed in a way that quickened his heart – and his blood.

'Oh, but I'm not surprised he married you,' Mama said, beaming at Tomasia. 'You're quite beautiful. Carlo always did have an eye for the girls, didn't you, *bambino*?' Mama pinched his left cheek between her thumb and fingers, giving it a squeeze.

'Please, Mama, you're embarrassing me.'

'Nonsense! What kind of mama would I be if I wasn't proud of my only *bambino*?' She let go of his cheek and slipped an arm round Tomasia's shoulders, guiding her through to the kitchen. 'So, tell me, how did you two first meet?'

Tomasia gave a panicked glance back at Strocchi. 'Ahh, well . . .'

He hurried after them. 'It was on the street in Florence,' Strocchi said, choosing his words with care. 'She stepped out of a doorway, and I knew I had to introduce myself.'

That was all true, but it was not all of the truth. The doorway Tomasia had stepped from was that of Le Stinche, the city's prison. She had been held there for failing to pay debts left by her dead brother. Cesare Aldo arranged for her release after Tomasia helped him while he was being wrongly held inside, but Strocchi was the one sent to pay off her debts. She emerged from the prison, and in that moment his heart was lost.

'Let her tell the story,' Mama protested, gesturing for Tomasia to sit opposite her at the kitchen table. 'Please, my dear, speak.'

Tomasia smiled. 'It was January. I was looking for somewhere to stay when we first met, and Carlo offered me his bed.'

Strocchi saw Mama's eyes widen, and hurried to explain. 'We didn't share the bed, Mama. I was leaving the city for several days, helping one of the officers search for a fugitive. I knew my room would be empty, and I didn't want to think of a good, God-fearing young woman having to stay on the streets overnight in the worst of winter.'

'So Carlo gave me the key to his room,' Tomasia said, with a grateful smile. 'That kindness, his kindness – it probably saved my life.' She gave his hand a squeeze.

Mama was watching them together. Strocchi held his breath. Once Mama made up her mind, nothing in Heaven could change it. If she disapproved of their marriage, he didn't know what they would do. Strocchi closed his eyes, offering up a silent prayer.

'And what do your *famiglia* think of all this?' Mama asked Tomasia.

'I have no *famiglia*,' she replied. 'Not anymore. My brother died a year ago, he was the last. Since then I have been on my own.' Tomasia smiled at Strocchi. 'Until I met Carlo.'

'My *bambino*,' Mama said. 'He's always had a good heart. If he loves you – and I can see that he does – then I'm sure I will love you too, Tomasia.' She threw out her arms. 'Come and give your mama another hug. Come, come!'

Tomasia got up and the two women embraced again, not as though they had just met, but as if they were being reunited after years apart. Strocchi realized he was crying. He wiped the tears away before either woman could tease him.

'Such a shame you got married in the city,' Mama sighed once she and Tomasia had stepped apart. 'I should love to have been there, to see my *bambino* wed.'

'Blame me for that,' Tomasia said, leaning forward to whisper in Mama's ear. 'We wanted to have our wedding night as soon as we could.'

Mama gasped and slapped Strocchi's hand from across the table. 'You little *diavolo!*'

Strocchi did his best to look innocent, but what Tomasia had said was true. Indeed, on their way to the village Tomasia had said she might be with child. But Strocchi did not regret their haste in getting married for a moment. Baby or no baby, he had never been so happy.

'But you must still have a blessing here in Ponte a Signa,' Mama went on. 'I'm sure Father Coluccio would be delighted to give you that, both of you.' She nudged Tomasia. 'The parish priest has known our *bambino* since the day he was born. It was Father Coluccio who baptized you, Carlo, so it's only right he blesses your wedding, yes?'

Strocchi found it all but impossible to resist Mama. She had a way of saying things so it sounded as if they were questions, yet the answer was always whatever she wanted. 'Yes, Mama, but we're only here for a day or two. I have to get back to Florence as soon as I can, otherwise the *segretario* will not be happy. Besides, Father Coluccio will be busy with the Palm Sunday services today; it doesn't seem fair to impose on him.'

'Impose? *Bambino*, he would be hurt if you didn't ask. The last service of the morning will have finished. Why don't you go and see him?'

'Now?'

'Of course,' Mama replied, laughing. 'When else?'

Strocchi rose from his seat. 'Very well. Tomasia, are you ready?'

Mama shook her head. 'No, *bambino*, your beautiful new wife is staying here with me. I want to get to know her better. This is the perfect time.' She slipped her hand inside Tomasia's, gripping it tight. 'We have so much to talk about, don't we, my dear?'

Tomasia nodded, a smile fixed on her face. Strocchi knew that look of panic in her eyes, but there was nothing else to be done. He gave her a kiss, and a peck on Mama's cheek before leaving. 'I'll be back before you know it,' he promised on the way out.

'Don't hurry on our account,' Mama called after him.

Strocchi made the sign of the cross as he left.

* * *

The prioress rose from her pew as Palm Sunday Mass ended. The nuns of Santa Maria Magdalena had their own chapel in the church, and their own entrance from the adjoining convent. It meant they could pray and worship without being seen by anyone else. If the convent followed this path in all matters, the prioress would be far happier. She believed the convent would be better enclosed, had believed it since she first took the veil and had adopted Suor Ortenza for her name as a nun. Many summers later she became the prioress of Santa Maria Magdalena, and stopped using the name Ortenza, but her beliefs remained the same.

The prioress was second only to the abbess within the convent walls. She had influence and importance, but was also required to show loyalty. This did not sit easily, not when the current abbess insisted the convent open its doors to the world, sharing what little it had with beggars and worse. The prioress had expected to be made Abbess when the chapter house voted five summers ago. She had already been prioress for ten summers by then, and had seen twenty more than her rival. But the old abbess urged from her deathbed that the convent remain at one with the world, and most of the nuns voted to confirm her last wish.

The prioress knew there were other reasons she had not been chosen. She did not suffer fools well and any convent had its share of the foolish. Those who took the veil were often devoted and godly, but there were also the unwanted younger daughters for whom a marriage dowry was not available. Some joined because no man would have them, others after becoming widows, and some because they lacked the imagination or wit to do anything else. They were often shown the sharp edge of the prioress's temper, much as she prayed for the strength to be tolerant. They had shared no wish to make her Abbess.

One other matter had been against the prioress: her younger sister, Violante. Siblings were not uncommon in convents. They could comfort each other in hard times, but Violante was another matter. Much of the time she remained in her private cell, a privilege usually set aside for those who held important posts. The prioress made an annual contribution to convent funds to have her sister sleep and pray away from the other nuns. It was better for Violante to be alone, better for everyone. But the fact that she had a private cell and rarely spoke to the other nuns had all counted against the prioress when the new abbess was chosen.

So for five summers the prioress worked alongside the new abbess, hoping to wear her down, to make her see the true path. But all that persuasion had fallen on ears which would not hear, all those arguments had been lost to eyes that could not see reason. The time for persuasion had passed. The abbess would be made to know sense, or to step aside.

The prioress watched the abbess departing the chapel, followed by those senior nuns who also believed in the convent remaining open to the world. The apothecary Suor Giulia stayed close behind the abbess, listening to the timid Suor Andriana whisper about whatever was occupying her today. Giulia must have the patience of a saint to tolerate such nonsense. Suor Paulina was next, the nun responsible for dispensing alms to the poor and sick of the parish. She was also acting as cellarer of late, after the death of her predecessor in that post. Paulina had a generous heart, but was even more generous when distributing the convent's provisions. Had nobody told her that being almoner did not mean giving alms to anyone who asked, whether or not they needed the help?

Last to leave was Suor Catarina, teacher to the girls in the guardianship of the convent, and those who came for lessons. She had a sharp mind, and often spoke in the chapter house that the convent played an important role by offering girls a place to learn. But Catarina had also objected to men being within the convent walls, such as when stone masons came to make repairs or a doctor was called to the infirmary. Of those who followed the abbess, Catarina was the one who appeared open to persuasion. Finding an opening was the challenge.

The prioress frowned. Enclosure was coming, whether the abbess and her disciples welcomed it or not. One day all convents would follow their true purpose, serving the Lord through prayer and contemplation, rather than helping those unwilling to help themselves. That day would come far sooner for Santa Maria Magdalena, if the prioress's prayers were answered. An anonymous *denunzia* sent to the archbishop had begun the process. Soon the convent doors would close for good. Then the abbess would have to stand aside.

'Prioress? Are you well?' The question came from Suor Fiametta, the sacrist of Santa Maria Magdalena, charged with keeping the convent books and vestments in good order. She had the pinched features of a woman who was always disappointed by others. It matched her manner – earnest, a stickler in many things, and quite without humour.

'Very well,' the prioress answered. 'Why do you ask?'

'You had a strange look on your face,' Fiametta replied. 'I was concerned.'

The prioress smiled. 'I was contemplating the days ahead. Come, let us return to the convent.' The prioress ushered Fiametta and the other nuns who favoured enclosure from the chapel. Better they not remain too long, it would arouse suspicion. The abbess was many things, but a fool was not one of them.

## Chapter Three

*A*ldo stalked north from the Podestà, both hands clenched into fists. *Palle!* Most days the petty indignities inflicted by Bindi could be ignored, childish games to be endured and forgotten. But the involvement of Ruggerio promised only one thing: trouble.

The merchant's reason for instigating this investigation was a lie, and a weak one at that. There were dozens of confraternities in Florence, companies of men who celebrated and venerated their chosen saint through good works and charity. Several of the confraternities helped to fund schools, while others contributed to orphanages or supported institutions such as the Foundling Hospital. Confraternity members were often seen processing through the city, distinctive emblems sewn into their robes. The more fervent members would flagellate themselves with whips of rope or leather, some doing so in public to show their bodies being purged of sin. This was Florence, after all. Doing good was not enough; it was even more important to be seen doing good.

Aldo counted any confraternity with Ruggerio among its senior members as suspect. The merchant had another motive hidden behind his tale of intruders scaling the convent walls, another reason why he wanted the Otto investigating Santa Maria Magdalena. Discovering that – and deciding how to act upon it – was the true test here.

Aldo marched towards the cathedral. High buildings lining the narrow road ahead hid the Duomo's terracotta bricks, but the closer Aldo got, the more crowded his path became. Why was everyone . . .? Of course. It was Palm Sunday. All streets near the cathedral would be choked with the faithful celebrating the start of Holy Week. Aldo considered pressing on, but forcing a way through the fervent throng held little appeal. He went east instead.

Bindi's other intervention was also vexing. Why couldn't the *segretario* accept Cerchi was gone and put a new officer in his post? The Podestà was a less poisonous place without Cerchi's insidious bullying, and the Otto would be better served by whoever replaced him. Aldo had hoped Strocchi might be chosen, though he would be young for such a post. The constable lacked the moral flexibility necessary to prosper in Florence, but showed plenty of promise as an investigator. Far more than anyone else serving the Otto, that was certain. But Aldo knew better than to suggest such a promotion to Bindi. The *segretario* had to believe such notions were his, and his alone, otherwise he would reject them out of wounded pride.

Aldo dismissed Cerchi from his thoughts and headed northeast towards the *ospedale* of Santa Maria Nuovo. It was an indirect path, but still quicker than facing the crowds around the cathedral. Very soon the Palazzo Medici, home to the city's new leader, loomed ahead. Aldo had played a small part in events that led to Cosimo being chosen. There was speculation the young Medici was little more than a figurehead with the real power in the hands of the Palleschi, a pro-Medici faction in the Senate. Aldo gave no time to such gossip. Cosimo was nobody's puppet. Anyone who thought him easy to manipulate had a harsh surprise waiting. Besides, Cosimo had his mother Maria Salviati close at hand to offer her counsel. She was a formidable woman, skilled in the ways of Florentine intrigues. Aldo considered himself fortunate to have emerged unscathed from his meetings with her. Maria had devoted ten years of her life to preparing Cosimo for the possibility of holding power. Now the city was his to command, she would ensure it remained so.

Aldo turned right after Palazzo Medici, marching towards the city's northern gate, Porta San Gallo. The buildings either side of the road became less grand, the three-level palazzi giving way to humbler homes of two levels, with wide stable doors below and living quarters above. Aldo skirted piles of horse dung, careful to avoid the channel of waste running down the centre of the street. Spring meant warmth and sunshine, life returning to Florence after the cold and wet months of winter. But it also brought the stench of piss and *merda* alongside more pleasing aromas. Sweat was sticking Aldo's tunic to his back when he reached the convents either side of via San Gallo. Which was Santa Maria Magdalena?

He found the church of that name first. Like many convents, the sisters of Santa Maria Magdalena shared their church with the surrounding parish. The church had a grand entrance on via San Gallo with the convent nestled behind it, away from the main road. Aldo found a plain, drab door to the convent on a side road. Nuns had little need of decoration, it seemed, and certainly not outside a building many of them might never leave in their lifetime.

Aldo walked round the convent to see if it had any other entrances, or obvious places where an intruder could scale the exterior. The convent was built on two levels, with plain stone walls that would offer limited assistance. There were a few windows, but most were on the upper level, narrow vertical slits with metal bars across them. No easy way in there. The back of the convent did have a sturdy set of wooden double doors, wide enough to admit a cart. Aldo peered through the narrow gap between the doors. A thick iron bolt secured them, with a heavy padlock for good measure. The only way to breach the convent without help from inside would be by climbing the walls . . . difficult, but not impossible.

Aldo studied the buildings opposite the rear of the convent. They were bleak houses of one and two levels. He doubted many summers had passed since they'd been built, yet the plaster was already crumbling. A wizened woman in a black headscarf was leaning from the shutters of one house, glaring at Aldo from the upper level. He gave her a nod, getting only a scowl in return. Ruggerio's tale of intruders attempting to climb the convent wall had to have come from somewhere. Those with little to do but stare out at the world often made able witnesses. Aldo made a note of where the woman lived before striding back to the convent entrance on the side road.

It was time to hear what the sisters had to say. Aldo doubted he would be inside Santa Maria Magdalena for long. After all, how much trouble could a convent full of nuns be?

Suor Giulia winced as she ground nutmegs inside her mortar. Both the bowl and pestle were sturdy, cast in metal to withstand generations of use. But doing the same task over and over sent pains shooting up her right arm. Nutmeg was time-consuming and difficult to grind, even after she had broken the seed into small fragments with a mallet. She paused to rub both hands together before massaging the warmed fingers into her aching shoulder. The sooner a reliable apprentice could be found, the better. It would leave her more time to devise better remedies. That would be a relief, though she would miss using her tools each day.

The mortar and pestle were among the few things she had brought to the convent. Taking the veil required the renunciation of worldly goods and possessions, but Giulia's skills meant she was allowed to keep her tools. Most apothecaries were male, but women – often daughters or wives – had long practised the craft alongside men. A female apothecary working alone would not be accepted in most parts of the city. But within the convent, her skills had been welcomed.

Giulia resumed crushing the nutmegs. They released a rich, vibrant aroma in her small, stone-walled workshop. She tipped the ground nutmeg into a ceramic jar, pouring oil over the powder until it was all submerged. A favourite cork sealed the jar tight, five sharp taps with the pestle making sure of that. She lifted the jar and shook it, forcing the nutmeg to mix with the oil. A knocking sound made her pause.

The novice Maria Teodora was hesitating in the doorway, her white veil evidence that she was still learning the ways of the convent. 'Suor Giulia, please accept my apologies for being late,' Maria Teodora said, crimson colouring her cherubic features. 'I was reciting prayers for sext with Maria Celestia and Maria Vincenzia, and we lost track of time. I ran—'

'So I can see.' Giulia handed the jar to the novice. 'If you are going to remain as my apprentice, you must be here when I say. Understand?'

'Yes, of course.' Maria Teodora stared with bewilderment at the jar in her hands.

'The fervour of your praying is commendable, but not at the cost of your studies.' Giulia nodded at the jar. 'Shake it.'

'Sorry?'

'Shake it.' Giulia clasped Maria Teodora's hands around the sealed jar, urging them back and forth, back and forth, before releasing her. 'Keep going. That's it. Good.'

The novice did as she was told, which was something. Finding a suitable apprentice had proven difficult. Not all nuns had an ability to blend the different ingredients in precise enough measures to create effective remedies. Some lacked the patience to spend days blending spices and oils. And others were simply lacking, or found their talents were better employed elsewhere in the convent.

Suor Catarina had been a diligent apprentice years ago, but preferred the communal aspects of teaching. Suor Andriana could not distinguish the different ingredients without constant supervision, a problem when working with potentially poisonous ingredients, so she had moved to the laundry and eventually become the convent's draper. The last apprentice before Maria Teodora was a servant nun, Suor Rigarda, who struggled to learn. Simple repetitive tasks were her strength, but she would never have succeeded as apothecary. Rigarda went to the infirmary instead, and seemed more content helping Suor Simona tend the ill and dying patients.

After working alone for a year, Giulia had decided to take on another apprentice. Maria Teodora was among a handful of novices to join the convent two summers past. She was a happy, somewhat plump young woman in need of guidance. Instead she had fallen under the influence of two other novices, the sharp-faced Maria Vincenzia and the sharp-tongued Maria Celestia. The trio soon became known as the three Marias, due to the fact each had chosen the same first name when taking the veil. All the other new novices had soon left Santa Maria Magdalena to make their devotions elsewhere. Giulia suspected Maria Vincenzia had driven them away, but the abbess had more pressing concerns. Giulia raised the matter with the prioress, worried that bullying was being ignored or even encouraged among the novices, but the abbess's deputy dismissed such fears. Girls would be girls, the prioress insisted. So Giulia had taken on Maria Teodora as an apprentice, hoping to guide the easily led young woman away from the influence of the others.

It was not going well.

'Why am I shaking this?' the novice asked.

'The better question would be to ask what is inside the jar.'

Maria Teodora nodded. 'What is inside?'

'Crushed nutmegs and oil. You are mixing them to make nutmeg oil.' Giulia smiled. 'You can stop now.' She took the jar back and placed it on a shelf. The mixture had to be shaken twice a day for the next two days. The contents would then be strained, used spices discarded, and the oil returned to the jar. Fresh nutmeg would be added and the process started once more.

Maria Teodora sniffed the air. 'That's what I could smell when I came in.'

'Yes.' Giulia massaged her aching shoulder again. She would have to make a salve for it otherwise sleep would be impossible, even allowing for the need to get up during the night to shake the mixture. She could ask her apprentice to take responsibility for that task, but was not sure Maria Teodora would remember.

'What is nutmeg oil used for?' the novice asked.

'A good question.' Giulia gave a smile of encouragement. 'It's part of many remedies, but the oil can also help those suffering with nausea, vomiting and stomach pain.'

'The food here never upsets me.'

'No, but this is a community of women. As sisters we have taken a vow of chastity, but our bodies do not recognize that. So we face some measure of pain and discomfort each month until we are no longer able to bear children. Nutmeg oil can ease that.'

Maria Teodora blushed. 'Suor, is it right to talk of this?' The novice was an only girl with five elder brothers, and had lost her mother to childbirth. It was no surprise she knew little about the realities of being a woman.

'We sisters are all creatures of Our Lord. Why would we bleed each month if he did not wish it to be so? We should not be ashamed of how we are or who we are. If you are to succeed me as apothecary, you will need to learn far more about this.'

Maria Teodora nodded, her brow furrowing. 'Yes, Suor Giulia.'

'Very well. Now I need you to clean the mortar and pestle before using it to crush some dried rhubarb and roses together. The infirmary needs some purgatives. Don't worry, it is quite simple to do. I'll keep watch on you while making some salve for my shoulder, yes?'

'Thank you.'

Giulia watched her apprentice struggle with the task. No, it was no good entrusting the novice with the nutmeg oil during the night. Besides, having seen fifty summers, Giulia found herself often rising at night to use the *latrina*. Why not put that time to good use?

Aldo knocked at the convent door, but got no reply. A second knock, firmer and for longer, still brought no response. There was a heavy iron circle fixed in the wood at waist height. Aldo took hold of it and twisted – the door opened. It wasn't locked. That made sense. What would there to be steal from a convent?

Aldo stepped through the doorway, leaving the warm morning sunshine. Inside was another world, one blessed with cooler air and soft light. Musty incense mingled with the cloying aroma of wilting lilies. Dust thrown up by the door caught in Aldo's throat. He coughed twice to clear it while studying his surroundings.

The room was a small antechamber of stone and timber, a single lantern flickering on the wall. Directly ahead stood a stern, heavy door, its wood stained so dark the surface was almost black. There was a lock but no handle, suggesting it only opened from the other side. To Aldo's left was an empty doorway leading into a candlelit parlour. Four wooden chairs were inside, close to an interior wall with short curtains hanging in front of them.

Aldo strode in, pulling aside the nearest curtain. That revealed a rectangular hole in the wall with a wooden grille across it. The effect was similar to a confessional in church, though it was a long time since Aldo had admitted his sins out loud. Through the grille he could see another parlour, almost a mirror to the room in which he stood, with four hard wooden chairs facing the connecting wall. This must be where families came to meet their sisters and daughters who had taken the veil. But no one was here now.

No, there was somebody. A nun was slumped in a chair against the far wall, head hanging down, chin against her chest. The dark blue of her habit bled into the murky light, shadows obscuring her white headband and wimple. Aldo might not have noticed her at all but for the snoring. The nun's breathing was heavy and regular, gentle snorts escaping her.

'Excuse me,' Aldo said, keeping his voice low so it didn't startle the nun. Her snoring continued, undisturbed. He tried again, louder this time. 'Excuse me, Suor?'

That got her attention. She looked up, eyes blinking, one hand wiping her mouth. It was not easy to be certain in limited light, but the nun appeared elderly, and had seen at least seventy summers. Outside the convent a person's hair colour and clothing helped show their age. But here only the face and hands were visible.

'Yes?' the elderly nun asked, peering at Aldo. 'Are you here to see someone?'

'Who is in charge?' he asked.

'In charge?'

'Who . . . leads you?'

She appeared to find the question both puzzling and amusing.

'Our Lord leads us. His words and his guidance are the way, the truth and the light.'

'Of course. I meant here, within the convent. Who makes the final decisions?'

The old nun rose from the chair, shuffling towards him. 'We are one body here. Any decisions that are made must be discussed first in the chapter house.'

'There must be someone who takes responsibility for what happens within these walls. Does this convent have a mother superior?'

'Ahh, you want the abbess,' she replied, a smile creasing her wrinkled face. 'I'm not certain she has time to see a visitor.'

'Perhaps you could go and ask her,' Aldo suggested. He introduced himself, explaining his role with the Otto, and the purpose of his visit.

'Intruders scaling the walls?' The old nun shook her head. 'That doesn't sound likely. Why would they want to come here?'

'That's what I am investigating. I would appreciate it if you could tell the abbess I'm here. And inform her I will be staying until I get some answers.'

'Very well.' She shuffled to a door in the far wall. As she opened it Aldo glimpsed a courtyard beyond, well-kept grass surrounded by stone cloisters and lavender bushes. Then the elderly nun was gone, leaving him alone in the parlour. There had been a twinkle of mischief in her eyes. She was certainly not so feeble nor so confused as she first appeared.

Strocchi strode up the dusty road to the only church in Ponte a Signa. The modest stone building rested on a hillside overlooking the village, amid vines and olive groves. The church had stood amid the rest of the village for generations, but persistent spring floods kept disturbing the bones of those buried in the parish cemetery. Eventually, it was agreed the graveyard should move to higher ground. The parish priest at the time – a self-important, vain man, according to Mama – insisted the church go with the departed to their new resting place. So the church was taken apart, moved stone by stone up the hill, and rebuilt on its current site. That had tested the fortitude and faith of everyone involved, but at least they no longer had to face their grandparents' bones floating by whenever the village flooded.

Strocchi couldn't imagine Father Coluccio making such a demand of his flock. The priest had been a faithful servant to Ponte a Signa for thirty summers, a kind and benevolent man full of forgiveness. He lived among the villagers, preferring to be with the people rather than using the house on the hillside built for his predecessor. That was given over to whichever *famiglia* was most in need, a simple gesture but one which showed how little time Coluccio had for believing himself superior to others.

Sweat was soaking Strocchi's new tunic by the time he reached the church, the sun baking the dusty road beneath his boots. There was no shade up here, and precious little breeze. By late afternoon thunder clouds would probably roll across the hills, bringing a torrential downpour. Strocchi couldn't help wishing the rain would come now, but all he could see overhead was a pure *azzurri*. He stepped through the sturdy church doors, grateful to escape the blazing sun.

Inside was dark as ink until he got used to his surroundings. They were simple, with few of the golden decorations and none of the marble found in Florence's places of worship. The church of Ponte a Signa was stone and wood, with a plain crucifix above the altar, a simple tapestry on one wall. Growing up, this was how Strocchi believed all churches would be. Giving praise to God did not require riches to be put on show. There were no fine frescoes on the walls, nor golden plate or chalices used to give Holy Communion.

'Carlo? Is that you, my son?' Father Coluccio strolled down the aisle, a broad smile creasing his sun-browned features. The priest's hair was silver these days, and his waist a little wider than Strocchi remembered, but his welcome remained as warm as ever. Coluccio reached out to shake hands, beaming at the constable. 'Your dear mama will be very happy to have you home. You've seen her, yes?'

Strocchi nodded, smiling back at the priest. 'It was Mama who sent me to talk to you. I visited your house first, but the door was closed so I came here.' He wiped the sweat from his forehead, puffing out both cheeks. 'I'd forgotten how steep that hill is.'

'It's the only thing making sure I still fit inside my cassock,' Coluccio replied, patting his belly. He gestured for Strocchi to sit on one of the wooden pews before joining him. 'Why did you wish to see me – nothing serious, I hope?'

'No, it's a happy occasion,' Strocchi said. 'I got married in Florence just before Lent.'

Coluccio beamed even more widely than before. 'Congratulations! That is wonderful news.'

'Thank you, Father. I brought Tomasia – my wife . . .' He stopped, shaking his head. It still sounded strange saying that out loud.

'You'll get used to it soon enough,' the priest said.

'I brought Tomasia home to meet Mama.' Strocchi explained the wish for a blessing. 'But we're only here for a night, or two at the most, and this is one of the busiest weeks in the year for you . . .'

'It is,' Coluccio agreed, 'but I can certainly find time to bless your marriage, my son.'

Strocchi let out a long breath, relief easing the tension in his shoulders and back. 'It will mean so much to Mama. And me too, of course. When—'

But Strocchi's reply was cut short by a burly man lurching into the church, his shabby tunic soaked with sweat, a shovel clutched in his grubby fists. 'It's hot enough out there – to roast your eyeballs – inside your skull!' the arrival announced between gasps for air.

'I'm sure it is,' Coluccio said, rising to approach the newcomer, 'but Carlo and I are busy discussing plans to bless his wedding. Perhaps you could give us a little privacy?'

'Carlo?' The intruder peered at Strocchi. 'Is that little Carlo, back from the city?'

Strocchi studied the man's face. It was nut brown from being out in the sun all day, a scratchy beard across the cheeks and chin. But that sneering expression and those grasping, greedy eyes . . . Strocchi would recognize them anywhere. 'Buffon.'

Neri Buffon had been the bane of Strocchi's boyhood, a brute who enjoyed bullying anyone smaller than him. Seeing Buffon again made Strocchi's belly lurch. Father Coluccio had heard the confessions where Strocchi admitted wishing God would strike down Buffon, so the priest knew how one boy had tormented the other. He ushered the new arrival towards the doors. 'I left some wine and food for you in the shade at the back of the church. Why don't you have it now, and go back to digging when the worst of the heat has passed?'

'Yes, Father,' Buffon agreed. He paused in the doorway to wave at Strocchi. 'Good to see you again, Carlo. Maybe I'll talk to you later, yes?'

But Strocchi wasn't listening. All his attention was fixed on the buckle securing a worn leather belt round Buffon's waist. It was silver, with a distinctive emblem etched into the metal: the lily of

Florence. The rest of Buffon's clothes were shabby and frayed, stained by sweat and dirt. But the buckle gleamed, its quality all too evident. Strocchi had seen a buckle like that many times, worn by Meo Cerchi, a corrupt and self-serving officer of the Otto. Cerchi had disappeared in January, vanishing one night without explanation. He was still missing, despite the Otto's officers and constables searching for him for weeks.

If that was his buckle, how in God's name had it come to be in Ponte a Signa?

*Chapter Four*

ore than twenty years of being a nun – the last five of those leading the Convent of Santa Maria Magdalena – had taught the abbess that unusual circumstances almost never heralded a welcome change. The life of a nun was one of routine, each day the same as the one before, and both the same as the days to come. Prayers were said at appointed times to mark the passing of the hours. Matins and lauds came before dawn, while sext marked the middle of the day, before vespers and then compline signalled the end of the day. Hymns and readings, prayers and psalms, all part of a cycle of daily devotions made to honour the Lord. It was a comfort to most nuns. It was the way of things.

Disruption to that rhythm was usually an omen of more disruptions to come.

There had been enough of that in recent days. The sudden and unwanted arrival of a visitation on behalf of the archbishop was the cause. Four outsiders – two priests and two men of the laity – had been sent to examine the convent, seeking to expose any serious misdemeanours or contraventions of rules. That first visitation was ocular; everything inspected by eye, and had lasted only a day. The abbess remained confident nothing untoward had been found because there was nothing for the visitors to find. But their failure to uncover misdemeanours or rule-breaking made a second inspection inevitable. And that would be an auricular visitation, with the nuns and novices individually subjected to questioning of their faith, their thinking, their way of life.

The abbess had far less confidence about what would emerge from that. There were some inside the convent with grudges against her leadership, and against her personally. The prioress had long wanted enclosure. Indeed, the abbess suspected the prioress was the person responsible for precipitating the visitation, via an anonymous *denunzia* sent to the archbishop by one of her acolytes – probably Suor Fiametta. The prioress was a burly woman whose certainty was as strong as her presence. If she could not get her own way by direct methods, she would be more than willing to employ less obvious approaches.

Sometimes the abbess found herself wishing the convent had chosen someone else as leader. Then she would have remained Suor Achillea, responsible only for her own devotions and duties. Instead she had become the abbess, responsible for all that happened within Santa Maria Magdalena. Five years of false smiles and wearying whispers from the prioress and her acolytes was a long time to bear any burden. But it was nothing compared to the pain borne by Jesus on the cross, the abbess reminded herself. That was a true burden. The machinations of the prioress and her acolytes were the bite of an insect in comparison.

Still, the last thing the abbess needed was another interruption, another intervention from outside. So the arrival of a breathless Suor Benedicta during a meeting in the chapter house was a worry. Benedicta was the listening nun, responsible for hearing all that was said in the visitors' parlour. She was there to ensure nothing unwise occurred, that none of the sisters or their guests engaged in ungodly conduct on either side of the dividing wall. Benedicta had seen close to eighty summers, with every year of that life visible in her careworn face. But despite those advanced years –

and a tendency to doze off while on duty – there was little that evaded her gimlet eyes or her hawkish hearing.

Benedicta bustled into the chapter house as the convent's humourless sacrist Suor Fiametta gave a lengthy report on the state of vestments under her supervision. Fiametta's face could not have been more sour if she'd sucked a lemon after each breath. The prioress and her acolytes nodded their approval as Fiametta lamented the rags and discarded cloths given away to the poor of the parish. Couldn't the convent find more use for such things before they were gifted to those outside the walls? The argument was all too familiar, and would change no minds. The abbess kept her gaze fixed on Fiametta as the listening nun approached.

'There's a man asking to see you,' Benedicta whispered to the abbess.

'This is one of the holiest days of the year. Send him away.'

'He claims to be an officer of the court, and says there have been reports of an intruder scaling the convent walls. He threatens to remain here until you speak to him.'

Across the room Fiametta paused her recitation, glaring at the interruption. 'Please continue,' the abbess urged, rising from her pew. 'I will be but a moment.' She led Benedicta out of the nearest door, nodding to the sacrist in apology. Not that it would shift the sour scowl of judgement that seemed to rest on Fiametta's face day and night.

The abbess questioned Benedicta on their way to the parlour, but there was little more to be learned about the new arrival. Benedicta did recall which among the dozens of courts in Florence the visitor represented – the Otto di Guardia e Balia – but that made little sense. The Otto was a criminal court, concerned more with violence and murder than religious matters. It certainly had no jurisdiction over what happened within the convent. Why would the magistrates send one of their officers to Santa Maria Magdalena? Unless . . .

A suspicion clawed at the abbess's thoughts. Was this some fresh *stratagemma* by those eager to undermine her leadership? A new attack on her belief that the convent should be an active participant in the life of the parish surrounding it, rather than a closed-off place of prayer, contemplation and little else? Perhaps the prioress had been dissatisfied by the visitation, and involving the Otto was her next *stratagemma*. But involving an authority from outside the Church seemed unlikely, even for someone so determined to get their own way as the prioress. That suggested another person was behind this fresh intrusion. But who else would seek to meddle with the convent?

The abbess's jaw clenched. Of course. It had to be him.

She paused at the parlour door, Benedicta by her side. 'Did this officer have a name?'

'I believe it is Cesare Aldo.'

Not someone the abbess had encountered before. She opened the door to look inside. A man stood behind one of the openings in the dividing wall. His face was lean and clean shaven, with a strong jaw. There were no needless movements, no fussing with his hands, and his taciturn features betrayed little. This man kept his own counsel. The abbess was aware of him studying her in turn, making his own judgements.

'Thank you, Suor Benedicta,' the abbess murmured to the listening nun, keeping her voice quiet. Let this officer guess at what she had said. 'I will see to our visitor. Please return to the chapter house, and make my apologies to Fiametta and the others. I suspect I will be busy dealing with this matter until our next prayers.'

As Benedicta shuffled away the abbess stepped into the parlour, closing the door behind her. She remained there until certain the listening nun had gone. Yes, her initial impressions were confirmed by what she could see now. His ice-blue eyes gave little away. Well, two could play at that game.

'I'm the abbess of this convent. You wished to see me?'

After Buffon left the church, Strocchi talked with Coluccio about Florence and how different it was to Ponte a Signa. Eventually, they agreed the blessing would be held the next day, after morning Mass. The priest was a good listener, with a talent for putting anyone at their ease. But Strocchi had questions he needed answered. 'Father, have you ever heard of the Otto?'

'I read about it in the letters you sent your mama. A criminal court in Florence, if I remember correctly. You work there, yes?'

Strocchi nodded. 'The Otto makes and enforces many laws in the city, but it also has authority out here in the Dominion. As a constable, I have to see those laws observed.'

'I understand,' Coluccio said. 'But what has this to do with me?'

'Neri Buffon is the parish gravedigger?'

'He got the job when old Baldovinetti died. I know Neri was no friend when you were boys, but he is able enough with a shovel.'

That explained Buffon's presence at the church, but not the silver buckle at his waist. 'I need you to be a witness while I ask him some questions. It's court business, Father.'

The priest frowned. 'You think Neri has broken a law?'

'I don't know. That's why I need to talk with him.'

Strocchi led the priest out into the roasting sun. The heat was a shock after the cool of the church, the humid air alive with the sound of insects. Strocchi's new tunic was clinging to him by the time they found Buffon, slumped against the back of the church.

There was wine on the gravedigger's whiskers and crumbs of food down his front.

'Neri?' the priest asked, his voice soft and gentle. 'Neri, are you asleep?'

A heavy snore answered that question.

Strocchi nudged the gravedigger with a boot. 'Wake up.'

Buffon opened his eyes, squinting up at them. 'Who is it? What d'you want?'

The priest cleared his throat before replying. 'Carlo – Constable Strocchi, here – needs to ask you some questions.'

Buffon flapped a dismissive hand before closing his eyes again. Strocchi had no patience for this. It was too hot to be out in the sun for long, and certainly too hot to waste time on an *idiota* like Buffon. The constable leaned over, slapping the gravedigger's face. 'Wake up!'

'What's going on?' Buffon slurred, his breath rancid.

'Your belt buckle, where did you get it?' Strocchi demanded.

Buffon wiped his whiskers. 'Was on a body, washed up in a flood. Nobody knew who he was, so I took the buckle. Get paid too little for doing this job. Only fair.'

'You are paid what you earn,' the priest said, exasperation in his voice. 'Who gave you permission to take the buckle?'

Buffon frowned. 'Didn't know I had to ask.'

Strocchi grabbed the gravedigger by the tunic, pulling Buffon to his feet. 'You stole from a corpse? What kind of man are you? What else have you taken?'

'Nothing, I swear—'

'Tell me the truth!'

To Strocchi's surprise, Buffon burst into tears. 'I didn't mean to –' he said between sobs, his eyes and nose running. 'It was so shiny and pretty, that's all.'

The priest rested a hand on Strocchi's shoulder. 'Let him go, Carlo.' Strocchi was happy to release the blubbering, pathetic figure. Buffon fell back against the wall, crumpling to the ground. The boyhood bully was now a weak and sad creature. Strocchi almost pitied Buffon. But there were more important things to be done.

He bent down to pull at Buffon's belt, undoing the buckle for a closer look. Yes, it was the same as the one Cerchi had always worn so proudly. The officer liked to hook his thumbs either side of the buckle, pulling it forward so nobody could miss the gleaming silver or the fine image of a Florentine lily etched into it. But there were doubtless other buckles like it, and Strocchi couldn't be certain this one belonged to Cerchi. Unless . . . He pulled the belt free from Buffon's tunic, ignoring the drunken gravedigger's objections. Turning it over, Strocchi found two letters crudely scratched into the silverwork: *M. C.* Meo Cerchi.

'I believe this buckle is evidence,' Strocchi announced. 'I'm taking it into the custody of the Otto until this matter can be resolved. If no one comes forward to claim it, then the buckle will be returned to you.'

'The Otto? What's that?' Buffon slurred.

'I'll explain it to you later,' the priest volunteered.

Strocchi rubbed a thumb across the initials scratched into the metal. There were many ways this buckle could have found its way downriver from Florence to Ponte a Signa, but one clear path was apparent. 'Father, tell me about this body that washed up.'

Coluccio frowned. 'It was early last month, I think. We had a week of rain, and the Arno burst its banks. When the waters receded, they left behind a body.'

'Can you describe it?'

Coluccio shook his head. 'Sorry. I performed the burial, but didn't see the body.' He leaned nearer Strocchi, voice low. 'Dado

Manucci found the poor soul. He said it must have been in the water some time. Probably trapped under a branch until the flood pulled it clear.'

'Were the remains male or female?'

'Male, Manucci said, definitely male.'

Strocchi nodded to the village graveyard. 'And it was laid to rest in there?'

'Yes. When nobody claimed the deceased, the parish paid for a proper burial in the pauper's grave. It is what we have always done for lost souls left behind by the river.'

'Thank you, Father.' Strocchi shook the priest's hand. 'I will see you tomorrow for Mass and the blessing, but I may well need to call on you again today.'

'Of course,' Coluccio replied. 'If I am not at home, I shall be in church. Holy Week is a busy time for a priest, even out here in the countryside.'

Strocchi strode away, the silver buckle clasped in one hand, intent on finding the man who discovered the body. The buckle belonged to Cerchi, Strocchi was certain of that, but was it Cerchi's body that had washed up on the riverbank? If so, that would solve the mystery of what happened to him. But how the missing officer's body came to be in the Arno, and whether Cerchi was dead or alive when he went into the water – that was another matter.

Aldo introduced himself and his reason for visiting the abbess, keeping the words unadorned and brisk. She had the look of a woman who wasted little time with pleasantries. She stood upright, her back straight and true, chin raised. Her habit and veil were dark blue, almost black, while her face was framed by a crisp white headband and a close-fitting coif that hid both ears before wrapping under her jaw. A simple wooden cross hung from a chain round her neck, and a knotted belt of rope was tied at her waist. It was difficult to know her age, but wrinkles at her piercing dark eyes and faint lines above her mouth suggested she was his age, or a little older.

'Have you had any intruders here?' Aldo asked.

The abbess took a long breath before replying. 'There have been times when men have sought to get inside after dark. A few succeeded by climbing an external wall and coming over the roof. Most were the worse for wine, acting on a whim or goaded by drunken fools. We guided them back outside, via the door that you came in.'

'And the rest?'

'One was a besotted youth who believed his beloved had been sent here against her wishes to prevent them being together.'

'Had she?'

'Not all those who take the veil in Florence do so of their own choice,' the abbess said, 'but this convent does not believe in confining women at the behest of their *famiglia*. A lifetime in the service of our Lord should be a choice, not an imprisonment. We proved to the youth that he was in error, and he left.'

Aldo nodded. The Otto had received a few anonymous *denunzia* against convents in the past, claiming a sister or lover was being kept against their will. The claims were passed on to the Church, which had authority over such matters. But Santa Maria Magdalena had never faced such an accusation. 'Any others?'

'There was a thief who had heard rumours of a treasure kept within these walls. His mistake was to climb onto our roof during a rainstorm in January. He slipped and fell into the courtyard.' The abbess looked over her shoulder at the internal door. 'His left leg was injured, so we treated him in our infirmary until he was able to leave.'

'I don't recall that being reported to the Otto.'

'Nothing was taken, so there was no need.' The hint of a smile played around her lips. 'As the Lord's prayer tells us, we must forgive those who trespass against us. Most of our prayers aren't usually quite so literal in their expression, but . . .'

Aldo found himself warming to the abbess, but he was no closer to knowing if there was any truth in what Ruggerio had reported. 'And in the last few nights? Has anyone attempted to get into the convent then?'

She frowned a moment. 'Not to the best of my knowledge.'

The abbess might not believe in lying, but it didn't mean she was beyond a sin of omission. Besides, her word alone would not satisfy Bindi, let alone Ruggerio.

'Could I look around the convent? I don't need to see all of it, but the *segretario* expects a full report on what I found here, as well as what I am told. Otherwise he will keep sending me back.' That sounded more of a threat than Aldo intended, but it was still true. Once fixed on a problem, Bindi kept worrying at it, like Cerchi's unexplained absence.

'I will show you the rest of the lower level,' the abbess said, her reluctance all too evident. 'The upper level is where my sisters in God rest and sleep. If you wish to see the dormitories and private cells, that will require permission from the archbishop.'

'Of course,' Aldo agreed.

'Then I shall fetch the key to admit you,' the abbess said on her way out.

Aldo was grateful for her co-operation. He had no wish to get entangled with Church politics. The present Archbishop of Florence was notorious for having bought his position from his predecessor with a large sum of coin. Since then Andrea Buondelmonti had devoted much of his time to reclaiming his considerable expense by various *stratagemmi*, such as imposing a bounty on those who sought absolution for missing Mass on Sunday.

The sooner Aldo could complete his investigation at the convent, the better.

# Chapter Five

*I*sabella Goudi stalked from the palazzo and climbed into the carriage waiting outside. She would have slammed the door behind her, but a servant was holding it open. Besides, the carriage belonged to the Contarinas, not her own *famiglia*, and there was no value in taking her anger out on somebody else's possessions. Her friend Chola Contarina saw the look on Isabella's face and stayed silent. The two were close enough for Isabella to share what was infuriating her when she was ready.

The carriage rolled away, heading east on its way to the Convent of Santa Maria Magdalena. When it was first proposed that Isabella should study at the convent, she had refused. Why waste her days being lectured by nuns? After all, nuns spent their lives praying and denying themselves even a moment of pleasure. Isabella preferred whispering secrets with her maid Nucca, gossiping with Chola or persuading Papa to buy her another gown.

That was fun. That was joy.

Not praying. Not studying. Not nuns.

But then Nucca mentioned the opportunities that might arise from doing what Mama and Papa wanted. First, it meant going out into the city. The palazzo could be like a gilded cage, especially when *Nonna* was in one of her moods. Isabella was fifteen and eager to explore, to see and experience new things. Most of the time she never went anywhere except to Mass, and even then she was surrounded by the whole *famiglia*.

Agreeing to study at the convent meant a chance to spend time with more girls her own age. That was exciting, much more exciting than learning about Latin and history and dusty old things in dusty old books. Isabella used to see her friend Chola Contarina every month, back when Chola and her mother were frequent visitors to the palazzo. But those happy mornings had become less and less frequent, no doubt because the *famiglia* business was struggling again. Papa and Mama thought Isabella didn't know, but she did. She might talk more than they liked, but she also knew how to listen and how to go unnoticed when important conversations were being whispered close by.

Attending classes at Santa Maria Magdalena also meant she could hear gossip from the daughters of other merchants, discover all those delicious secrets that never got spoken inside the palazzo. Isabella could learn who was in love with whom, what the newest gowns looked like, and what spring weddings were likely. Marriage was not unknown for girls yet to see fifteen summers, often to men much older than them. Mama had been betrothed by the time she was Isabella's age to ensure a favourable business alliance.

Having decided going to the convent might be useful after all, Isabella still resisted for another few days. That won the promise of a new dress from Papa, a pleasing reward for something she was going to do anyway. In a palazzo full of women who knew their own mind, Papa always gave way. He was a reed in the wind while those around him were storms and tempests. He would surrender anything for a quieter life, and Isabella enjoyed using this to her advantage. Mama and *Nonna* did it, why shouldn't she?

Three months into her lessons came the news Isabella most dreaded. She heard it first from Chola, whispered in the back of the Contarinas' carriage, bumping along the uneven streets to the convent. Negotiations were underway to form a partnership between Isabella's *famiglia* and another member of the Arte della Lana, the prestigious guild of wool makers and merchants – an alliance with Isabella offered in marriage as part of the deal!

She did not wish to believe it at first. Papa was easily bullied into doing what others wanted, but the notion that Mama had agreed to this bargain was much harder to accept. Yet Chola always had the most reliable gossip. And Isabella knew full well who must be behind all of this: *Nonna*. She would not hesitate to trade her granddaughter for a good alliance, just as she had done by marrying Mama to Papa. Isabella had long delighted in vexing *Nonna* whenever possible. Now the sneering old *strega* was getting her own back.

Well, not if Isabella could find a way to stop it.

Days turned into weeks, yet nothing came of the gossip. Chola was never wrong, Isabella did not dare to hope for that. But the silence did give her time to plan. Was there some *strategia* she could devise to avoid being trapped in an unwanted marriage? Isabella put all her energy and imagination into inventing an escape, but could see no way out. Then she was summoned by her parents and *Nonna* after they all returned from Palm Sunday Mass.

Papa stumbled over his words, while Mama stood by a window staring out at the city, unable to hold Isabella's eye. Eventually, *Nonna* lost patience and announced that Isabella had been betrothed to Ercole Rosso. He was a member of the Arte della Lana, just as Chola had predicted. Rosso was not a young man, *Nonna* smirked, so he would not bother Isabella often or for long once she had given him a son and heir.

'When?' Isabella had asked, not trusting herself to say more.

'Soon,' *Nonna* replied, her pleasure all too evident. 'A spring wedding is always best. You don't wish to be heavy with child during summer.'

That had torn Isabella's breath away. How could anyone be so callous, so cold? But before she could respond, a servant entered, announcing the Contarinas' carriage was waiting. Perhaps it had been for the best. Isabella would not have been able to stop her tongue once she started telling Mama, Papa and *Nonna* what she thought of their plan for her future. Yes, it was better to withdraw, to regather. She let Chola gossip as the carriage turned north. Isabella had no wish to share her news, not yet. She would wait until after classes, when they were back in the carriage and on their way home. It gave her a chance to think. There must be a way to escape this betrothal. There must!

Entering the convent cloisters was crossing a threshold into another world for Aldo. The walls around the courtyard were made of stone that recalled warm honey, each surface welcoming the sun – a stark contrast to the cold, forbidding hollow at the heart of the Podestà. The courtyard itself was given over to grass, a lush emerald sward surrounded by fragrant lavender on all sides and stone cloisters with vaulted ceilings. Aldo was surprised to see the distinctive purple flowers blooming so early, filling the air with their scent. A few nuns sat beneath the cloisters on benches, some reading prayer books, others with their eyes closed.

The convent's upper level rose above the cloisters. Aldo could see narrow windows dotting the walls, a glimpse of wooden shutters visible inside them. None of the gaps were large enough for a man to climb in or out of – a child would struggle to squeeze through. There was certainly no easy way for an intruder to climb from the roof to the courtyard. They would need to bring strong rope, and more than a little guile. 'Are there any other courtyards within the convent?' he asked. 'I've been inside the monastery at San Marco and that has two large courtyards, along with a smaller one.'

'There is a second courtyard on the other side of the chapter house, near the rear of the convent.' The abbess gestured to the far side of the cloisters. 'As you will see, it is given over to the kitchen garden, and a small orchard. We grow as much of our own food as possible. The garden also provides herbs for Suor Giulia to use in her remedies, and a drying place for our laundry during the warmer months of the year.'

'How many live here?'

'Forty-three, at present,' she replied, without hesitation. 'Thirty of us came when the convent was created as a daughter house to Le Murate, and our numbers have grown in the two decades since. Most of our sisters are chapter nuns, devoting their lives to good works and prayer. We also have servant nuns, plus six girls who board here under our guardianship. Another half a dozen girls come to the convent to study during the day.'

'And none of them has reported seeing an intruder in the last few days?'

'Of course not.' The abbess frowned as if the question was absurd. 'I would know should anything of that nature occur within these walls.'

It all seemed unremarkable, and much as Aldo had expected. Whatever Ruggerio was pursuing inside the convent, there was little of interest to report here. To the left of the parlour stood an infirmary. This long, narrow room occupied the rest of the south side of the courtyard, running parallel to the dirt road outside. The infirmary contained ten beds, but only a few were occupied, all by nuns of later years. 'The elderly and frail are a constant presence here,' the abbess said in a hushed voice as she led Aldo past the patients. 'Sometimes they are joined by sisters who become acutely ill. But all are well cared for by our infirmarian, Suor Simona.' The abbess nodded to one of three nuns tending the ill. She wore a similar habit but the two nuns assisting her wore black habits, rather than dark blue. One patient had a bowl beneath her left forearm to catch blood seeping from a cut across the skin. 'We had to summon a doctor for Suor Piera,' the abbess whispered. 'He insisted on bloodletting to ease her delirium, despite objections from our apothecary, Suor Giulia.'

As the abbess led him back to the cloisters, Aldo asked about the different colours worn within the convent. 'Girls in our guardianship and those who come here to learn wear pale blue. Servant nuns wear black,' she replied. 'They are usually from poorer families, or outside the city. They have a calling, but serve in a different way to chapter nuns.'

'How?'

'They work in our kitchen, or the laundry, and in the infirmary, as you've seen.'

'The more menial tasks,' Aldo observed. The abbess bristled.

'Chapter nuns all have duties of their own in this convent. Some labour long hours at the scriptorium, copying illuminated manuscripts. Others assist those in important posts, such as the sacrist and the almoner. It is important that such knowledge be passed on within the convent, to prepare those who may well fill these posts in future.'

'But how is it decided who becomes chapter nuns?'

'Those with education are better suited to certain roles,' the abbess replied, her face becoming stern. 'Those from humbler backgrounds are used to more . . . laborious tasks.'

Even here there was a hierarchy, Aldo noted, a divide between those who came from wealth and those who didn't. He wouldn't be surprised if families paid to ensure their daughters and sisters became chapter nuns. 'As it is in the city, so shall it be in the convent,' Aldo muttered as the abbess strode away.

She whirled round to face him. 'I permitted you to enter our convent despite the fact that you have no authority here. You have been inside our walls mere minutes, yet you see fit to judge a community about which you know nothing.'

Aldo's face flushed. 'I'm sorry, I did not—'

'Silence!' she snapped, her nostrils flaring. The abbess took a slow breath before speaking again. 'This convent is not perfect, but it aspires to do our Lord's work. Inside these walls my sisters and I are able to talk and pray together. We discuss and debate, we make our own decisions – regardless of whether we are chapter or servant nuns. We are a community. In return for being servant nuns, those sisters can learn to read and write if they wish – opportunities that would be impossible for them outside. Here they are treated with respect. Is that the life of most women in this city? Is that how life is for women from poor families?'

Aldo shook his head. Not for the first time, he found himself remembering a lesson too easily forgotten: more was learned when the mind remained open and the mouth stayed shut. 'Forgive me, Abbess. I spoke without thinking, and from a place of ignorance. I hope you will accept my apology for that error of judgement.'

She studied him for several moments before giving a curt nod. 'Very well.' The abbess spun round, marching along the western cloister, the side of the convent furthest from via San Gallo. Aldo hurried to catch up, wondering what had prompted her outburst. His comment had been ill-advised, but not enough to justify such a rebuke. Something else – or someone else – was angering the abbess. He would have to step more carefully here.

The abbess gestured to a room on her left. 'That is the refectory where we gather for meals. It is mandatory to eat together while listening to readings or the convent chronicle. We consider it a re-enactment of the Last Supper.'

They reached the cloister corner and the abbess paused outside two sets of wooden doors. She gestured at the doors nearest the corner. 'These lead to the kitchen, the apothecary workshop, scriptorium, our laundry, storerooms, and *offici* used by nuns in senior posts. The stairs up to our dormitories are also through there.'

Aldo pointed at the other doors. 'And those go into the chapter house?'

'Yes.' The abbess closed a hand round her small wooden cross. 'There are few places where women can make choices without the presence of men. We do that here in our chapter house. Everyone's voice is heard. For us, this is the important room in the convent.'

Aldo looked across the courtyard to the church of Santa Maria Magdalena, looming above the convent on its eastern side. There was a door leading into the church. 'More important than the church?'

'Yes,' she replied, without hesitation. 'Our Lord lives within everything, he is in all of us. We do not need to be inside a church to know him. But our chapter house, that is unique.' The abbess arched an eyebrow at Aldo. 'Do you wish to continue?'

He was fast coming to the conclusion that there was nothing to discover, but he nodded his agreement. Better to be thorough now, and avoid being sent back the next day.

The abbess pushed through double doors, leading Aldo into a stone-walled corridor. After the sunny warmth of the courtyard this was cooler and much darker, a few lanterns on the walls providing the only light. The abbess gestured to a door on the left. 'Our kitchen is in there, providing food for all those who live within these walls. Anything left over is offered to those going hungry outside. Santa Maria Magdalena is an open convent. I believe we have a duty to help the community around us, and many of my sisters agree.'

Aldo noted what she didn't say. There must be others within the convent who did not agree with her.

The abbess continued showing him the lower level. A *latrina*, the scriptorium and the apothecary workshop were on the left side, while another entrance to the chapter house and the door to her *officio* were on the right. As they reached the end of the corridor a chapter nun hurried from a doorway ahead of them, colliding with Aldo. She pulled back, staring at him in surprise and fear. She had a kind face but there was a timidity to her, like a mouse caught in the open. 'Suor Andriana,' the abbess said. 'Where are you going in such a hurry?'

'Forgive me,' the nun replied, a hand to her belly. 'I have not been feeling well.'

The abbess stood aside for Andriana to pass. 'Then do not let us stop you.' The nun scuttled by, disappearing into the *latrina*. The abbess sighed. 'She has a good heart, but a worried disposition, always afraid of making mistakes. I hoped being in charge of our laundry as the convent draper might help her overcome that, but so far . . .'

The abbess turned left, leading Aldo to gates at the rear of the convent. A small hand cart leaned against a wall, waiting to be used. The padlock securing the bolt across the gates was sturdy and well oiled. It showed no sign of force or damage. The abbess retraced her steps to the door from where Suor Andriana had come. 'That is our laundry.' Opposite it was a staircase leading upwards. 'We have four dormitories, and a handful of private cells.'

There was one last door on the left – the sacrist's *officio* – before the abbess led Aldo out into the convent's second courtyard. It was a lush area crowded with plants, flowers and fruit trees. The air was alive with sounds of insects, while scents of witch hazel and iris drifted on the breeze. Two servant nuns were hanging sheets and shifts on a line to dry. They whispered to each other as they worked, but a glare from the abbess silenced them.

Aldo turned a slow circle. The walls were high on all four sides. Two were external walls, facing out on to via San Gallo and the dirt alley north of the convent. The third wall had narrow windows on the upper level, while the last was highest of all. That was the back of the church, judging by the stained-glass window. There were no dislodged stones atop the external walls, no sign anyone had come over them. It would require considerable effort to get into the convent through this courtyard.

'I have seen enough,' Aldo said. 'Thank you, abbess.'

She acknowledged his words with a nod, leading Aldo back inside with brisk strides. But as they returned to the main court-yard, the unlikely sound of giggling echoed in the air. Young women in pale blue dresses spilled in through the door that led out of the convent.

'Girls!' the abbess called to them. 'Remember where you are!'

The new arrivals fell silent, nodding to the abbess before heading for the refectory. Aldo glanced at their faces, paying them little attention – no, it couldn't be. And yet . . .

'Excuse me, Abbess,' he said, hurrying towards the young women. Towards one in particular. What was she doing here?

'Where do you think you're going?' the abbess called, but Aldo ignored her. He had to know, had to be sure. The newcomers were already at the refectory door. He quickened his pace, determined not to lose sight of the young woman at the back of the group.

'Teresa?' he called out. 'Teresa!'

But she followed the others inside, and the door shut behind her.

Aldo stopped, certainty leaving him. The young woman had looked so much like Teresa, but his half-sister must have seen thirty-five summers by now, if not more, and that young woman was closer to fifteen. He realized every nun in the cloisters was staring at him. The abbess strode towards him, the dark blue of her habit billowing.

'Explain yourself,' she demanded.

'The last of the young women that went in here,' Aldo said, 'I thought I knew her.'

The abbess frowned. 'Has she been before the Otto?'

'No, nothing like that. It's – she –' He was struggling to put into words what had seemed so certain, but now was clearly a mistake. 'Can you tell me her name?'

'I don't see what this has to do with your reason for coming to the convent.'

'Please, Abbess. It would set my mind at rest.'

The nun sighed. 'Very well. She is one of the girls who study here most days.'

'Is she in the guardianship of the convent?'

'No, she still lives with her *famiglia*. Her name is Isabella Goudi.'

Of course. That was why she looked so much like Teresa. 'Would it be possible to speak with her?' Aldo asked more in hope than expectation. The answer was swift.

'Certainly not,' the abbess replied. 'I have been more than patient with you, but that is enough. Report to the court as you see fit. Unless you return with written permission from the archbishop himself, you shall not be allowed inside this convent again. Please leave. Now.'

The set of her face made it clear there was no value in pressing the abbess further. Aldo offered thanks for being allowed inside, bowed low to the abbess and strode to the antechamber door. But she followed him along the cloister, putting a hand on the door before he could open it. 'There's an old saying: They carry us in their mouths, spreading rumours about us wherever they go. Tell me, who made the *denunzia* claiming intruders had been seen scaling our outer wall?' she asked, her voice quiet so none of the nuns nearby could hear.

'I was sent here by the Otto's *segretario*, Massimo Bindi. No *denunzia* was made, but the report about intruders came from the Company of Santa Maria.'

Anger flashed in the abbess's eyes. 'From a member of that confraternity?'

'Yes.' Aldo recognized the fury she was struggling to suppress. The man responsible had caused the same effect in others. 'You already know who that was . . .'

She nodded, grimacing as the words left her mouth. 'His name is Ruggerio.'

'But how—?'

'It had to be him.' The abbess opened the door for Aldo to leave, ushering him into the antechamber. 'Girolamo Ruggerio is my brother.'

## Chapter Six

'Where have you been?' Tomasia asked when Strocchi got home. 'Visiting an old *amore*?' Her words sounded playful, but her gaze said otherwise. He could hear Mama humming in the kitchen, but knew she would be listening.

'Sorry I was so long,' he replied, kissing Tomasia. 'It took me a while to find Father Coluccio, but he can perform the blessing after Mass tomorrow morning.'

Sure enough, Mama came bustling in, wiping her hands on a cloth. 'He can? That's wonderful news. My *bambino*, being blessed in marriage – wonderful! A pity it's so soon. If we had more time, I could invite your cousins from San Jacopo, but—'

'Mama, it has to be tomorrow. I must go back to the city afterwards.'

'Already? But you just got here,' she protested.

Tomasia had been watching him. 'Something's happened, hasn't it? Carlo?'

Strocchi could hide nothing from her. It was one of the qualities he loved, her ability to see his troubles often before he knew what was worrying him. She listened in a way few others bothered to do – certainly more than Mama ever did. 'I found something.'

He showed them the silver buckle, explaining its significance. Tomasia already knew about Cerchi's disappearance. Strocchi had told her while they were in bed, talking about his hopes of becoming an officer one day. But she listened patiently as he told Mama. After coming down from the church, Strocchi had sought out Manucci. The villager confirmed what Coluccio had said. The remains were only part of a body, but Manucci had seen enough to know it was male. The silver buckle had been hanging from a belt round the waist.

'I saw Buffon wearing that,' Mama said, 'and wondered where he got such a thing. To stoop so low, stealing from a dead man.'

Tomasia shared a sad look with Strocchi. They'd both seen worse in the city. 'If the buckle came from this missing officer, what must you do?'

'I need to report back to *Segretario* Bindi, the administrator for the Otto – the sooner, the better. I must return to Florence tomorrow.'

'I will come with you,' Tomasia said, turning to smile at his mama. 'It has been wonderful to meet you, Mama Strocchi, but I would not dream of imposing on you by staying here while Carlo goes to Florence. A wife's place is with her husband, don't you agree?'

Strocchi fought back a smile. Tomasia was no delicate flower, content to live in anyone's shadow, let alone that of a husband. But she knew how to phrase things in a way that could not easily be rejected. Mama huffed and puffed but soon nodded her agreement.

'There is one more thing I must do,' Strocchi said. 'Tonight, if possible. I have to dig up the poor soul left by the flooding, and see if there is anything that proves his remains are those of Cerchi.' Mama and Tomasia both made the sign of the cross.

'You will need agreement from the parish council,' Mama said. 'Many of them will see it as desecrating a grave.'

'Talk to Father Coluccio again,' Tomasia suggested. 'Get his support. That will ease any concerns the council might have.'

'She's right,' Mama agreed, wrapping an arm round Tomasia's shoulders. 'You've chosen a good wife for yourself, *bambino*. Smart, as well as beautiful.'

Strocchi nodded, smiling. 'I wouldn't have married her otherwise.'

Aldo stood in the shade outside the convent, still untangling the threads of what he had learned. Ruggerio being the abbess's brother explained his eagerness to know what was happening at the convent, at least in part. So why invent a story about male intruders climbing the walls? The abbess had been adamant it was false, and Ruggerio's past lies supported that conclusion. But the *segretario* would still expect a full report, so the word of the abbess alone would not be enough.

Seeing Teresa's daughter had been far more of a shock, especially when Isabella was a living portrait of her mother as a young woman. Aldo had lived his first twelve years in Palazzo Fioravanti, a *bastardo* but raised as a Fioravanti at his father's insistence. Teresa was three summers younger than Aldo, the last child given birth by Lucrezia Fioravanti and the only one to survive infancy. That made Aldo her big brother, though Lucrezia had never missed an opportunity to mention his illegitimacy. It was Lucrezia who banished Aldo from the palazzo the day his father – her husband – died. And it was Lucrezia who forced Teresa to wed Bartolo Goudi six years later, despite the witless wool merchant being fifteen summers older. The betrothal secured a financial future for the Fioravantis' business, something far more important to Lucrezia than Teresa's happiness.

Unable to stop the wedding and unwilling to watch it happen, Aldo had left Florence to seek his fortune as a mercenary, riding with the great *condottiere* Giovanni delle Bande Nere. But Aldo never forgot Teresa or how affectionate she was to him as a child. Aldo returned to the city when injury ended his time as a mercenary, hoping to rebuild a friendship with his half-sister. But Lucrezia refused him entry to Palazzo Fioravanti and wouldn't allow him to see anyone from inside. One day, when the old *cagna* was dead, he might return to the home that had once been his – but not before, if he could help it. Aldo put Teresa, Isabella and the rest of that *famiglia* from his thoughts. There were still the supposed intruders to investigate.

He strode along the dusty side road to the crumbling homes behind the convent. The sun had passed its peak, yet the afternoon heat remained oppressive. In the centre of Florence the narrow streets had tall buildings on either side, providing plenty of shade. But here in the northern quarter, residences were far less imposing. There was little to stop the sun baking those foolish enough to be outside at this time of day. Aldo knew in which of the crumbling houses the wizened women in the black headscarf had been. The shutters on both levels of that building were closed now but the front door remained open, perhaps in hope of a cool breeze finding its way inside. All it actually did was allow flies to come and go.

Aldo stepped through the doorway into a fetid hallway, announcing himself to those within. 'Someone here claimed that men have been climbing the convent walls,' he called out. Aldo had no proof the report had come from this residence, but the words might provoke a reply. So could the chance of coin. 'There may be a reward for anyone with more to tell me.'

That got a response.

'How much of a reward?' a female voice called from above.

'Depends what I hear,' Aldo replied, pulling a pouch from his tunic and shaking it so the coin inside could be heard. 'And whether I believe it.'

'You'd better come up,' the woman said. 'Careful on the stairs.'

Aldo took her advice, testing each wooden step before putting his weight on it. The ripe aromas of cat piss and rotting fruit were making Aldo's nose run when he reached the upper level. How could anyone stomach this stench?

'In here,' a woman muttered from a doorway near the front of the building. She was younger than he'd expected from the sun-drenched face and widow's headscarf. Her clothes were shapeless, damp patches spreading beneath both arms. Aldo followed her inside, sweat running down his back. *Palle.* The sooner he got back outside, the better.

Shards of sunlight sliced between the shutters covering the windows, but it wasn't easy to see much. The woman introduced herself as Signora Ginerva Gonzaga. 'Well?' Aldo asked. 'What did you see?'

'Two men,' she said. 'One climbing the convent wall, the other helping.'

'When was this?'

'Two nights ago, after curfew. It was too hot to sleep.'

'You're sure they were both men?'

Gonzaga shrugged. 'What about the reward?'

'When I hear something I don't already know,' Aldo replied. The fact that there were two intruders was new, but not worth much. 'What did they look like?'

'Men.'

'Tall as me?'

'Hard to tell from up here.'

'You saw me by the convent wall earlier. Were they as tall as me?'

Gonzaga's eyes narrowed. 'The one helping was maybe your height. The other was shorter – and thinner.'

Aldo dug in his pouch, pulling out two *giuli*. The woman reached for the coins, but he lifted them out of her grasp. 'The one who was climbing – did you see him return?'

She shrugged again. That meant no, she had probably dozed off.

Aldo tossed the *giuli*, and Gonzaga snatched them from the air. Aldo paused on his way out. 'You told somebody else what you saw, otherwise I wouldn't be here. Who was it?'

'Our parish priest at Santa Maria Magdalena, Father Visconti.'

Aldo would have to question Visconti. For a man of the cloth to share a confession was a sin, but Aldo didn't doubt Ruggerio was capable of getting almost anything from a weak-willed priest – for the right price, of course. 'When did you tell him?'

'The next morning, after Mass. The Company of Santa Maria was visiting. I knew he would ask them to do something about it. They are important. Men of influence.'

Aldo nodded. Girolamo Ruggerio was one of them.

Gonzaga smiled, all too pleased with herself. 'Those nuns believe they are better than us, and yet they have a man visiting during the night. They give out alms to those who don't deserve it. People should earn their way, instead of depending on charity.'

'When do the nuns give out alms?' Aldo asked.

'Sundays,' she replied, gesturing towards the convent. 'They'll be there soon, outside the back gates. But you won't see me with my hands together, begging for help.'

'No,' Aldo said. 'You prefer to get your *giuli* by informing on others.'

* * *

The abbess had gone to her *officio*, hoping to address the many duties that came with leading the convent. No matter how many hours she devoted to such tasks, there was always more to be done. Urgent matters kept pushing aside the necessary, while the unexpected and the unwanted demanded attention ahead of those who deserved it, until all she could see were her own shortfalls and failures of leadership.

But instead of sitting at her desk the abbess paced the floor. Her outburst at Aldo had been regrettable. She would pray for forgiveness later, not to mention for the forbearance to withstand those who would see the convent enclosed. That was what had been clawing at her while she led Aldo around the convent. His comments about servant nuns had been clumsy and judgemental, but it was little reason to berate him. Doing so loud enough for nuns around the cloisters to hear was worse. No doubt word would have reached the prioress by now, one more mark against the abbess's suitability for the role.

Enough. It seemed she would get none of her waiting tasks done today. Better to see how her sisters in God were responding to all these disruptions. She could start with a visit to the refectory where Suor Catarina would be teaching boarders and visiting girls. Catarina was liked by her students, and had even offered to help guide the novices towards their final vows.

Normally, the abbess left the teaching nun to fulfil those duties. But Aldo had been interested in one of the visiting girls, Isabella Goudi. What was it about her that had caught the officer's eye, and why did he call her Teresa? The abbess opened a ledger with the names of all the visiting girls and their families. Yes, there she was: Isabella Goudi, daughter of Bartolo and Teresa Goudi. So Aldo had mistaken Isabella for her mother? The abbess could recall the Goudis' letter asking for Isabella to become a visiting student, but it was the prioress who met with the parents of prospective girls.

The abbess left her *officio*, heading for the refectory. It amused her to have the prioress, a woman so opposed to the convent's continued openness, be the one responsible for dealing with outsiders. Was it petty to also make the prioress responsible for the distribution of alms after Mass on Sundays? Yes. But the prioress delighted in making life hard for the abbess, so returning that courtesy seemed only fair. The abbess was happy to confess this to Father Visconti each week and accept whatever penance he deemed necessary.

Striding along the cloister, the abbess dismissed the prioress from her thoughts. The morning's intervention by the Otto was a greater concern. Not because the court could cause significant trouble, it had no meaningful jurisdiction within these walls, but because of the person responsible. The abbess had not seen her brother in more than a year, not spoken with him in two. Instead, letters passed between them, her brother expressing concern about the safety of items stored by his confraternity inside the convent. She had assured him more than once that there was nothing to fear, yet he would not accept her word. Now he was using his influence with the Otto to have an officer investigate.

It was as well she had not realized sooner who was responsible for Aldo's arrival, otherwise her outburst in the cloisters would have been far worse.

The abbess reached the refectory and slipped inside, doing her best not to draw attention. Catarina gave her a nod before returning to the lesson. The boarders and visiting girls were seated at two long tables, while Catarina stood before them with two of the convent's novices. Maria Vincenzia was a proud young woman, full of righteous self-importance, while Maria Celestia seemed happy to follow her example. Catarina was debating with them whether convents should all be enclosed.

'The outside world is a distraction,' Maria Vincenzia insisted. 'For us to truly devote ourselves to Our Lord, we should devote all our time to prayers and silent contemplation.' She was tall and straight of back with a hawkish face full of certainty.

'But what of those who depend on the alms this convent distributes?' Catarina asked. 'Would you have them starve or fall ill because of our devotion to prayer?'

'We do not need to be an open convent to dispense alms,' Maria Vincenzia replied, glaring down her sharp nose. 'Other orders distribute their alms through a small window.'

Catarina gestured at the visiting girls. 'And what about these students? They come to learn, acquiring skills that will help them the rest of their lives. Would you deny them that?'

Maria Celestia arched an eyebrow at the pupils. 'You assume they are all here to learn. From what I've seen and heard, many of them come to gossip.'

That brought a loud giggle from among the girls. The abbess looked to see who was responsible. One girl was being glared at by the others, the same girl Aldo had called to in the cloister: Isabella Goudi. It seemed she was almost as much trouble as he was.

Catarina turned towards the abbess. 'The leader of our convent has come to hear us today. Abbess, would you care to join our debate?'

'No,' she replied. 'I have no wish to stifle such a lively discussion. Please, continue.' She retreated to the door, smiling at Catarina. As she left, the abbess noticed a look of triumph pass between the novices. They seemed to believe their argument had driven her away, but the convent faced greater problems than the foolishness of two novices.

\* \* \*

Aldo was relieved to get back outside. The sun had moved on enough for shade to be found now, so he chose an empty doorstep opposite the back gates of the convent for a seat. Gonzaga was a bitter gossip. Had she lied to make trouble for the nuns? Possibly. But her words had the quality of truth despite their sourness. She claimed only to have seen men attempting to climb the convent's back wall. Had malice been her sole motive, Gonzaga would have added far more to the story.

So, if Gonzaga was speaking the truth, did that mean the abbess had lied? Not necessarily. The abbess might be unaware of whoever climbed or tried to climb into the convent after curfew on Friday. There was no shortage of gossip about men doing so after dark for secret meetings with lovers, but the truth was more mundane. Tales of convent passion were most often overblown *fantasie* spread by people like Gonzaga to cast a stain on godly women.

The abbess's fury when he questioned the jobs servant nuns took . . . That had been significant. Anger always brought the truth out of a person, for better or worse. His thoughtless comment should not have been enough to cause such a response, suggesting the abbess's mood was already a well-heated cauldron. Ruggerio had that effect, but the abbess didn't know then that her brother was responsible for the investigation. Something else was souring her mood. But was it related to the intruder? That was worth putting to the parish priest, but it would require a subtle approach to get the truth . . .

It was at least clear how the tale of men scaling the walls had reached Ruggerio. But why the silk merchant wanted an investigation of his sister's convent remained less apparent. Ruggerio never did anything unless there was advantage to be had. How could involving the Otto – and specifying that Aldo be the one who visited the convent – benefit Ruggerio? The man was unlikely to use a criminal court for some petty *vendetta* with a sibling.

There was something greater at stake here. But whatever that was remained behind the convent walls.

Aldo shook his head. Too often these hidden agendas led to bloodshed, especially when men such as Ruggerio were involved. The last time that happened it had almost cost Aldo his life, and caused several other deaths. The sooner this matter was finished, the better. He would talk to Father Visconti, and then report his findings to the *segretario*.

A small crowd had gathered outside the convent gates while Aldo had been thinking. Some were missing limbs, while others looked close to collapse from hunger or the heat. Most of the others were women, many with a small child on one hip and another holding their hand. These must be the needy Gonzaga held in such contempt. They looked no different to other citizens, despite their threadbare clothes and tired faces. All these people lacked was the fortune to be born into a wealthy *famiglia*. Needing help was not a sign of moral weakness, no matter what some might think.

The convent gates opened and a handful of nuns emerged. Two servant nuns set to work distributing food and coin to those most in need, while a younger chapter nun with a caring, open face spoke to each of the recipients. The waiting women clustered around another chapter nun, tall and upright. She listened to each one in turn, giving stoppered small bottles or twists of paper to the women. Aldo had seen Saul do the same for his Jewish patients; this must be the convent's apothecary.

A heavyset chapter nun stood apart from the others. She was older of face, her mouth twisted as if this giving of alms offended her. If she objected so much, why did she stand by observing it? Unless she had been made to do so. The abbess had implied some at the convent who did not approve of its openness. This glowering nun must be one of them.

But convent politics were of little interest to Aldo, and certainly of no relevance to his investigation. He rose from the doorstep and strolled away to find Father Visconti. Once the parish priest had been questioned, this matter could be concluded.

The prioress watched the stranger leaving. He had not come to beg for alms. Instead he watched what was happening outside the gates. Could he be the court officer that had angered the abbess earlier? The prioress had not seen what had happened in the cloisters, but word of it soon reached her from the convent's pompous sacrist. Suor Fiametta had argued for a conclave to hold the abbess to account for her outburst, until the prioress intervened.

To accuse the abbess over such a minor incident was too much, and too dangerous. She was a gifted speaker, able to win over anyone who might be wavering with the power of her words and her empathy. Instead of calling a conclave, the prioress had encouraged Fiametta and others to express their great sympathy for the abbess. Another intrusion, coming so soon after the unfortunate visitation . . . Little wonder the abbess was struggling to cope . . . Leadership was a privilege, but for some it could become too much of a burden . . .

'I'm sorry, that's all I have,' Suor Giulia announced to the women still gathered around her. 'Come back next Sunday, I'll have more by then.'

The prioress shook her head. The apothecary had been distributing remedies to the women of the parish for years, yet the need for such help continued to grow. When would Giulia learn? There would never be enough for everyone. As the disappointed women drifted away, the prioress went to offer her sympathies to Giulia. 'It is always the same.'

The apothecary nodded. 'Still, we do what we can.' She smiled at Suor Paulina who was handing small squares of poor man's candied quince to waiting children. The almoner beamed as the children ate their honey-preserved pieces of fruit.

The prioress had tried to make Paulina see sense, without success. The almoner was not a worldly woman, and far too gullible in how she dispensed alms. Every Sunday people came with a tale of woe and Paulina believed them all. But the apothecary was not so foolish.

'Do you think it will ever be enough?' the prioress asked Giulia.

'No. There will always be more need.'

'If that is true . . .'

'If that is true, why even try?' Giulia turned to face the prioress. 'We have spoken of this before. I believe one thing, and you another. We shall not change each other's mind.'

'Perhaps not,' the prioress agreed. 'But at least you are willing to talk. The abbess refuses to even discuss the convent's path with me anymore.'

'Do you wonder why?' Giulia asked. 'She knows the visitation was your doing.'

'I did not write to the archbishop.'

'No, it was probably Fiametta who put ink to paper, but the words and intentions . . .'

The prioress suppressed a smile. 'Our sacrist does what she can.'

Giulia pointed to the empty doorstep where the stranger had been. 'And the court officer, the man who was watching us from over there – was that your doing?'

'No. I'm not sure what prompted that,' the prioress admitted. But that would not stop her turning the unexpected into an advantage.

# Chapter Seven

ass was concluding as Aldo went into the church of Santa Maria Magdalena. The interior was not so grand as those closer to the centre of Florence, but still it had impressive stained-glass windows above the side chapels and ornate marble funeral monuments. As the faithful left, Aldo went to the nuns' private chapel. It denoted the transition from church to convent, a locked wooden door as the sole means of entry. There were windows high up in the chapel wall, but these did not allow anyone to see the nuns on the other side. They allowed Mass to be heard inside the chapel, and the nuns' singing to be enjoyed by those in the church. If any intruders had been tempted to get into the convent via the church, there were no signs of tampering around the lock on the heavy door.

'Can I help you?' a voice asked. The approaching priest was older than Aldo, grey hair swept back from a kind face, silver streaks in his beard.

'Father Visconti?'

'Yes. Are you new to the parish?'

Aldo introduced himself and the reason for his visit. The priest confirmed he had passed on Gonzaga's claims to the confraternity, but he seemed uncertain she was correct. 'Why would anyone wish to climb into the convent? Should a thief wish to find something worth stealing, he is far more likely to discover that within the walls of this church.'

'Is the nuns' private chapel beyond this door?' Aldo asked.

Visconti nodded. 'The nuns have the only key. When I go into the convent as their confessor, they open this door for me.'

It was much as Aldo expected. 'Could you tell me more about the convent? It would help me understand why intruders might go there. The abbess was rather . . . brisk.'

Visconti slid both hands inside the sleeves of his black cassock. 'The convent of Santa Maria Magdalena has long been a stone in the shoe of our diocese. The previous abbess was considered a troublemaker for suggesting convents be left to make their own rules and regulations. She believed her sisters in God were perfectly capable of determining what was best for a community of women.'

Aldo could imagine how the diocese had responded. 'And the current abbess?'

'Suor Achillea – that was her name before she was elected to lead – is kept busy by her own nuns. She believes in reaching out to help the needy of this parish.'

'Yes, I saw her nuns distributing alms,' Aldo said.

'Others within the convent favour enclosure, especially the prioress. She is second only to the abbess, yet –' The priest frowned. 'Their views could not be more different.'

Aldo thanked Visconti for his insights, even though the reason why intruders might climb the convent wall remained unclear. No doubt the *segretario* would complain about that, but Bindi was never satisfied, so it mattered little. Aldo still wanted to see one more person before returning to the Podestà, but she had nothing to do with his investigation.

When Isabella first arrived at the convent, it wasn't what she had expected. All of the girls had to wear a pale blue dress, cut in a modest style that hid almost everything. How was Isabella supposed to tease boys from a carriage when almost every part of her was hidden behind such a dull, drab thing? But classes were a surprise because the teacher was actually fun. Suor Catarina was demanding, and often frustrated with Isabella about her lack of study and her tendency to talk more than listen, but the nun also seemed to care.

Catarina wanted everyone to learn, whether they were visiting girls like Isabella or one of the boarders who lived under the convent's guardianship. The teaching nun even encouraged the girls to question what they read and what they were told. Today's class had been shortened due to Palm Sunday, but Catarina still found time to invite two novices for a debate on whether the convent should be enclosed. Isabella had other things on her mind, but she enjoyed hearing people argue about ideas. There were plenty of arguments at the palazzo, but no debate. Instead *Nonna* ruled the household as if it were her own private dominion.

When class was finished, Chola Contarina came bustling over to ask who the stranger out in the cloisters had been, and how he knew Isabella's *famiglia*.

'What are you talking about?'

Chola laughed. 'When we arrived, a man kept calling out to you, but he was calling your mother's name. Didn't you hear him?'

Isabella shook her head. 'What did he look like?'

Chola described the man – tall, lean, old enough to be their father – but that didn't help. Unless . . . Could he be the suitor *Nonna* had chosen for her? No, that made little sense. Such a man would call out her name, not that of Mama. People said she looked as Mama had done when a girl, but Isabella couldn't see it. As if she could ever look like Mama!

The visiting girls left the convent, eager to go home. But the

Contarinas' carriage wasn't waiting when Chola and Isabella emerged. Perhaps the servants had not realized class would finish early. Soon they were the last ones left.

'Isabella,' a male voice called.

She saw a stranger staring at her. 'He's the one from the cloister,' Chola whispered. The man was tall and lean, as Chola had said, but there was more to him than that. Isabella was used to men staring at her in church as if she was a meal to be devoured, a ripe piece of fruit they wanted to pluck before anyone else could have a taste. The lust of men, that's what Mama called it. She said many of them were no better than beasts.

But this stranger, he was different.

He was looking at her.

Rather than staring at her body his eyes were on her face. Instead of striving to picture her naked, this man seemed to be looking inside her. It was intrusive, but there was no sense of him being a danger. Not to her virtue, at least. No, it was more like he was – judging her.

'What do you want?' she asked.

The man came closer, but remained on the other side of the dirt road. 'My name is Cesare Aldo,' he replied. 'I'm an officer of the Otto di Guardia e Balia.'

'The criminal court?' Chola said. 'Is she in trouble?'

'No.' The man smiled. 'Nothing like that. Isabella, has your mother ever spoken of her brothers?'

Isabella frowned. What a question to ask. She would not dream of calling to someone in the street, wanting to know about their *famiglia*. Yet she could see no malice in this Aldo, if that was his name. He appeared to mean her no harm. He seemed curious about her. Yes, that was it. 'Mama told me she had two brothers, but both died before she was born.'

'Matteo and Giulio. She had a third brother, a half-brother.' The stranger put a hand to his chest. 'I grew up at Palazzo Fioravanti. I was three when Teresa was born. We played together until she was nine. Until our father died.'

'You never told me about this,' Chola whispered.

'I didn't know,' Isabella said. She wanted to ask more questions, but the Contarinas' carriage finally arrived, rattling along the dirt road to collect them. A servant jumped down beside the girls, full of apologies, pulling the door open. Chola got in first, Isabella following. Aldo came to her side of the carriage.

'Ask your mother about me,' he said as it rolled away. 'But don't mention me in front of Lucrezia. That old *strega* doesn't like hearing my name.'

The carriage rolled around the corner into via San Gallo, heading south, and Isabella lost sight of Aldo. She sank back into the plush seat, her thoughts a jumble of questions.

'Who was that man?' Chola asked, her delight at having such a tasty morsel of fresh gossip obvious. 'If he is your mama's brother, why isn't he called Fioravanti?'

Isabella didn't have any answers. But she remembered going with Mama once to lay flowers in the *famiglia* crypt. Mama's father lay in a tomb there. Isabella had run her fingers across where his name was carved into the marble. The *famiglia* name was Fioravanti, which *Nonna* still kept as her own. But his first name was shorter, easier for Isabella to trace: Aldo.


Aldo made his way to the Podestà, uncertain if it was wise to have approached Isabella. He had hoped to see Teresa once Lucrezia was in a crypt. But his stepmother clung to life year after year, her grip still as sharp as her tongue. No good would come of his intervention with Isabella, Lucrezia would see to that. But it was worth the trouble if his interest caused that old *cagna* a moment of discomfort.

The afternoon sun was dipping behind the palazzi and churches as Aldo reached the Podestà, the day's heat giving way to clouds that promised a thunderstorm. No doubt much of the rain would fall on the hills around Florence, but some might reach the city. He strode into the courtyard as Bindi descended from the administration level. The *segretario* came down one step at a time, struggling to see past that rotund belly to place his feet.

'What's taken you so long?' Bindi demanded.

'The abbess at Santa Maria Magdalena was reluctant to answer my questions,' Aldo replied. 'She denied any knowledge of male intruders scaling the walls of the convent in the last few days. When I pressed her, she said representatives of the Otto would not be allowed back inside the convent again without written permission from the archbishop.'

'You have been absent most of the day. Is that all you have to report?'

'No, *segretario*.' Aldo recounted what Signora Gonzaga claimed to have witnessed. It left Bindi with a problematic choice: take the matter to the archbishop, and in doing so accuse the abbess of lying, or tell Ruggerio he was wrong, and risk the merchant's wrath.

'Very well,' Bindi said. 'Visit Ruggerio and repeat your findings to him.'

Of course. Why should Bindi risk displeasing someone of importance when a proxy could be sent instead? If Ruggerio was angered by the message, his rage would be spent on the messenger, not the one who sent it. 'And if he isn't satisfied?'

'Remind him that the convent of Santa Maria Magdalena is under the jurisdiction of the Church, not the Otto. As the abbess stated, any further investigation by this court will require written permission from the archbishop.' Bindi gave a regretful smile. 'Alas, our hands are tied in this matter. Yes, tell him that, if you wish.'

Aldo bowed to the *segretario* before stalking from the Podestà once more. Whatever beauty the day possessed that morning, it had become the worst of spoils now.


Strocchi had been happy when the Ponte a Signa parish council finally approved his request to exhume the remains. Tomasia's suggestion of approaching Father Colucci first had proven wise. He agreed to permit the reopening of the grave, and summoned the council to discuss the matter. The members were unwilling to disagree with their parish priest, but insisted the exhumation must wait until dusk, so the digging did not attract unwanted attention. Strocchi agreed, having no wish to spend an afternoon working the ground under a blazing sun.

Now rain was lashing down, soaking the village and the hillside above it. Farmers might welcome the torrents for their parched soil, but it was turning Strocchi's task into a back-breaking burden. He plunged Buffon's shovel into the dirt, but no sooner had he made a hole than it filled with water. Father Coluccio stood to one side, rain running down his face, fingers working a rosary. Prayer alone could not stop sodden soil sliding into the grave.

Strocchi kept digging, his new tunic spattered with mud and sweat. Much more of this and he'd have blisters from the shovel slipping in his grasp. He was shivering too, the rain and black clouds making the air far colder than before. Strocchi stopped, calf-deep in mud and close to despair. He looked at Coluccio and the priest smiled back. In that moment the clouds parted, a beam of sunshine shining through. Strocchi made the sign of the cross and thrust the shovel deeper into the mud. It hit something solid, the handle ringing in his grasp. Strocchi dropped to his knees, not caring about the state of his hose, plunging both hands into the mud, clawing it away to reveal a long sack, secured with rope.

'That's it,' Coluccio said. 'That's what we buried the poor soul in.'

The remains came free in a rush, and Strocchi lifted them onto the ground beside the grave. He clambered from the hole, using the edge of the shovel to open the sack. The ripe stench of decay billowed out. He twisted away until the worst of it had gone.

The coarse sack ripped apart easily to reveal its grisly contents. Strocchi had seen bodies before, both the dying and the dead. As a boy he once encountered a corpse washed up on the riverbank, but that unfortunate had been in the water a few days, not a few weeks. Those remains were still recognizable as a young man.

This was worse, far worse.

Three of the limbs were missing, likely taken by strong currents or torn away by underwater branches. Part of one leg remained, but it was torn off at the knee. A memory of Mama's roasted chicken seeped into Strocchi's head, hands ripping away the wings at a feast. He swallowed down what was rising in his throat, pushing the recollection away. Look at this body, he told himself. Look at this body, and see what story it could tell . . .

Scraps of a tunic were still wrapped round the torso, shreds of rotting material coming away, revealing putrid skin and flesh underneath. Dark, curling hair matted the blotchy, mottled chest. So, the remains were definitely male. What else?

'Is it the man who owned the buckle?' Father Coluccio asked. The question startled Strocchi. He was so intent on studying the body, he'd almost forgotten the priest was there.

Strocchi forced himself to study what was left of the head.

Eyeless sockets stared back, empty and black. Rotting cavities in the cheeks haunted the face, while the lips had been torn or eaten away, exposing broken teeth. A thin beard sprouted across what was left of the chin. Was it Cerchi? It was difficult to be certain, not when damage and decay had taken so much. 'I'm not sure,' Strocchi admitted. Rather than straining to see a resemblance in what was left, Strocchi closed his eyes to recall how the officer had appeared. There was always something rat-like about Cerchi's features: those beady eyes, his sharp nose and that thin chin. Strocchi opened both eyes again, staring at the remains. Yes. Yes, what was left of the face and head bore a very strong likeness to Cerchi. 'Yes, I believe so.'

The priest shook his head. 'What happened to this poor soul, I wonder?'

It was a good question, and one *Segretario* Bindi would doubtless ask when Strocchi reported finding the body. His gaze was drawn to a gaping hole the size of a fist in the corpse's chest, just below the left nipple. Something had got in through a break in the skin to eat away at the insides. Strocchi could see several of the ribs where the bones had been picked clean. Was that –? He leaned closer, breathing through his mouth to keep the stench of rotting flesh from his nostrils. Yes, there was a notch in one of the ribs – no, two of them. Many things could have done that, but he'd wager a handful of *giuli* that a blade had passed between those two bones, metal slicing into them. He stood up, judging where the blade had gone. Close to the heart. A clean thrust would have been a mortal wound.

'I suspect he was stabbed,' Strocchi said. 'That suggests he was attacked, and then put into the water. He went missing a few days after the feast of the Epiphany. You said this body was left behind by flood waters in early February?'

The priest nodded, his ashen face still staring at the remains.

'Plenty of time for him to go into the Arno at or near Florence, and the body to make its way downriver to here.' Strocchi glanced at the sky. The gap in the clouds had vanished again, more rain was coming soon. Should he take the remains back to the city? They were evidence. But the prospect of carrying a rotting corpse into Florence on a cart or horse did not bear thinking about, and certainly not with Tomasia alongside him. Better to return the last of Cerchi to the ground. Give what was left a proper burial so he could rest in peace. If Bindi did want the body brought to the city, the *segretario* could send someone else to do that.

Strocchi rolled the remains into the grave before stepping aside so Father Coluccio could once more commit them to God's care. As the priest spoke, a thought struck Strocchi. Of all the places where the remains could have washed up, it was quite a coincidence they should find their way to Strocchi's home village. Even then, if Buffon hadn't stolen the silver buckle, the identity of the body would have stayed a mystery. And if Strocchi hadn't seen the buckle and persuaded the parish council to allow an exhumation, the mystery of Cerchi's fate – the fact he was probably murdered, and dumped into the river – would have gone unsolved. It was as if all of this was meant to be. As if it was a sign from God . . .

Coluccio made the sign of the cross, and Strocchi did the same. 'Amen.'


Palazzo Ruggerio was in the western quarter of Florence, giving Aldo's temper time to calm before he reached the grand residence. Its three levels were built of the finest stone and marble, every part of the design crafted to announce the richness and importance of those living within such beauty and splendour. Ruggerio was the last of his line, with no heirs to take his place. The merchant had married, but the union produced no children and the wife took her own life rather than remain with Ruggerio – or so gossips claimed.

Aldo knew better than to judge another man by where he sought pleasure. What made the merchant dangerous was his willingness to do almost anything to retain his reputation and influence. So why was Ruggerio meddling in matters at Santa Maria Magdalena? That question had been itching at Aldo all day, worse than any insect bite. Asking for a direct answer would serve no purpose. Better to feign disinterest and see what arose.

Aldo strolled in through the palazzo entrance, a pleasant smile fixed on his face. An eager servant bustled forward demanding to know Aldo's business. Soon Aldo was led upstairs to a richly decorated room, with brocades of many hues draped across the furniture and colourful plates displayed in open wooden cabinets. One entire wall was given over to a fresco of a biblical gathering, with all of those around the figure of Christ bearing similar features. They were generations of the Ruggerio *famiglia*, Aldo realized, with the last of their line at the far right. It was typical of the rich to have themselves painted into such scenes, but the abbess was missing from the fresco, despite being Ruggerio's sister.

'You like it?' Ruggerio asked from a doorway. The silk robe he had worn that morning was gone, replaced with a flowing gown of crimson and blue.

'I'm an officer of the Otto,' Aldo replied, still smiling. 'I leave art to others.'

'You do not need to have wealth to appreciate beauty,' the merchant said, gliding across the room to lower himself onto a golden chair. 'So, what did you discover at the convent? Are the sisters safe from intruders scaling their walls? Or have they been secretly entertaining men after curfew, perhaps?'

Aldo repeated what he had told the *segretario*. Ruggerio affected a mild interest in what was being said, yet none of the words changed his expression.

'And what will Bindi do about this?' Ruggerio asked once the report was complete.

'The convent is beyond the Otto's jurisdiction,' Aldo replied. 'Without proof that a significant crime has been committed, it is unlikely the court will take further action.'

'You mean it is unlikely the *segretario* will order further action.'

Aldo bowed his head a little, as if acknowledging the wisdom of that observation. All of this was a game, the words having less importance than what went unsaid. Ruggerio clasped both hands together in front of his narrow chest. 'The Company of Santa Maria supports the convent through donations and its members' influence. My brethren ask little in return. To be remembered in the prayers of the sisters, for example. To keep certain items related to the company safely within the convent. And yet . . .'

So that was the true reason for Ruggerio's interest. He or others in the confraternity had left items of significance in the safekeeping of the nuns. No wonder word of intruders scaling the convent's outer wall had brought Ruggerio to the Podestà. 'The convent is not as – cooperative as the members of the confraternity might have hoped?'

'Not the current abbess.' Ruggerio smiled, his eyes narrowing. 'Not of late.'

'*Famiglia* can be difficult,' Aldo agreed. Revealing he knew Ruggerio and the abbess were siblings was a risk, but could prove useful. A shadow crossed the merchant's face. 'Of course,' Aldo added as a reassurance, 'that is not something I shared with the *segretario*. He has little interest in such matters.'

Ruggerio gave a small nod of appreciation. 'Very well. If anything further emerges about difficulties within the convent, I would value hearing of them in good time.'

Aldo paused. Ruggerio was a venal, dangerous man. But he also possessed great influence. To make an arrangement with him was repugnant, but having only saints as allies was far from practical in Florence, and certainly not for an officer of the Otto. 'My first duty is, of course, to the court . . .' Aldo said, letting the promise of more linger in the air.

'Of course.' Ruggerio rose. 'Please, do pass my gratitude on to the *segretario*.'

A shiver ran down Aldo's back as he departed. Talking with the merchant was reminiscent of a fable about a scorpion and a turtle Aldo once heard while riding with a mercenary from Persia. The turtle had given the scorpion a ride across a river because the two creatures were acquaintances, yet when they reached the other side the scorpion tried to sting the turtle. As it was with the scorpion, so it was with Ruggerio. There was a threat lurking behind every word he spoke, a hidden meaning in all he said and did. Smiles and promises would mean nothing if there was a change in circumstances. When dealing with Ruggerio, it was wisest to prepare for the sting that would surely come.

Ruggerio could not help himself. It was in his nature.

### From a confession made at the convent
### of Santa Maria Magdalena:

*Forgive me, sisters, for I have sinned. I do not know if I will have the courage to share these words with you, but they must be written. This page shall be my confessor, and this ink shall bear my testimony. Better that I write now, while I have the clarity of mind to admit my sins. I ask for your forgiveness, sisters, but I expect no absolution.*

*Knowing the secrets I have kept, and the truths I have concealed, I fear what you will think of me when you read these words. I did what I felt was needed, what seemed necessary at the time – or so I told myself. Such justifications offer little armour against the truth of my trespasses. I have borne false witness, and I have been covetous.*

*But the worst of my sins is the worst of all sins: I have taken a life. I could write it was in defence of my physical self, and that would be true. I could claim it was to protect others, and that would not be false. I could argue what I did was just, and that would be correct. But the actions of my hands and heart I cannot deny.*

*I must now confess why I acted as I did. It will not be simple to admit these truths.*

*May God have mercy on all of us in the hours and days to come.*

*May God have mercy on all of you for what I have done.*
*May God have mercy on me, for I am a murderer.*

# Chapter Eight

❦

## Monday, March 26th 1537

*A*ldo's journey to the Podestà took longer than the previous day, but that was to be expected. Rain had swept down from the hills during the night, leaving the streets damp and a freshness in the air, but now only a few clouds remained in the morning sky. Ponte Vecchio was choked with hawkers competing for trade with the stalls. Having celebrated Palm Sunday, families were now searching for bargains. Aldo pushed his way through the throng, the waters of the Arno hidden from view by those crowding the bridge.

Using side streets and alleys to hasten his journey, Aldo arrived at the Podestà to find a carriage stopped outside the main gates. Grander members of the Otto often arrived by carriage, but it was rare to see one waiting as the road was too narrow for another carriage to pass with ease. Should a magistrate require their driver to remain nearby, there was ample room in Palazzo Firenze, just south of the Podestà. Besides, the Otto never sat this early. Bindi preferred having time to brief the magistrates on the cases before them, ensuring their judgement was aligned with his own. So whose carriage was it?

A servant was tending the horses, adjusting their harnesses. The carriage woodwork was equally well looked after, although it had seen many years of use. The style was familiar, but it was the crest on the carriage door that removed all doubt. Only one person still used the name Fioravanti, but the *famiglia* emblem endured – on this carriage, at least.

Aldo called to the servant. 'Has she gone inside?'

'No. She's still in the carriage. Waiting for someone, I think.'

Of course. Lucrezia Fioravanti would no sooner get out of a carriage to see him than she would walk to Pisa. He had been right to worry about the consequences of approaching Isabella outside the convent. Now those consequences were coiled inside the carriage, a bitter old *strega* full of piss and hatred. Time would have not withered her.

He strode to the carriage door. Let Lucrezia spit her venom and be gone. He banged a fist against the *famiglia* crest, bracing for what was to come. The door opened and a female face appeared, but not the one he expected.

'Cesare, is that you? When did you get so old?'

Teresa was much as he remembered, her delicate features set in an oval face. She was wearing a gown of gold and cream, with detached sleeves of the same fabric. Her fair hair was pulled back into an ornate coil, a few stray ringlets cascading over her ears. Worries and years were showing in her face, leaving small creases in her skin, and smudges of exhaustion under both eyes. But she was still beautiful, a woman in place of the girl he had known.

'I could say the same of you,' Aldo replied. They teased each other as children. He found himself doing it again, as if no time had passed. 'When I saw the carriage . . .'

'You thought Mama might be inside?'

'She was your mother, not mine. But, yes, I did.' Teresa still seemed to know his mind, despite the summers lost between them.

'Cesare, I need your help.'

Shouts heralded a cart approaching them. 'You're blocking the road,' Aldo said.

Teresa opened the door. 'Get in, and we'll talk on the way.'

Aldo hesitated. He should say no. Better not to get drawn into whatever *stratagemma* was being enacted here. His half-sister might be the emissary, but doubtless Lucrezia was lurking behind it. Teresa would be disappointed by a refusal, perhaps upset, yet she would understand. It was safer to walk away. Go inside the Podestà and do his duty there.

'Please?' Teresa asked, a tremor in her voice.

Aldo frowned, but climbed into the carriage nonetheless, calling for the servant to drive on. They jolted forward, rolling south before turning right. Aldo was relieved the carriage was heading west, rather than east towards Palazzo Fioravanti. 'So, you need my help. Or is it the *famiglia* that needs help, and she sent you to get it from me?'

'Mama doesn't know I'm here,' Teresa replied. 'She thinks I am visiting my friend, Nezetta Contarina. Our daughters both study at Santa Maria Magdalena.'

The carriage turned north. 'The convent?'

'Yes. That's where we think Isabella is now.' Her words faltered. 'She ran away from home this morning. The note Isabella left for me says she wants to become a nun.'

Aldo had spent too little time with Isabella to know the depth of her faith, but this story was incomplete, at best. Teresa lacked her mother's cunning, but was not without guile. And it was not unknown for young women to run away from home with a beloved. 'Could there be another explanation? Might she be somewhere else – or with someone else?'

Teresa shook her head. 'No. Her maid Nucca accompanied Isabella to the convent, made sure she went inside safely.' There was no trace of deception in Teresa's face. She was telling the truth about that much, at least.

'I was at Santa Maria Magdalena yesterday,' Aldo said, omitting the reason he had been there. If Teresa was not willing to share the whole story, why should he? 'Isabella will be safe there. I was told the convent offers young women a good education as well.'

'I know,' Teresa said, avoiding his gaze. 'That was why we started sending Isabella there. But she has become ever more wilful and headstrong. And now this nonsense about joining the nuns –' She fell silent as the carriage passed the Archbishop of Florence's grand residence, which faced the Battistero di San Giovanni and the Duomo.

Aldo lost patience with her hesitation and half-truths. 'I have spent my years since returning to Florence enforcing the law. If I'm to help, Teresa, I need to know everything. Otherwise I will stop this carriage and get out now. It's your choice.'

Finally, she looked into his eyes. This close, Aldo could see she had not slept the previous night, worry taking its toll on her. 'Our business is – failing. Twenty years ago, when I married Bartolo—'

'When Lucrezia forced you to marry him,' Aldo interjected.

Teresa nodded. 'Bringing the Fioravantis and Goudis together saved both businesses. But Bartolo is a shadow of the merchant my father was –' she smiled – 'that our father was.'

Aldo ignored the clumsy attempt to win his favour. 'So Lucrezia decided the solution was another betrothal, a fresh alliance.'

'It would have been Paulo to marry, if he hadn't –' Teresa's voice broke at that. Her son had died the previous summer, depriving the *famiglia* of an heir, and Teresa of her first-born. 'So Isabella is the one who must wed.'

'But she isn't as meek as you were. Isabella has refused to marry, yes?'

'How did you—?'

'I met her yesterday, as I'm sure she told you. Doubtless that is why you thought I might be willing to help now, in exchange for a promise of – what? Friendship? Kinship? You and I both know Lucrezia will never allow me back into the *famiglia*, not while she can draw breath. I was my father's *bastardo*, and she will never forget that.' Aldo looked out of the carriage window. They were on via San Gallo, nearing the convents clustered along the approach to the city's northern gate. He banged a fist on the ceiling. 'Stop here!'

The carriage came to a slow halt. Aldo opened the door and jumped out, his left knee protesting at the jolt. 'Aldo, please –' Teresa called after him.

He held up a hand to silence her. 'I will visit the convent and ask to see Isabella.'

'Thank you—'

'But I'm going for her sake, not for the *famiglia* or its business, and certainly not for Lucrezia. If the nuns let me see Isabella, I will listen to what she says. That's all. Perhaps if someone had listened to you all those years ago, things would be different now.'

Teresa's smile was wistful. 'Perhaps.'

'If there is anything to tell, I'll send a messenger.' He strode off. 'Goodbye, Teresa.'


Strocchi and Tomasia strolled hand in hand up the hill, Mama following them. It was still early enough to savour the cool of the morning, so the walk was a pleasure, not a chore. Word had spread about Strocchi's return, and the blessing that was to take place after Mass. Parishioners from Ponte a Signa lined the path to the church, applauding him and Tomasia as they approached. The day before villagers had watched them with suspicion. Now, thanks to Mama, he was being welcomed back as a prodigal son, with a beautiful bride as well.

Mama had found a silk gown that matched the blue of Tomasia's eyes. Strocchi chose not to ask where it had come from, suspecting the gown was borrowed from a palazzo up the hill. Mama would see it went back unmarked. Nobody but the villagers would be any the wiser, and none was likely to tell the owner. Besides, it took his breath away to see Tomasia in such a dress. She was already beautiful to his eyes, but now everyone could witness that too. He had never felt so fortunate to be at her side.

Father Coluccio was waiting for them in the doorway of the church, but there was someone with him whom Strocchi hadn't expected: Buffon. The gravedigger was holding a handful of wild flowers, which Tomasia accepted. 'May your days know only happiness,' Buffon said, his voice a whisper, 'and may marriage bring you great joy.'

'Thank you,' Tomasia replied, bowing her head.

Strocchi wondered if he was dreaming. The childhood bully was gone, replaced by a man trying his best. No doubt Father Coluccio had something to do with that, but it was heartening to see Buffon like this. It gave hope, real hope that people could change if they wanted, if the chance was open to them. Strocchi took Buffon's hand and shook it. 'Thank you for being here,' he said.

The gravedigger shrugged. 'Where else would I be?'

Coluccio called to all those lining the path. 'Everyone, please, come in. It is time for Mass, and then we can celebrate the marriage of our own Carlo to his new wife Tomasia. Let us share in their joy and happiness. Come, come.'

\* \* \*

Aldo was waiting in the convent parlour when the elderly nun came in from the courtyard, a scowl settling into her features. 'You again? The abbess said you were not welcome, not without a letter of permission from the archbishop.' The nun straightened her back. 'Do you have such a letter?'

'No,' Aldo replied. 'But I have no wish to enter the convent, nor to disturb you, the abbess, or your sisters in God.'

'Then why are you here?'

'I believe that my niece – my half-niece, in fact – is within these walls. I wish to visit with her. That is all.'

The elderly nun frowned. 'What is her name?'

'Isabella.'

She gave a sniff of dismissal. 'You are mistaken. I have spent every day in this convent for the past twenty years. There is no Suor Isabella here. I would know if there was.'

'My apologies,' Aldo said. 'She visits this convent as a student, but came here earlier this morning. As I understand it, she wishes to take the veil. Her name is Isabella Goudi.' He gave a brief description of Teresa's rebellious daughter.

'Oh. Her.' The elderly nun sighed. 'And she is related to you?'

'Yes.'

'That would explain a lot. The abbess is meeting with her. I will let them know of your request. The abbess shall decide whether to permit it. Wait here.'

She withdrew, leaving Aldo alone in the parlour once more. He doubted the abbess would be happy to hear of his return, but hoped she was fair-minded enough to allow a visit with Isabella, however brief. Should the abbess refuse, there was nothing else he could do but send a messenger to Teresa and then forget those still living at Palazzo Fioravanti. It had not been home since the summer his *palle* dropped, so there was little to regret from such a loss.

Isabella was sent from the abbess's *officio* when the wizened old nun came in, so she couldn't be certain what was being said inside. She tried listening at the door, but only mumbles and mutterings could be heard through the sturdy wood. Perhaps Mama had found the letter and had come rushing to the convent, demanding to see her? Mama and Papa would beg for her return, Isabella was sure of that. After all, they needed her for the wedding.

Another possibility nagged at her while she waited. What if her parents didn't come? What if they decided to leave her at Santa Maria Magdalena, to teach her a lesson? That didn't bear thinking about. Isabella had considered going to see Chola instead of coming to the convent, but her mother and Mama were close friends so that hadn't seemed a wise choice. Isabella knew the convent gave sanctuary to women in need of a new home. Suor Catarina talked about it in class one day, saying how proud she was of that. So the convent had seemed the best place to seek refuge. It wasn't meant to be forever. Just until Mama and Papa came to their senses, and *Nonna* Fioravanti calmed down.

The door opened and the abbess emerged. 'Do you know someone called Cesare Aldo?' she asked, the older nun behind her.

'He is my mama's half-brother,' Isabella replied. It was strange to talk of a man she had met for the first time a day ago as if he was *famiglia*. She'd mentioned him to Mama after getting home from Palm Sunday classes, eager to find out more. The mistake was doing that when *Nonna* Fioravanti was passing. Isabella had never seen the old *strega* get so angry so fast. She spoke of little else for the rest of the evening, demanding to know every detail of the chance encounter. *Nonna* claimed Aldo had stolen his last name from her late husband.

Whatever the truth, it had been decided the wedding plans must be brought forward. *Nonna* seemed sure Aldo would seek to interfere somehow, because he had done so before. Mama went very quiet, and Isabella knew something else was going on but nobody would answer any questions. She was a child. She had no say in the matter. She should go to bed before doing anything else that would be regretted.

Isabella sat up most of the night talking with Nucca, struggling to make sense of what was happening. She hadn't even met the old man she was betrothed to, and now everyone was in such a hurry to see her married. It reminded her of that time she knocked over a colourful plate much prized by *Nonna*. The ugly thing shattered into so many fragments she could never find them all, let alone put them back together. This was much the same. She knew there was a puzzle to be solved, but there were too many pieces missing to find the answers, let alone know their importance.

'Your mama's half-brother?' the abbess asked. 'You are certain of this?'

Isabella nodded. That she did know for sure.

'Very well,' the abbess said. 'Suor Benedicta, take Isabella to the visitors' parlour so she can talk to Aldo. You will listen, as is your duty, for anything that is improper or inappropriate. When they are done, bring Isabella back to my *officio*.'

'Yes, Abbess.' Suor Benedicta glared at Isabella. 'Follow me.' The old nun set off at such a pace Isabella had to run to catch up. Suor Benedicta might be even more wizened than *Nonna*, but she moved much faster. They strode out into the cloister, round the courtyard, and stopped at the door to the visitors' parlour.

'Conduct yourself properly,' Suor Benedicta warned, 'or else I will return you to the abbess immediately. Understand?'

Isabella nodded. She had seen the old nun a few times inside the convent, and there was usually a twinkle in her eyes. But not today.

Strocchi's head and heart were filled with joy at having his marriage to Tomasia blessed, with Mama and so many villagers there to witness his happiness. Afterwards they strolled down the hill for an outdoor feast behind Mama's house. People brought jugs of wine and whatever food they could spare. Platters laden with roasted fish nestled on the table beside bowls of polenta and fresh vegetables, bottles of oil and vinegar ready for pouring over the food. It was simple food, peasant food, Strocchi supposed, but it tasted of home.

Much as all this brought him joy, occasionally he would notice Buffon along the table, and the silver buckle fought its way back inside Strocchi's thoughts. He didn't want to recall Cerchi's remains, how they had looked. The stench of them still caught in Strocchi's nostrils, no matter how much he had scrubbed his hands and under his nails. He did not wish to be thinking about what had happened to Cerchi, not in the midst of the wedding feast. But once the question was asked, it seemed impossible to ignore.

Perhaps Cerchi had died after leaving the city? He could have been attacked outside Florence, and his body thrown into the Arno. But it seemed more likely one of Cerchi's enemies inside the city was responsible. *Santo Spirito*, there was no shortage of people with reason to want Cerchi dead. It was murder, Strocchi was certain of that. But who—

'Carlo?' Tomasia gave his right hand a squeeze.

'Sorry, my beloved.' He had told her about what was in the grave while they lay together the previous night. Tomasia was good at listening, good at letting him speak until his words ran as dry as a mountain stream in the heat of summer.

She leaned closer to whisper in his ear. 'We're leaving once the feast is finished. Be here now. Enjoy these moments with your mama and everyone else. It will take us the rest of the day to reach Florence. You can think about other things on our way back to the city, yes?'

Tomasia was right, of course. Cerchi had been dead for weeks, if not months, and would stay dead for a long time to come. Let the past stay in the past for now. Whatever tomorrow might bring would come in good time, along with the next sunrise.

Strocchi kissed his wife, and everyone else cheered.

Sometimes, life was good.

Isabella might look like her mother, but that was where the resemblance ended for Aldo. His half-sister had been a playful child around him, but shy in the presence of strangers. Isabella showed no hesitation in talking, no matter who might be listening. She sat opposite Aldo in the visitors' parlour, a wooden grille between them. The listening nun warned Aldo the visit would end if his words or actions were unsuitable.

Once Aldo made it clear he wasn't eager to take Isabella back to Palazzo Fioravanti, she spared no detail in describing why and how she had fled to the convent. 'I don't actually want to be a nun,' Isabella eventually admitted, glancing over her shoulder at Suor Benedicta. 'But I knew the sisters would take me in.'

'Have you met this man your parents and Lucrezia wish you to marry?' Aldo asked.

'Not yet. His name is Ercole Rosso.'

'Ahh. The wool importer.' It was no surprise that Lucrezia would select him as suitor. Rosso had married young, but had lost both his wife and son to childbirth. The grief of that would leave some men broken, unable to recover. The merchant responded by becoming one of the most successful importers in the city, bringing wool to Florence by means that others dared not risk. As his wealth grew so did his waistline, until Rosso was so fat he rarely left his palazzo. Now more than forty, Rosso needed a son to inherit. It was not uncommon for Florentine men to take a bride half their age, ensuring there would be plenty of childbearing years still ahead. A young beauty like Isabella would be enough to stir the *cazzi* of most men, even a bloated creature like Rosso.

'You know him?' Isabella asked.

'I know of him. Merging the *famiglia* business with his makes sense. And marrying him would certainly make you a rich young woman.'

'But is he handsome? Would I give myself to him, if I had the choice?'

Aldo did not reply.

'I understand,' Isabella muttered. 'Well, I'll not be bargained over like some cut of meat at the *mercato*. I won't be a chattel for Mama and Papa to sell.'

Her parents were not the ones making the deal, Aldo knew. 'Your mother said much the same to me, when she was your age. But Lucrezia had other ideas.'

'So what can I do?'

Aldo studied Isabella through the grille. She was doing her best to appear strong, but the arms folded across her pale blue dress told another story, as if she was hugging herself for warmth. There was no easy way out of this. Coming to the convent had delayed matters, but like most young women of means she had only two choices: the veil, or the wedding bed.

'I will send a message to your mother,' Aldo said, 'telling her your wishes. Beyond that I'm not sure there is—'

A scream cut the air. Aldo shot up from his chair. Isabella twisted round, and Suor Benedicta rose from her seat. 'That came from inside the convent,' Aldo said.

As Suor Benedicta went to the internal door, a female voice cried out beyond it: 'Murder! Murder!' A nun ran past the opening door, fear in her face. 'Blood, there's so much blood—' The words stopped, as if silenced or lost.

Suor Benedicta jabbed a bony finger at Isabella. 'Stay here,' she said before leaving, closing the door behind herself. There were raised voices in the courtyard, some crying out to God, others weeping and praying.

'I need you to open the door,' Aldo urged Isabella.

'What?'

'There's a door between the courtyard and the antechamber. I need you to open it.'

'But Suor Benedicta said—'

'Isabella, listen to me!' Aldo snapped. 'If there has been a murder inside the convent, it's my job to discover who did it and why. I need you to open that door so I can see the body before anyone interferes with it. Do you understand?'

## Chapter Nine

*A*ldo was waiting in the antechamber when Isabella opened the internal door to the convent. 'Thank you,' he said, striding past to reach the cloisters. Someone would be fetching the abbess. He had to reach the body first, otherwise she would never let him near it. Nuns were gathering on the far side of the courtyard, outside the doors in the north-western corner. Aldo hurried towards them, but Benedicta stepped into his path. 'What are you doing? How did you get in?' He brushed past. Ahead of him several nuns were comforting a novice with blood on her hands. She was shaking, her face drained of colour.

'Where is it?' Aldo asked, keeping his voice to a low, urgent whisper.

She pointed to the double doors. 'Left – on the left –'

He pushed by the remaining nuns and through the double doors, passing entrances to the kitchen and the *latrina*. The third door on the left was part closed, a coppery smell seeping out. Blood. But there was none on the stone floor outside. He pushed the door open.

It was the scriptorium where nuns copied and illuminated holy texts. Unlit candles stood on each desk. A single lantern, which hung from the ceiling, revealed the bloody mess below.

No wonder the novice had screamed.

A man's body was sprawled across the stones, naked and bathed in blood. More blood spread outwards from the corpse, pooling across the floor. Aldo had fought on battlefields, witnessing more death than he dared remember. But he could never recall so much blood around a lone corpse. It was . . . awash. Yes, that was the word. Awash with blood.

Aldo moved closer, careful to keep his boots clear of the pooling crimson. There were at least a dozen wounds to the chest and torso, but the face had suffered even worse.

It had been a frenzied attack. There was hate in this.

Picking his steps with care, Aldo moved around the corpse to the nearest desk, fetching a wooden chair. He took it to the scriptorium door, bracing the chair against the handle to stop anyone entering. The abbess would soon be in the corridor, expecting – no, demanding – to be let in. But the longer she and the other nuns were kept away, the more chance there was to study the evidence. Best to examine the body first. See what story it could tell.

The victim was closer to fifty than forty in age. There was grey in the hair above his ears, across the chest and around his un- circumcized *cazzo*. Jowls beneath the jawline and the curve of his belly showed the victim was far fonder of food and wine than hunting or horse-riding. The hands were pale and delicate, bearing no callouses or scars. Not a labourer, nor someone who worked outside, judging by the lack of colour on the skin. Not somebody who could easily climb up the convent's outer wall, so probably not the supposed intruder.

Aldo paused, his gaze returning to the victim's hands. Strange. The body had been stabbed again and again with the killer using a sharp, pointed blade – but there were no wounds to the fingers or palms. Fending off such a brutal attack would have been the natural response when facing such a threat. Instead, it seemed this man had let himself be killed. Had he wanted to die? No, that made little sense. More likely he was without his senses, unable to defend himself. Once metal had pierced skin the first few times, any fight left in him would have gone. The remaining stabs were born of malice, even madness.

This close to the body, the ripe aroma of blood choked Aldo's nostrils. He fought the urge to empty his stomach, but his legs were close to giving way. He put one knee to the floor, and dipped a finger in the blood surrounding the corpse. It was still wet. After wiping his finger clean, Aldo touched the dead man's skin. Cold. Cold as the stone beneath him. That prompted more questions than it answered. Aldo had spent enough time near corpses to know they could stay warm for hours after death, but spilled blood started to thicken and dry soon after leaving a body. So why was this body cold when its blood was still wet?

Voices outside the scriptorium door announced that Aldo wouldn't have much longer alone with the body. He peered at the victim's face, but it was difficult to see anyone familiar in such knife-ravaged features. The receding hair appeared dark brown, but was so stained by blood that couldn't be taken as a certainty. The dead man's eyes stared upwards, muddy brown around black. No beard, no moustache. Aldo frowned. It was no good. Until the body was cleaned, this could be one of a hundred men in Florence, if not more.

The scriptorium door shook but remained in place, held shut by the chair. 'Open up,' a stern voice commanded from outside. The abbess, and she was angry. Aldo couldn't blame her, but he had a task to complete. Enough of the body. He rose, knees creaking. What did the room around it reveal?

There was no blade nearby, no sign of the weapon used to stab the victim. Yes, blood surrounded and covered the corpse, but there were no splashes elsewhere. No flecks of red on the floor, no scarlet marks on the door or walls. Everything else in the room was neat and ordered. There were no signs of a struggle, nothing to suggest a murder had taken place here – aside from the bloody corpse on the floor. The scriptorium tools – quills, *stili* and brushes, rolls of vellum and parchment, pots of ink, rabbit glue and gold leaf – were all waiting in neat positions on each desk. There were knives among the tools, but they looked clean. Besides, those blades had wide, flat ends – not a good match for the wounds. Either the killer had taken their weapon with them, or the stabbing took place elsewhere and the body was brought here. But how to explain all the blood?

'Open this door!' the abbess demanded from outside. A fist hammered at the door.

Aldo took one last look around. The wooden beams of the ceiling were painted with an ornate pattern, rich and colourful. There was no other door or obvious entrance. Everything was in its place – no, there was something else. He had missed it at first, distracted by the corpse and all the blood. A scrap of parchment was visible beneath the victim's right arm, hidden in the shadow cast by the lantern overhead. Aldo pulled at the corner but it stuck under the arm. He lifted the limb, peeling the parchment away from the skin, noting that there was no blood beneath where the arm had been. Writing was visible on the parchment scrap, suggesting it had been torn from a larger document. Only a few words remained: *By Order,* it began; *the A* started the second line, and *shall* was all there was of the third. Aldo divided the scrap in half, folding it inward to shield the words before slipping it inside his tunic. Now it was time to face those outside.

* * *

The abbess had been upstairs praying in her private cell when one of the novices, Maria Vincenzia, burst through the door. 'Abbess, you must come! There's a body – a dead man – in the scriptorium . . . he's naked!' The abbess stalked to the staircase, demanding answers on her way down, but the breathless young woman had little more to add beyond saying it was another novice, Maria Celestia, who found the body.

The report sounded so absurd – a dead man, inside the convent? – that the abbess couldn't dismiss the possibility it was some elaborate jest. By the time she reached the hallway outside the scriptorium, the stone corridor was choked with nuns, their voices a babble of questions and confusion. She commanded them to silence, searching the faces for someone who could offer some sense about what was happening. Suor Giulia was standing to one side, her eyes fixed on the scriptorium door. The apothecary had a small workshop in the room next to the scriptorium; she might know what was going on.

The abbess beckoned her over, leaning close to whisper in the apothecary's ear. 'Is it true? Has one of the novices found a dead, naked man?'

Giulia nodded. 'It seems Maria Celestia discovered him when she arrived to light today's candles in the scriptorium. She staggered out with blood all over her hands, giving those passing by a terrible shock. I came out of my workshop when I heard one of them screaming. Nobody has dared go inside the scriptorium since. Well, nobody except a court officer. He's in there now, apparently.'

In all the tumult, the abbess had forgotten Aldo. He was meant to be meeting the Goudi girl in the visitors' parlour. How had he—? She banished the question. It did not matter. The fact he was with the body – the fact there was a body – was far more important. Glancing around, the abbess noticed Suor Andriana nearby. She was ashen-faced, a hand across her mouth. The draper's shock at what had been discovered was clear in her features. She would benefit from having a task to distract her. 'Giulia, I wish you and Suor Andriana to move everyone out to the cloisters. Once that is done, please find Maria Celestia and take her to the infirmary. She must be in great distress. I want Suor Simona to look after her.'

The apothecary nodded her understanding.

'Thank you.' The abbess went to the scriptorium, but the door would not open, no matter how hard she twisted the handle. 'Open up,' she said, but got no reply. Behind her Giulia and Andriana were ushering the others away, though the curious among them were not easy to persuade. The abbess waited until most had been taken out into the cloisters before hammering a fist against the wood. 'Open this door!' she demanded.

Still there was no reply, then there was a sound like wood scraping across stone and the door opened to reveal Aldo inside, blocking the entrance.

'You had no right keeping us out,' she snapped, looking past him to see what was inside the scriptorium. 'This is our convent. I shall be—' The words died in her mouth. A naked man lay on the floor, covered in blood and wounds. In the name of God, who would do such a thing? She whispered a prayer for the murdered soul, one hand clasping her small wooden cross while the other touched her forehead, chest and both shoulders.

Aldo stepped aside, letting her into the room. 'Do you know him?'

She entered, unable to lift her eyes from the body on the floor, its face cut to pieces. 'I . . . I don't think so.'

'It's not easy,' Aldo said, 'not with so much blood. Please. Look closer.'

The abbess forced herself to stare at the ravaged features, what was left of them. Who could be responsible for this horror? Nobody in their right mind, that was certain. There was something familiar about the face, but it was impossible to be certain. She shook her head. Movement outside the scriptorium caught her eye. 'Close the door.'

Aldo did so, resting his back against it. He was watching her move around the body, observing her. 'Yesterday, when I asked about intruders climbing in after curfew, you said there hadn't been any in recent days. Have men come to the convent at other times?'

Did he know about the diocese sending a visitation to Santa Maria Magdalena? the abbess wondered. Was this killing, this butchery, linked to that in some way?

'I need to know,' Aldo said. 'Have any men been inside the convent, besides myself?'

She hesitated. Better to speak the truth, no matter the price. 'Yes. The diocese sent an ocular visitation here three days ago. Two priests, and two laity.'

'An ocular visitation?'

Living in a convent so long, it was easy to forget not everyone had the same concerns, the same language for the promises and troubles that came with taking the veil. 'They inspect everything by eye to see if a convent and its nuns are following Church rules. We expect an auricular visitation in the next few days. Myself and my sisters in God will be questioned about our behaviour.' A second visitation had been likely. But this body, this – murder – made it certain. The future of the convent would be determined in the next few days.

Aldo nodded, falling silent. The abbess took the chance to

observe him. What was occupying the officer's thoughts? How did he even begin to discern the way forward when faced with such savagery? Aldo rubbed a hand across the silvering stubble on his jaw, but she could discern little more about him.

He gestured at the body. 'Was this man one of the visitors?'

The abbess gave a small shrug. 'Perhaps. If there was less blood, I could better answer that question. If the face was not so –' She trailed off, words failing her again.

He nodded. 'I need to send a message to the Podestà. The *segretario* must be notified. He will decide which officer from the Otto should investigate this, but I imagine—'

'You will do no such thing,' the abbess snapped. It was typical of an outsider, forcing his way into the convent, demanding they give way. It had been the same with the visitation, with everything that involved men intruding on convent life. She had seen it so often with the previous abbess, the battles fought with the diocese. If a nun dared speak her mind, she was accused of being difficult, a troublemaker. Yet when the archbishop expressed his views, that simply showed his strength of character. He had never shown any respect for the women of this convent, their lives or their autonomy. She got hold of her fury, forcing it aside to make this man see sense. 'Whatever occurs within these walls is a matter for the Church. It is not for your *segretario* to decide, not for your magistrates, and certainly not for you!'

Aldo scowled, narrowing his lips. 'Yes, all of that is true. The archbishop and the diocese have the final word in Church matters. But this is murder – a bloody and brutal murder – and that makes it a matter for the Otto di Guardia e Balia. You may not welcome the court here, but you cannot deny the reality of what lies in front of you.'

There was no condescension in his words, and no dismissal of her concerns. But that made the fact that he was correct no easier to accept.

'I came to the convent this morning to visit my half-sister's daughter,' Aldo continued. 'I can leave, if you wish, but that will only delay matters. Better to face them now, to take what control of the situation you can, before too many others become entangled here.'

Cramp in one hand made the abbess look down. She was still clasping her small cross, knuckles a stark white around the wood. She let go. 'What do you suggest?'

'Let me help you while others argue about who has jurisdiction here. That can be for the archbishop and the *segretario* to determine. You have more urgent matters to resolve, this corpse being one of them. It needs to be removed. I imagine you do not want a dead naked man carried through the convent in front of everyone.'

That made sense. It also showed Aldo was used to dealing with such situations. What a strange life he must lead, to be so unperturbed by the sight of violent death. 'I shall have one of my sisters fetch a covering,' the abbess said.

'We will also need some means of transporting it from the convent.'

'We have a hand cart for bringing heavy supplies from the *mercato*.' She frowned. 'Where will you take the body? To the Podestà?'

'No, to Santa Maria Nuovo. The nuns there can care for the remains.'

'Good,' the abbess replied. She knew some of those at the *ospedale* who cared for the sick and dying. They would respect the victim when others might not. 'Is that all?'

Aldo shook his head. 'That is only the beginning.'

\* \* \*

Giulia and Suor Andriana found Maria Celestia crouched in a corner of the cloister, her face ashen and both hands stained with blood. They got the novice to her feet, leading her to the infirmary where Suor Simona took charge. By the time Giulia returned to the scriptorium door, many of the other nuns had also come back to the narrow stone corridor. Convents were places of prayer and contemplation, refuges where murder was unknown. Such curiosity was understandable in the circumstances, if somewhat morbid.

The abbess emerged from the scriptorium, followed by a man in his middle years. He was careful to close the door behind him, ensuring nobody could see what was inside. It took Giulia a moment to recognize him. It was the man who had watched her and Suor Paulina dispensing alms at the back gates the previous day. He was a court officer – Aldo, that was his name. The dining table had been full of talk about him. If refectory gossip was accurate, someone claimed to have seen male intruders scaling the convent wall after dark, two nights before Palm Sunday. Now there was a dead man in the scriptorium. Were the two incidents connected somehow, or was Aldo's presence simple happenstance?

The stranger had an inquisitive gaze, studying the nuns while the abbess spoke. 'You will have heard whispers and rumours about what is in here,' she said, gesturing at the door behind her. 'The scriptorium will be closed for the day, perhaps longer. I will explain what is happening as best I can, but I prefer to do so only once. Where is the prioress?'

'Here.' The prioress pushed past Giulia to approach the abbess, her heavy frame forcing the apothecary out of the way.

'Please gather all those you can in the chapter house. I would speak to as many as possible before going to notify the archbishop about what has occurred.'

'Of course.' The prioress swivelled round to glare at those filling the corridor. 'Well, you all heard the abbess, did you not? Go to the chapter house.' The women beside Giulia moved away, many of them still stealing furtive glances at the scriptorium door. The abbess caught Giulia's gaze, motioning for the apothecary to stay.

The prioress was also pulling nuns aside. She commanded Suor Benedicta to go around the lower level, spreading word of the conclave. The prioress spoke to the sour-faced Suor Fiametta next. 'Please go upstairs to the dormitories and private cells. Tell anyone you find about the conclave. But do not disturb Suor Violante. I will see her later.' Fiametta nodded, bristling with her own importance at being given such a task.

Giulia stepped aside to let the eager sacrist hurry away. In the rare times Fiametta was happy, she still bore the face of a woman eating an unripe citron. Once the sacrist was gone, Giulia joined the abbess and Aldo by the scriptorium door. 'You needed me?'

'Quietly, without drawing attention, please fetch the small hand cart. I want you and another sister to cover the body, place it on the cart and remove it from the convent.'

'I –' Giulia hadn't expected this, but it made sense. Simona was busy with patients such as Maria Celestia, and there was nothing the infirmarian could do for a dead man. Short of a miracle, his condition was unlikely to change. 'Of course. Might I use my apprentice Maria Teodora for the task? She has . . . plenty of strength.'

'Very well.'

'And where are we taking this . . .' Words failed her. 'Where should the cart go?'

Aldo replied to that question. 'The *ospedale*, Santa Maria Nuovo. Deliver him into the care of the sisters there, until I can discover who he is and who should bury him.'

'I understand.' Giulia had left her apprentice grinding herbs in the workshop. Maria Teodora would have crushed them to oblivion by now. 'I heard the body is – unclothed.'

Aldo nodded, watching her face. Giulia refused to give him the satisfaction of seeing her turn crimson or white at the prospect of dealing with a naked man's corpse. This court officer knew nothing of her, or the life she had fled to join the convent. The body held no fascination or terrors for her. She gave a small nod. 'Then I shall bring something to cover him.'

# Chapter Ten

Satisfied with plans to move the body, Aldo asked the abbess if he could use her *officio* to write a letter. She agreed after he explained its purpose. While the abbess prepared to tell her nuns what had been found inside their convent, Aldo fetched Isabella from the parlour. She accompanied him to the abbess's *officio*. It was a simple chamber, furnished with a broad desk, several plain chairs and a heavy wooden cabinet against the far wall. Finding ink and paper atop the desk, Aldo asked Isabella to wait outside. He had a difficult letter to write and would rather do so without Isabella watching or asking questions.

*Saul,*

His hand shook a little. Should he scratch that out, replace the familiar with the more formal? No. Better to carry on, saying what must be said.

*I write in haste, and hope you will forgive these hurried words. I need your help. A man's body is being taken to Santa Maria Nuovo. He was killed in a brutal manner, but there are circumstances about this beyond my grasp. Your expertise and experience as a physician make me believe you can help*

*solve some of this puzzle. If you are willing, come to the*
ospedale *as soon as you are able and ask for me there.*

Aldo stopped. No, that was not enough. To send a letter like this without any better words was an insult. Saul deserved more after what had happened. Rather than start again, Aldo continued writing. Let the truth speak for itself.

*Forgive me for being so bold, but you once said you liked that.*
*I am sorrier than these simple words can express for my part*
*in the events that sundered us. I have respected your wishes,*
*and stayed away. You may have no desire to see me, and I*
*would understand that. If so, send your decision back by sealed*
*message.*

Aldo called Isabella into the *officio*. 'I need you to deliver a letter, can you do that?' She nodded. 'Have you been across the river to Oltrarno?'

The young woman frowned. 'Yes. Papa had a workshop near the Church of Santo Spirito; he took me there once.' Satisfied, Aldo added to his note.

*This letter is brought by my half-sister's daughter, Isabella Goudi.*
*Do not share my words with her. She is young and unworldly,*
*and would not understand. But please ensure she returns safely*
*to the convent of Santa Maria Magdalena.*
*Cesare.*

The ragged words would have to suffice. Aldo sealed the parchment with wax while describing to Isabella the best way of reaching the Jewish commune, and how to find Saul's home. Aldo made her repeat the instructions twice. She had a quick mind, restating his words without error or hesitation. Good. There was more to her than was obvious.

'I can do this,' she insisted. 'I'm smarter than Mama and Papa realize.'

'Once you are done, come directly back here. Promise me.'

Isabella smiled. 'I promise.'

The prioress had done as asked, gathering as many of the nuns and novices in the chapter house as could be brought there. Suor Simona remained at the infirmary with Maria Celestia and the other patients, none of whom were able to leave their beds. Suor Fiametta was last to arrive, shepherding those sisters who had been upstairs in the dormitories or private cells. Fiametta strode to the prioress, her nostrils flaring with righteous anger.

'Someone has taken a habit without my permission,' she hissed. Fiametta was forever disappointed by those who did not meet her high standards, but this incident was a fresh outrage. 'A complete set, gone – veil, wimple, all of it. I made a full accounting of the habits before compline yesterday. Who would do such a thing?'

The prioress placated Fiametta, promising to look into the loss once the conclave was over. By rights the matter should be reported to the abbess immediately. Theft was rare in the convent, so a miscounting was far likelier. But there were more urgent matters to resolve. The abbess rose to address all those on the benches either side of the chapter house. She looked tired, as if events were weighing her down. The prioress hid her quiet satisfaction.

'Sisters in God,' the abbess began, 'no doubt you have heard whispers about what was found in the scriptorium this morning. I am here to share the truth with all of you, in front of everyone and before our Lord, so that we may be as one in what we know and what we share. The coming days will not be easy, but if we abide together as a community, then we can support one another through these trials.'

The prioress nodded, careful not to be seen dissenting. When the time came for the abbess to step aside, the convent would favour someone who had been supportive of her.

'A terrible discovery was made this morning,' the abbess continued. 'One of the novices found the body of a dead man.'

This provoked gasps around the chapter house, nuns crossing themselves or whispering to each other, shock evident in all their faces. This was it. This was the beginning of the end for the abbess, and the start of a new beginning for the convent. The prioress looked upwards, offering a silent prayer of thanks.

'There is more,' the abbess said, raising her voice to be heard. The babble fell away, silence consuming the chapter house. 'It is clear that the dead man was killed. Murdered. Most likely here, last night, inside our convent.'

The babble rose again, wave upon wave, and the abbess did nothing to quell it. She let everyone say what they must to empty the rush of shock and dismay and fear. The prioress wished she had the ability to know when her sisters needed to listen, and when they needed to talk. The abbess seemed to have that awareness in her bones. The prioress knew it was not part of her own God-given gifts, but at moments like this she envied those who did. Envy was a sin, but none of them was without sin. Not even the abbess.

'I know you must all have questions,' the abbess said as the swell of noise abated. 'I shall answer all those I can, but my reply will often be that I don't know. Many of you will be afraid, worried about who committed this terrible sin. I share your fears. We do not yet know the name of the man who died, nor how he came to be inside the convent.'

The prioress watched those sitting opposite. They were listening and nodding, many praying. These would be testing times for the convent.

The abbess moved around the chapter house, reaching out to clasp the hands of those nearest to her. 'Before I hear your questions,' she said, 'I have several suggestions for us all to follow. Everyone should walk in pairs. We do not know if anyone else is in danger, but I wish us all to be safe until this matter is resolved. The scriptorium will remain closed today, perhaps for several days. Classes for visiting girls will be suspended. The fewer people coming and going from the convent the better, for all our sakes.' By now the abbess had reached the prioress. 'Lastly, I ask all of you to look after each other. We are stronger together if we are undivided.' The abbess turned away, raising her voice to address everyone. 'Let us pray.'

The prioress lowered her head, closing her eyes. Once this gathering was over, she would bring all those who believed in enclosure together. They must prepare for what was to come. The taking of a life was a terrible sin. But it was also an opportunity.

Aldo accompanied Isabella as far as the Duomo before they parted. He went south-west towards the Podestà, thoughts racing ahead in search of answers. Killings in Florence were usually simple to solve. The man responsible – it was almost always a man – was often found with the body or nearby. Victims were often known to their killer: part of the same *famiglia*, a neighbour from the same building or street, someone they worked alongside.

The body in the scriptorium . . . That was another matter. Until the dead man's name was known, it was difficult to know why he was killed, what motivated someone to plunge a blade into him again and again. Better to leave naming the victim to one side for now. There were plenty of other questions to answer. Why was he killed? Who took his life – and how? Who might benefit from his death? Why kill him in the convent, of all places – and why now?

How had the victim got inside the convent? There were three entrances and the abbess had said all were locked at night. That meant the victim had a key to get inside, or someone let him into the convent. The latter was more credible, but suggested his killer was a nun or a novice. Female killers were rare in Aldo's experience, and usually did so to save themselves – wives, daughters, mothers. Once a young woman in a *bordello* killed a visitor by accident, but it was his own fault for asking to be strangled with a belt while they fucked. Aldo doubted that was the case at Santa Maria Magdalena.

The *segretario* would demand answers when he heard about this killing, and there were not many to offer. The victim hadn't arrived at the convent naked, Aldo was certain of that, but where were the dead man's clothes? Hidden, burned, or removed from the building? A full list of those who had come and gone from the convent that morning would be needed. Had the victim been killed in the scriptorium? In most cases a body was found where it fell, but Aldo was less certain of that here. There had been so much blood, and yet no evidence of the attack taking place in the small chamber.

How the dead man was killed was the final question. All those wounds suggested a simple response: stabbing. But why had the victim not fought back? Who gave in to such a savage attack without any attempt to stop their killer? Was it even a single blade, or had more than one hand claimed this life? Aldo hoped Saul would set aside their differences and come to study the body. His clear-eyed view of such things – those warm hazel eyes that Aldo missed so much – would be invaluable.

The prioress had Suor Fiametta gather those who most favoured the convent's enclosure in the small courtyard behind the church. Getting Suor Simona away from the infirmary had not been easy, but Fiametta had succeeded in doing so. Suor Benedicta was also present. The listening nun might not be so forthright as others in wishing to see the convent enclosed, but it was still her preference. The gathering was small in number, but each nun was capable of influencing several others. Should the leadership of Santa Maria Magdalena be put to a vote in the chapter house, these women could tip the balance. The prioress looked at each of them in turn as she spoke, doing her best to match the abbess's oratory.

'What has happened inside this convent is a sin, and it is also a disgrace. We stand on holy ground, but that ground has been stained with the blood of a man. Who he was, how he came to be inside our walls after curfew – those are questions to which our abbess can offer no answers. But I know in my heart that it was her belief that we should remain open to the world that invited this event, this sin into our midst.'

Fiametta nodded, her thin nostrils flaring, and the other nuns followed her example.

'We have been patient. We have done all we could to persuade the abbess of her folly – but she would not listen. We asked her to think about the promise we all made to Our Lord, to be faithful unto him, to render all we are and all we have for him – but she would not hear. We pleaded with the abbess to see the path of righteousness lies in prayer and contemplation, not giving away our few resources to those who only come back for more – but she would not look at the truth and recognize her mistakes. Now we see the cost of her misjudgement.'

Those gathered were murmuring their agreement freely.

The prioress smiled. 'I agree with our abbess in one thing. The fewer people coming and going from the convent the better. You all heard her say that in the chapter house. From her own mouth does the truth come, though I doubt she realized her words would become our words. But she was right. We are stronger together if we are undivided. So I ask you now, my sisters in God, to reach out to those around us. Those who share your dormitory. Those alongside you when we pray in the chapel or eat in the refectory. Listen to them, hear their fears. Let them know you care about those worries, that you share their concerns.'

She paused, bringing both hands together. 'Our dream of this convent being enclosed is nearer than it has been in five years. So let us pray together and our Lord shall hear us.'

Isabella had been confident of finding her way, and that got her as far as the Arno. But the nearer she got to the Ponte Vecchio, the denser the crowd around her became. She was used to travelling in a carriage. Walking among people in the middle of the day was a very different experience, all noise and bustle and smells. Isabella was grateful for the modest blue dress worn by girls at Santa Maria Magdalena. The dull cloth and plain cut drew little attention.

She strode up the sloping bridge, stepping carefully between the puddles of blood and fish guts that littered the stones. Don't look anyone in the eyes, Aldo had warned her. Don't listen to anyone, and don't respond to questions. Keep walking and everything would be fine, Aldo insisted. But the hawkers on the bridge had other ideas. One of them stepped into her path, offering a golden ring for only a handful of *giuli*. The hawker saw her hesitate and moved closer, his fingers wriggling in the air, a ring on each of them. 'Like what you see, pretty girl? One of these would suit you very well.'

'Please step aside,' Isabella replied. 'I'm delivering a message.'

'Step aside, she says!' The hawker laughed, revealing a mouth missing most of its teeth. 'Step aside? Why yes, my lady, I certainly shall!' He bowed low, mocking her. Others around them were laughing, pointing at her and the hawker's comic display. She pushed past the ring seller. 'Hey, come back here!' he shouted. 'I haven't finished with you!'

Isabella ran, shoving through the crowd on the bridge, all thought of the careful directions Aldo had given her lost. She scampered down the other side and along the road south. As the press of people grew less, Isabella dared glance back. The hawker was gone, his tatty blue tunic and leering face lost in the throng behind her. But so were the landmarks Aldo had described. She had run too far.

The urge to cry was overwhelming, but Isabella fought it back. She must not weep. Not here, and certainly not in front of strangers. She'd promised to deliver the letter, so deliver it she would. But she dared not go back towards the bridge in case that hawker was still lurking. She needed help. Whom could she ask? Whom could she trust? Isabella was not much for praying, but she offered up a silent plea to the sky. No sooner had the words formed than she saw two nuns strolling towards her, deep in conversation. If prayers were always answered that fast, she would definitely pray more in future!

Isabella hurried towards the nuns, hoping her modest dress and best smile would win their favour. 'Excuse me, sisters, but can you help? I was sent from the convent of Santa Maria Magdalena and have lost my way.' She was sure the Lord would forgive her bending the truth a little. Why else send her these nuns? 'I am searching for the Jewish commune,' Isabella continued. 'Do you know if it is nearby?'

A few minutes later she was standing in via dei Giudei, a narrow street not far from where she had gone astray. The people here were different from those crowding Ponte Vecchio. The men all had long beards and wore small round caps on their heads, while the women were in long dresses and shawls. Few would meet Isabella's gaze. The strangeness of the commune reminded her of that first time she stepped inside the convent. It was as if she had blundered through a door to another world, a place unlike any she knew.

Were all the Jews in Florence squeezed into this one street? The walls were so close that she could touch both sides with her fingertips. A channel that stank of the *latrina* ran along the centre of the dirt alley. Isabella recalled how *Nonna* talked about Jews. She made these people sound like monsters, each one a grasping creature preying on those foolish enough to need a loan. But there were no monsters here. If anything, the people looked more afraid of Isabella than she was of them.

The doorway to each building had strange symbols above it. That must be the language the Jews used – Hebrew, wasn't it? Suor Catarina had talked about it in class but Isabella hadn't been paying attention. How was she supposed to find this doctor if – ahh, there it was! A sign above one doorway was in Hebrew, but it also had a name that she could read: Orvieto. Better still, the door was open. Aldo had said she could enter without asking permission.

Gathering her courage, Isabella went inside. The hallway was cooler than the street, and smelled nicer too: lavender and sandalwood, and another scent she knew, mulberry. There were several closed doors in the hall and wooden steps leading upwards. At the far end warm light spilled from an open doorway. 'Hello?' she called out, a tremble in her voice.

'Keep coming,' a man's voice replied from the open doorway. He sounded cheerful, someone who would be a friend. 'I'm in the back room!'

Isabella hesitated. She had never been inside a stranger's home before, and rarely went anywhere without Mama or *Nonna* escorting her. This house was very different from the palazzi where her *famiglia* and the Contarinas lived. There were no servants waiting to welcome her, no grand courtyard once you were inside the building, no frescos on the walls or statues adorning the corners. It was simple, even humble. But it was welcoming. It seemed . . . safe. Isabella ventured along the hallway, pausing at the open door.

The room beyond reminded Isabella of the kitchen at Palazzo Fioravanti, but this was not a room for making food. Jars, bottles and urns crammed the shelves, while blades of every shape and size littered benches round the walls. At the centre of the room was a long wooden table, where a kind-faced man was measuring powders into squares of paper before sealing them with a twist.

Doctor Orvieto looked much as Aldo had described, brown hair flecked with silver and a long beard full of autumn red. He wore a much-stained apron over his tunic and hose, sleeves pulled up to keep them out of his work. Like Aldo, the doctor was old enough to be her father, but there was none of Papa's sorry sagging. The doctor smiled at her while finishing his task. 'I don't think we have met before. How can I help?'

Isabella introduced herself, explained where she'd come from, and then offered Orvieto the sealed letter. 'This is for you.'

He hesitated, but accepted the document. 'Who is it from?'

'Cesare Aldo.'

'Cesare?' The doctor responded in a way Isabella had not seen before, as if his warm hazel eyes were surprised and happy and sad, all at the same time. His hands trembled a little as they turned the paper over inside them. 'Did he tell you what this says?'

Isabella shook her head.

Orvieto took a deep breath before breaking the seal, unrolling the paper and reading the letter within. His brow furrowed at first, before a frown stole away his happiness. Finally, Orvieto glanced up at her as his hands rolled the parchment back into a tight coil. 'Cesare says I must ensure you return safely to the convent.'

'That can't be all he says.'

'No, but much of it is private.' The doctor tucked the letter inside a pocket of his apron, which he then took off and draped over a chair, before throwing a short cloak over his shoulders. 'I'm going to Santa Maria Nuovo to help Cesare. Shall I escort you to the convent first?' Mischief creased Orvieto's features. 'Or would you rather come with me to the *ospedale*?'

Florence's city wall loomed ahead as Strocchi and Tomasia approached Porta San Frediano, the westernmost gate into Oltrarno, the southern quarter. Strocchi enjoyed having Tomasia's arms round him as they rode back from Ponte a Signa, but he would be glad to get off their hired horse. It was placid enough as a beast, but the saddle was poor and Strocchi hadn't been on a horse since January, making for a painful journey.

Saying goodbye to Mama had been exhausting, her tears making him weep as well. But Tomasia had not teased him about it afterwards. 'You are lucky to still have a mama,' she said, kissing the back of his neck. 'Weeping because you are leaving the place you call home is natural, Carlo. We will go back and visit your mama soon.'

He hoped Tomasia was right. But as Florence came closer, his thoughts turned to the reason they were returning early: Cerchi's murder. The more Strocchi mused on it, the more he believed the killing had taken place inside the city. Yes, Cerchi could have been slain elsewhere, but why dump his body in the Arno? Outside the walls of Florence a killer was more likely to bury the remains, or leave them to rot on open ground. Inside the city there were few places to hide a fresh corpse, unless you had a *famiglia* crypt. The smell of a rotting body was unmistakeable, and would soon be noticed. Dumping Cerchi's remains in the Arno offered a fair chance of the corpse being washed downriver and beyond the city walls, so long as it didn't get caught on one of the weirs.

'You're thinking about that buckle again,' Tomasia said behind him.

Strocchi laughed at how well she knew him. 'How could you tell?'

'The way you sit on the horse changed. You became more . . . upright.' She gave him a squeeze with her arms. 'Talk to me. When I was in Le Stinche, I found things easier when I talked about them with one of the other women.'

'Why would you want to hear about a murdered man?' Strocchi asked.

'It'll distract me from how sore my *culo* is on this saddle,' Tomasia replied. 'Who would have wanted this Cerchi dead?'

'Plenty of people. He wasn't well liked as an officer or as a man. Cerchi abused his position at the Otto, filling his pouch with coin whenever he could.'

'That's Florence. Everyone takes their chances.'

'Cerchi was worse than most, far worse.' Strocchi recounted how Cerchi used a murder victim's diary to extort money from wealthy merchants. 'That was a few days before Cerchi disappeared. Any one of those men might have killed him, or paid someone to do it.'

'What about at the Podestà? Did he have any enemies there?'

'It would be easier to name the friends he had, because there weren't any. He and Aldo were always clashing. The two of them hated each other.'

By now the gate was close enough for them to dismount and walk their horse through. Strocchi dropped to the dirt road before helping Tomasia down. 'You're always talking about Aldo,' she said, 'how much you think of him. But if he truly hated Cerchi . . .'

'You're suggesting Aldo killed Cerchi?' Strocchi laughed at her suggestion.

'What's so funny?'

'Aldo is far smarter than Cerchi ever was, knew how to deal with him. Besides, what reason could Aldo have for murdering Cerchi?'

Tomasia shrugged. 'You never know what is inside another person's head – or heart.'

'True,' Strocchi agreed. 'But if there is one thing I am sure about, it's that Aldo is not the person who killed Cerchi.'

# Chapter Eleven

The more Bindi heard, the more he wished Aldo had not spoken at all. The corpse of a naked man, found inside a convent? It was bound to be a jurisdictional nightmare. The Otto and its officers had a duty to enforce the laws of Florence, and bringing justice to those that committed murder was foremost among those duties. But the Church believed it should deal with all incidents on holy ground, regardless of the law broken.

'Do you know who the victim is?' the *segretario* asked.

Aldo shook his head. 'I've had the body taken to Santa Maria Nuovo. Once all the blood has been cleaned away, it may be easier to name the dead man.'

Taking the corpse away strengthened the Otto's claim to the investigation, though Bindi wasn't sure whether to be grateful. For this to happen in Holy Week only complicated matters. Should the archbishop deign to let the court investigate, he would probably demand the killer be found before Easter. Men of God had a limited grasp of the world outside their church walls, in Bindi's experience. The archbishop was another matter altogether.

The *segretario* answered to the city's leader, Cosimo de' Medici, and had little reason to encounter the archbishop directly. But Bindi's counterparts at other courts often told him about the archbishop. As leader of the Church in Florence, Buondelmonti might be expected to concern himself with the spiritual wellbeing of its people. But he was far more interested in how much coin he could extract from them. Churches could collapse, nuns and priests could starve, for all Buondelmonti seemed to care. So long as his purse was filled on a regular basis, so long as he was paid due homage in praise and coin, the archbishop was happy. Otherwise, his rages were terrifying.

'The Church must be notified at once,' Bindi said.

'The abbess is already doing so,' Aldo replied.

The *segretario* suppressed a smirk of satisfaction. Better her than him. But the matter of who was responsible for the investigation would still require agreement between the Otto and the Church. Sending Aldo to the archbishop's residence was tempting, but unlikely to have a favourable outcome for the court. Far better that someone of authority went, someone able to bend before the winds and will of others.

Bindi sighed. 'Very well. I shall visit the archbishop, and seek agreement that the Otto pursue justice for this unlawful killing. Until a decision is made, you will continue investigating. The faster you can find answers, the better.'

Tomasia offered to return the hired horse to its owner so Strocchi could report to the Podestà. He crossed the river at Ponte alla Carraia, pausing to look from the bridge down into the waters. Was this where Cerchi's body had entered the Arno? It must have gone in from a bridge. The current along the banks was not strong enough to carry a corpse over the weirs, let alone all the way to Ponte a Signa. Most of the river crossings within the city were open and visible to anyone on either bank. But Ponte Vecchio was crowded with buildings that would have hidden the deed from view.

Dumping a body from that bridge would not have gone unnoticed during the day, the stalls and traders were too busy. But at night, during curfew, the streets were empty and the stalls closed. It would still have been a risk, as there were homes built atop the shops on either side of the bridge, with families living inside them. None of those residing on Ponte Vecchio had come forward claiming to have seen a body put into the river, but nor had anyone asked them. For now Cerchi's absence was still considered a disappearance.

Strocchi headed north-east across the city, the silver buckle tucked inside his tunic. How would the *segretario* respond to news that an officer of the Otto had been murdered? Strocchi had little direct experience of Bindi, but there was no avoiding him now. The constable strode into the Podestà – and almost collided with Aldo on his way out.

'You're back,' Aldo said, clapping Strocchi on the shoulder.

'Yes,' the constable replied. 'But I discovered something while I was—'

'Tell me later,' Aldo cut in, moving past him. 'I have an urgent task at the *ospedale*.'

'Of course, but I need to ask your advice. When will you be back?'

'I'm not sure,' Aldo replied. 'Try Zoppo's tavern just before curfew. I will see you there, if I can.' He hurried away.

Strocchi watched him go, heartened by the possibility of a meeting later. Aldo had helped Strocchi find his way as a constable, offering wisdom and warnings in equal measure. It took a lot to earn Aldo's respect, and even more to secure his trust. But Strocchi liked to believe they were coming to understand each other.

The constable climbed the wide stone steps to the building's administrative level, willing his hands not to tremble as he knocked on the door to Bindi's *officio*.

'Come!'

Strocchi slipped inside, closing the door behind him. The *segretario* sat behind an imposing desk on the other side of the forbidding chamber. Bindi beckoned the constable closer, then ignored him in favour of a desk piled with papers. Aldo had once warned Strocchi about this, a *strategia* intended to make those waiting uneasy. Bindi enjoyed such games. Be patient and he would tire of the silence.

'Well?' the *segretario* eventually asked.

Strocchi reported what he had found in Ponte a Signa, and what it indicated. Bindi listened, fleshy hands clasped in front of his jowls, nostrils flaring in and out the only change to his permanent scowl. Strocchi took the silver buckle from inside his tunic and placed it on the desk, turning the metal over to show the initials *M. C.* on the back.

'And how far away is this village, this Ponta –?'

'Ponte a Signa,' Strocchi said. 'Two to three hours' ride.'

'If it was Cerchi's body, what makes you believe he was murdered in Florence?'

Strocchi explained his reasoning. When he ran out of words, Bindi let a long silence fill the air before speaking. 'It's not enough to have a body in a convent, now this . . .'

A body in a convent? That must have been why Aldo was rushing from the Podestà. Strocchi held his breath, waiting on Bindi's response.

'Very well,' the *segretario* said, at last. 'It seems likely the remains you found were those of Cerchi, and he was the victim of an unlawful killing. The murder of an officer of the Otto cannot go unpunished. Aldo was leading the hunt for Cerchi, but he is occupied with a more urgent matter, so I need someone else to take charge of this investigation.' Bindi glared at Strocchi. 'Do you believe yourself capable?'

'Yes, sir,' Strocchi replied. The words were out of his mouth in a moment, eager and ready to be spoken. What was he letting himself in for?

'Good. Find whoever it was that stabbed Meo Cerchi, bring this killer here to face justice, and I will consider promoting you to the post of officer.'

'Thank you, *segretario.*'

'Very well.' Bindi returned to his papers, waving a dismissive hand at the constable. Strocchi retreated towards the *officio* door. But as he reached for the handle, Bindi called to him. 'You can start by notifying Cerchi's wife that her husband is dead.'

'Yes, sir.' Strocchi stumbled out. *Santo Spirito!* Until a moment ago, he hadn't known the dead man was married. Now he had to tell Cerchi's wife that she was a widow.

The abbess had been waiting so long in the archbishop's residence, she feared the sounds from her stomach would disturb the dead. She'd left the prioress in charge of the convent, expecting to be back well before sext. Hours later, she was still sitting outside the archbishop's *officio.* The longer she stayed in the plush antechamber, the more her misgivings grew.

If she left now it would be another mark against her and the convent. Santa Maria Magdalena had been seen as a sanctuary for troublemakers during her predecessor's time, though the reputation was undeserved. All the previous abbess had done was argue that the convent had a right to welcome women seeking refuge, regardless of whether they wished to take the veil or not. Most of the women did not stay long, but it was how Suor Giulia first came to the convent, and she was now a senior nun.

Threatened with Santa Maria Magdalena's dissolution, the previous abbess agreed to stop providing sanctuary for women fleeing violent and abusive men. In truth, the convent continued to offer a refuge but was no longer able to ask for donations to fund that work. Dissolution had been avoided, but the diocese never forgave dissent and its clerics ensured successive archbishops never forgot. As always, the reputation of women rose and fell at the mercy of men, and that was doubly true within the Church.

The abbess had few doubts about the consequences of the murder for Santa Maria Magdalena. She had spent her five years as leader of the convent attempting to rebuild its good name with the diocese, but found her efforts often being undermined by the prioress and her acolytes. This killing would be the end. No matter who committed this sin, the convent would be deemed responsible. Enclosure was all but inevitable, while the threat of dissolution was suffocating. All her efforts, all her labours to keep the convent open and welcoming to the world, would be swept away once the prioress was in charge.

The abbess chided herself. Her efforts, her labours – such vanity. The future of the convent and its work was all that mattered. If she could persuade the archbishop to forego any final decision until after the killer was found and punished . . . But what she knew of His Excellency filled the abbess with more dread than hope. He was not a man to be gainsaid, not unless you brought plenty of coin and the promise of more. Clasping her hands together, she offered up a silent prayer. *Dear God, grant all thy servants the wisdom to see beyond themselves and their own needs. Show them that this—*

A bell chimed. The cleric behind the desk gave the thinnest of smiles, gesturing at the double doors on his left. 'His Excellency will see you now.'

She went in through the nearest door, her hands trembling.

The archbishop's *officio* was unlike anything the abbess had seen. The marble floor gleamed, ornate geometric designs set into the stone, while almost every other surface in the vast chamber was burnished or painted with gold. A lingering aroma of incense danced on the air, that unique whisper of prayer and scent. The coin needed to decorate in such a manner would sustain her convent for a lifetime. How could such opulence be serving God?

She strode across the expanse of marble to kneel before the archbishop. Monsignors and other clerics fussed in front of him, reminding her of busy insects on a hot day. Their black cassocks were all spotless, unlike her crumpled, dusty habit. But she would not be ashamed. She did not have the luxuries of those attending the archbishop.

At last the cluster of clerics parted to reveal the archbishop in full. He filled a golden throne atop a marble dais, a crimson canopy of silk draped around it. As a man he was more belly than torso; a white cassock struggled to contain his bulging gut. A short crimson cape draped across his shoulders and chest, while a gleaming silver crucifix hung down over it. Gold rings decorated each of his pudgy fingers, an impatient foot tapping the marble dais. The archbishop was clean shaven, his receding silver hair swept back beneath a black berretta. He glared at her with dark, unforgiving eyes. There was no welcome here, no warmth. 'Why have you interrupted my day?'

The abbess lowered her eyes. 'Your Excellency, I am—'

'Yes, yes,' he snapped. The attendants all stopped, as if frozen in place. 'I know who you are, from where you have come. My clerics have told me of your convent's past . . . conduct.' His lips curled with disdain. 'Why have you interrupted my day? I will not ask again.'

'This morning, one of my novices found the body of a dead man inside our convent. It was covered in blood, and had been stabbed many times.'

The archbishop said nothing. The silence lasted so long, the abbess wondered if the world had stopped. Finally, the archbishop spoke. 'If this is a jest, Abbess, it is a poor one.'

The abbess lifted her gaze. 'Your Excellency, I do not jest. There has been a murder at Santa Maria Magdalena. I wished you to know as soon as possible, so you could decide what should be done. An officer of the Otto di Guardia e Balia was visiting the convent when the body was discovered. He is claiming jurisdiction for the investigation of this killing.'

The archbishop's face hardened. 'The Otto – investigating on Church property? I think not.'

The abbess nodded, not daring to say more without being asked.

'Who is this dead man?' the archbishop demanded.

'We do not know,' she admitted, all too aware of the clerics watching her from either side of the dais. 'He was naked, with no clothes or belongings nearby to reveal a name. His face suffered many wounds, making it more difficult to recognize a likeness, and there was much blood as well.' The memory of that poor soul filled her thoughts. That ravaged face – that face . . . It would not come at the time, but something familiar about him had been nagging at her. She had seen him before, but when and where?

The archbishop was consulting with those around him, leaving the abbess free to recall the few men she had encountered in recent days. There was Aldo, and she had seen Father Visconti at Mass. A few days ago, the four men of the visitation had— that was it, the visitation. The dead man had been one of the two laity who had joined the two clerics for the ocular inspection. But what was his name?

'Are we boring you, Abbess?'

She realized the archbishop was glaring at her. 'Forgive me, Excellency. Seeing this poor soul in our convent, it was – I am still recovering from that, I fear.' Should she tell him the dead man had been a member of the visitation? Withholding this was a sin of omission, yet she had done worse and been granted God's forgiveness. But the truth would emerge eventually, and then she could stand accused of lying to the archbishop. No, she must confess what she knew now, and face the consequences. 'Your Excellency, I believe I may know which poor soul was killed in our convent.'

'A few moments ago you said you didn't know,' the archbishop replied, not bothering to hide his frustration. 'Which is it?'

'I do know him. Not his name, but I remembered where I'd seen him before.' The abbess explained that the dead man had been a lay member of the recent inspection.

The archbishop turned to the nearest cleric. 'I put Testardo in charge of assessing this convent, didn't I? Who did he take with him on the most recent visitations?'

'Father Zati,' the cleric replied.

'*Idiota!* I meant which members of the laity?'

The abbess was grateful the archbishop had found a fresh target for his anger. The unfortunate cleric was turning red with embarrassment. 'Cortese,' he spluttered. 'Testardo always takes Maso Cortese with him on convent inspections. But Cortese can't be the dead man; I saw him in the piazza outside less than an hour ago.'

'Then who was the fourth man?' the archbishop demanded.

The hapless cleric wiped sweat from his forehead. 'I believe a new man joined them for this visitation. Galeri, I think his name was. Yes, that was it – Bernardo Galeri.'

'Never heard of him.' The archbishop returned to scowling at the abbess. 'You said an officer of the court was at the convent when this body was found. Is he still there?'

'Not when I left,' she replied. 'He arranged for the body to be taken to Santa Maria Nuovo, and said he would report the murder to the Podestà. But that was some time ago.'

'Very well. You may go.'

The abbess was unable to conceal her surprise. 'Your Excellency?'

'Go,' he said, waving a dismissive hand. 'Return to your convent, to your nuns. I must discuss this matter with my advisors. You shall be notified of my decision.'

Knowing any argument would be wasted effort, the abbess got to her feet. Both knees had been chilled by the cold marble, but none of the clerics moved to help. She was only a woman, after all. The abbess bowed before leaving, her hands clenching into fists.


The prioress stumped upstairs to the convent's sleeping quarters. Chapter nuns occupied two large dormitories, while servant nuns shared two smaller dormitories with novices and boarders. The prioress strode past these towards the private cells, small chambers given over to a single nun, usually those who held an important post. To be granted one of those cells required a significant annual payment. The prioress had sacrificed her cell when Violante joined the convent, knowing her younger sister was ill-suited to dormitory life. It was better for all if Violante had a place of solitude, a place to be alone.

The prioress knocked at the heavy wooden door of her sister's cell. 'Violante, are you awake?' A low murmur of prayer was the only reply. The prioress went in, closing the door.

The cell was the same as any other in most ways, with plaster walls, a stone floor and high wooden ceiling. A narrow wooden bedframe nestled in the far corner, a mattress atop it. Nuns from wealthy families were known to fill their cells with tapestries and religious icons, but Violante had no such indulgences. Instead, she decorated the walls herself, scratching burnt wood into the plaster. Images of angels and cherubim danced along one side, surrounding the narrow, shuttered window. Opposite them were darker visions captured by Violante's hands. Demons. Monsters. Devils. For those she had added red to the blackness, though the prioress chose not to ask from where the colour came.

Violante was kneeling in the centre of the cell, her arms spread out sideways as if on the cross, eyes closed and lips murmuring prayers. She swayed from side to side, sweat falling from her face, soaking into the heavy fabric of her habit. How long had she been like this? Hours, perhaps, even all night. The prioress cursed herself for not coming sooner, but the body in the scriptorium had overtaken the day. She put a knee down on the cold floor to whisper into Violante's ear. 'Sister, can you hear me?'

The praying stopped, but Violante's eyes remained closed.

'I need to speak with you,' the prioress continued. 'May we get up from the floor? My old bones are not made for this, not anymore.'

Violante sat back on her haunches, bringing both hands together before rising. She was much younger than the prioress, a late child and a troubled birth. The prioress got up, and sat with Violante on the bed. 'There will be strangers coming soon. Men. I will do all I can to keep you safe from them.'

Violante nodded her understanding.

The prioress gave praise for the fact that her sister was having a good day. Let there be more, enough to fill the coming days. She rose to leave but Violante's voice stopped the prioress.

'There is something I need to tell you too.'

# Chapter Twelve

$\mathcal{B}$y the time Aldo reached Santa Maria Nuovo, the body from the convent had been taken to a small, empty room at the rear of the *ospedale*. Two nuns washed the corpse atop a stone table, afternoon sun streaming through a single opening high in the back wall, warming the bundle of mulberry twigs that hung in front of it. The women worked without words, moving with ease and efficiency – they had cleaned many a body before.

Grooves in the stone table caught the crimson water leaving the body. When the worst of the congealed blood had been removed, the nuns used cloths to clean folds and creases in the skin. The task was made more difficult by the body stiffening, as corpses did in the hours after death. Neither woman showed any shame or embarrassment at tending to a naked man's body in front of Aldo. They must have seen and dealt with far worse. Working with the sick and dying was not for the weak of will.

Their task complete, the nuns draped a sheet across the lower half of the corpse before departing. Once they were gone, Aldo moved closer to the dead man. It was easier to see his features without all the blood, but Aldo still did not recognize the face. The hair was brown, a lighter shade than it seemed in the scriptorium, chestnut with grey creeping in near the temples. Cleaning the body had made it more presentable, but not solved the problem of discovering who this man had been.

Footsteps were approaching the room, and a voice he recognized. What was Isabella doing here? The door opened and Saul entered with his satchel, Isabella by his side. But for her presence Aldo might have embraced Saul. But she was there, watching them. Besides, Saul's arrival meant he was willing to help as a doctor, not that he had forgiven what had happened. Aldo contented himself by nodding to Saul, appreciating the Jewish doctor anew. It was January when they parted in difficult circumstances. Saul had been furious, rightly so, exhaustion and anger making his kind face haggard at the time.

Now he looked more the warm, intelligent man Aldo had first met. Tall and upright, his body remained lean with wide shoulders and deft hands. Were there a few more strands of silver in his hair? Perhaps. But those hazel eyes were still full of warmth and kindness, even if Aldo could not tell whether Saul had arrived only from a sense of duty or obligation.

'You came,' Aldo said. Not the first words he had planned, but they would do.

'Of course,' Saul replied, eyes flickering to Isabella at his side. 'Always happy to help those who enforce the law.' He put down his satchel. 'So, what do you have for me?'

Aldo stood aside to let Saul and Isabella see the body. She gasped, making the sign of the cross, while the Jewish doctor arched an eyebrow at the multitude of wounds. 'Someone has been busy.' He moved past the dead man's feet to make a slow circuit of the stone table, leaning in for a close examination at times. 'Tell me about him.'

Among the many qualities Saul possessed, his directness was one of those that Aldo appreciated most. There was no need for ceremony or feigned reverence. A dead body was a dead body to the Jewish doctor. Aldo described where the body had been found, the way it was covered in blood, careful not to colour the words with his own suspicions and theories. 'The body was still loose when I first saw it this morning,' he added.

Saul gestured at the corpse. 'May I?' Aldo nodded. Saul closed both hands around one of the dead man's wrists, lifting it upwards. The body resisted, the arm rigid in his grasp. 'He's been dead at least twelve hours. Chances are, he was killed during the night.'

'How do you know?' Isabella asked. The young woman had stayed near the doorway. 'How can you be certain?'

'Two reasons,' Saul replied. 'First, I'm sure the sisters at the convent would have noticed a dead man in their midst if he was killed before last night. Even if hidden from view, a corpse begins to give off distinctive aromas as decay takes hold. Second, what happens to our bodies after we die follows a particular pattern, a predictable pathway, if you like. When life is ended, the body relaxes. Often whatever waste was held inside it leaves.'

Her face crumpled. 'That's disgusting.'

Saul smiled. 'Nonetheless, it happens. Warmth leaves the body too. Some hours later, perhaps half a day, the limbs become rigid as they have here. Two days after death, that tension leaves the body for the last time. It's part of who we are.'

'Oh,' Isabella said. She moved closer to the dead man. Curiosity seemed to be getting the better of her initial unease.

'With this body, there was something I hadn't seen before,' Aldo said. 'The skin was cold when I first touched it, cold as the stone floor underneath it. But the blood – and there was a lot of blood – was still wet, like wine. Shouldn't it have dried?'

'Usually,' Saul agreed. 'But there could be reasons for that. I have heard tell of a rare illness where wounds will not stop bleeding. The blood from such people remains wet for longer than is usual outside the body.'

'Would a person with such an illness know this?' Aldo asked.

'If they had ever been cut or their skin broken. I have never encountered a patient with such an illness myself, so I cannot tell you any more about it.'

'You said there were reasons,' Isabella interjected. 'What are the others?'

'How fast a body becomes cold after death depends on where it lies. You said this man was found on a stone floor?'

Aldo nodded. 'But if the surroundings made this body go cold faster, that should also have affected the blood on the—'

'I've seen him before!' Isabella blurted, pointing at the corpse's face.

'How?' Aldo asked. 'You were in the convent parlour when the body was found.'

'No, not today,' she replied. 'It was a few days ago. He was one in a group of four men at the convent. They interrupted one of our classes. Suor Catarina asked them to leave because they were disturbing the lesson. Two of them were priests, but this man was one of the others.' Isabella shivered. 'I remember because he was staring at us. At me. He looks different now, all those cuts to his face, but I'm sure that it's him. I never heard his name, but Suor Catarina told us the four men were called—'

'The visitation,' Aldo said. The victim had been one of the men inspecting the convent. Aldo remembered the scrap of parchment he found under the dead man's arm in the scriptorium. It was at the Podestà for safekeeping, but he could recall the text: *By Order, the A,* and *shall*. If Isabella was right, the scrap might be from the inspection papers. Such a document would start with the words: *By Order of the Archbishop of Florence*.

So why had the abbess not recognized the dead man when she saw the body? Yes, his wounds and all the blood made it difficult, but not impossible . . . Aldo pushed that question aside; it would have to wait for later. Identifying the dead man as one of the visitors was a significant step forward. 'Thank you, Isabella. Knowing who this man is – or was – should make finding his killer much easier.'

The young woman's face lit up. Knowing her *famiglia*, it was unlikely she got much praise except from Teresa.

'I need to talk with Dr Orvieto,' Aldo said. 'Isabella, could you wait outside?'

'Yes, of course.' She nodded to Saul as she left. Once Isabella was gone, Aldo reached across the corpse for Saul's hand.

'Thank you for coming. It's been too long, and I—'

'Shh,' Saul whispered, putting a finger to his lips. 'That girl is very curious. She will probably be listening to us from out in the corridor.'

Aldo nodded, raising his voice to reply. 'Now the body's been washed, I need you to examine it. Anything you can tell me about how this man died, and when, would be useful.'

Saul gestured at the victim's wounds. 'How he died will not take long to determine.'

'Most days, I would agree. But there may be more to this than we know.'

Saul nodded. 'Very well. I'll examine him thoroughly. Where will you be later?'

Aldo glanced at the doorway. Isabella's shadow was visible at the threshold. 'I can't be certain,' he announced. 'It's probably best if I come to your residence. Besides, you must have other people to see today, members of your own community that need your help.'

Saul nodded his agreement. He reached for his satchel, attention already turned to the body on the stone table. Aldo nodded to Saul before leaving, still unsure if the good doctor had forgiven him. The fact that Saul had come was a promising sign, but Aldo preferred not to hope too often. Survival was enough of a triumph in Florence some days.

The abbess returned to Santa Maria Magdalena not long before nones, the mid-afternoon recitation of prayers. She called all the senior nuns to her *officio*, leaving Suor Catarina to lead prayers in the chapter house. The infirmarian Suor Simona was also absent, but the urgency of her duties meant she often missed a conclave. After describing the archbishop's response, the abbess asked for reports on what had happened in her absence.

Suor Giulia confirmed that the dead body had been taken to the *ospedale* without incident, noting the assistance of Maria Teodora. 'My novice is proving an . . . able apprentice.'

The abbess suppressed a smile. Giulia had high standards, and limited patience. But having her guide Maria Teodora was a good deed, even if the novice would never succeed Giulia as apothecary. It had kept the young woman away from the other novices, who were not a good influence. 'What else?'

'I wonder if we could consider again the amount being distributed as alms,' Suor Paulina said, her comment bringing sighs from those who were standing near the prioress. 'Suor Ursia left us for our Lord's eternal grace, I have been fulfilling her responsibilities as cellarer for the convent since, while continuing my work as almoner. If anyone else wishes to lighten my burden, I would happily let them. But the truth remains the alms we give out are never enough for the needy of this parish. We should be doing more.'

Paulina's resolve was admirable. The prioress and others believed the almoner too kind of heart, too willing to give. Paulina had a young face, open and lacking in apparent guile, which served to strengthen such attitudes about her. But the abbess knew standing against those louder and harsher than yourself took courage. Paulina had plenty of that. 'I agree,' the abbess said, 'but that is a matter for another day, and one that must be agreed by the whole convent at the chapter house. For now, we have more urgent issues.'

The abbess noticed Suor Andriana was clutching a sack. The draper stood behind the other nuns, hiding herself away as ever. She seemed to have a need to say something but lacked the courage to speak. Before the abbess could invite Andriana forwards, Suor Fiametta chose to address those gathered.

'Someone has taken a habit without my permission,' she announced. 'As sacrist it is my responsibility to keep and care for the convent's books and clothing. To uphold that, I undertake a full accounting each day. This morning I discovered a set of garments had been removed without permission – habit, underskirt and wimple. Who would do such a thing?'

It was a valid question, and the abbess knew better than to suggest a miscounting. A nun as sanctimonious as Fiametta would have checked many times before making such a pronouncement. 'Can anyone offer an answer for our sacrist?'

Andriana raised a timid hand. 'I may know,' she said, her voice close to a whisper.

'Speak up,' the abbess urged. 'Tell us all.'

The draper reached into the sack. 'One of the servant nuns found these hidden in the laundry.' She pulled out a leather belt, woollen hose and a pale orange tunic. Andriana kept the garments at arm's length from herself, their ripe masculine stench filling the *officio*. These must be the dead man's missing clothes.

'Hold the tunic up,' the abbess requested. Andriana did so, but there was no blood evident on the cloth, front or back. That meant the dead man, Galeri, had been bare-chested when he was stabbed, or even naked. 'Thank you.'

Andriana then pulled a habit from the sack. This did bear blood, crimson staining the dark blue material in places near the hem. The wearer must have been close by when blood was shed for it to spatter her habit, yet none of the sisters had come forward to admit that.

'Was there a veil found with the habit?' the abbess asked. Every nun wore the same basic garments at Santa Maria Magdalena, but chapter nuns, servant nuns and the novices all had different-coloured veils. If the veil that matched the habit had also been found . . .

'I'm sorry, no,' Andriana replied.

The abbess nodded. 'So, having got blood on her habit, one of our sisters in God took another from among those in Suor Fiametta's storeroom, and hid the stained garment in the laundry, hoping it might go unnoticed. Keeping her veil suggests it bears no bloodstains, or else she realized its colour could help lead us to her.' The abbess studied the faces of those gathered. Each was glancing at the women around them, looking at veils for signs of blood. Whoever killed Galeri had now planted a seed of suspicion in all of their hearts. Taking a life was the far greater sin, but this doubt would still fester and grow unless it was snuffed out.

'What else?' Nobody responded. 'We must not let what has happened in our convent turn us against each other. Tell me, how are our sisters in God coping with all of this?' She turned to the prioress, who had stayed silent since entering the *officio*. The burly senior nun was not a woman who found it easy keeping her views hidden, but her thoughts seemed to be elsewhere. 'You know the mood of our sisters. How are they?'

The prioress hesitated before replying. 'Some of the younger nuns, those with less experience of the world, worry what this means for the convent.'

The abbess feared the same, but wasn't going to admit that. 'It is understandable. I wish I could offer assurances that nothing will change, but I fear that would be false hope. There shall be consequences we cannot yet foresee, but we must carry on. Now, does anyone else have matters to report before we join our sisters at nones?'

The prioress shook her head, and those around her did the same.

'Then let us go and pray,' the abbess said. 'More than ever, we need the guidance of our Lord. We need to be as one in our sisterhood of God.'

Finding Cerchi's wife – his widow – took longer than Strocchi expected. The Podestà held no record of where the dead officer had lived. The man in charge of paying those who worked for the Otto simply handed out coin; there was no need to know where each man resided. Strocchi asked other constables and guards, but Cerchi was a man without friends inside the Podestà. Nobody could recall visiting his home and, like Strocchi, few even knew Cerchi had been married.

It was Benedetto who provided the answer. The fresh-faced young constable strolled into the courtyard as Strocchi was leaving. Five months working for the Otto had done little to sharpen Benedetto's wits, but he was competent enough with simple tasks. To Strocchi's surprise, he knew exactly where the missing officer had lived. 'Cerchi has two rooms in Santa Maria Novella, down an alleyway, not far from the piazza. He sent me there once to fetch his spare boots. Why do you ask? Has he come back?'

Strocchi realized few in the city other than himself, Tomasia and Bindi knew that Cerchi was dead. The *segretario* had given no instruction whether or not others should be told what had happened. Perhaps it was better to maintain the story that Cerchi was missing. If he had been murdered in Florence, the killer would believe their crime remained unknown, the body undiscovered. 'No,' Strocchi said, choosing his words with care, 'not yet. But the *segretario* needs me to take a message to Cerchi's wife.'

Benedetto blew out his cheeks. 'I don't envy you that. She's an angry woman.'

Strocchi was less familiar with the western quarter of Florence, but Benedetto's instructions were good enough to find the building where Cerchi had lived. Up a set of creaking wooden steps he knocked at a door, preparing to face a woman who would soon be a grief-stricken widow. Rare were the occasions when constables from the Otto were required to tell a *famiglia* about a sudden death. He had been present for two such visits where the loss and grief were devastating. How would Cerchi's wife respond?

The door was ripped open, a furious woman inside. She was short, standing no higher than Strocchi's shoulder. Her face was careworn, nose twisted to one side as if it had been broken, while unruly curls of brown hair were pulled back in a severe knot to keep them out of her eyes. 'What the *diavolo* do you want?'

Strocchi removed his cap, clutching it in both hands as he introduced himself. 'Excuse me asking, but were – are you – married to Meo Cerchi?'

'Has that *bastardo* finally come back?' she demanded, still blocking the doorway. Her eyes narrowed. 'You said "were" – what's happened?'

Strocchi glanced around. None of the nearby doors were open, but the noises coming from behind them had stopped. 'Perhaps this would be better said inside –'

'No. Tell me, where is he?'

'I'm sorry to inform you, to tell you, that it seems likely—'

'Just say it!' she snapped.

'He's dead,' Strocchi blurted. 'Your husband is dead. Murdered, it seems.'

The woman did not respond at first. She appeared stricken, still as a statue. Then, when he feared she might collapse, the woman laughed. It burst out of her, laughter upon laughter, until tears were streaming down both cheeks.

Strocchi didn't know what to do. He had expected weeping, perhaps the numb nothingness of grief delayed, the way his mama had been the first few hours after Papa died. But this, this . . . joy – it was unlike anything he had witnessed.

Finally, the woman recovered enough to stop laughing. She sucked in a breath, wiping the tears from her face. 'Forgive me,' she said, 'but that's the best news I've heard in a long time. Please, come in.'

The room was small, a bed pressed against one wall, a wash basin on the floor beside it. A single chair stood beneath the only window. Through a doorway Strocchi glimpsed another room, some pans on a bench with chipped plates stacked on shelves above them. Everything had its place, everything was tidy. Together, the rooms were little bigger than the single one he shared with Tomasia. Strocchi knew officers were paid more than constables, and could add to that by collecting rewards and bounties. But none of that coin seemed to have come home to Cerchi's wife.

Strocchi waited until she had closed the door before asking her name.

'Grazia Cerchi,' she replied. 'How did he die?'

Strocchi told her about his discovery in the graveyard, the notches in the ribs.

'Did he suffer?'

A stab to the heart was a quick death, if the blade found its target. 'Probably not.'

'Pity.' Grazia sunk onto her bed, gesturing for Strocchi to have the chair. 'I meant it when I called him a *bastardo*. Meo only married me because he got me with child. But our baby – my little girl – did not breathe when she was born.' Grazia stared at the floor a while before continuing. 'After that, he wouldn't touch me, wouldn't come near me. Said it was my fault. Meo took his anger out on me, and his lusts out at the *bordello*.'

Shame coloured Strocchi's cheeks. He couldn't imagine treating Tomasia that way, though it was not his place to judge others. Let them confess their sins and seek forgiveness.

'All these weeks, expecting him to come home,' Grazia said, 'not knowing when he might walk back in that door, or what mood he would be in –' She took a deep breath, her back straightening. 'I can make a new life for myself now.'

Grazia seemed to feel only relief at her husband's demise. Could she have been involved with his murder? Perhaps. But her surprise, her laughter on hearing he was dead – that had all been genuine, Strocchi was certain. Her response granted him the opportunity to ask questions that would have been impossible if she was inconsolable. 'Can you recall the last time you saw your husband?'

She frowned. 'I told the other officer before, the one who was looking for Meo.'

'Aldo?'

'That was his name. He was kind, made sure I had enough coin to get by.'

That surprised Strocchi. Giving her coin had been kind, especially since Aldo and Cerchi had been near to *vendetta* several times. Strocchi was a little ashamed not to have done the same.

'I am investigating your husband's murder. His body was found downriver, but I suspect he was killed here in Florence. Knowing when you last saw him could help us find the truth.'

Grazia sighed. 'It was a few days after the Epiphany. He came home full of himself, not long before curfew. Claimed he was going to be rich at last, as he deserved.' She snorted. 'Meo never worked an honest day in his life, not if there was another way to fill his pouch.'

'Did he say how he was becoming rich?'

'No. He never shared anything with me, except his fists.' She pressed fingertips to her crooked nose. 'Meo went back out before curfew, and never came home again.'

'You said this was a few days after the feast of Epiphany. Can you remember how many?'

'Five, I think. It's hard to be sure, most days are the same. Meo often didn't come home until late, if at all, and when he did, his clothes stunk of the *bordello*.'

The feast of the Epiphany had fallen on a Saturday. Five days after that would have been Thursday, January 11th. That was when Strocchi had returned to the city with Aldo after several days away on court business. They had reported to Bindi, before going their separate ways. Strocchi remembered nodding to Cerchi on his way out of the Podestà. Was that the last time he'd seen the missing officer? Maybe. Cerchi did not report for duty at the Podestà the next day, or the day after, or ever again.

Before joining the Otto, Cerchi was a constable at the Office of Decency, which controlled the sale of sex for coin in Florence. Strocchi had heard Cerchi used that position to get what he wanted at one particular *bordello* without paying. It meant a visit to question the *matrona*. 'Victims often know their killer. Did your husband have any enemies?'

Grazia laughed at the question. 'Had you ever met him?'

'Yes.'

'Then you can put yourself on the list of his enemies. Meo hated most people, and the feeling was mutual. It would be easier to find those who didn't want him hurt, or dead.'

'Did he have *famiglia* in the city?'

'Not that he spoke of, and nobody ever visited. His father died years ago, I know that. But Meo only cared about himself.' The more Strocchi learned about Cerchi, the less there was to like. 'Did you have any other questions?' Grazia asked. 'I'm tired. I need to rest.'

'Of course,' Strocchi said, moving to the door. He paused on his way out. 'Do you have anyone that can be with you – *famiglia*, or friends?'

She shook her head. 'Not here in Florence. My sister lives in Friesole. I might go and stay with her. It's got to be better than this city.'

# Chapter Thirteen

The sight of the corpse on that table stayed with Isabella as Aldo led her through the city. The dead man had been still as a statue, but all the statues she had seen looked beautiful, even those of dying warriors. The body at Santa Maria Nuovo was so sad. All those holes in his chest and face. Ugh, it made Isabella's belly squirm. She didn't want to imagine how it must have been, dying like that. Poor man.

There were other things filling her head. Watching the Jewish doctor at work, how he talked about what happened to a body when life left it . . . that had been fascinating. She never knew such things. She would certainly pay more attention in classes if they were about things like that, instead of psalms and scriptures and God. Nuns talking about God was always dull, even when Suor Catarina was the one talking.

Recognizing the dead man had been a surprise. It was his eyes that made her realize. Isabella remembered the way he had stared at her during the visitation. Perhaps it wasn't so bad that he suffered? No, that was a terrible thought. But she could not find it in herself to weep for him. Aldo and Dr Orvieto had shed no tears for him, why should she?

The moment when Aldo thanked her . . . recalling it made Isabella's cheeks warm with pride. She never heard that from anyone in the palazzo. Well, that wasn't completely true. Her maid

Nucca was always grateful, but it was the maid's job to be her companion and friend. Mama called her beautiful often, but that wasn't the same. To be thanked . . . Isabella liked hearing those words. Perhaps she could find more ways to help Aldo . . .

Aldo kept striding ahead, Isabella scampering to keep up. He was at least a head taller than she was, with most of that extra height in his long legs. How quickly things could change when Aldo was around. In all of the excitement, she had forgotten how her day had started, fleeing to the convent, seeking refuge with the nuns. Now she was helping Mama's half-brother solve a killing on holy ground!

He seemed to be on good terms with Dr Orvieto, who was thoughtful and funny. Papa was always angry about what Jews charged him for loans. The way he talked, Orvieto should be a monster. But the doctor was nothing like that. How could Papa be so wrong?

There was something else Isabella didn't understand. Why had Aldo sent her out of the room so that he could talk with Dr Orvieto? She'd listened from outside the door but nothing was said they couldn't have spoken in front of her. They reminded Isabella of how she and Nucca were sometimes, whispering secrets when everyone was busy. It was good to have someone to confide in. Everyone needed a friend they could trust.

A servant nun called Suor Rigarda came to the abbess's *officio*, bringing a note from the infirmarian. It apologized for missing the meeting, and asked the abbess to come as soon as possible. She accompanied Rigarda back, afternoon sunshine filling the cloisters with the scent of lavender as they strode around the courtyard. At the infirmary, four elderly nuns were dozing in their beds. It seemed unlikely any would leave except to enter God's care. But there was a new patient in the far corner, separated from the rest of the room by a folding screen.

Letting Rigarda return to her duties, the abbess went to the screen. 'Suor Simona, you asked to see me?' The infirmarian emerged, crimson staining her white apron. She was a matter-of-fact woman, and offered no apologies for her bloodied appearance. Tending to those in pain or facing death had stripped Simona of all pretence.

'Thank you for coming,' the infirmarian said, her voice little more than a whisper. She took the abbess to one side. 'The novice that found the body –'

'Maria Celestia?'

'Yes. She was brought here, shivering and shaking, unable even to speak. When she sat down, I noticed her sleeves were stained with blood.'

'I saw the body too,' the abbess replied. 'There was a lot of blood.'

'But the blood on Maria Celestia is her own,' Simona said. The infirmarian came closer so nobody else might overhear. 'This novice has deep cuts to both palms, wounds not unlike those of . . .' She trailed off, her voice faltering.

'Are you suggesting Maria Celestia has the stigmata?' When he was crucified, Christ suffered wounds to his feet, wrists and hands. When someone spontaneously bore the same wounds as Christ – stigmata – it was considered a miracle. But few ever proved to be true.

'Of course not,' Simona replied. 'But when word of her wounds is heard by others –'

The abbess nodded. Though the convent's doors were still open for now, it was a close-knit community in which rumours were currency and whispers could take on a life of their own. Soon half the nuns would be talking about Maria Celestia's wounds and the possibility of a miracle in their midst. 'How is she?'

The infirmarian glanced at the screen. 'Her senses come and go. She speaks at times, but the words make little sense. Come and see for yourself.'

The abbess followed Simona behind the screen. Maria Celestia was resting beneath a sheet on the narrow cot. Her habit and veil had been removed, but her hair remained hidden beneath a white head cloth and her modesty by a white shift. The novice's arms lay on top of the sheet, by her sides. Bandages wrapped round both hands, blood soaking through. Her face was pale, her eyelids flickered, lips muttering, but no sound escaped them.

The abbess knelt by the cot. 'Maria Celestia, can you hear me?' There was no response. 'When did you suffer those cuts? Was it before, or after you found the body?'

Still the novice's lips moved, but she did not speak aloud.

Simona unwrapped one hand. There was a deep cut in the palm, piercing skin and flesh. Fresh blood seeped from the wound. 'The other is much the same,' Simona said.

The abbess placed fingertips on Maria Celestia's forehead. It was clammy, sweat soaking her head cloth. 'Does she bear any other wounds? On her wrists, or feet?'

'No. It is only her hands, or she would probably be far worse.'

The abbess got back to her feet. 'I will pray for her recovery. Until we hear what she saw and heard, it will be difficult to know who killed the man she found.'

Aldo knew there would be trouble when he reached the corner where via San Gallo met the side road to the convent. Two clerics in black cassocks were outside the convent, arguing with a workman on the best way to hammer a notice to the sturdy wooden door. Aldo could not hear all they said, but the word enclosure was clear enough. *Palle!* The archbishop was wasting little time in having the nuns shut away. Better to silence them than let word of a murder mar the ceremonies for Holy Week.

Aldo glanced at Isabella, still wearing the pale blue dress of a convent student. She was a wilful young woman who, no doubt, created much trouble for her parents. Isabella's natural curiosity meant she might be a useful ally inside the convent, but it could also put her in harm's way. Conscious of the clerics close by, Aldo lowered his voice to talk to her.

'I believe Santa Maria Magdalena is being enclosed. That means I will be locked out. But you could still go in, if you wish.' Isabella opened her mouth to reply but he motioned her to silence. 'If you do, it's likely you will have to stay several days, perhaps longer.'

Isabella bit her bottom lip. 'If I go in, will Mama and Papa be able to get me out?'

'Not easily, and not without special permission from the archbishop.'

Mischief crept into her face. 'Then I wouldn't have to marry Ercole Rosso?'

'Not while you remain here.'

'Then I choose the convent.'

'There is more at stake here than avoiding a wedding,' Aldo warned. 'You have no way of knowing how long this enclosure could last.'

She shrugged. 'Being in a convent can't be any worse than what is waiting for me.'

'You're forgetting something else,' Aldo insisted. 'There is a killer inside this convent. You saw the dead man, what they did to him.'

Even that didn't seem to stifle her enthusiasm. 'Perhaps I can help you find them. If you're stuck out here, I could be your eyes and ears inside.'

'That's too dangerous. Besides, you don't know what to look for—'

'You can tell me.'

'No!'

Isabella shrank back from his curt dismissal, and the nearby clerics swung round to stare at Aldo. He hadn't meant to snap but it was necessary to make her grasp the potential danger. He would not let Isabella put her life in danger for his investigation. 'Promise you will not do anything like that. Promise.'

She muttered to herself before giving a sulky nod.

'You will stay safe, stay out of trouble?'

Isabella rolled her eyes. 'Yes. I promise.'

Aldo didn't know whether to believe her, but it would have to do. 'If I can get you in, do you still wish to stay at the convent, at least for tonight?'

'Yes.'

'Then follow me, and say nothing.' Aldo led her to the convent door while assessing the two clerics. The older of the pair was gesturing at the workman, using both arms in the grand way of many Florentines. People in the city talked with their hands as much as their mouths, either making big movements full of *forza*, or the smallest of gestures for emphasis, often with just their fingertips. Judging by the coloured piping on his cassock, the older cleric was a monsignor. His face and hands were pale, suggesting he spent most days indoors, while grey hair was slicked back underneath his *zucchetto*.

The younger cleric was a priest, with no colour on his cassock. He had a kinder face, and sun-browned skin. He probably worked outside with the faithful. Where the monsignor had seen at least forty summers, the priest was two thirds that age, at most. He appeared less certain, remaining silent while the monsignor berated the workman.

'Excuse me,' Aldo said, stopping short of them. 'My niece Isabella is returning to the convent after visiting her poorly *Nonna*. May she go inside?'

The monsignor glanced at Isabella before staring at Aldo. 'A novice does not leave a convent. Her *famiglia* comes to visit her.'

Aldo nodded as if appreciating the surly cleric's wisdom. Better to placate him than to antagonise. 'Yes, of course, you are right. But my niece is not yet a novice.'

'And I probably—' Isabella begun, but Aldo cut her off.

'She is still praying for guidance about whether her vocation is strong enough. But my niece is boarding here at Santa Maria Magdalena, as you can see from her dress.'

The monsignor paid more attention to Isabella now. 'Then she may go inside. But any further trips out of the convent will not be possible for the rest of Holy Week.' He pointed at the notice now tacked to the door, ignoring the harassed workman beside it. 'The archbishop has ordered that Santa Maria Magdalena be enclosed while an investigation is carried out by the diocese, following an incident among the sisters.'

'Most wise,' Aldo agreed, offering his most benign smile. 'If I may ask, what is the nature of this – incident?'

Finally, the young priest spoke up. 'A man called Bernardo Galeri was murdered—'

'That is none of your concern,' the monsignor snapped, glaring at his colleague.

'A murder?' Aldo stepped back as if in shock before making the sign of the cross. 'What a terrible thing to have happened! The taking of a life on holy ground, that is a crime against God as well as a crime against the law. Are officers of the Otto coming to investigate, or has the killer already been caught?'

The monsignor's eyes narrowed. 'Why should that concern you?'

Aldo rested a hand on Isabella's shoulder. 'If my niece is returning inside the convent, I should wish to be certain that she is safe. I'm sure you understand . . .'

The priest nodded his agreement, but the monsignor frowned. However, he could not deny the logic of Aldo's argument. 'The archbishop has deemed this to be a matter for the Church authorities. As you say, it took place on holy ground. An auricular visitation will take place tomorrow to determine how this incident happened, and who should be punished for it.'

No doubt the abbess would be among those facing censure, regardless of whether she had any involvement with, or knowledge of, the killing. But the chances of a Church visitation solving the murder were smaller than those of a camel passing through the eye of a needle.

'If you are leading the visitation,' Aldo told the two clerics, 'I am confident whoever is responsible will be discovered and made to face God's justice.'

'Then you may be confident,' the monsignor replied, turning away.

'Forgive me,' Aldo said, 'but may I ask your names?'

'Father Zati,' the young priest volunteered. 'Father Pagolo Zati.' After that the other cleric had little choice but to respond.

'And I am Monsignor Luca Testardo. Now, if you will excuse us, Signor . . .?'

Aldo ignored the invitation to give his own name, instead

bowing to both men before ushering Isabella to the convent door. 'In you go, my dear. And remember what I said.'

The workman opened the door for Isabella. 'Yes, uncle, I will.' She winked before disappearing into the gloomy interior. Aldo was grateful only the workman saw it.

'Young women,' the man with the hammer said. 'Got a mind of their own.'

Aldo couldn't deny the truth of that, even with his limited experience. He strode to via San Gallo before turning south towards the Duomo, all the while sifting what the clerics had revealed. The fact that they knew the dead man's name meant the archbishop also knew – but how? So few people had seen the body. The abbess must have revealed the name when she reported the murder. Had she known the victim all along and kept his name from Aldo? If so, that brought her into question. Of course the abbess could have realized who the dead man was once the shock of seeing his body had passed. Nonetheless, her word was now in doubt. And, like every other nun inside the convent, she was a suspect for murder.

What of Bernardo Galeri? His name was not familiar, but tens of thousands of people lived in Florence. Unless they came before the Otto reporting a crime, or faced prosecution for committing one, Aldo had no reason to know them. At least having a name for the victim should make finding his killer simpler – assuming Bindi let the investigation continue. Persuading the *segretario* would not be easy, but there was a pathway that could leave Bindi little choice. The first step was securing entry back into the convent. That meant asking someone for help, a task Aldo did not savour. Worse still was the man he would have to ask.

\* \* \*

The abbess marched into the refectory, flanked by the prioress and Suor Giulia. The other nuns, novices and boarding girls all rose from their benches at the long wooden tables, bowing their heads. She swept round the top table to her chair, the prioress and Giulia on either side, before motioning everyone to sit.

The abbess smiled at the convent's draper. 'Suor Andriana, I believe it is your turn to lead us in prayer.' Andriana nodded, her cheeks flushing. The draper had a terror of talking in front of others. She preferred to go unnoticed, to do her duties without praise or regard. In some ways Andriana reminded the abbess of a timid mouse, hiding in corners and shadows. Speaking at the conclave of senior nuns earlier to show the dead man's clothes must have been difficult for her. But each woman was required to lead the others in prayer before meals were served in the refectory, and it was the draper's turn. Andriana rose, breviary held in trembling hands. By her side sat the teaching nun, Suor Catarina. The abbess could see Catarina murmuring to her friend, perhaps urging Andriana on or reassuring her all would be well. The draper opened her breviary and started to read aloud the day's prayer.

The words were audible but the abbess did not listen, her thoughts moving on to what had happened that day and what was still to come. The enclosure order had been expected, but the haste with which it was imposed still surprised her. The archbishop was not renowned for the pace of his deliberations, so it was probably prompted by one of his clerics. Outside of convents, the voices of women were never heard in places where the Church made decisions. There would have been nobody to argue against the enclosure. The reputation of Santa Maria Magdalena would not have helped and, besides, it was Holy Week. Better to seal the convent so word of what had happened could not embarrass the Church – or the archbishop.

The order might be temporary, but the abbess knew it was the tip of the sword. The visitation would return tomorrow, this time investigating a crime far worse than rule-breaking or minor misdemeanours. A murder inside the convent? That was reason enough for Santa Maria Magdalena to face dissolution, with the nuns and novices sent to Le Murate or any other convent that would have them. Avoiding such an outcome required a miracle. Even if Maria Celestia's wounds were stigmata, the abbess doubted they would be enough.

Far worse than that was a truth she had been pushing aside all day: one of her sisters in God was a killer. The body, all that blood . . . Someone inside the refectory was almost certainly responsible. Had the dead man found a way inside the convent, or did one of the nuns let him in, perhaps with murder already in her heart? But why kill him, and why inside these walls? Was this part of some *stratagemma* to force Santa Maria Magdalena into becoming an enclosed convent? If so, the plan had succeeded.

Since visiting the infirmary, the abbess had wondered if Maria Celestia's illness could be a way to avoid suspicion. Could the novice have killed Galeri? She claimed to have found his body, but there was only her word to support that and now she seemed incapable of speech. The cuts to her hands were also curious. How had she come by them? The abbess had seen no suitable knife in the scriptorium, and Aldo had not mentioned finding one. But what reason would the novice have for attacking Galeri? She and Maria Vincenzia were a difficult pair at times, but that was a long way from murder. Had something happened between Maria Celestia and Galeri when he came to the convent with the visitation?

If she was not the killer, it meant somebody else inside the convent had taken Galeri's life, had chosen to do so. The abbess let her gaze move from nun to nun. She knew all these women. She might not like each of them, but she loved every one of them as a sister in God. How could any of them have committed such a sin? It did not bear thinking about, but she must. Who among them was reckless enough – or ruthless enough – to kill?

The prioress was ruthless, yes, and burly of build, but she was more than sixty. How could she take the life of a man at least a decade younger than her without suffering injury? It strained the imagination. To dismiss the prioress on those grounds meant that all those nuns her age or older were also beyond suspicion. What about Suor Giulia? The apothecary's personal history before taking the veil was unknown to most inside the convent. She had experienced the violence of men. Might she have sought retribution? Perhaps. Yet the abbess saw no trace of guilt or remorse, nothing seemed to be troubling Giulia. To take a life and be unchanged by the experience, by the knowledge of what you had done . . . The abbess did not believe it was possible. Not for one of her sisters. But if she accepted that, none of the women around her could be guilty of this sin, this terrible breach of God's kindness . . .

The abbess studied more of the younger nuns. The sour-faced Fiametta, the earnest Paulina, the teacher Catarina – could any of them have killed Galeri?

She realized the refectory had fallen silent, Suor Andriana completing her prayer.

'Amen,' the abbess said, the others all echoing her words. Three servant nuns rose from their bench, carrying jugs of wine around to fill the cups. The abbess noticed gaps at two tables. Maria Celestia was absent from the novices, leaving an awkward space between Maria Vincenzia and Maria Teodora. The other empty seat was among the chapter nuns. Suor Violante always ate in her cell. It was for the best, but the prioress insisted a seat was kept should her sister decide to break bread with everyone else. Violante's troubles meant she could not be set aside as a potential suspect. If there was one nun within the convent who might be capable of murder, it was her.

# Chapter Fourteen

*R*uggerio beamed as Aldo was ushered into the *officio*. 'I had not expected to welcome you back to my palazzo so soon,' the merchant said. He was sitting behind an impressive desk, an exquisite fresco of muscular men at war adorning the wall. Bronze statues of naked heroic figures stood atop marble plinths in each corner. Ruggerio beckoned Aldo closer once the servant had gone. 'To what do I owe this pleasure?'

'You have heard about the body found at Santa Maria Magdalena?' With men like Ruggerio, it was always best to answer one question with another.

The merchant shifted in his high-backed golden chair, adjusting his imperial blue silk robe. 'The confraternity's senior brethren were notified not long after the archbishop. Do you believe this murder is related to the previous intruders?'

'Perhaps,' Aldo conceded, 'although the victim is unfamiliar to the Otto.'

Ruggerio licked his lips. 'Please, tell me more. Useful information is always welcome here, and those who bring it are well rewarded.'

There it was: an alliance waiting to be struck, if Aldo was willing. 'The dead man is – or was – one of the four men who conducted an ocular visitation of the convent a few days ago. His name was Bernardo Galeri.'

Ruggerio's eyebrows shot up at this, but he recovered his poise within moments. 'Galeri? How delicious!' The merchant rose to pace around, the ends of his robe fluttering. 'Buondelmonti must be furious. And that certainly explains why he ordered the convent be enclosed. I wonder how Galeri got—' The merchant stopped himself, but it was too late.

'You knew the dead man,' Aldo said. 'How?'

'That's not important –'

'How?'

Ruggerio stared at a fresco, avoiding Aldo's gaze. 'He was a member.'

'Of what?' Aldo put himself in front of the fresco. 'The silk merchant's guild?'

Ruggerio snorted. 'Don't be ridiculous.'

Aldo smiled as realization came. 'He was one of your brethren.'

'Not for long,' Ruggerio said.

Being part of a confraternity was an expensive way to display your faith. Members were expected to make large, regular donations to their favoured charity. In exchange, they joined an elite inner circle, giving them opportunities and allies otherwise unavailable. 'Let me guess. Galeri couldn't afford the price required to remain one of your brothers?'

Ruggerio gave a curt, reluctant nod.

'Why? If he was able to buy his way into the company –'

'The fabric-dying workshop he owned went out of business. There was talk of misspent funds – gambling, whoring.' Ruggerio sighed. 'The usual, tawdry vices.'

If that were true, it seemed unlikely Galeri would have paid the fee needed to join the confraternity. Not unless he believed it would bring a swift return, far swifter than escaping eternal damnation. The previous day, Ruggerio had said the confraternity used the convent as a place of safekeeping for unspecified items. And the abbess mentioned a thief who climbed into Santa Maria Magdalena after hearing rumours of a treasure there.

'A lack of coin wasn't the only reason you and the brethren dismissed Galeri, was it?'

Ruggerio did not reply, but his thin lips whitened.

'He asked too many questions about what was stored inside the convent, didn't he?'

Still the merchant stayed silent.

'So be it,' Aldo said, strolling towards the *officio* doors.

'He was curious,' Ruggerio called out. 'Too curious by far. That and his failure to meet our financial expectations left the brethren with no choice. He was dismissed.'

Aldo stopped by the doors. 'When you heard about intruders climbing the convent's outer wall, you feared it was Galeri or someone acting on his behalf. That's why you had me go there, to make sure he hadn't taken whatever you and your brothers keep in the convent.'

'Yes,' the merchant conceded.

Finally, the truth was emerging – or at least some of it. Trusting anything that came from Ruggerio's mouth was dangerous. Aldo considered asking what the confraternity stored inside Santa Maria Magdalena, but doubted he would receive an answer worth hearing. Better to pursue less sensitive areas where Ruggerio might be willing to talk with candour, areas where he had nothing to lose by replying. 'How long was Galeri in the confraternity?'

'A few weeks, perhaps a month—'

'Long enough to be considered as a convent visitor?' Judging by Ruggerio's face this had not occurred to him. 'If what you say about Galeri's character is true, there would be little chance of him being considered as a visitor. But if he was one of your brethren . . .'

Ruggerio nodded. 'He would have far less difficulty.'

That fit the facts, but Aldo knew that didn't make it correct. Galeri could well have had another reason for wanting to get inside, something unconnected to the confraternity. Still, the argument seemed to convince Ruggerio. Now to make best use of that. 'I understand the visitation is returning to Santa Maria Magdalena tomorrow. But it will be an auricular inspection, interrogating the nuns about what happened.'

'And with Galeri dead, the archbishop needs to appoint another lay member.' Ruggerio's eyes narrowed. 'You wish to be one of the visitors.'

Aldo smiled. 'It would serve both our interests. I can continue my investigation, and you will have someone there who understands the – needs of the confraternity.'

'Indeed.' The merchant resumed pacing. 'I have some sway within the archbishop's circle. I can suggest your name be considered as Galeri's replacement for the visitation. Will your *segretario* approve this? The Church has already asserted authority over the convent, so the Otto can wash its hands of investigating this murder. Knowing Bindi, he would be grateful to avoid any responsibility for finding the killer.'

'But he cannot object if one of his officers is seconded by the archbishop,' Aldo replied. 'Bindi's wrath will be considerable, but I can face that later.'

Ruggerio returned to his desk. 'Very well. I shall use my influence to have you named as the replacement member of the visitation.'

'Thank you, signor,' Aldo said.

'But I have two stipulations. First, you agree to intercede on my behalf – on the confraternity's behalf – should the abbess appear disloyal to her benefactors.' Meaning Aldo should intervene if the abbess sought to somehow implicate the confraternity in the murder.

Making any bargain with Ruggerio was regrettable, but Aldo had done worse. 'Agreed. And the second stipulation?'

'Answer one question for me, and be honest with your words. I am a shrewd judge of character. I shall know if you are lying.'

Aldo hesitated. There were many questions he had no wish to answer, and certainly not for the likes of Ruggerio. But if needs must . . . 'Ask what you will.'

'Why are you so intent on investigating this murder? Why come here and strike a bargain with someone you tolerate at best and despise the rest of the time?'

Aldo kept his face impassive. 'That's two questions.'

'Answering the first will suffice.'

Aldo knew his reason for persisting with the investigation, but he was not going to share it that easily – and certainly not with Ruggerio.

'Well?' the merchant asked.

Aldo smiled. 'The Church is demanding the Otto step aside. But I know the truth will never come out if the archbishop gets in the way.' He opened the *officio* door to leave. 'Besides, I don't like being told what I can and can't do.'

After taking his leave of Cerchi's widow, Strocchi spent a frustrating time talking to other residents in the building. Few of the residents had good things to say about Cerchi. Many were sorry for Grazia, sharing accounts of shouted arguments with her appearing bloodied and bruised afterwards. Some residents crossed themselves on hearing of the murder, but none shed a tear. *Diavolo* and a piece of *merda* were the most common descriptions of

Cerchi. Nobody recalled seeing the dead man after the feast of the Epiphany.

Strocchi had not been involved when Aldo investigated Cerchi's disappearance in January, but he had heard plenty about it from Benedetto. Among the gossip shared was the fact that Cerchi went to a *bordello* near the Mercato Vecchio every Thursday, the house run by Signorina Nardi. Strocchi had never been inside such a place, but leading the investigation into Cerchi's murder left little choice. The constable headed west from Santa Maria Novella, occasional glimpses of the Duomo in the distance helping him keep his bearings. A year of living in Florence had opened his eyes to many things, but the irregular nature of its streets and alleys still proved a puzzle at times.

When Strocchi found the *bordello*, it was not what he had expected. His imagination had pictured such places with half-naked women leaning from doors and windows, luring lost and desperate souls inside with the promise of illicit pleasures. The trading of sex for coin was legal in Florence, so long as the women abided by certain laws. Registration with the Office of Decency was one. Another was the restriction on where a *bordello* could – and, more importantly, could not – operate.

Signorina Nardi's place of business looked ordinary from the outside. Strocchi realized he had passed it numerous times without realizing what happened within. He stood across the street from the entrance, watching men arrive and depart. Some appeared furtive, slipping in with a hurried glance at those nearby. Others seemed unashamed, strolling to the door without bothering to see if anyone was watching. Taking a deep breath, Strocchi crossed the road. He was there on official business, seeking those who had murdered a court officer. Yes, going to a *bordello* in search of answers was embarrassing, but it was also his job.

Strocchi opened the door, grateful at not needing to knock and wait. If the outside appeared ordinary, the interior was unlike anything he had seen. The walls were adorned with frescoes, but altogether different from the tasteful paintings found in the palazzi of rich merchants. Instead of biblical scenes or artful depictions of the Tuscan countryside, here the walls were adorned with images of naked torsos and limbs, the faces of men and woman filled with rampant lust. Golden statues of nubile women stood in corners and recesses, pouting and posing as if aching to be touched. Then there was the smell: musk, sandalwood and other heady aromas. Strocchi could hear men grunting and women crying out as if overcome by joy, calling out names and obscenities with all their might.

It was overwhelming. Strocchi's senses urged him to flee. But before he could turn back, a woman emerged from an open doorway, her generous curves threatening to escape a scarlet silk robe, dark ringlets of hair cascading into the deep valley between her breasts. 'I haven't seen you before,' she purred, coming closer. 'Tell me, what is your pleasure? Do you wish to conquer and ravish? Or perhaps you prefer to be caressed and tormented, your *cazzo* teased till you can hold back no longer?'

'Actually,' Strocchi began, his voice much higher than usual. He coughed, reasserting his normal, deeper voice. 'Actually, I'm here on official business for the Otto.'

'Oh.' All playful pretence fell from the woman's face. 'How much do you want?' She spun round, marching back through the door from where she had come. 'Or do you want your payment in *fica* instead?' Strocchi went to the doorway. It led to an *officio* where the dark-haired woman sank into a chair behind a sturdy desk, pouring herself a cup of wine. 'Well?'

'I came here to ask questions,' Strocchi said. 'Nothing more.'

'Makes a change. Thought you might be looking to take up where Cerchi left off.'

'It's Cerchi I'm investigating. Well, his murder.'

The woman's gaze shot up. 'He's dead, then?' Strocchi nodded. 'I'm glad to hear it.' The woman glanced at a crucifix on the wall, and made the sign of the cross. 'I know I shouldn't wish ill on anyone, but Cerchi was the worst kind of *merda*.'

'So people tell me,' Strocchi said. 'May I ask your name?'

'Signorina Nardi,' the woman said. 'I'm *matrona* here. This is my house.'

'I've been told Cerchi visited every Thursday.'

Nardi nodded between sips of wine. 'He threatened to close me down unless I gave him a choice of girls, once a week. Never paid, but always expected to be treated like a prince. Beat my girls if he couldn't get aroused. Some of them couldn't work for days after his visits. None of us will be weeping any tears for Cerchi.'

Beating women, claiming sex as his due – it was surprising someone had not killed Cerchi sooner. 'When was his last visit?'

'The Thursday after the Epiphany,' she replied without hesitation, 'January the eleventh.'

'You seem very certain.'

'I am. By the next Thursday another officer came asking questions about Cerchi – but there was no sign of him. We haven't seen Cerchi since. And we haven't missed him.' Nardi put down her cup. 'How did he die?'

'I'm not able to—'

'Painfully, I hope,' she cut in. 'I pray he suffered the way he made my girls suffer.'

Strocchi kept his own counsel as she talked, letting Nardi empty herself of anger.

'Can you recall who Cerchi saw on January the eleventh?'

'Yes, it was Lisabetta.'

'Could I speak to her?'

'Probably, but it'll be a long journey. She went home to Bologna last month.'

Strocchi was finding it difficult not to despair of his task. 'I don't suppose you talked with Cerchi during his last visit here?'

'I did,' the *matrona* said. 'He was even more full of his own glory than usual. Came in gloating about how he had won a battle with somebody.'

At last, some fresh evidence! 'Did he say who?'

'No, but it made him very happy. I'd never seen Cerchi so satisfied with himself. He was like a bull with two *cazzi* in a field full of fresh cows.'

'Anything else you remember about that day?'

Nardi shook her head. 'Lisabetta took him to her room, and I was busy when Cerchi left. But he actually paid Lisabetta for her time, which was a first. Told her there was plenty more to come. He must have been expecting a lot of coin soon to open his pouch.'

It wasn't much, but the *matrona* had added to what Strocchi knew. He thanked her, turning to go. Nardi called him back. 'You can tell that officer I still haven't found those papers. None of the girls had them.'

'Papers?'

'When he came looking for information, the officer asked if Cerchi had left any documents here. The girls searched all the rooms, but there was nothing.'

Strocchi had no idea what she was talking about, but he kept it to himself. 'I will let him know. Again, thank you for your time.' He left the *bordello*, heading south. Before Nardi mentioned her final meeting with Cerchi, the constable had been ready to abandon the day and go home to Tomasia. He could always meet Aldo at the Podestà tomorrow. But those brief comments about Cerchi's mood on his last visit prompted fresh questions. Who had the dead man won a battle with, and why was Cerchi expecting so much coin? Strocchi couldn't be sure the answers would be linked to the murder, but they suggested a way forward. More than ever, he needed advice. If anyone could help him find Cerchi's killer, it was Aldo.

Aldo had passed by Saul's home most days since January. When the door was open, it told the world that Dr Orvieto was ready and willing to see anyone who needed his care, whether they were Jewish or not. If the door was shut, it meant he was asleep, or seeing a patient in their home. So many times Aldo had paused outside the door, uncertain if he should go inside to apologize for the events that had sundered their friendship. But the longer he hesitated, the harder it became to find the right words – no, to find the courage.

Now Aldo stood outside the doctor's home once more, willing himself to go inside. The afternoon sun was fading from via dei Giudei, the day's warmth abandoning the narrow street, but that wasn't why Aldo kept shivering. Saul had asked him to come, that much was certain. Yet Aldo still hesitated, his belly fluttering. Had that invitation been more courtesy, a doctor willing to help an officer of the court, or was Saul signalling they could be friends again, perhaps more than friends?

'Are you coming in?' Saul appeared in the doorway, studying Aldo. 'Or should I report my findings out here in the street? It'll be dark soon, and you probably still have things you need to do, people you need to see before curfew.'

'Strocchi is expecting to meet with me before the day's end,'

Aldo admitted. 'But the business of the Otto requires discretion, so it would be better if we talked in private.' The doctor hesitated a moment before gesturing at Aldo to enter, following him inside.

The back room where Saul treated his patients hadn't changed at all, the same aroma of drying herbs and sharp, astringent liquids blending in the air. A blue apron was draped over a chair at the long table, so Aldo sank into the other.

'You look thirsty,' Saul said, reaching for two cups. 'Wine?'

'Thank you.' It had been a long, hot day with little chance to drink or eat. Aldo emptied the first cup while Saul was still pouring his own.

'You've lost weight,' the doctor observed. He carried a chopping board over to the table, pulling away a cloth to reveal slices of cured meats, a generous bowl of olives, and an end of bread. There was a bone-handled knife amid the food, its sharp-edged blade glinting in the light of a nearby lantern. 'Here, eat while I tell you about the dead body.'

Aldo savoured the different scents rising from the board. 'You prepared this for me?'

'Blame my mother. She taught me never to let anyone you care about go hungry.'

Aldo smiled. 'You're not going to join me?'

'I'm not the one who needs more regular meals,' Saul replied, patting his belly. It pressed against his tunic a little. Aldo wasted no more time with questions, devouring the meat and olives while Saul talked. 'The dead man was about your age, or perhaps a little older. But he was heavy of gut, too heavy for his way of life. That indolence would have killed him soon, if someone else had not intervened.'

Aldo tore a piece of bread free, using it to soak up oil and herbs from inside the olive bowl. 'His name was Bernardo Galeri.'

'Well, you were right about Signor Galeri. There was more to his corpse than was first apparent. More accurately, there was more to his murder.' Saul sat facing Aldo. 'By my count he was stabbed at least twenty-seven times, perhaps more. The attack was so frenzied, I cannot be certain the blade wasn't thrust into some of those wounds more than once.'

'To keep stabbing and stabbing like that –' Aldo pushed aside the chopping board, only a few scraps of food left on it. 'Whoever was holding that blade didn't just want Galeri dead. They wanted to destroy him. The wounds to his face . . . they hated him.'

'So it seems,' Saul agreed. 'But I'm not sure that a blade was the murder weapon.'

# Chapter Fifteen

'*I* suspect Galeri was already dead before the stabbing.' Saul took hold of Aldo's right hand, turning it over atop the table, palm upwards. The doctor pretended to stab a knife down into the open hand. 'When any blade pierces the skin, blood escapes from the body through that wound. How much blood depends on how deep and how wide the cut is, yes?'

Aldo nodded. 'There was plenty of blood around Galeri's body.'

'Let's deal with his wounds first. Something else happens when a knife is thrust down into the skin, especially when the stabbing is as urgent and angry as it was with Galeri.' Saul let go of Aldo's hand to lift the knife from the chopping board, pointing to the small metal guard between the bone handle and the blade. 'Most knives have a protective piece like this to stop whoever is using the blade from cutting themselves.'

Aldo remembered the last time he had stabbed his stiletto into a man. 'If there's blood, and there usually is, the guard also stops your fingers slipping so much.'

The doctor put the knife back down. 'I'd forgotten you were a soldier once.'

'A long time ago. Tell me more about Galeri.'

Saul draped the cloth back across the board, covering the knife. 'Stab a blade into a body hard enough, and the metal guard punches the skin around the wound. That leaves a bruise like any blow – but the bruise doesn't colour the skin until several hours later.'

Aldo sat back in his chair. The first time they met, Saul was cutting open the carcass of a goat on this table to study what was inside, to learn more about how the body worked. The doctor was not content to accept all he had been taught about healing; he wanted to add to that knowledge. His curiosity was one of the reasons Aldo had asked Saul to study the victim. The doctor dealt in what could be observed, and analysed with all his senses. He dealt in facts. 'So what happens if you stab a body that's already dead?' Aldo asked.

'Good question,' Saul said with a smile. 'When a body is no longer alive, it stops responding in the same way. The bruising does not come. I've seen it myself, working with animal carcasses.' His smile faded. 'There were no bruises around the stab wounds on the corpse. That's what makes me believe Galeri was already dead when his body was attacked.'

If Saul was right, it explained why Galeri hadn't fought back when he was stabbed. Dead men didn't – couldn't – defend themselves. 'If the stabbing didn't kill Galeri, what did?'

Saul shrugged. 'That is something you will have to discover for yourself. If his body had borne any evidence of what caused his death, it was destroyed by the stabbing, or hidden by the blood, or washed away when his remains were cleaned at the *ospedale*. Whatever did kill him isn't obvious now. But if I should be asked to guess –'

Aldo waited, knowing Saul would not deny him an answer.

'I would say poison. I found no sign Galeri had been smothered, strangled, or slain by some other violence. Poison enables you to kill a man without him crying out or drawing attention. Tell me, do the nuns have an apothecary within the convent?'

'Yes, I believe so.'

'She will have plenty of ingredients that can take a life, just as I do – arsenic, aconitum . . .' Saul waved at the bottles of powders and oils lining his shelves. 'A small dose from some of these can help to quicken a sluggish heart, give a sick person back their liveliness. But increase that dose enough –'

'– and they die.' Aldo swallowed the last of the wine in his cup. 'How might such a poison have been given to Galeri?'

'If it was me, I would dissolve it in something strong, so the victim doesn't realize what they are drinking.' Saul refilled his own cup, and offered the bottle. 'More?'

Aldo shook his head. 'Remind me never to make you angry again. The convent also has its own infirmary, the abbess took me there.'

'That probably has remedies that could be fatal if administered in a large enough quantity. Poisoning is a guess, but it seems the most effective way to deal with Galeri. He was a big man. Most women would struggle to kill him by strength alone.'

That was something which had been troubling Aldo. Men were more likely to murder, and far more prone to using a blade for that purpose. Women needed greater guile to end a life, unless luck – or sometimes misfortune – was at their side. Poison would explain how one of the nuns had been able to kill Galeri without him fighting back. It also broadened the list of suspects, potentially. Any one of the nuns or novices could administer poison, assuming they had the means and knew how. 'If Galeri was poisoned as you suggest, there would have been no need to stab him?'

'None,' Saul agreed, 'and certainly not so many times. Whoever attacked him, whoever held the knife, may not be the killer. They desecrated his body and face, but I do not believe that was how his life was taken.'

'Even if the knife wasn't what ended Galeri, finding it could help uncover his killer. You've seen the wounds it made, what should I be looking for?'

'The blade did not pierce too deep, despite being stabbed into the body with force. I'd say it's about half the distance from the top of your middle finger to the base of your palm in length, and not much wider than your thumb. The tip is narrow and sharp. The handle could be any length, but it would need to be enough for someone to keep a steady grip.'

'What about the blood?' Aldo asked. 'There was blood all over Galeri, so much so that it had made a pool around him on the floor. Does a body still bleed after it dies?'

'Yes, but not for long in my experience. Without life to keep it moving inside the body, blood thickens and settles. At the *ospedale*, you said Galeri was cold to the touch but the blood around him was still wet?'

'Yes.'

Saul stood, taking the chopping board to a bench beneath the back window. 'Then I doubt what you saw was his blood.'

'You mean I should be looking for a second body?'

'I don't know. How much blood was there – enough to fill a cup? A wine bottle?'

Aldo closed his eyes, recalling what he had seen in the scriptorium. 'Enough to fill several cups.' He looked at Saul, who was frowning. 'What's wrong?'

'Just wishing I'd had the chance to see the body where you found it.' Saul came back to the table, but didn't sit. 'Was there blood elsewhere in the room, or only around the body?'

'The novice who found Galeri had blood on her hands, but there were no splashes of blood on the walls, or the ceiling. I've seen enough death to know if you stab somebody more than once, blood comes off the blade between each thrust. There was none of that. I wondered if Galeri's body was moved to the scriptorium.'

'Perhaps,' Saul said. 'But it still wouldn't explain so much blood. No, I think it was poured over him. He was killed, probably with poison. The body was stabbed after Galeri died, and may have been moved to the scriptorium, but we can't be certain of that or when. Then, finally, fresh blood was poured over the corpse.'

'But why do all of that?' Aldo stood, unable to stay seated with so many questions filling his thoughts. 'Could it be a ritual of some kind?

Saul shook his head. 'I don't know.'

The notion that the nuns at Santa Maria Magdalena were performing blood rituals was too fanciful for Aldo to believe. He had been inside Santa Maria Magdalena, had met the abbess. Her reaction when she first saw Galeri's body – that had been genuine, he was sure of it. There must be another explanation, a better explanation, for all that blood.

'What if someone did this to create confusion,' Aldo said. 'Most people finding fresh blood on a body will think the killing is a recent event. They would certainly believe the knife wounds must be the cause of death.'

'So the stabbing and blood were all a ruse?' Saul asked.

'Perhaps.' Aldo smiled. He rested a hand on the doctor's shoulder. 'You were right. There was more to this than I first realized. Thank you for being so diligent.'

'You're welcome. Besides, it made a change from the patients I see most days. What ails and sickens them is all too obvious. I enjoyed having a puzzle to solve.' Saul stared into Aldo's eyes. 'And I enjoyed seeing you again.'

Aldo pulled Saul into a kiss. When their lips met, it was as if no time had passed, as if the weeks and months they had spent apart were a moment of hesitation, not a chasm of loss and regret. Aldo's hand slid into Saul's hair, the other hand on the small of the doctor's back, pulling him closer. 'I'm sorry,' Aldo murmured between kisses.

'Why?' Saul asked.

'What happened – if I had listened to you –'

Saul leaned back a little, his hands resting on Aldo's hips. 'Then listen to me now. We made mistakes, both of us. But that's in the past. We start again, here and now. Both of us being honest with each other. No more surprises. Agreed?'

Aldo nodded.

A frail voice called out in Hebrew, accompanied by the sound of shuffling feet. 'That will be Esther,' Saul said, stepping away from Aldo. 'Every Monday she comes to complain about her pain. Always a new pain, always in a new place. Mostly, I think she wants someone to listen. Esther has been lonely since her husband died last summer.'

A stooped old woman dressed in black shuffled her way into the room. She peered at Aldo while muttering in Hebrew, her pudgy fingers jabbing the air. The words meant nothing to Aldo but her unhappiness at seeing him needed no translation.

'I shall leave you two together,' Aldo said, nodding to the old woman.

'Can I expect to see you again soon?' Saul asked.

'Tonight,' Aldo replied on his way out. 'Before curfew, all being well.'

Whenever Strocchi visited Zoppo's tavern, he was reluctant to touch anything. Florence had been spared an outbreak of plague in recent years, but if it came again, this tavern was likely to be the source. Tucked at the end of a neglected alley a few streets north of the Arno, it was an ugly hovel of a place. When the dank interior had last been cleaned was unclear, but Strocchi guessed probably not since plague had visited the city.

Despite that, the tavern possessed one reason to visit: its keeper. Zoppo's face was twisted by a sloppy leer, one of his legs ended at the knee and his skin bore more marks than a slab of limestone after a hundred years outdoors. Yet he had one of the shrewdest natures in Florence, along with an ability to coax secrets from every servant, whore and criminal in the city. Zoppo's wine might be rancid and his tavern closer to a *latrina*, but the quality of his information was always the finest.

Aldo had introduced Strocchi to the fetid tavern, and the usefulness of its keeper. As a constable of the Otto, Strocchi did not often have reason to call on Zoppo. Most days were devoted to patrols and other enforcement duties, such as assisting an officer when they were arresting a dangerous suspect. But investigating Cerchi's murder had made apparent why Aldo paid men like Zoppo for what they knew, and what they could discover. The Otto might be the most powerful criminal court in the city, but its authority was not recognized by everyone. It took the likes of Zoppo to reach those who did not fear the court.

Waiting for Aldo at the tavern, Strocchi had made the mistake of asking for a drink. The dim light made it hard to see what was in the cup Zoppo brought to the corner table, but the smell made Strocchi's eyes water. 'What can you tell me about Meo Cerchi?'

Zoppo peered down at Strocchi. 'Why do you want to know?'

'I'm sorry?'

'Why do you want to know? Is this you asking, or is it Aldo?' Strocchi wasn't used to having his questions answered with more questions. Drinking the wine would have been easier than getting a direct answer in here. 'Does that matter?'

'Does to the price. If you're here on behalf of the Otto, it costs more.'

'All I did was ask a question . . .'

'And if you want answers, I need to see some coin,' Zoppo replied. 'It's your choice.'

'I'm only a constable,' Strocchi protested, reaching for the pouch tucked in his tunic. 'I don't get coin for paying informants.'

'I'm not an informant,' the cripple hissed, glancing at two drunks slumped by the bar. 'I offer a service. Those who want to share what they know with others come to me, and I get them fair payment for that knowledge.'

'While taking a generous commission for your part in the transaction,' Aldo said from the tavern doorway. He strolled across, nodding to Zoppo before sitting opposite Strocchi.

'Man's got to eat,' Zoppo replied, his leer spreading wider. 'Drink?'

Aldo sniffed Strocchi's cup, wincing at the contents. 'Not if this is the best you have. But you can get me something else.' He put two *giuli* on the table. 'Find out all you can about Bernardo Galeri. He used to run a dying workshop, but it went out of business. Probably a gambler, so your friends may well have known him.'

Zoppo nodded. 'You said may have known him. Somebody's killed him?'

'More than once, it seems.'

'How fast do you need this?'

'Tomorrow.'

The cripple frowned. 'Takes time—'

Aldo silenced him by slapping down two more *giuli*. 'First thing.' Zoppo took the coin, grumbling all the way to the bar.

Once he was out of hearing, Aldo turned to Strocchi. 'Don't take any insolence from Zoppo. He only respects authority.' Aldo emptied the rancid wine onto the floor. 'And never drink in here. Not if you want to see another summer.' Strocchi nodded. 'So, what did you want to ask me?'

'It's about Cerchi.'

'Yes?'

'I found him.'

Aldo didn't respond at first. He remained quite still for several moments, before blinking. 'Sorry, I was thinking about something else. What did you say?'

'I found Cerchi.'

'Really? Well done. Bindi had me scouring the city for weeks trying to find that *bastardo*. So where is he?'

'I found him downriver, at Ponte a Signa. Well, what was left of him.'

Aldo's eyes narrowed. 'He's dead?'

'Has been since January, it seems.' Strocchi told the whole story: going home to visit his mama and recognizing the silver buckle on Buffon's belt; finding Cerchi's initials on the back of the buckle; how Cerchi's remains had been left behind by an early February flood; digging up what was left of him in the village graveyard; and the notches in Cerchi's ribs from a knife wound. 'I brought the buckle back today, and gave it to Bindi. The *segretario* said if I can find whoever murdered Cerchi, I could be promoted to officer.'

'Congratulations,' Aldo said.

'I haven't found Cerchi's killer yet.'

'No, but if anyone at the Podestà is capable of that, it's you.'

Strocchi beamed. Aldo did not give praise often. The officer believing in him meant a lot. 'You have far more experience with investigations like this. What should I do?'

'Certainly sounds as if Cerchi's been dead for a while. To discover who killed him, you need to determine when and where he died.'

Strocchi explained his belief that Cerchi was killed in the city, with the body going into the Arno from one of the bridges after dark. Probably Ponte Vecchio, because of the shops built along the bridge, making it easier to dump a body without being seen. All the other bridges were open spans, offering no such conceal-ment. 'I could be completely wrong,' he admitted. 'For all I know, he was murdered outside the city and whoever did it – bandits, I suppose – dumped him in the river.'

'True,' Aldo said. 'Cerchi did have an ability to make enemies wherever he went. But none of the gates ever reported him leaving. No, if you're right about him dying here, then the rest of what you say makes sense. What about when he died?'

Strocchi slumped back in his chair. 'That's where I'm struggling. I've talked to his widow, his neighbours – I even went to the *bordello* Cerchi visited on Thursdays. The last date that anyone can recall seeing him is January the eleventh.'

'That date sounds familiar . . .'

'It was the day the two of us rode back into the city. Nobody recalls seeing Cerchi after that day, and he didn't report for duty again. If I had to guess, I'd say he was killed that night. It would explain why you weren't able to find him.'

Aldo nodded. 'Makes sense. You'll have to look at the last few days he was alive. Did Cerchi do something before he disappeared that gave others a reason to kill him?'

'His extortion scheme,' Strocchi replied. It was the obvious answer, and a case in which the constable had been directly involved. He had found a murder victim's private diary which linked the dead man to several rich merchants. Strocchi had made a list of their names, but Cerchi used that and the diary as weapons for blackmail. One of the men – Agnolotti Landini – had killed himself as a consequence. Aldo helped end Cerchi's extortion scheme by stealing and destroying the diary and the list. 'Landini was the first name on that list,' Strocchi said, 'but he took his own life several days before Cerchi disappeared.'

'A tragic case,' Aldo agreed. 'Even so, the Landini *famiglia* had good reason to blame Cerchi for what happened. The widow or one of Landini's sons could have paid someone to kill Cerchi. The rumours about why Landini died have been bad for their business.'

Strocchi nodded, adding a visit to the Landini *famiglia* to his plans for the next day. 'I've been struggling to recall any of the other men on that list. I wrote it in such haste . . .'

'The dressmaker Renato Patricio was the second name,' Aldo said.

'Yes, that's right! Thank you. I will seek him out tomorrow.'

'That won't be easy. Patricio left the city.'

'When?'

Aldo brushed a hand across the greying stubble on his chin. 'Last month, I think? Apparently Patricio sold his workshop near Piazza delle Travi and went north, announcing he had grand plans to create beautiful gowns for the merchant wives of Milan. Said he hoped to turn that city into a new leader in dressmaking.'

'How do you know that?'

Aldo gestured at the tavern around them. 'Not all my informants are as disreputable as Zoppo. It helps to have sources in high and low parts of the city. To succeed as an officer, you need to find favour with people from every part of Florence. What you think of them doesn't matter. What they can tell you does.'

Strocchi could see the sense of that, but something else Aldo had said caught his attention more. He leaned forward. 'You think I could be an officer?'

'Yes, sooner or later. Sooner, if Bindi has the wit to promote you.'

Strocchi offered up a silent prayer that Aldo was right. The extra coin from being an officer would make a great difference if Tomasia was carrying a baby. No Strocchi had ever been more than a country farmer working a rented field. To be made an officer for a powerful Florentine court . . .

'Can you remember any other names on that list?' Aldo asked. 'Cerchi was greedy, he would not have stopped after extorting money from Landini and Patricio.'

Strocchi shook his head. He had burned the list after Aldo retrieved it from Cerchi. 'What if Patricio left the city because he paid someone to kill Cerchi? Whoever murdered Cerchi must have known the remains would be found eventually. Bodies that fall into the river float back to the surface in a few days.'

'How do you know that?'

'The village where I grew up is downriver from the city. More than once I saw a body floating in the water. The fields by the river often flooded in the spring. Sometimes bodies are left behind. That's what happened to Cerchi.' Aldo shook his head. 'What? Am I wrong?'

Aldo held up a hand. 'No. I was simply – The chances of Cerchi washing up there –'

'I know,' Strocchi said. 'Tomasia says it is happenstance, nothing more. But I keep wondering if God meant me to find him. What do you think?'

'That God has more important things to do than this,' Aldo replied. 'As for your question about Patricio, I met him a few times over the years. He never struck me as someone ready to murder. Men who love making beautiful dresses don't often get involved with violence. But if someone was looking to pay for Cerchi to be killed, I know who might have helped –' He reached in the air, snapping his fingers several times.

Zoppo stumped over to them. 'Yes? I'm a busy man, you know.'

Strocchi fought back a laugh. He and Aldo were the only people in the tavern, aside from two drunks snoring in the far corner. Aldo held out more coin. 'The constable needs information. He's liable to be an officer soon, so you'd be wise to help him.'

Zoppo's grubby features twisted into an ingratiating smile. 'Of course. Any friend of Aldo is a friend of this tavern, so long as there's coin. How can I help?'

'I believe an officer of the Otto was murdered in January,' Strocchi said, 'not long after the feast of the Epiphany. Stabbed in the heart, and his body dumped in the Arno. It's likely the person holding the blade was paid to do so. I want to know if anyone hired a killer in the days after the Epiphany. Can you help?'

Zoppo took the coin from Aldo's open hand. 'When do you need to know?'

'Before curfew tomorrow, if possible?'

The cripple glared at Aldo. 'See? This is how you treat a friend.'

'We're not friends,' Aldo told Zoppo before standing up. He nodded to Strocchi. 'I've someone I need to see tonight, before curfew. Good luck with your investigation.'

Aldo strode from the tavern, fighting the urge to quicken his pace. *Palle!* Even when Cerchi was no more than food for worms, he found a way to soil the day. He remained a festering sore, his name poison on the tongue. How had—

'Wait!' Strocchi called out. Aldo forced himself to stop, letting the constable catch up. 'When I went to see Nardi, she gave me a message for you. She hasn't found the documents you were looking for. None of the girls had them.'

Aldo's belly lurched. 'Documents?'

'Yes. Nardi said you asked if Cerchi had left any documents at the *bordello*. Her women searched all the rooms, but there was nothing.'

'Thanks for passing on the message.' Aldo strode on, the food and all that wine Saul had given him threatening to come back up.

'It made me wonder what the papers were,' the constable said, hurrying to keep pace. 'I thought they might be to do with Cerchi's death.'

'They weren't.'

'No?'

Strocchi would keep asking until he was satisfied, so Aldo stopped. 'Cerchi was not a good officer. He was sloppy, losing court documents. He even took some from the Podestà without permission, and forgot to bring them back.' It was a lie, but sounded believable.

'You thought he had left them at the *bordello*?'

Aldo nodded, willing his body not to betray him. 'When Cerchi disappeared, I had to take charge of all his cases. Bindi discovered two *denunzie* were missing for a trial due before the magistrates. I went to Cerchi's home, I tried the *bordello* – both without success. I finally found the damned things under a bench at the Podestà, in the officer's cell off the courtyard.'

Strocchi's face fell, his disappointment obvious. 'Oh.'

Aldo clapped a hand on the constable's shoulder. 'You will find whoever killed Cerchi. It may take a while, but I know you will find them.' Aldo's belly heaved again. 'Now, let me go. Something I ate is not sitting well, and I need to find a *latrina*.'

'Yes, of course.' The constable stepped back. 'Forgive me, I didn't realize.'

Aldo stumbled away, his discomfort growing by the moment. Round a corner he found a dark alley. Then everything he had eaten and drunk came back up. Half-chewed olives and scraps of meat spattered the ground, stained crimson by Saul's wine. Spasm after spasm bent Aldo double, till there was nothing left to come. Still the roiling inside him would not cease . . .

Strocchi did not know it yet, but much of his speculation about Cerchi's death was accurate. The killing had taken place on Ponte Vecchio, and it was a knife that ended the officer's life. Extortion was the reason behind his killing. If Strocchi could deduce all that, it might not be many more days before he discovered the rest.

Finally, blessedly, the turmoil subsided inside Aldo. He sank to one knee, gasping for fresh air and spitting to clear his mouth. Staring at the crimson mess around him, Aldo's thoughts slipped back to that night in January . . .

He had been down on one knee then too, coughing and choking while Cerchi strutted around, threatening to expose what kind of man Aldo was. Cerchi claimed to have two *denunzie* as proof. But before revealing Aldo's secret to the world, Cerchi wanted to extort all the coin he could. To make matters worse, Cerchi was more than ready to make others suffer for what he saw as Aldo's sins. 'Orvieto – he's like you, isn't he? Tell me, does the Jew like to put it inside you, or do you put it into him?'

Aldo had insisted Cerchi was wrong, begged for Saul to be left alone. But Cerchi would not listen, would not see reason. 'I'll do whatever I want. And as of tonight, you'll do whatever I say, whenever I say it. From now on, you're my whore.'

That was when Aldo had buried his stiletto in Cerchi.

# Chapter Sixteen

𝒜ldo found his way to the river and turned east, towards Ponte Vecchio. The setting sun was painting the clouds overhead yellow and orange, while the waters of the Arno glistened. Already the heat of the day had faded, pushed aside by cool breezes as twilight came for Florence. Soon the city gates would be locked and night would fall.

Aldo had seen more lives ended than he could remember, many taken by his own hand. Most of his killings had been as a soldier for hire. But some were during his time as an officer of the Otto, defending his own life or that of others. Of all the ways to end a life, stabbing a man was among the most intimate, even more so when done face to face, close enough to embrace. That was how it had been with Cerchi. A moment of surprise as the stiletto pierced skin; Cerchi's small gasp of pain. Aldo had smelled Cerchi's foul breath as it steamed the air, witnessed the anguish twisting those narrow, rat-like features.

Aldo had given the stiletto a hard quarter-turn, the blade resisting as it scraped across bone. It was a trick learned from being a soldier, a way to ensure the enemy went down and stayed down. Twisting a knife inside a wound made it harder to staunch the bleeding, the injury more likely to kill. Cerchi had not realized he was dying in those first moments, disbelief still consuming him. How had his moment of triumph become his undoing?

It had been well after curfew, Strocchi was right about that too, clouds covering the moon. The butchers' stalls and other shops were all long closed, blood from the day's trade freezing on the bridge's stones. There was nobody nearby, nobody watching. Cerchi had lurched to the side of the bridge, flailing at the stone parapet for support.

All it took was one hard shove, and Cerchi toppled over the side, falling through the gap between buildings. He sank beneath the water at once, the Arno claiming him in a single swallow. Aldo had strolled away, knowing the butchers' boys would wash away any evidence the next morning. Sometimes killing was necessary, or so he had told himself . . .

Aldo stopped at the northern end of Ponte Vecchio. It was close to curfew, traders shutting their stalls for the night. There was a second level above many of the shops, with the top half of the buildings providing humble homes for some of those who worked below. Few of these dwellings had windows that looked down on the bridge, and those that did kept their shutters closed. The stench of meat and blood and offal was usually ripe on Ponte Vecchio, though not during Lent when the Church expected people to forego meat. Living above the butchers' stalls must be all but unbearable during summer. Back in January the smell had been less oppressive, but none of the shutters were open the night Cerchi died, Aldo was sure of that.

He strode up the curving bridge, savouring the last of the spring day. Aldo stopped at Ponte Vecchio's highest point, where the gap between buildings gave a view of the Arno. The last of the day's sun was sliding beneath the horizon, throwing one last glorious splash of colour across the clouds before surrendering to darkness.

Aldo had returned here the day after Cerchi died, expecting to see a body caught on one of the weirs downriver – but there was none. The current must have been strong that night, the waters high enough to carry Cerchi's corpse away. Aldo had gone to the Podestà, waiting for – no, expecting – a citizen to make a *denunzia* about two men arguing on the bridge, or claiming to have seen a body fall from Ponte Vecchio. But nobody did.

Days passed and Cerchi did not report for duty. His body was not found by fishermen further down the river, and his remains did not wash up on the banks of the Arno. Meo Cerchi was gone, and the world was no worse. In fact, it was a better place. But Aldo also knew that Cerchi's disappearance had not put an end to his threats. There were still the two *denunzie* Cerchi claimed to have given to someone Aldo did not know. If anything happened to Cerchi, the *denunzie* would be sent to the Otto.

For days after Cerchi died, Aldo waited for the inevitable summons to face those accusations, the trial that would follow. But when he was summoned by the *segretario*, it was to be given the task of finding Cerchi. Aldo had almost laughed. The investigation gave him the chance to search for the *denunzie*. He found them hidden inside the dead man's home after searching the two rooms while Grazia was at the *mercato*.

Cerchi's claims had all been lies. There was only one signed *denunzia*, written by Patricio. The other document repeated the same accusations, but bore no signature. Cerchi had been unable to read or write, so someone else had written it for him. A brief comparison made clear why the documents were so similar – Patricio's hand was responsible for both. Cerchi must have planned to coerce someone into presenting the second *denunzia* as their own words, or to submit it anonymously as proof the first was true.

Aldo burned both documents. To ensure the problem never arose again, he visited the dressmaker's palazzo. Patricio begged for forgiveness, breaking down as he recounted the threats Cerchi made. Aldo couldn't be sure Cerchi had not hidden further copies of the *denunzie* elsewhere. To counter that, he had Patricio make a fresh *denunzia* accusing Cerchi of extortion and recanting any prior claims as false, written under duress. Aldo had one last demand: the dressmaker must leave Florence. Permanently.

After Patricio departed for Milan, Aldo believed himself free of Cerchi's shadow. The *merda* would not trouble anyone again. So Strocchi's proud announcement that he had found Cerchi's remains in a village graveyard – it had brought all those fears back up again, along with the food and wine. Of all the people to find the body, why must it be Strocchi? The chances of him stumbling on the silver buckle Cerchi wore, and then following that to the bones, let alone recognizing the signs of a knife wound in the remains . . .

Was all of this happenstance? Yes. Was it ill fate, playing a trick? Possibly, though Aldo refused to believe the path ahead of him was written before he took a step each day. Perhaps this was all part of God's plan? Strocchi might think so. He was young, a man whose faith had not been shaken by the realities of life. Strocchi was still innocent in many ways; he still truly believed – something Aldo had not done for years. Perhaps Strocchi would say all of this was God's punishment for the way Aldo lived and loved. *Palle!*

Aldo turned his back on the setting sun. Self-pity would not help him. Whatever had brought this about did not matter now. There was a simple truth to recognize. He did not, would not, regret killing that *merda*. No matter what others might think, it had been necessary. But he did have to decide what to do about

Strocchi's investigation. It might take the constable days, perhaps weeks, but eventually he would find enough threads to follow until he deduced what had happened on Ponte Vecchio that night. The fact that Strocchi had already deduced so much of the truth showed how good an officer he would be. Aldo had done his best to lead Strocchi astray while they talked in Zoppo's tavern, pushing the constable towards the names on that list. It was tempting to go further, to suggest other false leads for Strocchi to investigate. But if he was too helpful the constable might become suspicious. Better to let him stumble along alone, for now at least.

There was another path ahead that Aldo could see: leaving the city. He could resign from the Otto, gather what coin he had, and ride away from Florence in the morning. By the time Strocchi had enough evidence to make a *denunzia*, Aldo would be beyond the court's jurisdiction. His abrupt departure might be seen as proof of his guilt – no doubt Bindi would enjoy making that argument to the magistrates. They would convict Aldo in absentia and issue a warrant for his arrest. But so long as Aldo remained outside the Otto's reach, he would face no further punishment.

Yet fleeing the city sat uneasily with him. Why run? Why leave behind the life he had made for himself? After two months apart he and Saul were healing their rift. To go now meant leaving behind all the tomorrows they might have, all the happiness they might know. Aldo could ask Saul to come too, but that meant explaining why – and he wasn't sure Saul could forgive a killing, no matter how justified it seemed. Besides, Saul had a whole community that depended on his care. Asking him to surrender all of that for the uncertain hope of a new life many miles away . . . no, it wasn't fair.

Running from Florence also meant leaving other things unfinished.

Seeing Teresa had brought back a wealth of memories, happier times when they had been as close as brother and sister. He had not appreciated Teresa's attempt to get his help in marrying off her daughter – the cold grasp of Lucrezia was all too evident in that. But part of him still missed being part of the only real *famiglia* he had known. The day had been so frantic, he forgot to send a message about Isabella. Still, a night of worry might make Teresa rethink the marriage plans for her daughter. And then there was Isabella, caught up in the convent's enclosure. What would happen to her?

It was vanity, but Aldo doubted the murder would be solved without him. The Church already had a culprit it could blame: the convent, and the women inside it. They would all be held account-able for Galeri's killing, no matter who was actually responsible. The abbess and her sisters in God deserved answers and that required a proper investigation, not some hasty pretence performed to satisfy the archbishop. No, that was not good enough.

So, the decision was made. The next few days would be devoted to finding whoever murdered Bernardo Galeri. Once that was resolved, it should be apparent whether Strocchi was close to the truth about Cerchi's death. In the meantime preparations could be made to depart the city, if that became necessary. Aldo nodded. So be it.

When Isabella had fled to the convent to escape her unwanted marriage, she had not planned on spending the night at Santa Maria Magdalena. Her parents would obviously realize they were in the wrong, and come to beg for her return at once. Well, not at once, *Nonna* would not allow that, but certainly within a few hours. Isabella had expected to be back in her own bedchamber by nightfall with Nucca tending to her every need, the maid eager to hear gossip about life inside the convent.

Instead, Isabella found herself preparing to sleep in a dormitory alongside the six girls who boarded at the convent, and several servant nuns. The room was on the convent's upper level, near the stairs. It was much larger than Isabella's room at home, but crowded with many narrow beds. A stale, disagreeable odour hung in the air that made Isabella crinkle her nose. Palazzo Fioravanti had the finest embroidered bed linens, and Isabella went to sleep in a nightdress decorated with beautiful bows. Here the beds bore a lumpy mattress and plain, coarse sheets. One of the servant nuns, a dutiful and dumpy girl called Suor Rigarda, showed Isabella where to find a plain sleep shift. Isabella had never shared a room with anyone else before, let alone eleven others.

All the servant nuns seemed to do was yawn and pray, while the boarders were busy in their own corner. Isabella joined them, hoped for secrets and speculations about the body found in the scriptorium. But the abbess had forbidden all talk of such things. Instead, the boarders kept whispering about someone called Maria Celestia and her wounds that would not stop bleeding. The boarders seemed to think this a miracle, but to Isabella it sounded disgusting. She returned to her allotted bed, aware of a growing discomfort in her belly. That might be due to the food in the refectory. Plain would be one word for it, and dull another. She looked under her bed, but found no pot in which to relieve herself. Isabella crept across to Rigarda who was kneeling nearby.

'Where do I go to – you know?' Isabella pointed below her belly.

Rigarda did not reply, her lips too busy whispering a prayer.

'The *latrina* is along the hallway,' another servant nun said. She had darker skin than most of the others, and a weary smile. 'Come,

I'll show you.' Isabella followed her out into a bare wooden hallway, dimly lit by a few candles. Further along stood a heavy wooden door. A draught blew beneath it, chilling Isabella's toes. 'It's in there.' The servant nun took a lit candle from a sconce on the wall, handing it to Isabella. 'You'll need this.'

Isabella nodded. 'Sorry, I don't know your name.'

'Suor Dea.'

'Thank you, Suor Dea.'

The servant nun headed back to the dormitory so Isabella ventured inside the *latrina*. It was clean, but cold air came whistling up through the ovals from below. Isabella dripped wax onto the floor to fix her candle. The last thing she wanted was for it to fall over and go out. After relieving herself, she retrieved her candle and went to the door, eager to leave before someone else came in. But when she peered out, there were two nuns in the hallway having a disagreement. They were looking away from Isabella, veils of different colours hiding their faces. But she knew enough of the convent to realize one was a chapter nun, the other a novice.

Isabella put an ear against the door, hoping to hear what they were saying. But their voices were low whispers, only a few words reaching her. 'Hidden' was one thing she did hear, 'mistake' was another, and 'they can't know' a third. Isabella leaned closer, certain—

'Oww!' she cried out. Something was burning her foot! She looked down and realized it was hot wax, dripping from the candle. Footsteps hurried away. By the time Isabella got the door open, the hallway was empty. She put the candle back in its sconce and returned to the dormitory. All the others were in their beds. Dea sat up as Isabella went past.

'Are you well? I heard someone call out.'

Isabella explained about the candle wax, showing the red mark on her foot. She was about to ask if anyone had come in before her, but remembered the chapter nuns and novices slept in other dormitories, or their own cells. It was impossible to know for certain who had been arguing in the hallway, but one of them had a distinctive scratchiness to her voice. Isabella was sure she had heard that voice before, but couldn't recall when or where. Still she was certain she would recognize it if she heard that nun speaking again.

Saul was closing his front door when Aldo strode along via dei Giudei in the twilight. 'I was wondering if you would be back before curfew,' the doctor said with a smile.

'It has been quite a day,' Aldo replied, stopping at the doorstep. He was all too aware how close the windows of other homes were, and how inquisitive Saul's neighbours could be.

'Do you require more medical advice?' Saul asked, his eyes twinkling.

'No, I came to convey the Otto's thanks for your expertise earlier at the *ospedale.*'

'You're welcome. Please, come in – I should like to hear how the case is progressing.'

It was tempting, but Aldo doubted either of them would emerge before morning. Much as he wanted that – much as he wanted Saul – it must wait until he found the words to explain what had happened with Cerchi. Saul deserved the truth. If he could forgive what Aldo had done, they might be together. If not . . . Aldo didn't want to consider that, not after waiting so long. 'Another time.' He offered a hand to Saul, pulling him close to whisper in an ear. 'Soon. I promise.' Aldo stepped back. 'I hope the Otto can call on you in future, if needed?'

'Of course.' The shadow of a frown crossed Saul's face, but he seemed to understand. 'If you want me, you know where I'll be.'

Aldo marched away, not letting himself look back. It was better this way.

*From a confession made at the convent
of Santa Maria Magdalena:*

I am ready to face whatever punishment is deemed necessary
for my acts, knowing I shall face a greater judgement. I pray
for myself, and I pray for all of you, my sisters in God.

I pray you can forgive me for my trespasses, though I
cannot forgive myself.

I pray that those who remain when this is over are able to
lead us from temptation.

Most of all, I pray that there will be a tomorrow for all
those who dwell within this place of God – chapter nuns and
servant nuns, novices and boarders. Most of you have good
hearts and pure spirits. I pray that you can find the strength to
retain that goodness and purity. You will need it to find the
path out of this darkness.

Yes, I murdered Bernardo Galeri.

It was the only way, I truly believe that – even now.

I prayed for him at the hour of his death. And I shall pray
when my last hour comes.

I have sinned against you, sisters, those whom I should love
above all things.

Know that our Lord is with all of you.

May God have mercy on us.

# Chapter Seventeen

## Tuesday, March 27th 1537

*A*ldo woke early. Beyond his wooden shutter the first glimmers of dawn were painting fresh colours across the bruised sky. Soon the city would stir from its slumber, grateful for the warmth of spring and the promise that brought. But Aldo was already pondering how to make best use of the opening he had secured from Ruggerio. It would require cunning and guile. It would also need a fresh tunic and hose, along with clean boots.

Lay members of a diocesan visitation were expected to be men of good standing in their faith, their manners, and their appearance. There was little Aldo could do about his beliefs, but a boyhood spent in Palazzo Fioravanti had been an education in presenting the right face to the world, while a wash and shave could take care of the rest. He scraped a blade across his chin, fingertips finding the bristles along his jawline in the early morning murk. The tunic and hose he wore for hearings of the Otto were clean, kept ready in case of being summoned before the magistrates. Lastly, Aldo pulled on his best boots, a shiver running up his spine. Taking a dead man's place was uncomfortable. Galeri had also traded favours to join a visitation to Santa Maria Magdalena. He was murdered for that – poisoned, stabbed repeatedly, and covered with blood. Hopefully that pattern would not be repeated.

Departing the *bordello*, Aldo went west rather than taking his usual path east. That would have meant passing via dei Giudei. Better to avoid the temptation. Instead, Aldo crossed the Arno and went on to the tavern. Zoppo did not open before noon, so it took several minutes of hammering to summon the cripple. He opened the door a crack, peering out with tired eyes. 'Already? It's not even light yet.'

'First thing means first thing,' Aldo replied, shoving his way in. The tavern reeked even worse in the morning, but at least the poor lighting hid whatever was causing the stench. 'What have you heard about Galeri?'

'Not much,' Zoppo grumbled, stumping across to the bar. 'You didn't give me long.'

'Not much is better than nothing.'

The cripple pulled himself onto a wooden stool. 'Well, you were right. Galeri was a gambler, and a bad one. He owed money to at least three men, none of who have my natural charm. Galeri wagered his worker's wages away. And then he wagered the business away.'

'What about his home?'

'He lived above the workshop. It's in the eastern quarter, between Santa Croce and the river. Word is spreading about his death, so it will have been ransacked by now.'

Aldo grimaced. 'Meaning you told Galeri's gambling friends about the murder in exchange for a cut of whatever they found at his home.'

Zoppo shrugged. 'Business is business, and your coin doesn't cover all my costs.'

'Anything else?'

'Not long before his death, Galeri had been looking to hire a thief good at climbing. Way I hear it, he was too fond of *dolce* and that showed round his middle. He needed someone who could go where he couldn't. Not really the sort of thing I arrange, so I only heard about that from a friend of a friend. Don't know if he found the right thief . . .'

That solved one puzzle. There was no way to be certain, but Aldo knew in his *palle* that Galeri had been one of the people Signora Gonzaga saw trying to get inside the convent a few nights ago. His hired *complice* must have failed, otherwise why would Galeri return on Palm Sunday after curfew? Aldo sighed. Answer one question and another took its place. He slapped coin down on the nearest table. 'There are two more things I need. First, where was Galeri's workshop?'


Isabella had never known such a poor night's sleep. Servant nuns getting up early had woken her long before dawn, while snoring from several nearby boarders ensured she could not get back to sleep. The filling in her lumpy mattress had parted during the night, leaving her lying on top of hard wooden boards. But worst of all was the itching. At first it was a few niggles, but soon her body seemed to be on fire, forcing her to scratch and claw at the skin. There were bumps dotting her legs and belly, clustered behind her knees and across her midriff. Isabella shuddered at the thought of what she would find when she lifted her shift.

A chapter nun entered the dormitory, clapping her hands to rouse those still asleep. 'Come along, sisters. Time to raise our voices in worship to the Lord!'

As one the servant nuns and boarders rose, stretching and yawning. Some dropped to their knees to pray alongside their narrow beds, Suor Rigarda among them. Isabella wasn't in a rush to join them. Her belly was rumbling. The nuns must break their fast soon, or would she have to suffer through more prayers before there was any food?

The tired, cheerful face of Suor Dea stopped on her way past. 'It'll be prime soon. You need to be ready before we're called to chapel.'

'Prime?'

The servant nun laughed. 'The early service. This time of year it's before sunrise.'

'Do we eat first?'

Dea shook her head. 'Sorry.'

Isabella scratched inside her elbows. 'Oh.'

'You shouldn't have slept there. That mattress is always full of fleas.'

'What?' Isabella sprung from the bed, flapping at herself, imagining hundreds of tiny creatures biting and crawling all over her body. 'Why didn't anyone tell me?'

'Come with me to the *latrina*,' Dea said. 'We'll see how much you've been bitten. If it's bad, I can take you to the infirmary. Suor Simona has a salve that stops you scratching.'

'Thank you,' Isabella muttered, following Dea out of the dormitory. Coming to the convent had seemed a good idea the previous day, a way to escape marrying some old man. Now Isabella was starting to wish she could go home. Her own bed, her own maid, her own life – it seemed much more appealing. Even if she did have to marry Rosso, at least she would get a new dress for the wedding.

But the convent was enclosed by order of the Archbishop of Florence, with nobody allowed to leave the grounds. Isabella sighed. So much for escaping.

* * *

Galeri's residence had been ransacked, as Zoppo predicted. Aldo found the workshop door hanging from its frame, and anything of value gone from inside. All the dyes and cloth were missing. Only empty benches and vats remained, too heavy to carry away and of little value on their own. Wooden steps led to the upper level where the dead man had lived and slept. Again, anything worth taking was gone. There were no tapestries, no art on the walls, no fine porcelain. But there had been more than thieves at work here.

Everything was in disarray. Simple furniture had been broken apart. The mattress on Galeri's bed lay in shreds, its filling spilled across the floor. His clothes were in tatters, the linings split, the seams torn apart. Robbers were not this thorough. Someone had come here to search everything Galeri owned. Yet the amount of the devastation suggested the quest had not been successful. If they found whatever they sought, those searching would have stopped before scouring every possible hiding place. What did they believe Galeri had? His murder was not commonly known yet. How had those searching even been aware—

Ruggerio, it had to be Ruggerio. Aside from those Zoppo had alerted, few others in the city knew Galeri had been killed. Fewer still had any reason to scour the dead man's residence. But Ruggerio did know of the murder, and he certainly knew the victim. His reaction on hearing what had happened now made more sense. Ruggerio feared Galeri had gone to the convent after curfew, intent on stealing something the confraternity kept there.

Knowing the depth of Ruggerio's ruthlessness, he would have sent men to ransack the residence as soon as he heard Galeri was dead. If they had not found what Ruggerio sought, it was likely still inside the convent, which was now enclosed by order of the archbishop.

No wonder Ruggerio had been so willing to help.

Aldo stepped outside. Was there a link between the scrap of parchment he found under Galeri's body and whatever those who ransacked Galeri's property had been seeking? Aldo had thought the torn parchment corner might be from the official documentation for the first visitation, but that was clearly wrong. Any such document would be of no use when Galeri returned to the convent after dark on Palm Sunday. There must be another explanation.

What if the torn corner was actually from a document stored at the convent by Ruggerio's confraternity? That made more sense. Perhaps Galeri had found what Ruggerio and his brethren kept there. He couldn't remove the complete document – why, Aldo didn't know – so Galeri tore off a corner and stuck it inside his tunic. Maybe he planned to use it as means for extorting coin from the confraternity. If so, he didn't know how dangerous men like Ruggerio could be. Before Galeri could attempt it, he was murdered inside the convent. The parchment must have stuck to his skin and gone unnoticed by whoever killed him . . .

Aldo shook his head. That was all guesses and leaps of reasoning. There was no value in mentioning this to anyone else, not until he had some supporting evidence.

Strocchi bore no wish to return to Palazzo Landini. The last time he had ventured inside the grand residence, the *famiglia* patriarch – overcome by grief and guilt – threw himself from one of the windows in the upper levels. Agnolotti Landini died from injuries sustained when he fell, but in truth it was Cerchi's extortion that killed him.

Now the quest to find whoever murdered Cerchi, or paid for

him to be killed, brought Strocchi back to Palazzo Landini – a bitter irony. Normally the main double doors would stand open, inviting customers and other visitors into the residence. Today only a small door to one side of the main entrance was ajar. The constable went through it.

He found Palazzo Landini in disarray. Trees that once grew tall and proud in the central courtyard were neglected and dying. Most merchants conducted their business on the lowest level of their residence so a functionary was always waiting to greet visitors, but here there was none. Strocchi had to shout several times before an elderly servant appeared, looking gaunt and tired. At first he insisted the *famiglia* were not receiving guests.

'What if I wished to conduct business?' Strocchi asked.

'Then you have come to the wrong palazzo,' a bitter female voice replied. A grey-haired woman was glaring at Strocchi from an inner window overlooking the courtyard. There was something familiar about her, the piercing gaze, the tilt of her head.

'Signora Landini?' Strocchi bowed. 'My name is Carlo Strocchi, I am a constable—'

'You're from the Otto,' she cut in. 'You're the one who killed my husband.'

Strocchi reddened at the accusation. 'That is not true, signora.'

'You didn't stop him,' she retorted.

'I did not know what was in his heart.'

That put a stop to her accusations. She stared down, the constable expecting to be dismissed at any moment. Instead, she gestured at the elderly servant. 'Alfredo, escort our guest upstairs. I will be with you in a moment, constable.'

Strocchi was ushered to the middle level, where the *famiglia* resided and entertained guests. But there was no grand furniture anymore, no tapestries on the walls, no colourful plates on display.

It had been stripped bare, a hollow chamber where a home should be.

When Signora Landini did emerge, he heard her approach by the tapping of a cane on the cold marble floor. She leaned on it for support, her face sagging on the same side. Strocchi had seen old farmers in Ponte a Signa stricken in much the same way, made weak by a sudden illness that cleft their strength in two. He offered to fetch a chair.

'You will not be staying long enough for me to sit,' she said. 'Ask your questions.'

The words blurted out before the constable could stop them. 'What happened?'

'You did,' Signora Landini replied. 'You came here, accusing my husband. A few hours later he was dead. We have been suffering for that ever since.'

'I don't understand,' Strocchi admitted. 'Your *famiglia* had a strong business—'

'Agnolotti killed our business when he killed himself,' she hissed. 'The shame of that was a stain on anyone with the name Landini. Then the whispers began about why Agnolotti died, and our shame became ten-fold. But worse was still waiting. He had borrowed against future earnings. The creditors saw we could not trade and demanded their coin. Everything we own will soon be sold to pay those debts, including this palazzo. My husband – may God curse his name – left us with nothing. No name, no business, no home. Nothing.'

Strocchi studied the widow as she spat and raged at what had happened. Signora Landini had good reason to seek vengeance, but this anger was all for her dead husband. Their marriage, their *famiglia*, their life together – all of it was a lie, she snarled. Worse still was his cowardice. In taking his own life, Agnolotti Landini condemned those left behind.

The constable waited until her anger was spent before speaking again. 'Your husband was being blackmailed, that is why he stepped from that window.'

'I know,' she said, her voice a sneer of condescension. 'The fool told me what he had done, why he was like a tapestry fraying from both ends.'

'Did he tell you the name of his accuser?'

'He had no need. I saw the man when he first came here, bringing his snide little threats and his nasty little vermin face.'

'That man –' Strocchi watched the widow's face – 'he is dead. Murdered.'

She shrugged. 'I hope he suffered, but his death will not save my *famiglia*. It will not turn back the storm that has ruined us.' Signora Landini stalked past Strocchi, her cane tapping a staccato rhythm on the floor. 'You may leave.'

Strocchi watched her go before retreating down the palazzo's internal steps. Fury was all she had left. But he found it difficult to believe she was behind Cerchi's murder. The dead officer held no interest for Signora Landini, despite his role in events.

No. Whoever had killed Cerchi resided elsewhere.


From Galeri's workshop Aldo went north towards the church of Santa Croce, a place of worship so large its name had become that of the entire eastern quarter of Florence. The surrounding streets and piazze were familiar to Aldo, who had spent his boyhood in this part of the city. But he had done his best to avoid Palazzo Fioravanti in the years since returning to Florence, knowing what lurked inside, the coiled venom that waited there.

Seeing Isabella in the convent and mistaking her for Teresa had brought back many childhood memories, things that had long since been buried. Sharing a carriage with Teresa, letting himself be pulled into the *famiglia* intrigues, those were mistakes. Now, against his better judgement, he was returning to the palazzo that had been his home for twelve years. Like an insect attracted to a flame, or a fool unable to resist a game of chance, he was giving in to a lure that could only bring pain and suffering.

But when Aldo passed the stone lion on its corner plinth outside Santa Croce, he saw Palazzo Fioravanti was far different from the grand residence of his youth. It still occupied pride of place opposite the church's side entrance, but the stone walls were not so sturdy as they had once been. No merchants were outside waiting to be admitted. Several wooden shutters hung askew. The palazzo appeared tired, weary.

No wonder the *famiglia* was so eager to marry Isabella to Ercole Rosso.

Aldo knew better than to present himself at the main doors. Do that, and Lucrezia would hear of his arrival long before he could speak to Teresa. Instead, he used the narrow alley on the western side of the palazzo to reach the servants' entrance at the back. There he waited for several minutes until a young woman about Isabella's age came out carrying an empty basket. Aldo introduced himself, and asked her to take Teresa a message. The maid soon returned, inviting Aldo inside. Teresa would see him, but he must hurry.

Aldo had sworn he would never set foot in Palazzo Fioravanti again. Not after what Lucrezia had done. He could tell the maid what Teresa needed to know. But some part of him wanted to go in, wanted to see if the palazzo was as neglected within as it looked outside. Part of him needed to touch the flame and see if the pain was still as exquisite.

He followed the maid through the kitchen and up a set of

internal stairs at the rear of the palazzo. Only servants came this way, she explained. As a boy Aldo had used the same stairs to escape Lucrezia's gaze whenever his father was away. The maid led him to a small chamber at the back of the middle level. There were papers stacked against all four walls, piles as high as Aldo's waist in places. Some had tipped over, spilling across the tiled floor. A tired odour of neglect filled the chamber. Aldo tried to open a shutter, but the wood was stuck fast.

'That has not opened in years,' an imperious voice announced behind him.

*Palle!* Aldo recognized those icy tones, the utter disdain. Lucrezia Fioravanti, the woman who had cast him out the same hour his father – her husband – had died. The maid had gone to Lucrezia first, or his stepmother had spied him from a window. It didn't matter which was true. His need to touch the flame had brought its exquisite reward.

Clenching himself for what was to come, Aldo swung round.

Lucrezia was as upright and coiled as he remembered. She wore a richly embroidered gown in mourning colours, her high hairline hidden behind a veil – but time had not been kind. She was at least seventy, if not more, and every year of that showed in her age-mottled skin and sunken face. The cheeks were hollow, her lips pulled taut by so many years of disappointment. Her eyes remained piercing, the gaze that of a hungry carrion-eater, but they were retreating into her skull, dark shadows haunting them.

'Signora Fioravanti,' Aldo said, giving the slightest bow of his head.

'*Bastardo*,' she replied, not dignifying him with anything more.

'My name is Cesare Aldo.'

'Yes, I heard you stole my husband's first name.'

'You forbade me from using Fioravanti.'

'I also forbade you from entering this palazzo again, yet here you are.'

Aldo dug fingernails into the palms of both his hands. This poisonous *cagna* would not get the satisfaction of seeing his anger. 'I came to see my sister.'

'Half-sister. And you have no more right to call on her than you do to enter here.'

'Teresa asked for my help,' Aldo replied, and enjoyed the twist of dismay in Lucrezia's lips. So, Teresa had been telling the truth. Her mother had not known. 'She asked that I intercede with Isabella. See if her daughter – your granddaughter – could be persuaded to come home. Or didn't you know that Isabella had run away to a convent?'

'I am quite aware of that spoiled child's foolishness. She is so wilful and obstinate, it is hard to believe we share any blood at all,' Lucrezia sniffed.

'On the contrary,' Aldo said, smiling. 'Isabella reminds me of you. But she lacks your bitterness, that sour spirit that curdles everything you say and do and touch.'

Lucrezia stiffened. 'I've heard more than enough of your opinions. You were my husband's greatest mistake, and you grew into his greatest disappointment. He wept on his death bed when I told him what I had discovered, what sort of man you would become.'

She was lying, Aldo knew she was lying. Her words were intended to wound, like a barb on an arrow that caused more damage when it was pulled free of the flesh.

Aldo strode the few paces towards her, causing Lucrezia to back away, a shadow of fear on that wizened face. 'Tell Teresa her daughter remains inside the convent, and she will probably be there for several days more. It has been enclosed by order of the archbishop. Even if Isabella wished to come home – which I doubt – she has no choice in the matter. Should that change, I shall send a messenger. Now, stand aside so I may leave.'

Lucrezia glared at him, tiny tremors making her head tremble. But eventually she moved out of his way. A single word followed him out, hissed from dry lips.

'*Buggerone.*'

Aldo paused, letting the silence swallow his stepmother's venom. 'If you want to see my father's greatest disappointment,' he said, not bothering to glance at Lucrezia, 'all you need to do is find a looking glass. The answer will be staring back at you.'

And then he stalked away.

# Chapter Eighteen

*B*indi had to read the letter three times to be certain his eyes were not deceiving him. But there was no denying the ink scrawled across the missive, nor the meaning of those words. His Excellency, the Archbishop of Florence, had decreed in his wisdom that an officer of the Otto should be seconded to a diocesan visitation. The officer would join three other visitors to help determine who was responsible for an unlawful killing inside the convent of Santa Maria Magdalena. Most galling of all, the archbishop had chosen Cesare Aldo as that officer.

How was this possible? By what means had Buondelmonti come to this decision? The archbishop was notorious for his grasping attitude. Crimes committed on the grounds of a church, convent or any other diocesan property were kept strictly within the jurisdiction of the Church. Why would the archbishop choose to relax that grip? Why would he call on the Otto for an officer to assist with the investigation? And why choose Aldo?

Someone had Buondelmonti's attention. They had been whispering in his ear, bending him to their will. That same person had chosen Aldo as their pawn to go inside the convent.

Of course.

It had to be Ruggerio.

It was not enough that he had forced the court into serving

his will. Now Ruggerio was extending his grasp further, all the way to the archbishop. And why? Bindi had heard the rumours about what the Company of Santa Maria kept at the convent: treasure. But the *segretario* knew it would not be treasure in the usual sense of that word. There would be no gold, no coin or precious works of art stored inside Santa Maria Magdalena. Men like Ruggerio and his brethren would not permit such things to leave their own safekeeping.

No, it was far more likely the convent was being used to store holy relics alongside documents relating to the confraternity's creation and control. Most religious brotherhoods were built on charitable intentions, alongside the wish to be seen to be doing good. The Company of Santa Maria was different. Its leadership had not changed in decades. Time had taken a few of the senior brethren, but it was said the remaining founders, such as Ruggerio, still made all the significant decisions. Something bound those men together. Was it their collective lust for power, or was it a past transgression they had committed together?

On another occasion, the *segretario* would admire such a taut hold on the power. But not when it interfered with his own domain. The archbishop's order to enclose the convent had left a smile on Bindi's features. It spared the Otto from investigating any further. All fault would fall on the diocese should the matter go unsolved. Bindi could have shared his regrets at this unfortunate outcome while escaping any blame. A perfect solution.

But now the Otto remained culpable, even if only by association. The *segretario* sent word to the guards outside the Podestà gates: the moment Aldo approached, he must report at once to Bindi. All too often Aldo came and went as he wished. It was intolerable from any other officer as none of them had Aldo's ability to unknot the most insoluble cases. But a reckoning was overdue. When

Bindi heard knocking at his *officio* door, he did not bother making Aldo wait. The anger could be contained no longer. 'Enter!'

Aldo came in, closing the door before approaching the broad desk. He bowed his head, a show of respect that served to irk Bindi more. 'You wished to see me, *segretario*?'

'Whom do you serve?'

'I'm an officer of the Otto.'

'I'm glad you remember that much, at least. And do you believe a servant of the Otto should have more than one master?'

'No, *segretario*.'

'Then explain this.' Bindi flung the letter so it landed in front of Aldo, making him bend over to retrieve it. 'You have been seconded by the archbishop himself to assist a diocese visitation to that convent, Santa Maria Magdalena!'

Aldo took his time reading the letter before replying. 'So I see.'

As if he didn't already know what it would say! Bindi snapped his fingers, gesturing for the officer to return the missive. 'Well? Do you have an explanation?'

Aldo shook his head. It seemed he preferred a sin of omission to an outright lie.

'You will, of course, abide by the wishes of the archbishop,' Bindi said, folding the letter before resting his hands atop it on the desk. 'This court serves the Church and the people of Florence with equal skill and authority. But while you are busy helping with the investigation, I expect a full report at the end of each day on your progress. Once the visitation is concluded, you must return here so that we can discuss your future with the Otto. I shall not tolerate having an officer trade favours with those outside the Podestà to further his own interests, not without my prior permission. Is that understood?'

Aldo nodded, his face impassive as ever.

'Very well. You may go.'

Bindi waited until Aldo reached the *officio* door before calling to him. 'One more thing. A note from Monsignor Testardo arrived with the letter. The visitation is gathering outside the archbishop's residence. Run, and you might just get there in time.'

The anger that caused in Aldo's eyes was quite delicious.


Aldo refused to run. The *segretario* had deliberately withheld the time and place where the visitation members were gathering to secure a petty victory. It was typical of a need to show his power, a way to overcome his impotence. If striding to the meeting place meant being late, so be it. Aldo would not arrive red-faced. Gaining the trust of the other visitors was going to be difficult enough.

Testardo was pacing in front of the archbishop's residence as Aldo approached. The monsignor had been curt and dismissive outside the convent the previous afternoon. Now he appeared angry and impatient, his boots scuffing up dust. The younger priest, Father Zati, was keeping out of Testardo's way. Beside him stood another man wearing a rich red tunic and blue hose. He was at least forty, if the thinning hair beneath his blue cap was any guide. That must be the other non-cleric who had accompanied Testardo, Zati and Galeri on their first inspection. He had a weak chin and gentle eyes, suggesting he might lack the monsignor's steel. Time would tell.

Aldo introduced himself to the trio, professing sorrow for his late arrival. The lay visitor – Maso Cortese – accepted the words with good humour. Zati was equally forgiving. Testardo held his tongue until the others fell silent, studying Aldo with hawkish eyes. 'You were outside the convent yesterday,' the monsignor said, accusation in his voice. 'You claimed not to know what was going on at Santa Maria Magdalena.'

'Are you sure, monsignor?' Cortese asked.

'His clothes are different, but I never forget a face,' Testardo said. 'Why the pretence? Was that young woman actually your niece?'

'Isabella Goudi is my step-niece,' Aldo replied, ignoring the other question.

'Now you expect us to take you – an officer of the Otto – onto Church property?'

'I believe it was the archbishop who decided that,' Zati said, getting a glare from Testardo in response.

'I am as surprised as you,' Aldo lied. 'The *segretario* of the Otto only told me this morning.' That much had the virtue of being true, even if it wasn't the whole truth.

Testardo bristled but could do nothing more. 'Very well,' he snapped. 'But I lead the questioning when we enter the convent. If your – assistance – is required, I will ask for it. Otherwise your role will be to listen and observe. Nothing more.'

'Of course.' Aldo bowed to the monsignor, keeping his face blank as an empty page.

'We have but a single day to discover what happened at the convent, and who was responsible for the murder of Bernardo Galeri. If a confession cannot be secured before curfew tonight, the future of Santa Maria Magdalena shall be forfeit. Let us go.' Testardo marched north, Cortese hurrying to catch up.

Aldo fell into step alongside Zati as they passed between the Battistero di San Giovanni and the Duomo. 'I understand there was a visitation to the convent on Friday,' Aldo said to Zati, his voice loud enough for the monsignor to hear. 'Were you part of that?'

'Yes,' Zati replied. 'All of us were, along with the unfortunate Signor Galeri.'

'Did you know him well?'

'Not at all. I believe it was his first time being a visitor for the diocese.'

'Indeed?' Aldo affected polite interest in what the young priest had to say, despite already knowing the answers to his own questions.

'Signor Galeri accompanied me as we inspected the convent,' Zati continued. 'But he showed little interest in much of what we saw. In truth, I was not quite sure why he had sought to become a visitor. He only paid attention a few times.'

The four men turned on to via San Gallo, heading north towards the convent. Aldo slowed his pace a little, not wishing to reach Santa Maria Magdalena before the priest could finish his recollections. 'Is that so? And where in the convent was Galeri attentive?'

Zati frowned as he replied. 'We interrupted a class in the refectory. He took a strong interest in the girls' studies, which did not please Suor Catarina, their teacher. Signor Galeri also lingered at the infirmary for a short while, and he was most eager to visit the *officio* of the abbess, although she was not present at the time.'

Why would Galeri want access to her *officio* while she was absent? Unless that was where the confraternity's possessions were held for safe-keeping . . . Aldo smiled at the priest. 'You said Galeri paid attention a few times. Was there somewhere else?'

Zati laughed. 'Well observed, Signor Aldo. You would make an excellent inquisitor.'

'Perhaps, but I lack the fervour.' Aldo noticed Testardo glancing back over his shoulder at them. The young priest did not have the guile of older Florentines, which made him a willing source of information, but the monsignor would not tolerate that much longer. 'Was there another place that caught Galeri's eye?'

'Not so much a place as a person. A group of chapter nuns passed us on their way to chapel for nones. Signor Galeri stared at them. It was almost as if he knew one of—'

'Father Zati,' Testardo interjected. The monsignor stopped, twisting round to stare at them. 'I believe our new observer has heard sufficient gossip for now.'

'But I was simply telling him—'

'Enough!'

Zati fell silent, his face becoming crimson at the rebuke. Testardo gestured for Aldo to come forward. 'Signor Aldo, come and walk alongside me. Signor Cortese can keep Father Zati company the rest of the way, yes?'

Aldo did as he was told. With any luck, the monsignor would insist on Cortese and Zati remaining as a pair for the day, meaning Aldo could see and hear all that Testardo did inside the convent. Far better to be near the visitation's leader for what was to come.


The abbess was not surprised by the visitation's arrival, but the presence of Aldo was less expected. Such roles were given to members of the laity, men close to the Church or part of an important confraternity. To have an officer of the court among the visitors was strange, to say the least. How had he won such a concession from the archbishop?

No, that did not matter. Besides, Monsignor Testardo would be enforcing whatever edict the archbishop had decided, with the young priest and Cortese dutifully doing as they were told. Judging by Aldo's behaviour the previous day, he would be seeking the truth. For the convent to survive this visitation, any hope rested with the officer.

She welcomed the quartet, escorting them towards the chapter house. In the main courtyard the morning air was already thick with the scent of lavender, bees darting from flower to flower beneath the warm sun. 'Signor Aldo, I owe you an apology,' the abbess said. 'When I saw the body in the scriptorium yesterday, I did not recognize him beneath all the blood. It was only later that I recalled where I had met Signor Galeri. I hope you will forgive my error. I had no intention of misleading you.'

'There is nothing to forgive,' Aldo replied. 'What you saw was shocking, especially for someone unused to encountering such violence.'

'Is there anything else you wish to share, Abbess?' Testardo asked, his voice heavy with disdain. 'Any other admissions you need to make before we can begin?'

The abbess paused outside the chapter-house doors. The monsignor had arrived angry. If the abbess indulged in the sin of gambling, she would have placed a wager on Aldo's presence as the cause. Her apology had only added to Testardo's ill mood. But she had little doubt his decision about the convent's future was already made. Helping Aldo find the truth was what mattered now. The dead man deserved no less.

'Actually, yes, there is.' She told the visitors about Suor Andriana discovering the dead man's clothes in the convent laundry. 'They were neither ripped nor cut, and there was no blood on any of his garments.'

'Is that important?' Cortese asked.

'It means Galeri was already naked when he was stabbed,' Testardo said, 'otherwise the blade would have damaged his clothes and there would be blood on them.'

'A doctor examined the remains after they were removed to Santa Maria Nuovo,' Aldo added. 'He believed Galeri was stabbed more than twenty times.'

'Quite,' the monsignor agreed. 'I went to the *ospedale* to see for myself this morning. The fact Galeri had undressed before he was attacked – and that he was inside the convent after dark – indicates that he came here for carnal pleasures.'

The abbess gasped. 'My sisters in God would never break their vows of chastity!'

Testardo scowled. 'Can you offer another explanation that fits the circumstances?'

'I—'

'Or are my words too close to the truth for you to accept?'

The abbess kept hold of her anger. 'I respectfully disagree with you, monsignor,' she said, lowering her voice so nuns nearby did not hear. 'But there is something else I must share. A bloody habit was also found in our laundry. The blood was still damp.'

Testardo nodded. 'Then that removes all doubt. Galeri was lured to the convent after curfew, it seems with the promise of sinful pleasures. Once he was undressed and vulnerable, one of your sisters attacked him with a blade, stabbing Galeri over and over until he died.'

The abbess searched the faces of the other visitors. Cortese was ashen, a hand to his mouth, while Zati made the sign of the cross. Only Aldo appeared to disagree, shaking his head. But he did not contradict the monsignor. Why was the officer holding his tongue?

Testardo glanced at the other visitors. 'Our duty is clear. We shall question each of the nuns until one of them admits to this unholy crime. If no confession is obtained by the day's end, everyone within the convent shall be held responsible.'

'That is not fair,' the abbess protested. 'That is not just!'

'I am acting upon the direct edict of the archbishop himself,' Testardo replied. 'If you wish to protest this course of action, I suggest taking it up with him.'

'How can I do that when the convent has been enclosed at his behest?'

'That is far from my concern. Perhaps you should try praying for help instead.' The monsignor turned his back on her. 'Father Zati, you and Signor Cortese will conduct a full inspection of the convent. Go into every room, every storage space. Find the blade that was used to kill Signor Galeri.'

'Might I make a suggestion?' Aldo asked.

'What?' Testardo snapped.

'Galeri came into the convent after curfew. Either he obtained a key, or someone let him in. Perhaps our fellow visitors could begin their inspection by discovering whether any of the keys for the three entrances are missing, and confirming whether any of the locks have been tampered with or forced? That would help confirm your – deductions.'

The abbess watched Testardo bristle, but he could not seem to find any reason to refute the suggestion. 'Agreed. While that is taking place, I will lead the questioning of the nuns, with Aldo by my side as an observer. We gather here again at sext.'

The concession gave the abbess the smallest reason to hope. It seemed that if Aldo could find a way to uncover the truth, he would. Perhaps all was not lost. Not yet.

Aldo waited until Cortese and the young priest had departed before speaking again. Men like Testardo did not enjoy having their authority challenged in front of others, especially when the challenge was one of merit. 'I have another suggestion,' Aldo said, 'one that could make our task quicker, and ensure this matter is concluded today.'

'Yes?' the monsignor replied, not bothering to hide his impatience.

'Abbess, where do your nuns sleep?'

'Most share dormitories on the upper level,' she said. 'The two larger dormitories are used by chapter nuns, while the servant nuns share two smaller dormitories – one with our novices, and the other with the girls who board here. We have seven private cells which are mostly given over to those of us who hold senior positions within the convent.'

'I saw all that when the previous visitation made its inspection,' the monsignor complained. 'How is this relevant?'

Aldo ignored the question, continuing to address the abbess. 'Could a sister leave one of the dormitories during the night without another nun noticing?'

She shook her head. 'Not easily. The dormitory doors tend to creak. Two amongst us must rise each night to say lauds, the early morning service. They always wake the others coming and going. My sisters in God often complain of this in the chapter house.'

'So whoever sleeps closest to the door in each dormitory—'

'Could tell us whether anyone left that room the night Galeri died,' Testardo cut in. 'Good. That would quicken our task. Tell me, who occupies the private cells?'

The abbess pointed to the upper level of the convent above the infirmary and visitors' parlour. 'I have the cell at the far end, by the church. Suor Paulina, our almoner, sleeps in the cell next to mine. I can hear her snoring most nights through the shared wall. Next to her is Suor Andriana, the convent draper—'

'I remember her,' Testardo interrupted. 'A quiet, unworldly young woman.'

The abbess waited for him to finish before continuing. 'Beside her is Suor Giulia, our apothecary, and beyond her is the sacrist, Suor Fiametta. By rights Suor Simona should have one of the cells but she prefers sleeping in the infirmary to stay close to her patients. So Suor Benedicta has the next cell.'

The name sounded familiar to Aldo. 'She is the nun who listens to all conversations in the visitors' parlour?' If Galeri had returned after the first visitation during daytime, the listening nun would know of that.

'Yes,' the abbess said. 'The final cell was occupied by the prioress for some years, but she asked for it to be given to her younger sister when Suor Violante joined the convent.'

Testardo nodded. 'Suor Violante was unwell during our first visitation. Her cell was the one room we were not able to inspect. I trust that will not be a problem today.'

'No, monsignor,' she replied, but Aldo noticed a hesitation in her voice. What was inside Suor Violante's cell?

'Very well,' Testardo said. 'I shall require an *officio* in which to do my questioning. Arrange for the nuns who sleep beside the door in each dormitory to come forward first, one by one. After that I will need to see each nun who occupies a private cell. That should answer many of my questions.' He glanced at Aldo. 'Unless you have any other suggestions?'

'Actually, yes. Abbess, you said Suor Simona sleeps at the infirmary. How many patients are in the beds there at present?'

'Five,' she replied, looking across the courtyard to the infirmary. 'But the novice Maria Celestia was only taken to the infirmary yesterday, with shock. She was the one who found the body. Our infirmarian found deep cuts to both of Maria Celestia's hands, but we do not know what caused these.'

'Why not?'

'Maria Celestia has been in a fever since she was taken to the infirmary. You will have to wait for her to recover before she can be asked any questions.'

Aldo nodded his understanding, while hiding his frustration. The novice was an obvious suspect or, at least, a key witness. Not being able to question her would hamper efforts to find Galeri's killer.

'The other four patients –' the abbess continued. 'None of those poor souls can leave their beds. They are close to death themselves.' She made the sign of the cross before squaring her shoulders. 'You may use my *officio*. I would ask that Suor Violante be questioned last. She has not been well, and it would be better if she was not disturbed.'

'That will depend on another nun confessing to their guilt first,' Testardo said. 'If not, Suor Violante must face our judgement like everyone else.'

# Chapter Nineteen

Suor Giulia pulled the jar of nutmeg oil down from its shelf in her workshop. She had been dutifully shaking the contents every twelve hours, once during the day and again at night. It would soon be time to drain the nutmeg fragments from the liquid, before starting the whole process again. Another three days and the remedy should be finished – assuming the convent had not already been dissolved by the archbishop.

The refectory was full of gossip that morning as the nuns broke their fast. Suor Fiametta and others who favoured enclosure welcomed the order imposed on the convent, not bothering to keep the triumph from their faces. The prioress was not present to keep her acolytes in check. She sometimes chose to spend time with her sister before the day's work. The result was a sour mood in the refectory.

Now a second visitation had arrived. Officially, the men were meant to discover who was responsible for the body found in the scriptorium. But Giulia had few illusions about a diocesan investigation pursuing justice. She knew how laws could be twisted and bent to suit the needs of those in power – and that was almost never women. A miracle would be required for the convent to reopen its doors before Easter Sunday. Despite the whispers about Maria Celestia's wounded hands, miracles were hard to find in Florence.

Giulia was still shaking the nutmeg oil when her apprentice arrived, red-faced and out of breath as usual. 'Suor Giulia, please forgive me,' Maria Teodora panted while pulling on her apron. 'I was praying at the infirmary and got lost in my rosary . . .'

'Your fervour is commendable,' Giulia replied, 'but so is good work done in the service of our Lord. I must make a sleeping remedy for the abbess. She says Suor Paulina's snoring is worse than usual. Fetch me the devil's helmet from over there.' The apothecary gestured to a heavy ceramic jar on a shelf at head height behind the workshop door.

'The devil's helmet?' Maria Teodora asked, her face full of fear and doubt.

'Yes, the aconitum. In that black jar.'

The novice took the right jar from the shelf, carrying it across to the work bench with great care, as if afraid the *diavolo* himself would burst from inside.

'Good, now see how much there is.'

'You want me to look inside?'

'Yes.'

'But – isn't that dangerous? You called it the devil's helmet.'

Giulia wondered how such a timid creature got through the day. It was little surprise the novice's *famiglia* had chosen the veil for their daughter. Life in most parts of the city would crush Maria Teodora. 'Aconitum has many names – monkshood, wolf's bane, and the devil's helmet. It is highly poisonous.'

The novice backed away from the jar. 'Then why do you have it in your workshop?'

'Many of the things I keep here are dangerous if used incorrectly. Aconitum is a plant, it grows in our garden courtyard. The flowers are blue and purple, they look like the hood a monk wears – hence the name monkshood. Each year I harvest one plant, dry it and grind it into a fine powder. A tiny portion goes into some of my remedies. Remove the stopper and look inside the jar, there should be plenty.'

Maria Teodora edged back towards the jar, her hands shaking. 'Are you sure?'

'Yes, I have not had much need of it since the last harvest.'

'No, I meant . . . are you sure it is safe to look inside the jar?'

'Yes, quite safe.' Giulia watched the novice grip the stopper with trembling fingers. 'But breathe in before you remove that, just to be sure.'

After a long inhale, Maria Teodora pulled the stopper free, her eyes squeezed tight shut. Eventually, she opened them again, and peered into the jar. 'It's nearly empty.'

'Are you sure?'

'Yes.' The novice tipped the open rim towards Giulia. 'See?'

Perhaps half a cup of powder remained inside the jar, not enough to cover the bottom. 'How can that be?' Giulia asked, taking the jar. 'I keep a careful record of all poisons. The devil's helmet was half full at the start of Lent, and that was the last time I used any—'

There was a knock at the partially open door. 'Suor Giulia, may I come in?'

Giulia put the stopper back into the jar. 'Yes.'

The sharp-faced novice Maria Vincenzia entered. 'Pardon my interruption, the abbess sent me. The visitors are in her *officio*. They wish to question those who have private cells.'

'Thank you,' Giulia replied. 'I will be there as soon as I can.'

Maria Vincenzia nodded and withdrew, closing the door after her. How long had she been standing outside before knocking? Had she heard them talking about the aconitum? If so, word of the missing poison would be all around the convent before sext.

Giulia returned the aconitum to its shelf and removed her apron, draping it over the jar of nutmeg oil. Her apprentice lingered by the workshop bench.

'What should I do?' the novice asked.

'Go to the chapel and pray for your friend, Maria Celestia. In fact, I suggest you pray for all of us. We need our Lord's mercy more than ever. I will fetch you soon.'

Strocchi had hurried from Palazzo Landini to the Podestà, believing the *segretario* would expect a full report on the search for Cerchi's killer. There was little to tell, but Bindi kept the constable waiting more than an hour before finally sending him away unseen. Holy Week had brought forward a planned sitting of the Otto and preparing cases for the magistrates took precedence. Strocchi was both angry and relieved. Waiting had wasted much of his morning, but at least it meant not having to face Bindi.

The constable headed south before turning east to find Renato Patricio's former workshop, not far from Piazza delle Travi. The new owner was a Jew called Elijah Farissol. Short in height but full of gossip, Farissol couldn't wait to share his triumph in acquiring the workshop. 'There are many in this city who would not sell their place of business to one of my kind,' he said. 'They would rather we stayed in our little street south of the Arno, that we did what we have always done – lending money and tending bodies. But my father was a cloth maker, and his father before him. I intend to make them proud.'

Strocchi smiled, happy to listen but eager to learn what else Farissol knew. 'Why do you think Patricio was so willing to sell?'

'Desperation.' Farissol took Strocchi's arm, leading him away from workers stretching cloth to a small *officio* nearby. 'Patricio needed coin to leave the city. If he had not been in such a rush, he could certainly have sought a better price. But something was forcing him out of Florence. He wouldn't reveal what – or who – that was.'

That answered Strocchi's next question before he could ask it.

'Patricio went around saying he had plans to introduce the grand wives of Milan to his dresses,' Farissol continued. 'I'm only a humble Jew, but even I know Milan is the dullest city in the north for clothes. Patricio will struggle to sell a single gown up there.'

'So why go?' Strocchi asked.

The Jew shrugged, but there was a twinkle in his eyes. Farissol wanted to say more, but needed to have it teased out of him. Strocchi glanced from the *officio* door to the busy workshop. 'Patricio cannot have made his dresses alone. Tell me, what happened to his workers? Did they go with him to Milan?'

'No. Some of them didn't wish to work for a Jew, but a few remained. They had quite the tales to tell about Patricio and his last few weeks in the city . . .'

'Such as?'

Farissol leaned closer, lowering his voice to a whisper. 'Patricio was in trouble with the Otto. An officer of the court visited several times, and left poor Patricio in tears.'

That must have been Cerchi, extorting coin from the dressmaker. Strocchi described the dead man, but Farissol didn't know what the officer looked like.

'When was the last time Patricio had one of these encounters?'

'Not long before he left the city.'

That didn't make sense. All the evidence suggested Cerchi had died in January, but Patricio hadn't departed Florence until several weeks later. 'In February? Are you certain?'

'I think so.' Farissol shrugged. 'I don't pay much attention to gossip.'

After thanking Farissol, the constable questioned a few of the workers but got nothing further from them. He went outside to Piazza delle Travi. Had his deductions been wrong? Had Cerchi still been alive weeks after January 11th? If so, where had he been hiding and why had nobody seen him? Aldo and several constables had scoured the city for Cerchi. They would have found him. And Cerchi's body had washed ashore in Ponte a Signa in early February, after days or weeks in the water. No, Farissol must be mistaken.

Either way, it was best to keep investigating and trust the truth would emerge. Better that than going back to the Podestà and admitting he had been wrong.

Aldo had not paid much attention to the abbess's *officio* the previous day. Then he had been seeking paper, ink and a place to write – the top of her desk provided all three. Now he was seeking answers, and a murderer. But Testardo insisted on asking the questions. While the monsignor prepared to face the first nun, Aldo studied their surroundings to see why Galeri had been so eager to gain entry to this chamber.

A heavy wooden cabinet against the far wall drew the eye. Numerous drawers filled most of the cabinet. Inside these Aldo found ledgers detailing the many nuns of Santa Maria Magdalena past and present, along with the items surrendered by each woman when they took the veil. Some were covered in dust, untouched for decades; others were more recent.

One large door stretched the full height of the cabinet's right side. This was secured by a sturdy metal lock that refused to give way, despite Aldo's efforts. There were scratches around where the lock met the wood of the cabinet. Someone had tried to force it open, without success. The scratches appeared recent, the edges of each one still fresh in the wood.

'Shall we start?' Testardo asked, settling in the abbess's chair behind the desk.

'Yes,' Aldo replied. But something stopped him leaving the cabinet. An edge of torn parchment was jutting out beneath the cabinet door. Aldo crouched for a closer look, putting one knee on the cold stone floor. A few letters were visible on the parchment, forming part of three consecutive lines: *of Giro*; *uthority*; and *be given*. 'A moment,' Aldo said, aware that Testardo was watching. 'I have a problem with my boot.'

'It can wait,' the monsignor said before raising his voice. 'Enter!'

Aldo stood, nodding to the abbess as she escorted a chapter nun into the *officio*. Those words, where had he . . .? Of course, the scrap of parchment under the dead man. It must have been torn from the document caught in the cabinet door. Had Galeri been trying to force the lock? Was that why he came back to the convent after curfew? Aldo combined the words from both pieces and they made more sense: *By Order of Giro. . . the Authority . . . shall be given.* That confirmed the parchment was not an authorization for the first visitation. The archbishop's first name was Andrea, not Girolamo.

So who had issued the parchment, and why would Galeri risk his life to steal a corner from the document? Ruggerio's first name was Girolamo, but that was common in Florence. Aldo could not conceive the circumstances in which Ruggerio would issue a written order. The merchant was notorious for only giving commands and orders verbally. He never trusted anything to parchment in case it could become evidence against him. The order must have come from someone else named Girolamo. The answer was behind the locked cabinet door . . .

'This is Suor Giulia, our apothecary,' the abbess announced. Aldo retreated from the cabinet, but not before the abbess noticed on her way out.

'Be seated,' Testardo told Giulia. Aldo moved to a corner where he could observe Giulia while remaining to one side of the monsignor.

It was difficult to know the apothecary's precise age. The shape of her body was hidden by her habit while the veil and wimple concealed all but her face. Wrinkles clustered at the corners of her watchful eyes while lines across her forehead suggested she was near fifty. Her back was straight and her shoulders square. Giulia showed no fear of the visitors.

'Before answering any questions, there is something I must tell you,' she said. 'A quantity of aconitum has been taken from my workshop.'

'Aconitum?' Testardo asked.

'It's a poison,' Aldo interjected, recalling what Saul had said. 'You keep a supply?'

'Yes.' Giulia's attention shifted to Aldo. 'It is used for some remedies, but in the smallest of amounts. The quantity taken from my workshop was considerable.'

'Enough to kill a man?'

'Enough to kill a man many times over,' she replied.

'That is of little consequence,' Testardo announced, impatience in his voice. 'I have seen Signor Galeri's body. He was stabbed to death; that much is certain.'

Aldo knew better but kept that to himself. 'How could someone take poison from your workshop? Was it not locked?'

Giulia shook her head. 'We are a community built on trust,

devoting our lives to God. No internal doors are locked. Theft does not happen here. We trust each other with our lives.'

'That did not save Bernardo Galeri,' Testardo said, not bothering to conceal his rising anger. 'One of you killed him. That is beyond dispute.'

'Do you know when the poison was taken?' Aldo asked.

'Since the beginning of Lent,' the apothecary replied. 'My new apprentice, Maria Teodora, discovered the loss today. I haven't had cause to check it before.'

'What effect would the poison have if someone swallowed it?'

'That depends on the amount. A creeping numbness in the arms, legs or face would be the first signs.' The apothecary pressed a hand to her belly. 'Then they would feel pain and illness here. The person would become weaker, struggling to breathe, as if a weight was pressing on their chest. If the dose of aconitum is great enough, it will claim their life.'

'How long would the poison take to weaken a man? How long to kill him?'

'Again, that depends on the dose. It could be very swift, if enough is consumed.'

'Thank you,' Testardo snapped at Aldo. 'Now, Suor Giulia, I understand you occupy one of the private cells on the upper level, is that correct?'

'Yes, the middle cell of the seven, between Suor Andriana and Suor Fiametta.'

'Did you leave your cell after curfew on the evening of Palm Sunday?'

'Yes.'

Testardo leaned forwards, studying her closely. 'Why?'

The apothecary smiled. 'The need to use the *latrina* during the night becomes more familiar at our age, as I'm sure you know.

And I have a jar of nutmeg oil that needs shaking each noon and night to make sure its contents are being properly mixed.'

'You came down to the convent's lower level to do that?'

She nodded. 'My workshop is next to the scriptorium.'

'What time was this?' Testardo asked.

'I can't be certain. It was well before dawn.'

'Did you see anyone while you were out of your cell?'

Giulia shook her head.

'What about voices? Did you hear anyone?'

She hesitated. In Aldo's experience that meant a witness was either recalling what had happened, or was crafting a lie. 'Matins,' the apothecary said. 'I could hear the service being said in the chapter house. That means it was early morning on Monday, not Sunday evening.'

'Did you recognize the voices saying matins?' Testardo asked.

'No, but I believe two of our novices, Maria Celestia and Maria Vincenzia, were due to say matins and lauds that night. You would have to ask them.'

'Thank you, Suor Giulia. You may go.'

Aldo waited until the apothecary had departed before speaking. The monsignor had been thorough, but he had omitted an obvious question. 'You did not ask if she knew Galeri.'

'What?'

'You did not ask Suor Giulia if she knew the dead man.'

Testardo rose from his chair. 'And you did not have my leave to ask any questions at all. I agreed to your presence as an observer, Aldo, nothing else. I do not know how you came to be part of this visitation, but I shall not have my methods challenged or my authority undermined. From this moment you will stay silent when I am asking questions unless I give leave to speak. If you cannot abide by that, leave the convent now. Do you understand?'

In his life Aldo had been confronted by men far more dangerous than Testardo. Better to let the monsignor blow himself out like any storm. Let all that anger have its moment. Testardo was an impediment, yes, but one that could be endured.

Aldo gave a respectful nod. So, Saul had been correct, Galeri was poisoned. Could the apothecary have been the one responsible? She would know the amount required, know how to handle the poison without suffering any illness from it herself. And coming forward to say the aconitum had been taken from her workshop was a clever *strategia,* if she were responsible for the murder. The admission made her appear more honest, willing to admit a mistake and accept responsibility.

Giulia mentioned she had an apprentice, Maria Teodora. If the apothecary proved not to be the one responsible, her student was another potential suspect. And Giulia had said the novice was her new apprentice, suggesting there had been others. They would know about the poisons in the workshop. It could be useful to know names of her past apprentices.

Then there were the two novices who had been up saying prayers before dawn on Monday, Maria Vincenzia and Maria Celestia. Both were potential suspects, with the cuts on Maria Celestia's hands of particular interest. A pity she was not fit to be questioned. Not yet.

Aldo wished he had intervened to ask if Giulia knew Galeri. The nun's response – whether a lie, the truth or an evasion – would have been instructive. Her knowledge of poison was certainly impressive for an apothecary working in a convent. As with Galeri's corpse, it seemed there was more to Giulia than might at first be apparent . . .

# Chapter Twenty

❧

$\mathscr{P}$onte Vecchio was thronged with people as Strocchi approached it, the rising curve of the bridge hidden from view by the crowds pushing past each other. It would be better to come back when the best bargains were gone, but the constable could not wait. The needs of the Otto had all of Bindi's attention for now, yet he could turn to other matters without warning. The *segretario* lacked any patience with those who failed to fulfil his orders.

Strocchi studied the homes above the shops and stalls. They were simple dwellings, two rooms at most, built precariously on top of the businesses below. Most were occupied by those who worked on Ponte Vecchio, the constable knew that much, but he could not imagine how the air must smell when the hottest days of summer came. By July, those who could leave the city did, retreating to their country estates, while those left in Florence sweated and sweltered and suffered. Then the air here would be fit only for flies.

Strocchi plunged into the crowd, forcing his way towards the first stall on the eastern side of the bridge. There was no separate door for the home above it, so whoever lived there must come and go through the shop. The fish-seller inside confirmed this after Strocchi had shouted his question across the heads of impatient wives. 'Nobody's up there now,' the fish-seller said. 'My son lived over the shop, but he got married and his new wife refused to stay there. Not good enough for her.'

It was a similar response in the next shop, and the next. Some homes were occupied, but the people that lived there were busy working. Come back before curfew, come back tomorrow, or don't come back at all. Most of those Strocchi did find at home had not lived on Ponte Vecchio long, a few weeks, perhaps, and they were already eager to leave. He didn't blame them. Some residents refused to talk at all, having no interest in getting involved with the court. Others were grateful for the coin Strocchi offered, but had nothing useful to say.

Frustration wore at the constable's patience. *Santo Spirito*. He had been so certain Cerchi met an end on the bridge. But if Cerchi had died on January 11th, it was still many weeks ago. Strocchi knew where he had been that day because it had been so significant – riding back to Florence with Aldo, that incident with the moneylender's killer, before returning home to find Tomasia waiting. Strocchi's life changed in more ways than one that day. But for most citizens of Florence, January 11th had been a cold Thursday in the middle of a long winter and nothing more . . .

Strocchi was close to abandoning his quest when he knocked at the door of a home above the largest butcher's stall on the bridge, not far from its highest point. The stall was closed, but that didn't mean the home above it was empty. A young woman answered, a beaming baby balanced on one hip. She had smudges of tiredness under both eyes, but her smile was warm and welcoming. Strocchi explained his reason for visiting, struggling to conceal his weariness at saying the same words for what must be the twentieth time. To his surprise, the woman – Salvaza Fideli – was happy for him to come in.

Her home was cosy, just one long room with a low ceiling. The marital bed occupied the end of the room, a cradle beside it for the baby, with a nursing chair and trunk the only other pieces of furniture. Salvaza and her husband had moved in two days after Christmas. Leonello had been learning his trade as a butcher, otherwise they would never have such a home. During Lent he was working long hours for a fish-seller, leaving her to care for their new child, Gasparro. They had no *famiglia* in the city, and visitors were few. 'Nobody wants to come here most of the time,' Salvaza said, resting the baby against her chest, little Gasparro lying his head on her shoulder. 'The smell.'

Strocchi nodded. Even though the butchers' stall below was closed until the end of Lent, the stench of blood and stale meat still seemed to fill the air. Yet the young signora seemed not to notice. Perhaps a person became used to it in time?

'I have no sense of smell,' she explained. 'I lost it when I fell ill as a child.'

The constable could not help watching the baby, wondering about the child Tomasia believed she was carrying. Should God bless them, it would be many months before the child – their child – was born. Let it be as happy and healthy as this little one.

'Do you have children?' Salvaza asked.

'Not yet, but perhaps soon.'

'Then get all the sleep you can now.' She held up the baby boy, shaking her head at him. 'This one never stays asleep through a night. You don't, do you, *bambino*? I'm lucky Leonello gets up sometimes to rock him back to sleep.'

Strocchi asked if they had been home on the night of January 11th. 'It was the Thursday after the feast of the Epiphany. A cold night.'

'We would have been here,' she said. 'But when you have a young baby all days and nights seem the same. You remember other things, like the first time your baby smiles.'

'I believe a murder happened on Ponte Vecchio that night. A

man was stabbed on the bridge sometime after curfew – or his body was dumped in the river from here.'

Salvaza gasped, making the sign of the cross. She moved the baby from one shoulder to the other, her brow furrowing. 'I don't know what night it was, but Leonello told me he heard two men arguing on the bridge after curfew. Gasparro had a cough, so Leonello got up to try and soothe him back to sleep.'

Strocchi struggled to hide his excitement. After a long morning of little success, this was a break in the clouds at last. 'Did your husband say what the men were arguing about?'

'Sorry. You will have to ask Leonello when he gets home.'

'Do you often hear people on the bridge after curfew?'

'No. I think that's why Leonello noticed. I've heard patrols passing some nights when I get up to feed Gasparro, but nothing more. Curfew is the only time the bridge isn't busy.'

'Did your husband see the men?'

Salvaza shook her head, patting the baby's back. It wanted her attention. 'No. We keep the shutters closed at night.' She reached for her dress buttons. 'I need to feed Gasparro.'

'Of course,' Strocchi said, before realizing what that meant. His cheeks became hot as Salvaza continued unbuttoning. 'I'm . . . I didn't . . .' He stumbled towards the door. 'What time will your husband get home?'

'Not long before curfew,' she replied, reaching inside her dress to pull out a breast. The baby pressed its face into the soft mound, complaints forgotten. 'Should I tell him that you will be coming back?'

'Y-yes,' the constable stammered on his way out. 'Thank you, signora.'

Strocchi clattered down the stairs, his cheeks hot and no doubt crimson. He had no reason to be embarrassed, a mother feeding her baby was the most natural thing in the world, but still it unmanned him. Strocchi pushed a way through those crowding the bridge to the gap between buildings where he could look down at the Arno.

At last he had a witness. If one of the men arguing was Cerchi, that would prove . . .

No. Don't leap ahead to the conclusions you crave, Aldo often said. Gather evidence and the truth should emerge. To be an officer of the court, to be just, required dispassionate judgement when the truth was soiled or stained.

Strocchi stared down at the river flowing beneath the bridge.

By curfew, the truth would be clearer.


A salve from Suor Simona had calmed Isabella's many bites. As thanks, she spent much of the morning helping Dea tend patients at the infirmary. Four were old – even older than *Nonna* – but one was a novice, Maria Celestia, who kept bleeding from both hands. Isabella watched Dea bringing bowls covered with crimson-stained cloths from behind the screen where Maria Celestia lay.

'What happened to her?' Isabella asked Dea while they were folding bed sheets.

'Nobody is sure. She found the body yesterday,' the servant nun whispered, glancing over a shoulder to be sure nobody else could hear. 'She's been drifting in and out, saying things that don't make any sense. Some of the other nuns –' Dea leaned closer – 'they think her wounds may be stigmata.'

Isabella nodded, not wanting to show she didn't understand. 'That's terrible.'

Dea stared at her. 'It would be a miracle.'

'Yes, of course. I meant . . . the pain must be terrible.'

'Nothing to what Christ suffered on the cross. Wounds to his feet, his hands.'

Isabella paid little attention in church, but Dea talking about wounded hands did sound familiar – 'Oh yes, the stigmata. Is that what Maria Celestia has?'

Before the servant nun could answer, a sharp-faced novice strode into the infirmary. She spoke to Suor Simona for a moment before disappearing behind the screen round Maria Celestia's bed. 'That's Maria Vincenzia,' Dea whispered. 'She and Maria Celestia are close.'

Isabella nodded. She remembered the two novices sneering in front of the class on Palm Sunday, especially Maria Vincenzia. Isabella took fresh sheets to all the unoccupied beds in the infirmary, pausing at the empty cot by the screen that shielded Maria Celestia. A voice was murmuring on the other side.

'Another visitation is here now,' someone was saying. 'This will soon be over.'

That voice! It had the same scratchiness that Isabella had heard the previous night. She hadn't been able to remember where she knew the answer from then, but now it was obvious. Maria Vincenzia must have been the secretive novice talking in the corridor after dark.

Another voice spoke behind the screen. 'My hands –' Dea had said Maria Celestia was not making any sense, but the bedridden novice sounded like anyone else to Isabella.

'Shhh,' Maria Vincenzia said. 'No one must hear you.'

Isabella moved closer, eager to hear more – and knocked over a wooden cross on a bedside table. It clattered to the floor, making everyone look round. 'Sorry,' Isabella said.

Maria Vincenzia emerged from behind the screen, glaring at

Isabella. 'My friend is ill. She may even be dying. The last thing she needs to hear is your clumsy mistakes.'

'Sorry,' Isabella repeated, staring at the floor.

'I've seen you before.' Maria Vincenzia loomed over Isabella. 'You were in the refectory two days ago. Who are you?'

'She is a day student staying at the convent for now,' Dea said, joining them by the empty cot. 'Her name is Isabella, and she's not doing anyone any harm.'

Maria Vincenzia glanced at the servant nun. 'If she's a student, teach her to be quiet. This is a place of healing. The sisters need rest.' The novice stalked out.

'Don't worry about her,' Dea told Isabella. 'She comes from a rich *famiglia*, so she expects everyone to treat her like a Medici.'

Isabella nodded, but her head was full of what she had heard the previous night: 'Hidden', 'mistake', and 'they can't know'. What had Maria Vincenzia hidden, what mistake had been made? Just what had the two novices done?

So many questions, but the answers were eluding Isabella. She couldn't help wishing Cesare Aldo was here. If anyone would know what to do, it was him.

Aldo watched Testardo building a list of those who had been out of their beds after curfew the night Galeri was killed. The monsignor began by questioning those who slept next to the door of each dormitory. Suor Dea and Suor Rigarda were absent from the dormitory shared by servant nuns and boarders because they were helping Suor Simona at the infirmary; nobody else came or went between the night of Palm Sunday and the next morning.

It was a similar response from the nun who slept by the door of the other small dormitory, the one shared by novices and servant nuns. Maria Vincenzia and Maria Celestia had left during the night to say matins and lauds at the appointed hour, but nobody else came or went during the night. Next Testardo summoned the women who slept by the doors of the two larger dormitories, home to all chapter nuns. The first to be questioned was the prioress. She stalked into the *officio*, refusing to sit, and instead demanding answers from Testardo.

'Is it true you are threatening to question my sister, Suor Violante? She is not well, and subjecting her to an interrogation will only make that illness worse!'

Aldo knew such a *strategia* would only anger the monsignor. Sure enough, Testardo was up on his feet, bristling at the accusations from the prioress. 'What gives you the right to question my judgement?' he snarled at the prioress.

'You have not answered my question,' she replied, crimson shading her face.

'This visitation is acting upon direct orders from the archbishop,' Testardo said. 'I have the full authority of the diocese to question whomever I choose in whatever manner I decide. You may consider yourself fortunate that this is merely a visitation, and not an inquisition. And if your sister is so ill, why is she not being cared for in the infirmary?'

That made the prioress hesitate. 'Her sickness is of the mind, not the body. She is better in solitude than being among others.'

'Be that as it may, Suor Violante will face the same questions as any other nun at this convent, if I deem that necessary,' the monsignor said. Aldo studied Testardo struggling to get back control of his temper. It seemed the monsignor was not used to being challenged. But he was wise enough to realize antagonizing the prioress would do the visitation little good. Testardo sat back on the chair behind the abbess's desk. 'But I give you this assurance:

if we find whoever was responsible for the murder of Signor Galeri before the end of the day, or if someone confesses to his killing, then your sister shall be spared our questions.'

The prioress scowled at him before giving a curt nod. 'I understand you want to know if anyone left our dormitory during the night on Sunday.'

'That is correct,' Aldo said, hoping to ease the tension between them. Instead Testardo glared at him.

'Nobody came or left,' the prioress replied. 'Does that satisfy you?'

Aldo wanted to ask more but stopped himself.

'It does,' the monsignor announced. 'Thank you for your time, prioress.' She stalked from the *officio*, not giving either man a second glance. Aldo saw her pause outside the door, whispering something to the next nun waiting to come in. Nothing helpful would come of that.

The chapter nun from the final dormitory repeated what the prioress had told them. Nobody came or went during the night. Aldo willed Testardo to ask more, to press harder, but it was apparent the monsignor had little interest in the answers he was hearing. The future of Santa Maria Magdalena had been decided, and the investigation was simply a precursor to announcing that decision. If the killer did confess to their crime – to their sin – all the better. But it would make little difference to the archbishop's decision.

Testardo moved on to interrogating the nuns in positions of authority, and those who had private cells. But his superior attitude was not helping, as became clear with Suor Catarina. She was young, thirty at most, but was still responsible for teaching the young women who boarded at the convent and those who came in for classes. Catarina had won Isabella's respect, which could not have been an easy achievement. But the monsignor treated the teaching nun like a child, or an *idiota*.

It took only a few questions for the teaching nun to lose her patience. 'Why are you asking me this?' she asked, her cheeks reddening. 'I sleep in the dormitory above the refectory, away from the door. I would wake the sisters around me if I got up in the night.'

'I simply asked if you knew Signor Galeri before he came to the convent—'

'And I told you, no. The first time I encountered that man was when you brought him into my class as part of the first visitation. It was bad enough you interrupted my teaching, but that man leered at my pupils. Several were disturbed by the way he stared at them.'

Aldo wished Testardo would think before speaking. Aggravating another nun would do the investigation little good. No doubt the prioress and others already questioned were telling those sisters preparing to face Testardo about his attitude, putting everyone still to come on their guard. But the monsignor continued to be dismissive with Catarina. 'You made your views known then—'

'And you did not listen,' she snapped. 'This convent is a sanctuary for women and girls, a place where we should be safe from men like Signor Galeri.' Her face twisted when she said the name. 'Too many of us have suffered at the hands of men before coming here. Visitors are supposed to be men of faith, holy and pious, without favour or prejudice. That man was like a fox let loose in a hen house.'

'Do you deny killing him?'

'Of course I do!' Catarina rose from her seat. 'Only our Lord may take a life. I am here to teach young women to think for themselves, nothing more.' She stalked out.

'The last thing young women need to do is learn how to think,'

Testardo said once Catarina was gone, leaning back in his chair. 'Well, she's certainly angry enough to kill.'

'I doubt Suor Catarina would show us her anger if she had murdered Galeri,' Aldo observed. 'Only a fool would do so, and she is no fool.'

'Perhaps.' The monsignor frowned, as if something was troubling him. Catarina's barbed words about the visitation seemed to have struck home.

'You did not select Galeri as the fourth visitor, did you?' Aldo asked.

Testardo shook his head. 'Our usual fourth withdrew, and Galeri was suggested. He was a member of the Company of Santa Maria, a confraternity that is bonded to the convent.' The monsignor changed topic. 'But Signor Galeri is not the one being investigated here. He is the victim, and he deserves our best efforts to find his killer.'

So long as those efforts were completed by curfew – but Aldo kept that to himself.

Suor Paulina was next to face Testardo's questions, but the convent almoner was of little help. 'I slept through the night,' she said when asked, 'as I always do. I have been told my snoring is quite loud, but it never disturbs me. Those without sin have nothing to trouble their conscience, I believe, or their slumbers.' Paulina denied knowing Galeri, from the first visitation or in any other way. 'I'm not sure I met him when the previous visitors came. It was that young priest – what's his name?'

'Father Zati,' Testardo replied.

'Him,' she continued. 'And the other one, Cortoldi?'

'Cortese. Signor Cortese.'

'Alongside my duties as almoner, I have been managing our provisions since my predecessor was taken to our Lord's grace. It was Father Zati and Signor Cortese who inspected the provisions store. I spent quite some time answering their questions.'

The monsignor persisted with his own questions but eventually sent Paulina away. The abbess was next to be interrogated. She admitted being awake much of the night that Galeri died, but denied leaving her cell. 'I struggle to sleep because my cell shares a wall with that of Suor Paulina. Her snoring is particularly loud when she has been testing the convent wine.' The abbess claimed to have heard nothing but snoring until dawn.

The convent's draper, Suor Andriana, struggled to hold their gaze as she came in, her hands worrying the beads of her rosary. Aldo recalled meeting her outside the laundry the first time he had come to the convent on Palm Sunday. She reminded him of a mouse hiding in the corner of a room, as she had then, hoping to go unnoticed.

Andriana confirmed the loudness of Paulina's snoring. 'I am deaf here,' Andriana said, tapping her left ear, voice little more than a whisper. 'I sleep on my right ear. Otherwise I would get no sleep at all.' The draper had visited the *latrina* on Sunday night after curfew, but saw and heard nobody else. 'I'm sorry, I wish I could help you more.' She paused on her way out. 'It is nearly sext. Will you be needing a midday meal?'

'Yes,' the monsignor replied, rising from his seat. 'But first I—' he acknowledged Aldo with a glance – 'but first we need to meet with our fellow visitors.'

Aldo followed Testardo outside. The scriptorium stood opposite the abbess's *officio*, its door ajar. A faint tang of metal hung in the air. Someone had been washing the floor, doing their best to remove that blood. The stain might be removed, but the consequences of what happened would remain. No amount of scrubbing could dissolve that.

Zati and Cortese were waiting in the cloister by the chapter-house doors. Before they could report any progress, a voice called out to the visitors. Suor Benedicta was waving from the far side of the courtyard. A messenger hurried round the cloister to greet the four men, a youth clutching his cap in one hand and a sealed document in the other. 'Is one of you Monsignor Testardo?' the messenger asked. 'I have an urgent letter.'

Testardo took the letter, gesturing for Cortese to pay the messenger. The monsignor broke the wax seal, shielding its contents from the others. His brow furrowed, a grimace settling on his lips. 'It seems my sister has fallen gravely ill. Her doctor fears she may not last the day.' Zati murmured a prayer under his breath, while Cortese made the sign of the cross.

'Where is your sister?' Aldo asked, doing his best to sound sympathetic.

'Our *famiglia* has a country palazzo, outside the city. It will take me two hours to ride there –' Testardo hesitated. 'I have no choice. I will hasten there now, to see what can be done and to give her the last rites, if needed. Father Zati?'

'Yes, monsignor?'

'You will lead the visitation in my absence. I shall return before curfew when this matter will be brought to an end.' Testardo stalked away, taking the messenger with him.

Zati and Cortese bid the monsignor a safe and swift journey. Aldo echoed them while keeping a smile of satisfaction from his face. He had paid Zoppo handsomely to find a way of making Testardo leave the convent. How that was done, Aldo had left to the tavern keeper's cunning and guile – two attributes Zoppo did not lack. Now Testardo would be absent for at least four hours, perhaps longer. That wasn't long to uncover Galeri's killer.

# Chapter Twenty-one

*O*nce Testardo was gone, Aldo turned to Zati and Cortese. 'The monsignor asked you to see if keys for the convent's three entrances were missing, and whether any of the locks had been damaged. What did you find?'

The young priest appeared surprised by the question. 'I'm sorry?'

'The keys, the locks – what have you found?'

Cortese cleared his throat. 'I thought the monsignor left Father Zati in charge.'

Aldo feigned a smile. 'I have the greatest respect for Monsignor Testardo's wishes, and nothing but faith in you, Father Zati. But I am an officer of this city's most powerful criminal court. Do either of you have experience in catching killers?'

Zati and Cortese shook their heads.

'I share your concern for the monsignor's sister. Would it not be the greatest service we could do to find who killed Signor Galeri before the monsignor returns?'

Cortese's mouth flapped like a fish pulled from the Arno. 'I – I –'

Zati proved himself more decisive. 'Yes, I believe so.'

'Thank you,' Aldo replied, resting a hand on each man's shoulder. 'Now, what have you discovered about the convent's locks and keys?'

'There are three entrances,' the priest said. 'The sisters' private chapel has a connecting door only used by their confessor, Father Visconti. We talked to him. He confirmed only the abbess has a key to that door, which is in her possession.'

'The lock of the connecting door was undamaged,' Cortese added.

Aldo ignored him. Though lacking in experience, Father Zati seemed the more useful. 'What about the other entrances?'

The young priest pointed to where Testardo had departed. 'The abbess and the listening nun each have keys to that door. Both are accounted for. The lock is worn from use, but otherwise undamaged. The other entrance is the doors at the back of the convent. Again, the padlock and bolts are worn but show no damage. The abbess and cellarer both have keys for the padlock. The abbess has hers, we have yet to speak to Suor Paulina.'

'She was with you and Monsignor Testardo at the time,' Cortese explained.

'You've been very thorough,' Aldo said. 'Well done. The monsignor also asked you to search every room and storage space for the blade used to stab Signor Galeri.'

The priest's eyes slide sideways to Cortese. 'Checking the doors and keys took all morning.' It was clear whom Zati held responsible.

'That is understandable,' Aldo said. 'But you have done well – thank you. Father, you are leading us until Monsignor Testardo returns. Can I make a suggestion?'

'Of course.'

'Finding that blade is more important than almost anything else. It could lead us to the person responsible for the wounds Galeri suffered.' Whether that was the same person who poisoned Galeri was another matter, but Aldo kept that to himself. 'You and Signor Cortese inspected the convent a few days ago. You are far more familiar with Santa Maria Magdalena than I. Tell me if I am being too bold, but I suggest you work together to find that blade. I believe it would gladden the monsignor's heart to know you were following his instructions.'

The young priest agreed, and Cortese concurred. The pair strode away, eager for their task. Aldo smiled. Good. He would make faster progress with them occupied elsewhere.

'That was impressive,' the abbess said once the pair were out of hearing. 'Anyone who can be that persuasive . . .' She emerged from the chapter-house doors to stand beside Aldo. 'You should be giving sermons.'

'I don't have the strength of faith to be a preacher,' he replied. 'And the last time this city surrendered itself to someone who gave good sermons, it didn't end well.' Forty years ago a Dominican friar named Savonarola had risen to a position of power in Florence thanks to the power of his oratory. He preached that divine justice would save the city and its people from the indulgences of the wealthy, making everyone equal before God. Women and their daughters began taking vows and entering convents to save their souls. Those who valued their place in society made sure they were seen going to church often. Even young men and boys fell under the sway of Savonarola, forming gangs dressed in white to demonstrate purity. They marched the streets and hammered on doors, demanding those within surrender their vanities – wigs, gowns, paintings, secular texts and more. But when the friar challenged the divine authority of the Church itself, he was excommunicated and eventually executed.

'Are you old enough to remember Savonarola?' the abbess asked.

'No, but my papa told me of the hold the friar had over the city. Apparently, I was conceived while his followers were hurling their vanities onto a bonfire . . .' Aldo's words died away, realization striking inside him like a hammer against a bell. Savonarola's first name had been Girolamo. At his ascendency, he had commanded significant authority in Florence. Could that explain the scrap of parchment found under Galeri's body, a scrap torn from the locked cabinet in the abbess's *officio*? Had the Company of Santa Maria originally been created by the authority of Savonarola? Ruggerio and his senior brethren would have been fifteen or sixteen when the friar's dominance was at its peak, the right age to have been among the *piagnoni,* as they were known.

Had the confraternity's leaders been one of the bands of Savonarola's boys? Dark tales were still whispered of acts committed in the friar's name. That could explain what had bound Ruggerio and his brethren together for so long, a secret history they shared. If there were documents proving that, why would such men keep their incriminating papers inside the convent? Why not destroy the proof? Unless there was something within the documents that also empowered them? By keeping the papers out of reach in the convent, it meant none of the confraternity's leaders could use the documents against any of their brethren. That raised the question of how Galeri had found all this out, and whether his murder was related to it . . .

'I cannot allow you to wander this convent alone,' the abbess said, forcing Aldo to focus on his current investigation. 'You are not a confessor, nor a man of the cloth, so you cannot be left alone with any of the nuns.' She peered at him. 'Does that amuse you?'

Aldo realized he was smiling. The nuns had little to fear from Aldo, but there was no reason for the abbess to know that. 'Not at all, I fully understand. What do you suggest?'

'I will accompany you until Monsignor Testardo returns.'

'We should visit the infirmary first.' He strode away, the abbess hurrying after him. With Testardo absent, there was at last an opportunity to question the novice who claimed to have found the body. A bird swooping over the convent courtyard cried out, attracting Aldo's attention. He watched it fly away south towards the centre of Florence. Somewhere out there Strocchi was hunting whoever had killed Cerchi. Aldo could not help but wonder how the constable's investigation was progressing. Hopefully, not too well . . .

Strocchi was footsore and weary, his spirit faltering. The morning had been a wasted effort under a hot sun, and his tunic was soaked with sweat. He went home, hoping to find Tomasia. She worked at a stall in the Mercato Vecchio, but returned when it sold out. Some days, that happened before noon, on others, it took longer. Happily it had been a busy morning and Tomasia was back early. They rented the middle level of a small wooden house in the city's western quarter. Mama had been impressed when Strocchi described their dwelling. 'A whole level just for the two of you? Must be doing very well in the city, *bambino* . . .'

The truth was more modest. That whole level was a single, narrow room. Tomasia had divided it in two by hanging a curtain, with the kitchen at the front by the door and their bed at the back. It was humble but clean, a decent place to raise a *famiglia*. If he became an officer, they could move – Strocchi sighed. There was little chance of that, not while his efforts to find Cerchi's killer were as empty as a dry creek in summer.

They had a salad, and half a spiced pie one of the stall keepers was going to throw away. Tomasia always brought home more than their coin could buy. She had a talent for seeing potential where others saw little. Strocchi sometimes wondered if that was why she had agreed to be his wife. That, and the baby, if it came.

Tomasia made him recount his morning. 'The witness above Ponte Vecchio sounds promising,' she said when Strocchi had finished.

'I already know he didn't see anything.'

'But he heard them arguing. He can tell you what they were arguing about – and that will tell you more. Can't you see, Carlo? You're so close to the answers.'

Strocchi took her fingers in his own, kissing them one by one. He inhaled the smell of spices and pastry on her warm hands. 'What would I do without you?'

'Starve,' Tomasia replied, with a laugh. She leaned over the table to give him a kiss, her tongue darting between his lips. 'How long before you have to go?'

Isabella was enjoying herself, even if the infirmary was full of smells and sights that made her belly lurch. Cleaning a patient was . . . disgusting. No, her enjoyment came from working along-side Dea. The servant nun treated Isabella as an equal, as if she was useful. At home she was a burden, or a nuisance, or a posses-sion to be traded. Isabella liked to believe Nucca was her friend. Before coming to the convent, Isabella had never wondered if she and her maid would be close in another place, in other circum-stances. Even Isabella's friends from class . . . They considered her their equal. But did they ever think of her as useful?

Dea emerged from behind the screen shielding Maria Celestia, bringing a handful of blood-stained bandages. Isabella offered to help.

'Thank you,' Dea said. 'These all need scrubbing before they can be dried and used again. There's a brush and bowl of water by the door.' Isabella took the bandages, blood squelching between her fingers. A rich, metallic smell filled her nostrils, making her cough. 'Breathe through your mouth,' Dea whispered, 'and you'll be fine.'

Isabella started scrubbing. She was searching for water to rinse them when the abbess strode in, a man close behind her. 'Aldo!' Isabella put a hand to her mouth, the startled shout still echoing around the infirmary. 'Sorry.'

The abbess glared. 'I did not know you were working here.'

Isabella shrugged. 'I wanted to be helpful.'

'Indeed?' The abbess's gaze shifted to Aldo. 'Shall we see how Maria Celestia is?'

Aldo smiled at her. 'Could I have a moment with Isabella first?'

'Very well. I will consult Suor Simona about her patients.' She swept away. Isabella shivered. The abbess was almost as formidable as *Nonna*. Almost.

Aldo ushered Isabella away from the other nuns. 'How are you?'

'Good,' she replied, stifling a yawn. 'Tired. The beds here are terrible.'

'I've been told suffering is good for the soul, though usually by those who don't suffer.'

Isabella hadn't expected to see him so soon, let alone inside the convent. 'Are you part of the visitation? Everyone fears what it will find.'

'They should. One of these nuns is a killer, but in the eyes of the Church, that makes all of them sinners.' He studied the infirmary. 'What can you tell me about Suor Simona?'

'Not much,' Isabella admitted. 'She cares for her patients, that I do know. Dea told me Suor Simona sleeps here in case anyone needs her.'

'Dea?'

Isabella nodded to the dark-skinned servant nun. 'I've been helping her.'

Aldo smiled. 'And the novice who found the body . . .?'

'Maria Celestia. She's behind the screen. The wounds on her hands won't stop bleeding. Some of the nuns are saying those are stigmata.'

'What do you think?'

Isabella wasn't used to being asked what she thought. She frowned, gathering together what she had witnessed, what it might mean. 'The bleeding – it's no miracle.' Isabella recounted the whispers she heard between the two novices; about recognizing Maria Vincenzia's voice from the night before; and what had passed between the novice and a chapter nun then.

'You're certain that's what they said?' Aldo asked.

'Yes. Hidden, mistake and they can't know.' Isabella described being berated by the novice. 'She looked at me as if I was dirt from the street you would wipe off your boot before going inside.'

The abbess beckoned Aldo to join her. He nodded but lingered by Isabella a moment longer. 'Remember what you promised me yesterday?'

'That I would not try to help you find the killer.'

'And what else?'

'That I would stay safe, and stay out of trouble.' Isabella flung her hands in protest. 'I wasn't trying to find the killer last night; I was going to the *latrina*.'

'And in here today?'

'It's not my fault if I overhear things, is it?'

Aldo shook his head. Was that a rueful smile she saw? Maybe, but he hid it well. 'When this is over, I don't want to be going to your funeral.'

Fear ran a cold finger down Isabella's back. 'I'll be careful.'

'The closer the investigation gets to finding who killed Galeri, the more desperate they will become. They could kill again. Remember that.'

Aldo was eager to question the novice who found Galeri's body. Had the investigation been his alone, he would have started with her. Testardo had prevented that, but with the monsignor gone Aldo could follow his own path – or at least try. But the abbess insisted on checking first with Suor Simona whether Maria Celestia could cope with being questioned. It gave Aldo a chance to study the infirmarian. She was one of the few nuns in a senior post he had yet to question about Galeri.

Simona was brisk of word and manner, keeping her answers to the abbess brief. No, it would do no harm for them to question Maria Celestia. The novice was still drifting in and out of her senses, so they should not expect much. Aldo saw no reason to waste Simona's time with anything but direct questions. 'Where were you after dark on Palm Sunday?'

'Our lives are divided by the hours, the prayers we read each day,' she replied, resting a damp cloth on the forehead of an elderly nun. 'Compline is the last service of the day, while two among us rise each night to read matins and lauds.'

'And where were you after compline on Palm Sunday?'

Simona gestured around herself. 'Here. I sleep in one of the spare cots, in between tending our patients. Suor Rigarda and Suor Dea were also here on Sunday night, they can confirm that. I was with Suor Piera most of that night,' she added, nodding at a patient.

Aldo would need to see if the servant nuns agreed, but the infirmarian showed no sign of guilt or nervousness. 'What about the dead man, Bernardo Galeri – did you know him?'

'No, not until he came here with the visitation. From what I can recall, he had little interest in the infirmary, though I did notice him observing our servant nuns. I was about to challenge him when the visitation moved on. I did not see him again.'

'Do you keep any poisons here? Aconitum, or others like it?'

'No. Suor Giulia provides all our remedies. She is the expert in such things.'

This was not what the abbess had expected. Suor Simona said Maria Celestia was still quite ill, but the novice seemed to be recovering. Yes, she looked pale, and her lips were muttering without making any sound. But her veil and shift were no longer soaked with sweat, and far less blood coloured the bandages round her hands.

The abbess knelt beside the narrow cot, motioning for Aldo to join her on the cold floor. 'Maria Celestia,' the abbess said, keeping her voice a whisper. 'Can you hear me?' The novice continued mouthing silent words. 'This man wishes to ask about what you found in the scriptorium. Can he do that?' There was no response. 'Ask your questions,' the abbess told Aldo, 'but don't expect many answers.'

He nodded. 'My name is Aldo. I need to see your wounds. May we unbind them?' Maria Celestia said nothing. 'She does not object.'

'Silence is not consent,' the abbess replied.

'No, but your infirmarian agreed it would cause no harm. If you do not wish to do so, I can wait until one of the servant nuns comes to change the bandages.'

The man was infuriating, but he was also right. Against her better judgement, the abbess unbandaged the novice's right hand.

The skin of Maria Celestia's palm was split open side to side. Blood oozed from the exposed flesh. The abbess twisted her face away, but Aldo leaned nearer. The abbess saw his gaze narrow. He had noticed something.

'Turn the hand over,' Aldo said, his voice a low murmur.

The abbess did as asked, but could not bring herself to look.

'The wound is only on the palm,' Aldo said.

The abbess let her gaze return to Maria Celestia's hand. He was right. Whatever caused the wound, it was not stigmata. Such wounds pierced all the way through the hand, not just into the palm.

'I need to see the other one,' Aldo said.

The abbess unwrapped the novice's left hand, forcing herself to look at what was there. The wounds were similar, a livid slice across the palm. Aldo pointed to the skin. The palm had been cut more than once. Again, there were no wounds on the back of the hand.

The abbess rewrapped the bandages while Aldo asked his questions. 'Maria Celestia, I need to know what happened in the scriptorium. Did you see anyone else? Was anyone leaving the room as you approached it?'

But the novice remained silent, lips moving without making any sound. Aldo leaned closer, tipping his head to listen. Again, his eyes narrowed. He retreated from the cot, pushing up from the floor with a groan, knees cracking as he did.

'We will leave you to rest,' the abbess said before rising. Aldo gestured for her to follow. They went to a quiet corner. 'Well?' the abbess asked. 'What was she saying?'

'Prayers in Latin,' Aldo replied. 'Those wounds are not stigmata.'

'Clearly.'

'I've seen cuts like that before. I suspect – no, I believe – your novice made some of them. Does she have a history of hurting herself?'

'No. Not Maria Celestia.' Conscious of the other patients nearby, Abbess lowered her voice. 'She and Maria Vincenzia are bullies. They hurt others, never themselves. The two of them wound with words, not knives.' The abbess frowned. 'You said Maria Celestia made some of her wounds. Why only some? What did you mean?'

'I doubt all those cuts were self-inflicted. As a soldier, I saw men hurt themselves in the hope of escaping a doomed battle. It is easy enough to slice open one hand, but far harder to do it again to the other. You have to use your wounded hand to hold the blade, and all that blood makes it slippery. No. If Maria Celestia is unused to pain or seeing her own skin split open, I doubt she could have managed to cut both her own hands.'

'She asked someone to do that?'

'Or they did it to her. But if that was the case, I would expect to see bruises on her wrists, injuries to show she fought back. There were none. That means it was her choice. She wanted her hands cut open. She wanted to bleed like that.'

The abbess took a step back. Holy Madonna, what had happened in her convent? 'The blood on the body – you think some of it came from her?'

'Yes.'

'But why? Why would she do that?'

'To create confusion, perhaps. The fresh blood made it seem as though the murder happened not long before Maria Celestia came out of the scriptorium.'

A tightness was closing round the abbess's temples, affecting her sense of balance. She put a hand against the nearest wall to steady herself. When word of this reached the archbishop . . . What hope could they have now?

'Abbess, are you unwell?' Aldo asked.

'I – I need to sit.' The infirmary was whirling around her . . .

# Chapter Twenty-two

*A*ldo caught the abbess as she slumped sideways, lowering her onto an empty cot. The infirmarian bustled towards them. 'What happened? What did you do to her?'

'Nothing,' Aldo said.

Simona pushed past, leaning down to listen to the abbess's breathing before pressing a hand to her forehead. 'She's fainted. Hopefully that's all.' The infirmarian called to Suor Dea. 'Fetch water and a cloth.' The servant nun hurried away, taking a bowl with a puddle of blood inside it. 'I feared this would happen,' Simona said. 'The abbess hasn't been eating, and she struggles to sleep. The cares of this convent weigh heavy on her.' The servant nun returned with a cloth in a bowl of water. Simona laid the cloth across the abbess's brow.

Aldo followed the dark-skinned servant nun. 'May I ask you a question?'

Dea glanced at Simona, but she was busy with the abbess. 'Yes, I suppose.'

'You were here on Sunday night, with Suor Simona.'

'Yes. So was Suor Rigarda,' she added.

'Before, I noticed you were tending one of the elderly nuns . . .'

'Suor Piera.'

'You took a bowl with blood away from her bed.'

Dea nodded. 'Blood-letting sometimes helps patients, especially those with a fever.'

'Have any of the patients been bled in the last few days?'

'Piera was, the night of Palm Sunday.'

'And what happens to the blood?'

'Usually it is poured away,' Dea said. Again, her eyes slid towards Simona.

'Usually?' Aldo asked.

'We had to bleed Piera that night. But the bowl went missing.'

'When was this? Sunday night, or early Monday morning?'

'Not long before dawn on Monday,' Dea replied. 'I was exhausted, we all were. I thought I must have emptied it and forgotten. But I found the bowl by the door later, clean and empty. I asked Suor Rigarda but she knew nothing.'

That confirmed Aldo's suspicions. Maria Celestia cutting both her hands open would have spilled some blood, but not enough for what was poured over Galeri. Combining her blood with that from the elderly nun would have been. That suggested Maria Celestia was trying to conceal something when Galeri was murdered in order to protect herself or someone else.

But the novice had not acted alone.

'Do all novices have duties to perform,' he asked, 'in addition to their studies?'

Dea nodded. 'Maria Celestia assists those who illuminate texts in the scriptorium. She prepares the room each morning. That's probably why she found the body.'

'And where does Maria Vincenzia work?'

'She is meant to help in the kitchen.' Dea scowled. 'I know it is wrong to judge others, but I have friends there, other servant nuns. They have little good to say about her.'

Aldo pushed Maria Vincenzia up the list of those he most

needed to question before Testardo returned. He thanked Dea for her candour before returning to the abbess. She was upright on the cot now, colour returning to her cheeks. Simona did not appear happy.

'You should remain here and rest,' the infirmarian insisted.

'Thank you,' the abbess replied, rising from the bed. 'But I have duties to perform.' Her gaze shifted to Aldo. 'Have you seen all you wish?' He nodded. 'Then let us move on.'

Aldo followed the abbess outside. When she reached the cloisters, the abbess sank onto a stone bench. Aldo sat beside her, unsure if she was unwell again. They remained in silence a while, the abbess gripping her wooden cross.

'My fainting –' she eventually said. 'It wasn't the sight of those wounds, or even all the talk of blood –' The abbess fell silent, nodding to a pair of nuns as they passed, one reading from a breviary. Once the nuns were out of hearing, the abbess continued. 'Until today, I hadn't believed any of my sisters in God could be part of this. The taking of a life is for our Lord, and him alone. I would not let myself believe any among us could do that.'

'Now you know there is a killer here,' Aldo said.

She nodded. 'What can you tell me of Signor Galeri? Was he a good man?'

'No.' Aldo revealed what he knew, sparing her few details. 'I suspect there is more to learn about Galeri, why he came to the convent after dark. Discovering that could help explain his murder. But you should know Testardo's decision is already made.'

'I feared as much,' she said. 'Our convent has been a stone in the archbishop's shoe for years. He would prefer we were shut away from the world, unable to ask questions of what the diocese does with its wealth. I had thought perhaps Galeri was killed elsewhere and brought into the convent to disgrace us. But now . . .' The abbess shook her head, shoulders slumping. She should still be a suspect, but Aldo could discern no reason for her to kill Galeri. She had nothing to gain from his death, and everything to lose. Aldo believed he could trust her.

'Before you fainted, I asked if Maria Celestia was known to hurt herself. You said no, not her. Is there someone else that does?' The abbess did not reply. Aldo could see he needed to show himself worthy of her trust. 'I am an officer of the court, but I was born a *bastardo*. Despite that, my father insisted I be brought up as one of his own. Isabella's mama, Teresa, she was – is – my half-sister. I was twelve when my father died. Teresa's mother banished me from the *famiglia* and its palazzo that same day. I spent six years on the streets of Florence, living from one day to the next, doing whatever I must to survive. I used to beg outside the church I had gone to every Sunday of my life, but the priests would not let me inside. There was one person – a nun – who took pity on me that first winter. She gave me alms when nobody else would. If not for her, I would have died. She is the reason I am here, the reason I made a pact with a *diavolo* to get appointed to this visitation. Let me repay her kindness. Tell me what I need to know so I can find this killer.'

Aldo fell silent. He was not used to sharing such things. It left him hollow, as if speaking so much truth emptied him out inside. Had the abbess believed him?

'Very well,' she said eventually. 'We have seven private cells. Most are given to those who hold positions of responsibility. Our listening nun sleeps in the sixth—'

'I know all this,' Aldo cut in. 'I was there when you told Testardo.' His patience was fraying. Bad enough he had shared parts of his childhood that no other living soul had heard. Now she was repaying him with common knowledge.

'Let me finish,' the abbess said, determination slipping into her voice like a blade. 'The seventh cell belongs to the prioress. But when her younger sister joined us, the prioress insisted her cell be given to Suor Violante. The prioress's sister is a woman of intense faith, but she does not fit easily into a community.' She glared at Aldo. 'Any community.'

Aldo cursed himself for a fool. Too many men rushed to display their own wisdom rather than letting a woman reveal what she knew. He had never thought himself such a man. 'Forgive my interruption, I did not realize what you were trying to tell me,' he said. 'The prioress's sister hurts herself?'

The abbess gave the smallest of nods. 'Violante is troubled. She would never hurt another. I do not think she means to hurt herself. But she believes there are demons in this world others cannot see, concealed within the skins of men, lurking behind their lusts and longings. Faith alone is not enough to turn these monsters away. Most days she is the kindest, gentlest of women. But when she sees the demons, when she hears their voices or feels them under her skin . . . It is safer for Violante to remain in her cell, away from blades and any other – temptations.'

Aldo nodded. Now the abbess's wish to keep the visitation from that cell made sense. She was not hiding something; she was protecting someone. The reality of the convent being enclosed by the archbishop now took on a more dangerous prospect. In some ways, it might be safer for everyone if Santa Maria Magdalena was dissolved.

Bindi had been relieved when the Church asserted its jurisdiction over the murder at Santa Maria Magdalena. Being forced to step aside was irksome, but the *segretario* knew there were no thanks to be had for uncovering this killer. Proving a murderous nun had claimed a man's life would be a source of scandal and shame, both for the convent and the diocese. Far better the Church take responsibility for that, and deal with the consequences.

Having escaped that burden, Bindi ought to have been pleased. The eight magistrates currently comprising the Otto were conscientious in their duty and compliant in following his guidance. For once the court finances were in balance, with fines and other incomes meeting the cost of administering justice. And it was Holy Week, when Florence shook off the last vestiges of the winter to commemorate the death of our Lord. Yes, Bindi ought to have been pleased. But it was not to be, not with Strocchi standing in front of him.

Those who served the court frustrated the *segretario*. First, there had been Aldo's secondment to the diocesan visitation. Bindi had no proof Aldo was responsible for that, but his impassive face when told the news said enough. He had somehow arranged it. The court was already short an officer, due to Cerchi's disappearance – his murder, it now seemed. He had been a blunt weapon, more intent on filling his pouch than serving the city, but still effective. Losing Aldo to the diocese, however briefly, left the Otto with few capable officers. The others were bullies or buffoons, without talent or shrewdness.

Bindi had wondered if Strocchi might make a good officer. The constable was young for such a promotion, his features yet to show the lines and cares of a man's character. Yet in his year with the court Strocchi had revealed a stern moral core many constables lacked. He was respectful, diligent and appeared to care as much about seeing justice done as about the appearance of doing so. And there was nothing hidden behind Strocchi's face, no masks worn by the young constable. All of that made it clear Strocchi had not grown up in Florence. He was an honest son of the Tuscan countryside. But his resolute nature and the glimmers of a deft mind showed Strocchi had promise. Yes, he could make a good officer one day.

But the more Strocchi reported of his efforts to find Cerchi's killer, the less sure Bindi became of the young constable's potential. He seemed unable to still his tongue in front of the *segretario*, truth escaping like wine from a broken bottle. When the disappointments finally ran dry, Bindi made a single observation. 'So, you've found nothing?'

'I wouldn't say that, *segretario*—'

'Are you denying the truth of my words?'

'No, sir, but—'

'Are you calling me a liar, constable?'

Strocchi had the good sense to cease talking. He shook his head instead.

'So, as I was saying,' Bindi continued, 'you have found nothing. You believe Cerchi was killed on Thursday, January the eleventh, but have no proof. Indeed, one witness seems to indicate Cerchi visited the workshop of this dressmaker—'

'Renato Patricio,' Strocchi said.

'. . . visited this dressmaker in February, weeks after Cerchi died.'

The constable opened his mouth to protest, but stopped himself.

'You have no suspects, and no witnesses,' Bindi said. 'In short, you have spent the better part of two days proving nothing and finding less.'

Strocchi grimaced. 'I do have a potential witness, sir, someone who may have seen or at least heard Cerchi and another man arguing on Ponte Vecchio after curfew that night.'

'A potential witness? So you haven't questioned them yet?'

'No, sir.'

'And when do you expect to do so?'

'Later today,' Strocchi replied. 'By curfew tonight, I will know what they know.'

'Assuming that is anything at all.'

The constable's gaze dropped to the floor. No, Strocchi was not a son of Florence. His feelings were as plain as his face. 'You have until first thing tomorrow. If you are unable to present fresh evidence – or a compelling reason to continue – the matter shall be closed.'

Strocchi bowed to him. 'Thank you, sir.'

Bindi dismissed the constable with a gesture. Strocchi retreated to the door, but did not leave. 'May I ask a question?'

The *segretario* made no effort to conceal his displeasure. 'What now?'

'Did Cerchi ever take court documents away from the Podestà?'

Bindi frowned. He did not know the answer, but was not admitting that in front of a constable. 'Why do you ask?'

'One of those I spoke to suggested Cerchi did so sometimes. I thought it might be relevant, that a suspect in a case before the Otto killed Cerchi to get such court documents –'

'Then you thought wrong. This court does not mislay or misplace official papers.'

Still the constable persisted. 'I understand that, sir, but if Cerchi—'

'Enough!' Bindi snapped. 'You have your answer. Go.'

Strocchi bowed once more before leaving.

No, Bindi decided, Carlo Strocchi would not make a good officer. He had the tenacity of a hunting dog, but lacked the wisdom to know when to let go. And his heart was too pure. He needed to learn there were no good choices, only lesser evils. Once that was burned into him, he might become an officer. Until that day, Florence would always have the better of Strocchi.

Suor Giulia climbed the wide wooden stairs to the convent's upper level. Rising each night to tend the nutmeg oil was more exhausting than she had expected. How mothers coped with babies was beyond her. No doubt some deep instinct to care for the child must help them. But Giulia had never felt that pull which persuaded so many women to have a child. Perhaps if her husband had been a loving man, then she might have known the same urge other women did. But all she'd had from him was pain and shame.

Reaching the upper level, Giulia strode along the corridor to the private cells. On her left, small wooden shutters offered a view of the main courtyard, its sun-drenched grass and beds of lavender. A few nuns were sitting on the stone benches beneath the cloisters, but most were in the refectory, enjoying a meal after the recitation of prayers at sext. Who knew how many more times they would break bread together? A murder, and now the visitation . . . The life they knew at Santa Maria Magdalena was under threat.

Giulia noticed a novice hurrying towards her, head down, hands clasped together as if praying. But there was no reason for a novice to be in that part of the convent. Giulia stepped into the younger nun's path, forcing her to stop. Maria Teodora looked up, surprise and fear in her face. 'Suor Giulia!'

'Why aren't you in the refectory?'

'I –' Crimson coloured the novice's cheeks. 'I – I was on an errand for the prioress.'

'What errand?'

Maria Teodora couldn't hold Giulia's gaze, a sure sign the novice was lying. 'The prioress asked me to see if Suor Violante wished for a meal. I got no reply.'

That sounded more truthful. Giulia knew she should press the novice for more, but she was tired to her bones. 'On you go. I will expect you in the workshop before nones.'

'Yes, Suor Giulia.' Maria Teodora scuttled away.

Giulia went on, pausing when she reached the door of the first cell. 'Suor Violante, are you there?' Inside a single voice was whispering prayers. Giulia wanted to know if Maria Teodora had spoken true. But a pained sobbing seeped beneath the door, caught in the breaths between whispers.

It was cowardice, but Giulia could not face someone else's tears. Not today. Better to let Violante find solace in prayer. What harm could there be in that?

Having witnessed how Testardo's dismissive attitude had brought few results, Aldo sought advice from the abbess on how best to question the remaining nuns. He knew what was needed, but involving her would show a willingness to listen. Word of that should spread through the convent. Besides, it was always harder to get answers from a closed mouth.

The abbess proposed having Suor Benedicta fetch those Aldo wished to question. With the convent still enclosed, the listening nun had little to do. Her age brought respect from the others. And Benedicta was a terrible gossip, the abbess revealed. If anyone was talking, Benedicta would hear it. Besides, she slept in one of the private cells so the listening nun also had to be questioned to determine whether she was a true suspect.

Aldo suggested the abbess sit behind the desk. This was her *officio*, the other nuns were used to seeing her there. It would be disquieting if he took her place. Besides, Aldo preferred to stand. When questioning a witness or a potential suspect – and all those to come were potential suspects – it was better to have them sit while he moved around. Standing offered the chance to see a suspect's body shift and move, to note what they did with their hands. Answers were not simply what was said, but how it was spoken and what else a suspect did.

When Benedicta arrived she sat opposite the abbess, back firm and upright, her eyes twinkling. 'You wished to see me?' There was nothing coy about the listening nun, so the questioning did not take long. No, she did not know the dead man. Yes, the night of Palm Sunday she slept in the private cell between those of Suor Violante and Suor Fiametta. No, she had not got up during the night, nor did she leave until it was time to get ready for prime service.

'You did not leave your cell during the night?' Aldo asked. He was standing behind Benedicta. She did not turn round to reply.

'As I told you,' the listening nun said, a hint of impatience in her voice.

'Did you hear anyone?' He moved round to watch her face. She was frowning.

'Suor Violante does not sleep soundly, or for long,' Benedicta replied. 'She tends to pace her cell at night, whispering prayers to herself. I find it quite soothing.' Benedicta smiled. 'But there was someone else up that night. I heard voices in the corridor.'

'Whose voices?' Aldo asked. 'What were they saying?'

'Sorry, I don't know. I could not hear them clearly, they were whispering.'

'But you're certain it was more than one voice?'

'Yes.' Benedicta nodded, showing no hesitation.

Her certainty was compelling. A single nun in the corridor by the cells would have confirmed what previous witnesses had said. It could have been Suor Giulia on her way to mix the nutmeg oil, or Andriana going to the *latrina*. But two people having a whispered conversation outside the private cells was fresh evidence.

Benedicta had a gleam in her eye that Aldo recognized. It meant she knew something, but wanted to be asked before revealing it. 'The dead man was Signor Galeri, who came to the convent on Friday as part of the visitation. Had you met him before?'

'Not before that day, no.'

Aldo suppressed a smile at her quiet glee. 'Did he come back after the visitation?'

'Yes, the following day. He claimed to have left something in this *officio*. I did not let him in, of course. Even in an open convent, men cannot come and go as they wish. So Galeri asked to speak with one of the servant nuns. He claimed to be part of her *famiglia*.'

'Why did you not mention this earlier?' the abbess asked.

'Nobody asked me.'

Aldo smiled at Benedicta. 'And who was this servant nun Galeri asked to see?'

'Suor Rigarda; she helps at the infirmary. I saw no reason to refuse the request, so I brought her to the visitors' parlour.'

Aldo had yet to question Rigarda, but already he knew she was working at the infirmary the night Galeri was killed. Now it seemed she had a personal link to the victim.

The servant nun was fast becoming a significant suspect.

# Chapter Twenty-three

❦

'What did Suor Rigarda and Galeri speak about?' Aldo asked.

'They did not talk long,' Benedicta replied, 'and I heard little of it.' The listening nun straightened her shoulders, as if to justify her answer.

'You didn't hear them at all, did you?'

The listening nun could not hold his gaze. 'No,' she admitted. 'I was – distracted.'

Benedicta did not wish to confess she had either fallen asleep, or had left the servant nun alone with Galeri. Whatever the reason, it made little difference. To know what was discussed, Aldo would have to question the servant nun. Using paper on the abbess's desk, he wrote a handful of names, including Rigarda. 'Inform all of those on this list that they will need to be questioned.' Benedicta looked to the abbess for approval before accepting the list.

Once the older nun was gone, the abbess rose from her chair. 'The more I hear, the more I realize how little I have known about what happens in this convent.'

Suspecting they had time before the next nun arrived, Aldo pointed to the wooden cabinet. 'Your brother told me his confraternity stores items in the convent for safekeeping – yet you have no locked internal doors. The only such door I have seen is on that cabinet.'

The abbess's lips thinned. 'Girolamo spoke true. The convent does keep confraternity possessions safe in return for regular, generous donations to our funds.'

'Who has the key to the cabinet?'

'I have the only one.' She turned the cross that hung from a chain round her neck. A small key was secured behind the wood. 'This never leaves me, day or night. And the lock on that door is sturdy. It would require considerable force to open it.'

'Someone has tried, and recently.'

The abbess went to the cabinet, running her fingers across the metal and wood.

'I suspect it was Galeri,' Aldo said. 'I believe he came to your convent to get at whatever is inside that cabinet. During the first visitation, did he come to this *officio*?'

'Yes, they all did.' The abbess stepped back, her eyes widening. 'That afternoon, I was going to nones but realized I had left my breviary behind. I came back, and found Galeri by this cabinet. He was embarrassed, but it did not seem important at the time.'

'Did he appear embarrassed – or guilty?'

The abbess took a moment before replying. 'Guilty.'

Aldo nodded. He needed to know what was inside the cabinet but doubted the abbess would open it simply because he asked. 'There is something I have not shared with Testardo, or the others. Galeri was not stabbed to death.'

'But his body – all that blood –'

'You saw what someone wanted you to see: a man with dozens of stab wounds, his body awash with blood.' Aldo told her about Saul's belief that Galeri was killed with poison. 'I found a scrap of parchment under the body. It matches the torn parchment jutting out beneath this door. I suspect Galeri came here the night he died to open this cabinet. When that failed, he tore off a corner of the parchment.'

'Why?'

'To answer that, I need to see what is behind this door.'

The abbess hesitated. Before she replied, there was a knock from outside. 'It's Suor Fiametta,' a voice called. 'You asked to see me.'

'I will consider your request,' the abbess told Aldo.

It was mid-afternoon, the sun still bathing the streets as Strocchi marched west across the city. Most people had retreated indoors to escape the hottest part of the day. But the constable did not have that option. Unless he found something to satisfy Bindi, the chance of bringing to justice Cerchi's killer would be lost – and so would the chance to become an officer.

Strocchi turned into the alley where Zoppo's tavern lurked, a drunk sprawled in the dirt outside the open door. Acrid smells assaulted Strocchi's senses as he went in, though whether they came from the drunk or the bar was unclear. At least it was cooler inside.

'Back so soon,' Zoppo said. 'Thought you wouldn't be returning until near curfew?' The cripple was pouring drinks for two hunched figures at the bar. It was the first time Strocchi had seen any customers who still had their senses.

'I need your answer now.'

Zoppo glared at Strocchi. 'Told you already, I can't pay what you want.' The cripple smirked at his customers. 'What's an honest tavern keeper meant to do? Constables demanding payment for doing their jobs. It's a disgrace.'

Strocchi didn't understand. 'What are you talking about?'

'Outside.' Zoppo jabbed a crooked finger at the alley. 'I'll talk to you outside.'

The constable retreated back through the doorway, stepping over the drunk. Moments later Zoppo stumped from his tavern, calling over a shoulder to those inside. 'Help yourself to another drink when you're ready!' He led Strocchi away from the entrance, hissing at the constable. 'What kind of *idiota* are you? Never come in my tavern announcing you want answers. You want to get me killed?'

*Santo Spirito!* Strocchi kicked himself for being a fool. In his haste he had put Aldo's best informant in danger. 'Forgive me, I didn't think –'

'It'll cost you coin, and me bruises,' Zoppo replied. 'Hit me.'

'What?'

'Hit me. That way nobody believes I tell you anything about them. Hit me.'

Strocchi shook his head. 'I can't –'

'Hit me,' Zoppo hissed, 'or else I never help you again.'

The constable didn't want to, but he couldn't see what else to do. He punched Zoppo in the stomach, doubling the tavern keeper over. Strocchi leaned over him. 'How was that?'

'The face,' Zoppo gasped, leaning against a wall for support. 'You're supposed to hit me in the face. How else do people know I've been hurt?'

'Oh. Sorry.'

Zoppo pulled himself upright. 'Come on, then. Hit me.'

Strocchi lashed out again, connecting hard with Zoppo's right eye.

'*Merda!*' The cripple staggered back, clutching a hand to his face. 'Not that hard.'

'Sorry,' Strocchi said. 'I didn't know –'

Zoppo took the hand from his face, revealing a broad grin. 'No,

I'm jesting with you. Good punch, though.' He looked to see if anyone was watching. 'You bring more coin?'

'Aldo gave you plenty last night,' Strocchi replied.

The tavern keeper leered at him. 'Can't blame me for trying. Right, I've been asking around. Nobody remembers anyone offering money to stick a blade in Cerchi. That *bastardo* wasn't popular, so there would have been a line of men from here to the Arno for that job. But you were right about one thing.'

'What's that?'

'Cerchi hasn't been seen or heard of since the middle of January. He was filling his pouch from all sorts of *strategemmi*. That stopped when he disappeared.' Zoppo pressed two fingers to the eye Strocchi had punched. 'Ohh, this is swelling up nicely. I'll have a good bruise there in the morning. Remember that the next time you want something.'

The abbess was happy for Aldo to question Suor Fiametta. The sacrist had an earnestness that made her difficult to appreciate, and few of the other sisters could recall seeing her smile. Fiametta was most meticulous in her duties, keeping a strict accounting of the convent's vestments and books. Aldo was certainly finding her a hard stone to turn.

'So you had not met or heard of Signor Galeri before the first visitation?'

'As I said, no. He was not known to me,' Fiametta replied, her lips pursing.

'What did you do on the night of Palm Sunday?'

'The night that led to Palm Sunday, or the night that followed Palm Sunday?'

The abbess suppressed a smile. Having spent five years dealing with Suor Fiametta, it was a quiet joy to see someone else bear that burden.

'The night that followed Palm Sunday,' Aldo said through gritted teeth.

'I spent that night the same as I spent the night before, and the night after, and every night since. I was alone in my cell. I prayed, and then I slept.'

'Did you hear anyone else? Your sisters in God that occupy the cells on either side of you, perhaps? Or one of the other nuns in the corridor outside your cell?'

Small creases formed between Fiametta's eyebrows. The abbess leaned forward. It was unusual to see the sacrist pause for thought. Fiametta was even more certain of her beliefs than the prioress. If Fiametta had her way, the convent doors would never open again.

'No,' Fiametta finally said. 'I heard no one that night. But I sleep well each night.' She smiled at the abbess, pale blue eyes glinting. 'Those who follow the true path of our Lord have no reason for their slumbers to be restless.'

The abbess feigned a smile in response. 'Thank you, Suor Fiametta. Was there anything else you wished to tell us?'

'No,' the sacrist replied, rising from her chair. 'Though I am surprised you have not questioned me about the stolen habit. It was taken the same night this man died, I believe.'

'The abbess already told us about it,' Aldo replied. 'There was nothing further to ask about, unless you have since learned who took it. Have you discovered that?'

Fiametta bristled at the question. 'No. No, I haven't.'

'Then you may go,' the abbess said, gesturing to her *officio* door. The sacrist gave the briefest of nods before leaving. The abbess waited until the door shut before speaking again. 'Thank you for intervening on my behalf,' she said to Aldo.

'It was my pleasure,' he replied. 'How you stand her company is beyond me.'

'We are a *famiglia* in this convent, and you cannot choose your *famiglia*. You learn to live with them, or you find another.' The abbess recalled what Aldo had said about being banished by his stepmother. 'I'm sorry, I didn't mean –'

He raised a hand to show no offence had been taken. The abbess frowned. 'I don't understand why someone chose to hide their bloodstained habit with Galeri's tunic and hose. It was inevitable they would be found, just as his body was found.'

'But concealing them gave the killer time to prepare for that discovery,' Aldo said.

There was a knock at the door. 'Come in,' the abbess called. Father Zati and Signor Cortese entered, nodding to her and Aldo in turn. 'What is it?' she asked.

The priest spoke first. 'We know how Signor Galeri got into the convent.'

Aldo watched the abbess as Zati and Cortese revealed what they had discovered. Suor Paulina was missing her key for the padlock on the back gates. The two men had been busy searching for the blade that killed Galeri, but had paused to ask about the key. She'd had no reason to use it since Palm Sunday, especially now the convent was under an enclosure order. Paulina took the visitors to her cell so the key could be retrieved – but it was missing. A thorough search confirmed the key was gone.

'Suor Paulina recalled last using her key after Mass on Sunday, it must have been removed from her cell later that day,' Zati said. 'Someone used it to open the back gates so Galeri could get inside. One of the sisters, a novice or one of the boarders.'

The abbess remained calm through all of this, listening carefully, her face betraying nothing. But she shook her head when Zati suggested a boarder might be involved. 'No, the girls were in their dormitory all night. We would know if one of them had done this.'

'I agree with the abbess,' Aldo said. 'We already know the person responsible for Galeri's death comes from a small number of suspects: the nuns who have private cells, the three nuns who were tending patients at the infirmary, and the two novices who recited lauds and matins that night. Everyone else was sleeping in a dormitory, where leaving after dark would have been noticed by the nun nearest to the door.'

'Could a nun by a dormitory door have slipped out?' Zati asked.

'Perhaps, but everyone agrees the doors are noisy. They would have been noticed.'

'Then we are close to knowing who killed Signor Galeri?' Cortese asked. His haste to see the matter closed was evident. Either he was hoping to share in the glory, or he feared what would happen if Testardo came back to find the visitation no further forward.

'Perhaps,' Aldo replied. 'Have you found the blade used on him?'

The two men's expressions sagged. 'No,' Zati confessed. 'There are so many rooms here, each with many potential hiding places. For all we know whoever killed Signor Galeri threw the blade into a drain or down a *latrina*.'

Aldo smiled at them. 'Then you must hope to find it before the monsignor returns, otherwise he might tell you to inspect both of those possibilities.'

Zati and Cortese trudged out. When the door closed behind them, the abbess burst out laughing. 'Forgive me.' She put a hand across her mouth. 'I shouldn't laugh, not at a time like this, but the looks on their faces . . .'

Aldo nodded. 'Father Zati has a good heart but is not a natural investigator. And as for Signor Cortese –' He glanced at the cabinet. 'Abbess, have you considered my request?'

Her smile faded. 'I have.' One hand closed around the cross she wore. 'You can look inside, but must not touch anything. Agreed?'

It was better than nothing. 'Agreed.'

The abbess strode to the cabinet, removing the key from her cross. She opened the door, revealing three shelves within. On the top lay a collection of oddly shaped cloth bags, some made of velvet and others of brocade. All had drawstrings pulled tight to conceal their contents. 'What is inside those?' Aldo asked.

'Holy relics, if I remember correctly.'

The middle shelf was given over to a small wooden casket secured by two heavy padlocks, its corners and joints protected by brass fittings. A thin layer of dust showed it had not been touched of late.

Documents, parchments and scrolls filled the bottom shelf. Most were sealed with wax, hiding whatever was written within. But others had been resting against the cabinet door, their edges caught beneath the wood when it was last shut. These must have been what Galeri was tugging, trying to pull them clear. The top three had resisted him, but the fourth document down was the one Galeri tore.

Aldo crouched for a closer look. He was able to piece together the first few sentences: *By Order of Girolamo Savonarola, the holders of this document have the Authority to search any and all homes for sinful objects. These shall be given—*

The documents above masked the rest of it. He looked at the abbess, but she shook her head. Aldo got to his feet and she locked the cabinet once more. He had still seen enough. He now knew why Galeri had joined the first visitation, and what brought him back after Palm Sunday. The dark legacy of Savonarola loomed large over Ruggerio and his brethren, with the proof of that lurking inside this cabinet. Returning to steal that had cost Galeri his life, but it was doubtful the document in the cabinet had been what motivated his killer.

Who murdered him was still in question.

# Chapter Twenty-four

❧

*M*aria Vincenzia came into the *officio* and sat opposite the abbess, ignoring Aldo. Isabella's description of the tall, thin novice had been perceptive; she did look at other people as if they were *merda* to be scraped from her boot. The abbess introduced Aldo, explaining why he would be asking the questions. Maria Vincenzia nodded, as if granting them permission. Yes, this novice had a high opinion of herself. Would it be the same after all his questions?

'On the night of Palm Sunday,' Aldo said, 'you and Maria Celestia were to be in the chapter house, reciting the prayers at matins and lauds.'

'We were there,' the novice replied, still keeping her gaze on the abbess.

'I understand all novices are required to undertake work assisting others in aspects of convent life, while also undertaking studies to prepare for their vocation.'

'Yes. I help in the kitchen.'

'And Maria Celestia?'

'She assists in the scriptorium.'

'Where the murdered man's body was found.'

'Yes.'

Aldo moved so he was standing just to one side of the abbess, where the novice could not help but see him. 'Were you there when she found the body?'

Maria Vincenzia hesitated before replying. 'I happened to be passing and heard her cry out. I went in to see what had distressed her.'

The novice's account contradicted what Aldo had heard the previous morning, a distant scream and a female voice crying out the word murder twice. Maria Vincenzia was not going to be a reliable witness. So be it. 'You say you happened to be passing?'

'That is correct.'

'On your way to where?'

The novice frowned, her gaze shifting to Aldo's face. 'I'm sorry?'

'Where were you going when you heard Maria Celestia cry out?'

'I . . . I can't recall.'

'Interesting. We'll come back to that, in case your memory improves.' Aldo moved away from the abbess, passing the novice so that he could stand behind her. 'Your voice, it sounds as if you have been ill. There is a scratchiness to it.'

'It is simply my voice,' Maria Vincenzia said, a little impatience creeping into her reply. 'I have sounded this way for years, as the abbess can confirm.'

Aldo ignored the suggestion. 'I mention this because you were overheard in a corridor of the convent last night, talking to a chapter nun.' The novice stiffened in her chair. 'It was a hushed conversation, but that scratchiness in your voice was still recognized.'

'Whoever claims that is mistaken,' Maria Vincenzia replied.

'Perhaps. They did not hear much of what was said, only a few words: "Hidden", "mistake", and "they can't know". I was going to ask if you knew what that meant.'

'I have no—'

'But since you say this person was mistaken, we shall move on.'

Aldo shifted again, coming round to the other side of the novice to stand in front of the *officio* door. 'Maria Celestia has remained at the infirmary since discovering the body in the scriptorium. She is overcome with shock, according to Suor Simona. You also saw the corpse covered with all that blood, and yet you seem unaffected. Can you explain why?'

The novice folded her arms. 'Each of us is as our Lord made us. Some are better able to cope with seeing such things, however shocking.'

'Of course,' Aldo agreed. 'Tell me, did Maria Celestia cut her hands before or after she found the body?' The novice gave no reply. 'It's a simple question. When you went into the scriptorium to see why Maria Celestia had cried out, were her hands already cut open?'

'I – don't recall.'

'Something else for us to come back to, if we have time.' Aldo smiled at the novice. 'Would you say that Maria Celestia is your friend?'

'We joined the convent at the same time. We support each other.'

'Have you been to see her at the infirmary?'

'Several times.'

'That's right. In fact, you were heard talking with her there earlier today. That voice you have, it does catch the ear, even when you try to be quiet.'

Maria Vincenzia twisted to sneer at Aldo. 'A clumsy girl was nearby when I was visiting, but you shouldn't trust anything she says. I saw her in one of the classes on Palm Sunday. She would rather gossip than listen to Suor Catarina's wisdom.'

'I can only agree with you . . .'

'Good.' The novice rose from her seat. 'Abbess, may I go now?'

'But that clumsy girl is my niece,' Aldo continued. 'So I listen when she tells me something interesting, such as hushed conversations between you and Maria Celestia, especially when one of you is supposed to be beyond her senses.'

The abbess gestured for Maria Vincenzia to sit, which she did.

'This will soon be over, that's what you said to Maria Celestia.' Aldo stepped closer to the novice, looming over her. 'What will soon be over?'

'I don't know what you are talking about.'

'You don't know?' Aldo asked. 'Or you can't recall?'

Her head snapped round to glare at him.

He smiled at her. 'You can go.'

'I'm sorry?'

He gestured at the *officio* door. 'Go. I've asked all my questions – for now.'

The abbess nodded her agreement. Maria Vincenzia pushed past Aldo on the way out, the door slamming after her.

The abbess arched an eyebrow at Aldo. 'You never mentioned any of that to me.'

'A good inquisitor does not reveal all their tools before starting work.'

'You think Maria Celestia and Maria Vincenzia killed Signor Galeri?'

'No. I believed they poured the blood over him. The killer – that was someone else.' Aldo rubbed his hands together. 'Shall we get our next suspect in?'

When Strocchi returned to the one-room residence above the closed butcher's stall, Leonello Fideli was still not back. His wife Salvaza said she was expecting him soon. Their *bambino* kept crying, his face red with frustration. Questioning Fideli there would be difficult. Better to take the husband somewhere Strocchi could have his full attention.

The constable explained this to Salvaza, and asked her to describe Fideli. 'He has the kindest eyes,' she said, 'the eyes of a man you know you can trust. When he smiles, dimples appear in his cheeks. And when he laughs, he makes me laugh too.'

Strocchi nodded. 'I meant, how might I recognize him when I see him?'

'Oh.' Salvaza giggled. 'Sorry. He's as tall as me. He has brown, curly hair that needs cutting. Leonello keeps trying to grow a beard, but –'

Strocchi thanked her on his way down the stairs.

'He's missing the top of this finger!' Salvaza called, holding up the forefinger of her left hand. 'Cut it off his first day working for the fish-seller, the poor thing. They've had him running errands ever since.'

The constable made his way back to Ponte Vecchio, finding a locked door where he could keep watch. Most of those coming and going from the nearby fish-seller's stall were women, but a few men went in – servants, judging by their clothes. As the throng grew thinner, Strocchi feared he had missed Fideli. Perhaps it would be better to wait inside? He stepped from the doorway to cross the bridge when a short man with brown curls appeared. Strocchi caught a glimpse of a wispy beard. 'Fideli?' he called. 'Leonello Fideli?'

The short man stopped, looking round. Strocchi crossed the bridge, shoving aside a toothless hawker with a ring on every finger. The constable introduced himself, before leading Fideli away in search of somewhere quieter. Strocchi wanted no distractions.

Fideli's testimony was the last chance to find whoever murdered Cerchi.

Aldo assessed Suor Rigarda as the servant nun shuffled into the *officio*. The servant nun couldn't be more different from Maria Vincenzia. Where the novice had been all sharp angles and arrogance, Rigarda was hesitant in manner and appearance, as if she didn't deserve to be noticed. She mumbled an unsought *apologia* for making them wait before sitting. While he was being introduced, Aldo found a chair and sat to one side of the desk, lowering himself to the level of Rigarda's gaze. 'I understand you help at the infirmary?'

She gave a small, frightened nod.

'And you were there the night of Palm Sunday?'

Another nod.

'Did you see or notice anything unusual?'

Rigarda shook her head.

'Are you sure?'

The nod was quicker this time.

'A few days ago a visitation came to the convent. Do you recall that?'

Rigarda nodded.

'Did they visit the infirmary?'

Another nod.

'Did you speak to them?'

The servant nun seemed about to shake her head, but spoke instead. 'No,' she replied, her voice little more than a whisper. 'But one of them spoke to me.'

'Which one?' the abbess asked.

'He said his name was Galeri.'

'Why did he speak to you?' Aldo asked quickly, to stop the abbess continuing.

'He saw me – take something.'

'What?'

The servant nun burst into tears. She crumpled forward, sobs wracking her body. Aldo looked to the abbess. She shrugged and shook her head, seeming as surprised as he was by this outburst. The abbess pulled a clean handkerchief from a desk drawer, pushing it across to Rigarda. The servant nun got the sobbing under control, wiping her eyes and begging forgiveness. Aldo motioned for the abbess to take over the questioning. The last thing this young woman needed was a man demanding answers from her.

'Rigarda, what did you take?' the abbess asked, her voice gentle and quiet.

'I – I was so hungry – and one of the patients wasn't eating, so I –'

'You took some of their food.'

'Only when they didn't want it.' Rigarda wiped more tears from her cheeks. 'But that man, he said I was stealing food from those who needed it.'

The abbess shook her head. 'You did nothing wrong. Nothing. That food would have gone to waste if you had not eaten it. Better you did, and had strength for your duties.'

The servant nun looked up, hope in her sad eyes. 'Do you mean that, Abbess?'

'Yes.'

A little hope crept into Rigarda's face. Aldo leaned forward. 'The man who accused you, he was not a good or kind man.'

'Our Lord says it is not for us to judge others,' she replied.

'Of course. But I also believe you see who people are by their actions and by their words. This man, Signor Galeri, he came back to the convent after the visitation. Suor Benedicta told us he asked to see you in the visitors' parlour.'

Rigarda nodded.

'Did he try to coerce you into assisting him?'

The servant nun frowned. 'Did he . . .?'

'Did he ask you to do something for him?'

She nodded, close to tears again. Aldo feared the abbess would end his questioning if Rigarda broke down again. He had to go carefully, delicately.

'We know someone took Suor Paulina's key to the back gates so this man could get into the convent on Sunday night. Is that what he asked you to do?'

The servant nun nodded, her eyes brimming. 'If I didn't, he would write to the abbess about me stealing food. But I told him no. I wouldn't do it.'

That was not the answer Aldo had expected. 'You refused?'

'Yes. I said he should write to the abbess.'

'And what did Galeri do?'

'He laughed at me.' Rigarda broke down in tears again. 'He said – he didn't need me – he had someone else to help him,' she said between sobs. 'I was only—'

Aldo finished the words for her. 'Only in case his other plan failed.'

She nodded. To Aldo's eye her guilt and shame were true. Galeri had manipulated the servant nun, sought to bend her to his will – without success. Someone else helped Galeri get into the convent after dark, but who had done so and why?

Aldo was willing to wager his own coin that whoever helped Galeri get inside was probably the one who poisoned him. Galeri believed he could use that person to get access to the locked cabinet. Instead, he got a cup of poisoned wine, and twenty-seven stab wounds.

Out in the cloisters a bell rang for nones, the mid-afternoon prayers. Testardo would be back soon, and Galeri's killer was still to be found. Time was running out.

Suor Giulia refused to sit when brought back into the abbess's *officio*. She had already been questioned, there was no reason for her to be summoned again. But Suor Benedicta insisted the summons had come from the abbess, not the visitation, so Giulia did as she was asked. The convent faced enough challenges without her adding to them.

There had been whispers at sext about Testardo leaving, so Giulia was not surprised to find Aldo leading the questions. He promised to be brisk. 'In fact, I only have one question that needs an honest answer,' he said, with a bland smile.

'I have sworn vows of poverty, chastity and obedience,' Giulia replied. 'All my answers are honest.'

'Very well,' Aldo said. 'Did you know Signor Galeri before he came to the convent?'

Giulia hesitated. This was the question she had feared. It was a question she had expected earlier but which the monsignor had not asked. Having announced all her answers could only be honest, to lie or evade would be the worst hypocrisy. 'Yes. Galeri was my husband.'

Aldo took a step back, one eyebrow arching. Most men seemed to believe nuns only came to their vocation as girls or young women. It did not occur to many of them that a woman could be married or even have children before taking the veil. The abbess was less startled, but even she had not known the name of Giulia's husband – only what he did to her.

'When was this?' Aldo asked.

'Many years ago,' Giulia said. 'We married young, far too young. Signor Galeri – Bernardo – was not the man I believed him to be. He gambled, he drank – and often took his losses out on me. One night he came at me with a broken bottle –'

She stopped. It had been so long ago, yet talking about that night brought everything back. Most of the time she could keep the fear and pain at the back of her thoughts. But it always lurked, an old wound waiting to be torn open, a weakness that could give way at any moment. Skin healed, bruises faded, but loss and shame lingered. So did anger – at herself, at those who never came to help, at those who didn't want to see. And at her husband, for what he did. For what he had broken.

Giulia swallowed all that down, keeping her voice as even as she could. 'So I fled. I wandered through the city after curfew, banging on doors, but nobody answered me. I needed a refuge, a place to recover. I found it here.'

Aldo's attention shifted to the abbess. 'Did you know this?'

She was staring at Giulia. 'I'm sorry?'

'Did you know this?' he repeated.

'I –' The abbess reached for the cross hanging round her neck. 'Some of it, but not who Galeri was. I thought Giulia had learned her apothecary skills from her husband.'

'He preferred hurting to healing,' Giulia said. 'No, my father was an apothecary, so I learned at his elbow. My brothers did the same, they were apothecaries as well – they may still be. I have not seen them since coming here.'

'What happened when Galeri arrived at the convent with the visitation?' Aldo asked.

'He did not seem to know me, not at first. And this –' she gestured to her habit – 'visitors only see our hands and faces. It is not much to recognize a person by, if you haven't seen them for many years. I remembered him, of course. It was –' She paused. 'He came to my workshop with the monsignor. They did not stay long. Galeri seemed bored, as if his thoughts were elsewhere. I thought my danger had passed. That I was safe again.'

'But he came back.'

'Yes. I had been wrong. He did know me, but couldn't recall from where – at first.'

'What did Galeri want?' Aldo asked.

'To be let into the convent after curfew. He said there was something in the abbess's *officio* that he needed. If I helped, he would let me be. If not . . .'

'He would find a way to hurt you again.'

'Yes.'

'But how?' the abbess asked. 'You are a respected member of this convent, in a position of responsibility. What could Galeri do to you from outside these walls?'

'He could make a *denunzia* accusing me of whatever he wished. Galeri was never much troubled by the truth. He could influence the visitation's report to the archbishop. He could destroy this convent, if he wished. See it enclosed, or even dissolved. All of that to hurt me.'

'You agreed to help him,' Aldo said.

Giulia shook her head.

'You stole Suor Paulina's key, and let Galeri in through the back gates after curfew.'

'No,' Giulia insisted. 'I told Bernardo to do his worst. He was always a hollow liar. I knew that whatever he threatened me with was a means to an end and nothing more. Why should Monsignor Testardo listen to a fool like him? Bernardo was angry, cursing at me. He pulled back a fist to hit me, but the young priest came looking for him.' Someone knocked at the door. 'I didn't see him again until the abbess asked me to take his body to the *ospedale*.'

Aldo crouched beside her. 'Suor Giulia, did you—?'

The door opened and the prioress strode in, clutching several pages of parchment. 'Put an end to this inquisition,' she announced. 'No more of my sisters in God need face any more your questions. Everything that you need is here.' The prioress put the pages on the desk.

'I did it,' she said. 'I killed Signor Galeri.'

### Statement by Leonello Fideli, written on his behalf by Constable Carlo Strocchi of the Otto di Guardia e Balia:

*I live with my wife Salvaza and our infant son Gasparro in a room on Ponte Vecchio above a butcher's stall where I was working in January. Gasparro was only a few months old then, and not sleeping well due to a cough. I looked after him if he woke before his midnight feed, so Salvaza could get some rest. That was why I was awake to hear two men arguing on the bridge beneath our room. I cannot be certain of the exact date, though I know it was a handful of days after the feast of the Epiphany.*

*I had been sitting in our nursing chair with Gasparro in my arms, letting him suckle my little finger. It was not his mother's milk, but still seemed to soothe him. I must have been dozing because a gruff voice woke me, demanding answers. Gasparro shifted in my arms but he did not wake, thank the Madonna. The voice outside spoke again, demanding more coin the next day, and more after that.*

*I heard another man's voice, much quieter. He sounded weak, broken.*

*The first man was sneering. There was a heavy thud, followed by coughing sounds. I put Gasparro back in his cot before going to our wooden shutters. They creak if moved, so I peered between them. But it was dark and I struggled to see much below. One of the men was strutting about as if he owned Ponte Vecchio, while the other was hunched over as if in pain.*

*'I should have guessed what kind of man you are much sooner, I suppose,' I heard the cocksure man say.*

*Gasparro started coughing again. I feared he was going to wake, but he snuffled himself back to sleep. I put an ear back to the shutter, straining to hear what was happening below.*

*The louder man said he had been talking to someone. He said that person didn't seem like much, but they watched and listened. He mentioned a name but not one I recognized. I think it was Benedetto, although I may have misheard that.*

*Whatever this person had seen or heard, it seemed to be important. The man hunched over was begging for mercy, but it didn't seem to do him any good. The cocksure one said that from now on, the other man was going to be his whore.*

*Something happened I couldn't see, and the two men moved out of my sight. But there was a sound I recognized. I heard it all the time when the butcher was cutting meat at the stall. It's the sound a blade makes when it pierces flesh.*

*After that there were only noises, no voices. I thought I heard a heavy splash in the river, but can't be sure. The last thing I heard for certain was the sound of someone walking away. One man strolled south towards Oltrarno. It sounded as if he didn't have a care.*

*I listened for a while longer but there was nothing else. Gasparro's cough came back and he kept us awake most of the night. Next morning I told my wife Salvaza about what I had heard. She suggested I go downstairs to look on the bridge but I couldn't see any signs of what had happened. I thought about reporting what I had heard, but Gasparro was very ill and that took all our attention. I forgot about what I'd heard until a constable from the Otto came to ask me about it. He has written this statement for me.*

*I confirm this is a true and correct record of what I saw and heard that night.*

# Chapter Twenty-five

*A*fter thanking Fideli for his statement, Strocchi hurried to the nearest river crossing. As he strode, Strocchi pieced together what had happened on Ponte Vecchio that cold night in January from what he already knew and what Fideli had said. Cerchi was extorting coin from the man he met on the bridge; that was now certain. This meant the killer was not somebody sent there to murder Cerchi on the behalf of others, not a hired blade or a willing criminal.

The sound Fideli heard of a blade piercing flesh – that must have been the moment when Cerchi's extortion victim became his killer. Strocchi could not help wondering what the dying man had felt as the knife slid into him. Surprise? Anger? Dismay? Had Cerchi even realized his life was over, or had his arrogance refused to let him consider such a possibility? The splash was probably Cerchi falling into the Arno. The killer was fortunate the waters were high that night, strong enough to carry the evidence of his crime over the weirs and down the river towards Ponte a Signa.

Yet having ended another man's life, the killer had not run. He had not fled the crime, had not raced from the bridge. There was no fear, no panic. This killer had brought a blade to his meeting with Cerchi, and had been ready to use it. Once Cerchi was gone, his killer strolled south to Oltrarno. What was it Fideli said? As if the killer did not have a care.

Two further things the witness had said made the breath catch in Strocchi's throat. The first was Cerchi accusing his target of perversion. The man hunched over on the bridge did not deny preferring the company of other men. That secret had become Cerchi's weapon. Yet a nagging voice at the back of Strocchi's thoughts told him not to include that in the statement. It was unnecessary, the voice said. Fideli could not read or write so he was none the wiser.

The second thing that had chilled Strocchi was the revelation about who had provided Cerchi with the means for his extortion. What could Benedetto have seen or heard that was so helpful to Cerchi? To find out, Strocchi headed for the Podestà where Benedetto was due on guard duty. A suspicion about who killed Cerchi had been clawing at Strocchi all day. Now it coiled inside him with all the slyness of a serpent, whispering poisonous suggestions. You know who did this, the sibilant voice seemed to be saying. You already know . . .

Aldo read the prioress's confession twice. There were several pages, all written by an urgent hand, the ink blotting in places. The opening words caught his eye: *Forgive me, sisters, for I have sinned.* But it was not until the bottom of the first page that the prioress confirmed her claim: *May God have mercy on me, for I am a murderer.* Aldo studied the remaining pages before handing them to the abbess, who had ushered Suor Giulia from the *officio*. The abbess sunk into her chair, reading each page while the prioress waited in the seat opposite.

'Is this true?' the abbess asked when she had finished.

The prioress nodded.

'Why? Why did you kill Signor Galeri?'

'Suor Catarina told me about him leering at our pupils. I thought she was imagining it – you know how Catarina feels about men in the convent. But later I found him in my sister's cell. He was –' The prioress shook her head. 'Violante is troubled, but this place is her sanctuary from the world. For him to intrude on that, violating her refuge –'

'So you decided Galeri must die?' Aldo asked.

'I realized what kind of man he was,' the prioress replied. 'The thought of killing him did not enter my head – not until I saw him inside the convent after curfew on Sunday.'

'How did he get in?'

'I do not know,' she admitted. 'He was sly of tongue, willing to lie without a moment of hesitation. He must have persuaded someone to admit him, or he stole a key.'

Aldo pondered that answer. It did not match what the apothecary had said, but two testimonies often disagreed on details. 'Where did you see Galeri on Sunday night?'

'The upper level. I heard someone passing the dormitory where I sleep. If you live in a convent, you learn the sounds that others make after dark. I feared someone with impure motives had found a way inside our walls. The intruder was returning downstairs,' she said. 'It was a man. I slipped out of the dormitory to follow him. I don't know if any of my sisters in God heard me go. I confronted the intruder outside the scriptorium. That's when I discovered it was Signor Galeri.'

Aldo was not convinced. Other nuns who slept near the doors to each dormitory had insisted nobody could come or go without being noticed. The prioress's confession might satisfy Testardo and the archbishop – the Church loved a sinner admitting their transgressions – but it was not proof. Too much about this tale did not stand up to scrutiny.

'How did you kill him?' Aldo asked, wanting to see how the prioress responded. There were raised voices in the corridor outside, both male – two, no, three of them. Testardo must have returned already. *Palle!* The truth must come now, or it might never emerge. 'How?'

'He had a blade,' the prioress said. 'I don't know where it came from, he must have brought it. We struggled, and I got the blade away from him. He laughed at me. Galeri didn't believe I would use it. He came at me, and –' She fell silent, her gaze on the floor.

No mention of poison, and the dead man's hands had showed no sign of any struggle for a knife. Nor did those of the prioress. 'You're saying his death was an accident?'

The prioress nodded.

'But Galeri had dozens of wounds. Are you claiming those were also unintended?'

'He spat at me. Bragged about what he would do to the young girls who study here. I – lost myself. When I found my senses again, he was on the floor, covered in blood.'

The prioress was lying. Her written confession was equally false. That meant—

Testardo stormed in, his face full of righteous anger. His black cassock was dusty from riding, the collar soaked with sweat. 'What is going on here?'

The abbess rose to greet him. 'Monsignor, it is customary to knock before entering. I appreciate your visitation is important, but—'

He held up a hand for silence. 'I have just made a round trip of several hours to see my sister, whom I had been told was gravely ill. Instead, I found her well, with no knowledge of sending for me. That message was either an elaborate jest,' Testardo glared at

Aldo, 'or an attempt to usurp my leadership of this investigation. Whatever the truth, I have little good will left. I would appreciate a direct answer to my question. What is going on here?'

'The prioress has just confessed to killing Signor Galeri,' Aldo replied.

Confusion furrowed the monsignor's brow. 'Abbess, is this true?'

'Yes.' The abbess held up the written pages.

'You admit your guilt?' Testardo asked the prioress. 'You murdered Signor Galeri?' She nodded. 'Then this investigation is at an end,' Testardo announced. 'I will report my findings to the archbishop immediately. In the meantime, this convent shall remain enclosed. Abbess, I urge you to lock this woman away where she can harm nobody, including herself.'

'Monsignor, you cannot do that,' Aldo said.

'Are you challenging my authority?' Testardo demanded. 'Galeri's murder is a matter for the Church, not the court. You have no jurisdiction here.'

'I agree, but my challenge was not to your authority. It was to your grasp of the facts. The prioress has confessed to murder, but she is not guilty. She may have stabbed Galeri, but not in the way she says. And even if she did, he died by another's hand.'

'Nonsense,' the monsignor replied. 'She confessed. That is the end of it.'

'Not if the prioress is lying,' Aldo insisted. 'Galeri was poisoned, most likely with aconitum. He was dead before any blade pierced his skin. The stabbing was cruel, an act of hatred, but it was not what killed him.'

Testardo folded his arms. 'What proof do you have?'

Aldo revealed what Saul had observed about the wounds, how they indicated the stabbing happened after Galeri was dead. 'I believe he was poisoned, and his body hidden while the killer sought a way to get the corpse out of the convent. I suspect someone else found Galeri, and attacked him with a blade.'

'But – why stab a dead man?' the abbess asked.

Aldo didn't have an answer for that. Not yet.


Strocchi approached the Podestà, hoping his suspicions were wrong. Benedetto and another constable stood guard outside the entrance. Benedetto had been with the Otto for only a few months, yet his initial enthusiasm was already souring. Officers could fill their pouches with coin from rewards and bounties, but constables had few such chances. Progressing to officer took years, if it happened at all. Some men moved to other, less demanding courts – Florence had dozens, each with jurisdiction over a different aspect of life. Others embraced laziness, corruption or bitterness. Benedetto had chosen the last of these.

Strocchi forced a smile as he reached the gates. 'Benedetto, are you busy?'

Benedetto glanced along the road. Few people were visible as the late afternoon sun sunk behind the looming Podestà walls. 'What does it look like to you?'

'That you can spare a few moments. I need to ask some questions.' Strocchi led him inside to the courtyard. Benedetto slumped onto a stone bench against a wall.

'Well?'

'I'm trying to discover what happened to Cerchi,' Strocchi said.

'Since when do constables investigate murders?'

'The *segretario* told me to, after I found the body and brought him proof.' Benedetto scowled, as if nothing would satisfy him. 'The last time anyone saw Cerchi was a Thursday in January,' Strocchi continued, 'five days after the feast of the Epiphany.

Aldo and I had been out of the city. We came back late that afternoon.'

'And?'

Strocchi didn't want to push Benedetto into a false answer. He might concoct a tale just to play the *diavolo*. 'Before he disappeared, Cerchi was busy with an investigation of his own. I've heard he was asking constables about people they knew.'

Benedetto frowned. 'What was Cerchi investigating?'

'That doesn't matter. Did he ask you any questions?'

'If it doesn't matter, why are you talking to me about it now, two months later?'

Strocchi couldn't tell Benedetto the whole truth, not when he wasn't sure himself. But he could offer some of it, and see where that led. 'I've tried everything, and got nowhere. Bindi is ready to end the investigation. This is all I've got left.' Strocchi sunk down on the bench beside Benedetto. 'Cerchi could be a *bastardo*, but he was murdered and that deserves investigating. Otherwise, what are we for?'

The guard they had left by the gates was calling for Benedetto. The constable got back to his feet. 'Standing sentry is all I'm good for, according to Bindi.'

Strocchi watched Benedetto stroll away, frustrated but also relieved. Maybe it was better if Bindi ended the investigation. Nobody was mourning Cerchi, and nobody cared who killed him. Maybe it was best to forget, to leave this matter to rest.

Benedetto paused, turning back to Strocchi. 'I can't remember what day it was, but Cerchi did ask me a lot of questions not long before he disappeared. Took me to a tavern and got me drunker than I've ever been. It was strange, I'd always thought he despised me . . .'

'What did you talk about?'

'Can't remember. All I know is he kept asking me about one person.'

Strocchi feared the answer but still asked the question. 'Who?'

'Aldo. Cerchi kept asking me about Aldo.'


Aldo presented his strongest arguments, but Testardo responded with derision. 'You have no evidence. Just the word of some Jewish doctor, and an apothecary misplacing a measure of poison.' He brandished the prioress's confession. 'This woman has admitted to murder.'

'Then where is the knife?' Aldo asked. 'Where is the blade she used to kill him?'

The monsignor nodded. 'Finally, some sense from your mouth.' He loomed over the prioress. 'Well? Where is this blade?'

'Hidden,' she said. 'I will tell you where, but only if you end this investigation now.'

'You are in no position to strike bargains,' Testardo retorted.

The prioress folded her arms but said nothing. It was clear the monsignor would get no further with her. They were threads from the same tapestry, each as stubborn as the other. Testardo rounded on the abbess instead. 'The prioress shares a dormitory with other chapter nuns, but she used to have a private cell, didn't she?'

'Yes,' the abbess said. 'She asked for that to be given to her sister, Violante.'

Testardo strode to the door, pulling it open. 'Father Zati, Signor Cortese!' The two men appeared. They must have been lurking outside, listening. 'Go to the private cells, and find the one occupied by Suor Violante.'

'No!' The prioress rose from her seat, fear invading her face. 'You can't do that.'

The monsignor ignored her. 'Search the cell. I believe you will find the blade used to murder Signor Galeri.'

Zati and Cortese nodded their understanding before leaving.

'Call those men back,' the prioress said, but the monsignor ignored her. She turned to the abbess. 'Please, we have our differences, but Violante – those men can't go to her cell.'

'Why not?' the abbess asked.

The prioress collapsed to the floor. 'She's ill –'

Aldo watched her crumple. The prioress had been as stern as a statue until now. Why was she . . .? Then the pieces fell into place. Aldo pushed past Testardo. 'Where are you going?' the monsignor snapped.

'Violante is why the prioress confessed,' Aldo said. 'It was to protect her sister. She believes Violante killed Galeri!'

Testardo's eyes widened. 'What if she still has the knife? What will she do with it?'

Aldo ran for the stairs. He took them two at a time, ignoring the pain in his left knee. Reaching the upper level, he sprinted towards the private cells. Ahead, Zati stood by a doorway as Cortese pushed his way inside.

'Stop!' Aldo shouted at them.

But it was too late.

# Chapter Twenty-six

he sound of a man screaming always cut Aldo cold. A woman's scream was disturbing, but the scream of a man was somehow worse. It was unnatural to the ear, an unnerving collision of surprise and distress. Women suffered pain too often, they seemed to have a tolerance for it few men possessed. When a man screamed, it was a fresh torment for most of them. Their cry came from discovering how fragile life was. Women had no such illusions.

Aldo had heard the screams of men while a soldier, both from the enemy and from those fighting alongside him. It came with the pain of blade and bolt piercing flesh, the cracking of bones and the tearing of skin. It came from the heart and it came from the *palle*. It burst from men's mouths, eerie and high-pitched. It sounded like nothing else.

That was how Cortese sounded.

Before Aldo could reach Violante's cell, he saw a glinting blade flash through the air – once, twice, a third time. Then Cortese was screaming, staggering backwards, his hands flapping at the air. He twisted round, the reason for his distress revealed. His right cheek had been cut open, skin sagging below the wound, a glimpse of teeth visible through the gap. Cortese's right hand was also cut deep into the flesh below the thumb. His tunic had been sliced open, a red line livid across his pale chest.

Cortese fell into the priest's arms, both of them tumbling to the floor. The screams died away, replaced by Cortese coughing a crimson mist into the air, scarlet spattering a nearby wall. Zati whispered a prayer, hands shaking as he comforted Cortese.

Aldo stopped, aware of Testardo behind him. 'Stay back,' he hissed, willing the monsignor to listen. For once, it worked. 'Stay still. All of you. Let me go in.'

None of the men sought to stop him.

Aldo moved closer to the doorway. Violante was kneeling inside the cell, a bloody blade in one hand, her breviary in the other. She was tall, and strong of build. Aldo could see a resemblance to the prioress in her face. Yet where her older sister bore a scowl, Violante was angelic. Her eyes were wide, cheeks rounded and rosy. But the blood across her face was proof of something else, as were the frantic prayers.

Reaching the doorway, Aldo lowered himself to one knee. She had cut Cortese when he had burst into her sanctuary. Safer to enter slowly, carefully. If Violante was startled, there was no knowing where that blade might go. Aldo edged forward, hands down by his sides.

'May I come in?'

She did not reply, but her muttering ceased. There was the smallest of nods.

'Thank you,' Aldo said, keeping his voice to a gentle murmur. He moved inside. The cell was small, with a single narrow cot. Large, lurid paintings dominated the walls. Angels and cherubim danced on one side, while demons and *diavoli* writhed across the others.

Aldo wondered where she had found the pigment – perhaps the scriptorium? – until he saw the circle of crimson dotted around Violante on the stone floor. The cuts to her hands removed any doubt. The abbess had said Violante sometimes hurt herself. No wonder Cortese's sudden intrusion had led to bloodshed. Knowing her history, Aldo doubted the convent let Violante keep a blade. The question of where the knife in her hand came from, and whether it was the one used on Galeri, could wait. All that mattered was getting the blade from her without any more bloodshed.

'I know you don't want to hurt anyone. I believe your only wish is to be left to pray and paint and devote yourself to our Lord, yes?'

She nodded again.

'For that to happen, you need to empty your hands.'

Violante stared up at the high wooden ceiling.

'You are in pain. Let me help, if I can.'

She lowered her gaze, seeing Aldo for the first time.

'Will you let me help you?'

Violante nodded.

'Then you need to empty your hands.'

Slowly, with great care, she lowered the breviary to the stone floor.

'Good. Now . . . the other hand.'

Violante hesitated before lowering the bloody knife to the floor.

'You can let go now,' Aldo whispered. 'It can't hurt anyone anymore.' Someone moved behind him, distracting Violante. Aldo reached back, pushing the door shut. 'It's just us here. You can do this.' Aldo smiled at her. 'I believe in you.'

She lifted her trembling hand from the knife, small drops of blood falling on the blade. Aldo waited until Violante was upright once more before speaking.

'I'm going to take it away from you. May I do that?'

The nun nodded, tears running streaks through the blood on her face.

'Thank you.' Aldo leaned forward, slowly reaching out one hand. His eyes never left those of Violante as he closed his fingers round the knife. He slid it back across the floor. There were two letters cut into the handle, near where it met the blade: *BG* – Bernardo Galeri. So he had brought the knife into the convent, not knowing it would be turned on him later that night. Aldo slid the blade up into his tunic sleeve, out of sight.

'It isn't mine,' she said. Her voice was gentle, almost childlike. 'Someone pushed it under the door while I was praying.'

Aldo glanced over one shoulder. There was a narrow gap between the door and the floor, enough for a blade to slide through. 'When was this? Yesterday?'

'Today. Not long after sext.' Violante rested a hand on her breviary. 'I say the midday prayers here. I had not long finished when . . .' Her words died away.

If she was telling the truth, this blade had to be the one used on Galeri. Zati and Cortese must have been close to finding it, so whoever had the knife sought to shift the blame by pushing it under Violante's door. Maybe they hoped she might use the blade on herself – or anyone coming to her cell. It was a shrewd *strategia*. Lashing out at Cortese had turned Violante into the obvious suspect for Galeri's murder. No wonder the prioress made her false confession. She must have visited her sister, seen the blade and believed Violante was a killer. The prioress offered herself to save her sister.

Retrieving her breviary, Violante retreated to the cot. 'I want to be with my sister.'

Aldo stood, knees creaking. Perched on her bed, Violante seemed no threat to anyone but herself. Hard to believe she had stabbed Galeri so many times. Very hard indeed.

\* \* \*

The abbess almost fainted when she saw Signor Cortese. The cuts to his hand and chest would heal, but the wound to his cheek . . . To witness such horrors once in a convent was unheard of; to see bloodshed twice in two days . . . What sins had been committed to visit such devilment upon this place? And what consequences would that bring?

Testardo was helping Father Zati get Cortese to his feet, hands pressed to the poor man's face where the blade had done its worst. The monsignor locked eyes with the abbess as he passed, leading Zati and Cortese away. Enclosure would not be enough to save them now. Testardo would see the convent dissolved within days, if not sooner.

The abbess heard someone approaching. 'Is my sister hurt?' the prioress asked.

'I don't know,' the abbess admitted, unable to lift her gaze from Cortese's blood on the floor. The wall needed washing too. One of the servant nuns could be asked, but the abbess wanted to do it herself. She needed to find some way of being useful.

The door to Violante's cell opened and Aldo emerged. His face was impassive, giving away nothing of what he had seen. The prioress hurried to him. 'My sister, is she –?'

'She's hurt, but that will heal,' he replied. 'Violante is asking for you. If you can, keep her in there. It is better she stays where she is, for now.'

The prioress went into the cell, closing the door behind her. The abbess could hear muffled voices, the sounds of reassurance. Despite her flaws, the prioress loved her sister.

Aldo pulled a knife from inside his tunic sleeve. It was red with blood, the tip sharp and narrow. 'Saul was right,' Aldo murmured.

'Saul?' the abbess asked.

'The Jewish doctor who examined Galeri's body. He told me

what sort of knife was used to make all those wounds. This matches what he described.' Aldo showed her two letters cut into the handle, near the blade: *BG*. Bernardo Galeri.

'So Galeri brought his own knife into the convent – and Violante stabbed him with it.' She leaned against the nearest wall. 'That's why the prioress was so eager to confess.'

'Galeri was poisoned,' Aldo said. 'The stabbing came later, after he was already dead – and I do not believe Violante was responsible for either of those acts.'

The abbess struggled to untangle this twisted knot of violence. 'Then who –'

'That will have to wait.' Aldo strode for the staircase, the knife in his grasp. The abbess hurried after him.

'Where are you going?'

'To make Testardo see reason before he leaves,' Aldo replied. 'Otherwise Violante will be blamed for murder, and the true killer will escape justice.'


By the time Aldo reached the cloister, Testardo was stalking towards the convent entrance. Zati and Cortese were close behind, the wounded man clutching a bloody cloth to his face. Aldo tucked Galeri's knife inside his right boot for safekeeping. 'Wait!' he called, running after them. 'You're not taking Cortese to the infirmary?'

Testardo whirled round, crimson with anger. 'This visitation is at an end. Signor Cortese will go to the nearest *ospedale*. I am withdrawing us from the convent before anyone else is attacked.'

'Cortese forced his way into that cell on your orders,' Aldo said, catching up to the monsignor. Nuns were spilling out from the infirmary, the refectory and from other rooms, watching him and Testardo. Good. It might offer a chance to force the killer's hand.

'The abbess had told us that Suor Violante was not well. Cortese terrified her, so she lashed out. He should never have entered without another nun being present.'

'She attacked him!' the monsignor said. 'Just as Galeri was attacked here. I wouldn't be surprised if the same blade was used both times.' Testardo stared at Aldo's hands. 'Where is the knife? Tell me that nun no longer has it.'

'No, she surrendered it to me. The knife is safe,' Aldo insisted. 'Suor Violante says someone else pushed the knife under her door today, not long after sext. They wanted her to be blamed for what happened. But Galeri was poisoned. His stabbing—'

'Yes, I've heard what you think. That doesn't mean you're right.'

'I know who killed Galeri,' Aldo lied, raising his voice to ensure everyone nearby would hear him. 'Give me time and I'll find proof—'

'No!' Testardo's voice echoed around the courtyard. 'The investigation is done. I will report my findings to the archbishop tomorrow, and that shall be an end to this matter.'

'What will your report say?' Aldo asked.

'That Signor Galeri was murdered here, on diocesan property, by someone from within these walls.' Testardo grimaced. 'We do not have enough evidence to be certain who did this, so the convent as a whole must bear responsibility for it.'

*Palle!* It was much as Aldo had feared. At least the monsignor was not making a scapegoat of Violante. Being brought before the archbishop to face an accusation of murder would break what was left of her. 'And what will you recommend?'

Testardo tilted his chin upwards. 'Dissolution. This place has long been a sanctuary for women eager to undermine the authority of the archbishop. The previous abbess was a troublemaker, defying the will of the diocese for years. It is clear her successor is equally unable or unwilling to control the women of this place.' The monsignor glared at the nuns watching him from around the cloisters. 'The faithful of Santa Maria Magdalena shall be divided among whatever convents can house them – within Florence, or out in the Dominion. Boarding girls shall be moved to another order, or returned to their *famiglia*.' The monsignor surveyed the beautiful courtyard and stone cloister. 'There are several monastic orders in need of a new home. This could be just the place for them.'

'Perhaps,' Aldo said, 'but I imagine the Company of Santa Maria will object to its bond with this convent being so summarily severed.' Ruggerio would not be happy to see the confraternity lose the hiding place for its secrets, let alone risk those secrets being revealed.

'Perhaps,' Testardo agreed, 'but that influence only reaches so far. The archbishop prefers those who follow his judgement, rather than seeking to bend his will.' The monsignor gestured at Zati and Cortese to leave the convent. He watched them depart before glaring at Aldo. 'All members of the visitation must leave together.'

Aldo still had one last *stratagemma*. 'I wish to stay. My niece Isabella is here in the convent, but she is not a boarder.' The abbess approached them, a hand clasping the cross hanging from her neck. 'If the abbess is willing, I should like to talk with my niece, persuade Isabella to return to her *famiglia*. She can be quite headstrong.'

The abbess nodded. 'So long as Aldo departs before nightfall, I have no objection.'

'Very well,' the monsignor said, not bothering to hide his exasperation. 'Abbess, this convent remains enclosed by order of His Excellency, the Archbishop of Florence. No visitors are permitted within these walls without his permission, and none after sunset.'

'I understand,' she replied.

'Until a decision is made about the future of this convent, I recommend you keep Suor Violante confined to her cell – for the safety of everyone.'

'Of course.'

Testardo strode away. In moments he was gone, the door slamming shut behind him.

'So?' the abbess asked. 'Is the diocese dissolving us?' Aldo nodded. Her shoulders slumped. 'Then there is nothing more that can be done.'

'I still need to discover who killed Galeri,' Aldo said, 'and why. First, I need to talk with Isabella. Do you know where she is?'

'Still helping at the infirmary, I believe.'

'Thank you.' Aldo noticed all those who saw and heard his argument with Testardo were already gone, but what he had said went with them – especially his lie about knowing who killed Galeri. That would spread through the convent until it reached the murderer.

Aldo strolled to the infirmary. He had turned himself into a target. How long before the killer responded to that?

# Chapter Twenty-seven

Suor Giulia was waiting by the *officio* door when the abbess came in from the courtyard. 'Is it true?' the apothecary asked. 'Did Violante attack one of the visitors with a knife?'

The abbess nodded, but showed little other reaction. Leading the convent often sat heavy on her shoulders. Now she seemed crushed by the responsibility. Giulia wished there was some way she could lift the burden, but what she had to say would only add to it. The apothecary followed the abbess inside.

'I fear that . . . I know who gave her that knife.'

'Who?' the abbess asked.

'My apprentice, Maria Teodora.' Giulia told of her earlier encounter with the novice. 'I should have challenged her at the time but I was tired, and –' Giulia stopped. Regrets were wasted tears in her experience. 'I knocked at Violante's door. I heard praying, but she did not respond.'

'Where is Maria Teodora now?'

Giulia took the abbess to her workshop where the novice was sweeping the floor. The abbess abandoned her usual gentle approach. 'Maria Teodora, I understand you went to Suor Violante's cell earlier today. What were you doing there?'

The novice stopped sweeping, her gaze lowered. 'The prioress asked—'

'No,' the abbess cut in. 'You have heard what happened to one of the visitors?' Maria Teodora nodded. 'Tell us the truth. Why did you go to Suor Violante's cell?'

Maria Teodora burst into tears. Giulia took the broom, setting it aside. She found a clean cloth and gave it to her apprentice. 'You did not mean for anyone to get hurt, did you?'

The novice shook her head, tears still streaming down her rosy cheeks.

'You pushed the knife under Violante's cell door, yes?'

A nod.

'Who told you to do that?' Giulia asked. 'Who gave you the knife?'

Maria Teodora wiped her eyes before replying. 'If I say, do you promise not to tell her? She mustn't hear how you found out.'


Strocchi wandered the city, not noticing or caring where he was going. What Benedetto had said . . . Strocchi's suspicions had been growing a while, but he kept denying the possibility. Yet putting what Benedetto told Cerchi alongside what Fideli had witnessed . . .

Could Aldo be the man who had stabbed Cerchi on Ponte Vecchio, then pushed his body over the side of the bridge? The swollen winter waters had finished the job, carrying Cerchi downriver. It was a perfect murder, until an early spring flood dumped Cerchi's remains on the banks of the Arno, close to Ponte a Signa. Even then, the body was soon buried and forgotten, a poor soul laid to rest in the village graveyard. If Buffon had not taken Cerchi's silver buckle . . . if Strocchi had not recognized it when he went home . . . if, if, if. So many tiny moments, so many chances, all coming together to lead him to this apparent truth.

Strocchi remembered what he thought after uncovering Cerchi's remains: somehow all of this was meant to be, that it was a sign from God. Had that only been two days past? It seemed a lifetime ago. His arrogance that evening was shameful. As if God would reach down to help him attain a promotion. It had been nothing more than ill chance, fickle happenstance.

If Aldo killed Cerchi, that would explain his behaviour at the tavern. He seemed a man undone when told of the body's discovery. As if his certainty had been kicked away, leaving him to swing like a prisoner in a noose . . . And that story of Cerchi taking documents for a case before the Otto. Bindi refuted it, but the significance of that was only becoming clear now. Had Aldo even been ill the previous night? Or was he trying to flee the truth?

Then there was what Fideli heard Cerchi say, the phrase Strocchi had omitted from the witness statement. 'You did a good job of hiding your perversion,' Strocchi said out loud. Cerchi believed Aldo was a man who – Strocchi shook his head. No, he could not think about that. Not yet.

It would be curfew soon, and he was not far from home. Tomasia would help him understand all of this. Strocchi recalled what she had said as they neared the city gates, that Aldo could be responsible for Cerchi's death. Had she been joking? Or had she known what loyalty had made him too blind to see? Either way, Tomasia would know what to do.

She was in a chair by the window when Strocchi got home, the shutters open wide. 'You're back early,' she said, a smile spreading across her face. 'Had enough for one day, or unable to resist your new wife? Give me the right answer and you could be well rewarded.'

Strocchi wanted to join in her playfulness, but could not bring himself to do so. 'You were in Le Stinche with Aldo. What was he like there?'

Tomasia's smile faded. She did not enjoy talking about her months in the prison, kept there by her dead brother's debts. 'Why do you ask?'

'I need to know what kind of man Cesare Aldo is.'

She rose, closing the shutters. 'A man of honour.' Strocchi didn't understand what that meant, and said so. Tomasia sighed. 'Tell me why you need to know, and I'll explain.'

Strocchi recounted what Fideli heard and saw that night in January, and what Benedetto had said. Tomasia poured wine as she listened, bringing them both a cup. 'I don't want to believe Aldo capable of murder,' Strocchi said, 'but the more I think on it –'

Tomasia sipped her wine. 'Aldo saved my life in prison, and more.'

'How?' Strocchi asked.

'Are you sure you want to hear this?'

Strocchi nodded. Whatever Tomasia had to say, he needed to know.

'One of the others in the women's ward had stolen from me – I can't even recall what, though it seemed important enough at the time. I knew better than to walk the courtyard alone, women went everywhere in pairs. But I was angry enough to be foolish.' Tomasia put her cup down. 'There was a brute of a man called Maso. He dragged me into the condemned man's cell. I fought against him but he was too strong . . .'

Strocchi wished he hadn't asked now. 'You don't have to—'

'Aldo saved me, or he tried to. Nobody else came, not even when I screamed for help – not the guards, not the other inmates. But Aldo did. He got Maso away from me, and I ran.'

'Did Aldo . . . kill Maso?'

'No, that *bastardo* is still alive, but he won't be hurting anyone else.' Tomasia grimaced. 'I knew Maso would kill Aldo, so I went back and hit Maso with a stone. Last I heard he's still in the *ospedale* at Le Stinche, with the mind of child. I hope he rots there.'

Strocchi had known life inside Le Stinche was dangerous, but not how dangerous.

'Aldo was not there long,' Tomasia said, 'but he fought for his life more than once. He could kill a man, I'm sure. But from what I saw, he fought to save himself or others.'

'Is that why you suggested he might have killed Cerchi?'

'Did I?'

'Yes, when we were riding back from visiting Mama. I was so sure you were wrong, I even laughed. But now –' Strocchi sighed. 'And what about the rest of it, Cerchi accusing Aldo of perversion? I mean, this is Florence, a city full of sinners. I have arrested men like that as part of my duties for the Otto. I even read about such things once, in a murder victim's private diary. But I never thought that Aldo was . . .'

'Was what?' Tomasia asked. 'A man who lies with other men?'

Strocchi shuddered at that. It was wrong. Such acts, they went against everything he had been taught in church, against how he had been brought up. How could Aldo be such a man? Even if he did not believe as Strocchi did, it was still against the law. How could Aldo be an officer of the court, how could he enforce its laws, when who he was and what he did broke those laws? The constable had believed he was getting to know Aldo, to understand him. But that could not have been further from the truth.

Aldo lived his life outside the law – and outside the mercy of God's love.

Strocchi tried to explain all this to Tomasia, but kept stumbling over his words. 'How can I ever work with him again, knowing what I know – who he is, and what he is?'

'Which bothers you more?' she asked. 'You talk as if one is the equal of the other.'

'No, it's . . .' Strocchi sank onto their bed, not knowing what to think anymore. Tomasia came and sat beside him.

'When I was a girl,' she said, 'our parish priest was a kind man called Father Capire. He often gave sermons on the teachings of Jesus, how the son of God preached about love and tolerance. Jesus did not judge those who were sinners, Father Capire told us. Does it matter who Aldo loves? He is still the same man as he was before you heard this.'

'I know, but—'

'Perhaps the problem is not with Aldo,' Tomasia cut in. 'Perhaps it is with you.'

As ever, she could see through the clouds in his head, make sense of what was eluding him. 'Perhaps you are right. I need time to think about that. But what of Cerchi's murder?'

'Well, do you think Aldo is capable of murder?'

'I've seen what anger can do to him. I know he was a soldier before joining the Otto. To survive that you have to be capable of killing.' Strocchi remembered riding from Florence with Aldo in January while they hunted a killer. When they found him, Aldo let the murderer live – but only because that was the wish of Cosimo de' Medici. Strocchi had little doubt Aldo could have buried his stiletto in the killer's throat that night, without hesitation. 'Aldo would take a life if he had to, if he thought it necessary. But murder . . .'

Tomasia took Strocchi's hand in her own. 'There's another way to look at this, Carlo. Even if it was Aldo who stabbed Cerchi, you don't know what reason he had for doing that.'

'What justification could there be for murder?'

'After Maso attacked me in Le Stinche, I wanted to kill him. He was not a threat to me anymore, I had escaped. But when I hit him with that stone, I wanted to murder Maso.'

'You didn't.'

'I tried. Yes, I was saving Aldo's life. But I wanted Maso dead.'

'That was in prison,' Strocchi said. 'You were locked in Le Stinche with Maso and more men like him. You were defending yourself.'

'If Aldo killed Cerchi – and you don't have proof of that – what makes you think Aldo wasn't defending himself, or someone else? This Fideli told you what he heard, but it was months ago. You don't know enough to be certain of anything.'

She was right. As ever, Tomasia was right. 'So what do I do?'

'What do you have to do?'

'Bindi is expecting my report in the morning. If I don't have fresh evidence, he will end the investigation. I stay a constable. And whoever murdered Cerchi escapes the law.'

Tomasia pulled him closer. 'And do you have the evidence to convince Bindi?'

'Not yet.'

'Then the investigation will end.'

'And what about Aldo?'

'What about him?' Tomasia turned Strocchi's face to her own. 'If you really want to know what happened, there's only one person alive that can answer your questions.'

Isabella was surprised when Aldo returned to the infirmary, more so that he was there to see her. She had spent the afternoon working alongside Suor Dea. It was exhausting but Isabella made herself a promise: when she got back to Palazzo Fioravanti – if she got home – she would look for ways to be helpful. That didn't mean she was in a rush to get married, and certainly not to some *grasso* old man, but Isabella could see now how easy her life had been. Maybe she could give something back . . .

Isabella was pondering what that might be when Aldo approached her. 'I don't have long,' he said, the words quiet. 'Is there somewhere we can talk?'

'The refectory. The abbess cancelled all classes, it should be empty.' She led him along the cloister to the refectory. Inside, Isabella pointed to double doors at the far end. 'Those go to the kitchen, but the next meal is after vespers so we won't be disturbed.'

They sat either side of a table, Aldo studying her for a few moments. 'Is something wrong?' Isabella asked. 'Have I got something on my face?'

'No,' he replied. 'I was . . . You look like your mama when she was your age, but you are different from her in many ways. Teresa was a happy girl, but she could not withstand her mama. Lucrezia always got her way. Always.'

Isabella shook her head. '*Nonna* doesn't frighten me,' she lied. 'Were you the cause of all that shouting out in the cloister?'

Aldo told her some of what had happened since their last meeting, though Isabella knew he was keeping part of it back. He chose his words with too much care. Even so, Isabella could see the convent would not stay a refuge much longer. 'What will happen?'

'Some of the nuns may return to Le Murate, in the western quarter. The rest will be scattered among other convents, some outside Florence.'

Isabella hoped Dea was not be banished from the city. And what would happen to classes if Suor Catarina was sent away?

That was all in the past, it seemed. If *Nonna* got her way, there would be no more classes. A wedding, the marriage bed and raising children was all Isabella could expect. That, and being a widow. There must be more to life, surely?

Suor Rigarda came through the kitchen doors, carrying a plain pottery jug, cup and plate. She seemed surprised to see Aldo in the refectory. 'You're here,' she said, bringing the jug, cup and plate over to put down beside Aldo. There were three small sugar and almond cakes on the plate, alongside pieces of candied quince. 'The abbess thought you had not eaten or drunk all day. She asked kitchen staff to bring something to the refectory, in case you were hungry.' Rigarda held up a scrap of paper with 'For Cesare Aldo' written on it.

'Thank you.' Aldo smiled at her. 'You're not working at the infirmary anymore?'

'I asked for new duties,' Rigarda said before returning to the kitchen. Aldo tried a cake, but it crumbled in his hand. 'Be careful,' Isabella said. 'The food isn't very good.'

'It's a convent,' Aldo replied. 'You can't expect much if they don't have much.' He pushed the candied quince around the plate. 'With the visitation withdrawing, I have to leave soon myself. I want you to come with me.'

'Why?'

'It isn't safe here. I should not have let you come inside last night, it was a mistake. I thought you would be in no danger, but they may know we are related. That puts you at risk.'

Isabella shook her head. 'Why would someone hurt me?'

Aldo told her about his announcing that he knew who the killer was. 'I hoped it might force them into action. But I may have made you a target too.'

She sighed. 'If I leave the convent, where will I go? I cannot return home. *Nonna* would have me married before the end of Holy Week.'

Aldo lifted a piece of cake to his lips, but his nose wrinkled at its odour. He returned the cake to the plate, pushing it aside.

'Could I come and stay with you?' Isabella asked. She knew nothing about Aldo's home, but it had to be better than her flea-riddled mattress in the dormitory upstairs. 'Until Mama and Papa agree to postpone the wedding.'

'I don't think so, Isabella.'

'Where do you live?'

'Oltrarno.'

Not the most respectable of quarters, but her friend Chola said it was becoming more popular, thanks to all the artisans living there. 'That wouldn't be a problem.'

'Perhaps, but the house where I live . . .' Aldo seemed unsure how to continue. 'It's not suitable for a young woman from a respectable *famiglia*.'

'Why not?'

'It's a *bordello*.'

The word sounded familiar, but Isabella could not recall why. 'A *bordello*?'

Aldo rolled his eyes. 'It's where men go to – to –'

Then Isabella remembered. 'Oh!' Chola had told her about such places, and the sort of men who visited them. It sounded . . . 'You live there?'

'Yes.'

'But why?'

'It suits me. I have an arrangement with the *matrona*. I get a room for a few *giuli*, and she has an officer of the court as her tenant. It means no man ever causes trouble.' Aldo poured wine into his cup. 'You understand why that wouldn't be suitable for you, yes?'

She nodded.

Aldo sipped the wine. 'The nuns may not cook well, but this is very good.' He drained the cup, and poured another. 'So, will you come with me when I leave?'

Isabella didn't know what to say. Though she found it hard to believe, Aldo seemed certain that staying at the convent any longer would put her in danger. But going home to Palazzo Fioravanti meant marriage to some bloated old man. Perhaps the Contarina *famiglia* would let her stay a few nights? Chola was her best friend, after all. Yes, that might be the answer . . .

The cup dropped from Aldo's grasp, spilling wine across the table. He stared at his fingers, as if unable to understand what was happening.

'What's wrong?'

'My hands . . . going numb . . .'

'Why would they—'

'Poison,' Aldo gasped, one arm flailing at the jug on the table. 'Aconitum . . .' He slumped sideways before sliding to the floor. Isabella got up, unsure how to help. Aldo doubled over, hands clutching at his belly. 'I'll get Suor Simona!' she volunteered.

'No –' Aldo gasped. 'Find – Suor Giulia –'


Giulia was outside her workshop talking with the abbess when a girl in a pale blue dress burst through the doors from the courtyard. 'You have to come! Aldo's been poisoned!'

Giulia hurried after her, the abbess close behind. The girl led them to the refectory where Aldo was sprawled. He had vomited across the floor, a purple puddle beside him. Wine was dripping from a table. Giulia knelt beside Aldo, listening for any sound.

He was breathing – just.

But when she pulled back his eyelids, only the whites were showing. His lips were stained by the wine, but the rest of his face was drained of colour. 'Aldo, can you hear me?'

He did not reply.

Giulia sat back. The girl was standing to one side, clasping and unclasping her hands. She must be his niece, Isabella. 'You said he was poisoned. What makes you think that?'

'He told me before –' She gestured at him.

'Did he say anything else?'

'A word I hadn't heard before . . .'

'Aconitum?'

She nodded. 'Does that help?'

Not really, but Giulia wasn't going to admit that. 'Did he eat or drink anything?'

'Just a cup of wine.'

Giulia dipped a finger into what was dripping from the table. She sniffed it, but there was nothing unusual in the smell. She put the finger to her tongue –

'Careful,' the abbess said.

Giulia tasted the wine, then spat it back out. Something had been dissolved in it. 'Why poison him now?' Giulia murmured. 'The visitation has gone.'

Isabella answered. 'Aldo told me about announcing he knew who killed that man. He thought turning himself into a target might make a difference.'

'And it did,' Giulia said, shaking her head at Aldo's foolishness.

Isabella approached the abbess. 'Suor Rigarda brought the wine and cakes. She said you asked her to because Aldo hadn't eaten or drunk all day.'

'I did no such thing,' the abbess insisted. 'We must find out who—'

'That can wait,' Giulia said. 'We need to help Aldo first. Isabella, go to the infirmary. Tell Suor Simona what has happened.'

The girl dashed from the refectory. The abbess came closer. 'What can you do?'

'He's already got most of the tainted wine out of his belly, but there is no treatment for aconitum poisoning,' the apothecary replied. 'Aldo's survival depends on how much he swallowed, and how strong his will to live is.'

'Is there nothing else we can do?'

'What we do best: pray.'

# Chapter Twenty-eight

❦

## Wednesday, March 28th 1537

*T*he abbess made no attempt to sleep. She had prayed for hours. When prayers were not enough, she sought answers. She could not remain idle while the convent waited to be dissolved. In the past, the abbess would have sought help from the prioress. Despite their disagreements, they made a strong pair when working towards a common purpose. But the prioress was busy caring for her sister. So the abbess woke Suor Giulia early to ask for her help. She was the one who had seen Maria Teodora leaving Violante's cell. Besides, there were few others the abbess trusted to stay silent about what might be uncovered. Giulia had kept her husband's name secret for years; she would not indulge in refectory gossip.

They worked from the apothecary workshop. It was smaller, and less intimidating than the abbess's *officio*. The workshop was alive with scents and spices – nutmeg and cinnamon, the sweetness of honey and the florid fragrance of rosewater. It also had a sturdy door that fit well in its frame – a quality that kept conversations inside the workshop private.

Suor Rigarda was first to be brought from her bed for questioning, though she seemed not to have slept. The servant nun was distraught about the poisoned wine. 'I did not know,' she insisted, eyes red-rimmed from crying. 'The message came from you, Abbess.'

'What message?' Giulia asked.

'A note came to the kitchen. It was my first day helping there. The others were busy cooking, so I found some cakes and wine.'

'Do you still have the note?'

Nodding, Rigarda reached inside her sleeve. 'I tucked it here, for safekeeping.' Giulia took the note, handing the parchment to the abbess. It had been written in haste, ink blotting the page. That suggested the poisoning was devised without thought for the consequences.

'This was not written by my hand,' the abbess said. 'And this parchment – I believe it comes from the scriptorium, not my desk.'

'But the scriptorium is still closed,' Rigarda said.

The door was closed, but it had no lock. 'Who brought this to the kitchen?'

'I did not see, abbess.' Rigarda was close to tears again.

Giulia rested a hand on the servant nun's shoulder. 'You have done nothing wrong. But if there is poison in any more of the convent's wine, we need to know so it can be poured away. Where did you find the wine that you took into the refectory?'

'I didn't. Maria Vincenzia offered to fetch some for me. She would know.'

'Then we shall ask her,' the abbess said. 'Thank you for your honesty, Suor Rigarda. Please keep what we have discussed here to yourself.'

'Of course.'

Giulia ushered Rigarda out. When the apothecary returned, her face had the anger of a thundercloud. 'Maria Vincenzia. Why am I not surprised?'

The abbess nodded. 'You warned the prioress and myself about her. Perhaps if we had listened –' Maria Vincenzia must know the poisoned wine would soon lead to her. She would be preparing her excuses. Let her wait. There were others with questions to answer. 'Giulia, find your new apprentice and bring her here.'

The apothecary soon returned with Maria Teodora. The novice stared at the floor, unable to look either nun in the eye. The abbess was angry, but knew letting that show would not help. There was one chair in the workshop, a plain wooden seat. The abbess brought it to the novice, smiling at her. Maria Teodora sank onto it, fingers working her rosary beads.

'I – I didn't know what would happen,' she stammered. 'That poor man – I never meant anyone to be hurt. I didn't know – I didn't know –'

She broke down, and it took Giulia time to calm the novice. Eventually, she was able to answer questions. Yes, she had pushed the knife under the door. No, it hadn't been her idea. No, she didn't know where the knife had come from, or whose it was.

'Tell us, who gave you the knife?' Giulia asked in a soft, quiet voice. 'Who told you what to do with it?'

The novice shook her head. 'She'll know if I say.'

The abbess crouched by the chair. 'You don't have to tell us. All you need do is nod when we say the name of the person who gave you the knife. Do you understand?'

'Y-Yes . . .'

'Was it Maria Vincenzia?'

The novice hesitated before nodding.

'Did she tell you what to do with the knife?'

A second nod.

'And did she tell you what to say if somebody challenged you?'

A third nod.

The abbess got back to her feet. 'I know that can't have been easy. Thank you.'

The novice's face was full of doubt. 'How can I ever be forgiven for what I've done?'

'You must confess what you did to Father Visconti, and make whatever act of contrition he deems suitable. Our Lord knows your heart is pure, that you never intended anyone to be hurt.' The abbess exchanged a grimace with Giulia. 'The Lord will forgive you, as he forgives all of us sinners. Now, and at the hour of our death.'

'Amen,' Giulia said.

Maria Teodora made the sign of the cross. 'Amen.'

'There is something you must do for us,' the abbess said. 'As part of your penance.'


Isabella spent the night at Aldo's bedside, away from the other patients. She was accustomed to praying, had grown up mumbling and muttering her way through the usual dull words in church, but never paying much attention. She believed, everyone believed. But her own prayers had always been frivolous lists of wishes and hopes. Now she was praying for someone else, a man she had known only a few days. Praying for him to live.

She dozed off at times – even God couldn't expect her to stay awake all night – but when awake, Isabella did her best to keep praying. Suor Simona came to Aldo's cot often to see how he was, while Suor Giulia visited twice while it was dark outside. Isabella couldn't see any change in Aldo. His skin was as pale as old bread soaked in water, and his breathing little more than a low rasp, but Suor Giulia gave a reassuring smile both times she visited.

It was Aldo's mutterings that woke Isabella. She straightened up, her back and neck protesting at having been slumped on an old wooden chair for so long. The first glimmers of a new day were beginning to light the courtyard.

'I'd do it again,' Aldo murmured, his words startling her. 'I'd do it again . . .'

Isabella found a small bowl of water and a cloth by the cot. One of the servant nuns must have left it. Noticing Aldo's lips were cracked and dry, Isabella used the cloth to moisten them before pressing it to his forehead. 'Saul,' he whispered. 'Saul —'

Why would Aldo be thinking of the Jewish doctor? The two were friends, and Dr Orvieto had been kind to her when there was no need to be. She hoped the doctor was being a comfort to Aldo as he slept. If only there was something she could do . . .

'It was necessary,' Aldo sighed as she removed the damp cloth. Isabella returned it to the bowl, and clasped her fingers together, ready to pray for him again. 'Necessary,' he said again, the knuckles on his hand tightened until the skin stretched taut across them.

Isabella made the sign of the cross.


Giulia had stayed with the abbess until matins, discussing what they might do next. Finally, the abbess had sent Giulia to rest. But no sleep came, thanks to the rumble of Suor Paulina's snoring in the next cell but one. It was almost a relief when the abbess tapped on the cell door. Giulia followed her downstairs. Maria Teodora was waiting for them below.

'She's still in there,' the novice whispered.

Giulia wanted to ask who, but the abbess did not linger. She marched along the corridor, stopping outside the *latrina* door to push it open. Inside was dark, a single lit candle illuminating the long, narrow room. 'Come out,' the abbess called, 'and bring it with you.'

There was a long silence before Maria Vincenzia emerged, the sleeve of one arm held across her nose and mouth, a heavy pottery jar under her other arm.

'Give it to Suor Giulia,' the abbess commanded.

Scowling her reluctance, the novice relinquished the jar. Giulia peered inside. It held the missing aconitum. She pushed past Maria Vincenzia to look inside the *latrina*. The room was ripe with the smell of waste, but there was something else in the air, a familiar pinch at the nostrils. The tell-tale stain of poison lined each of the holes. The novice had been pouring it away, hoping to destroy the proof of her guilt.

'How did –?' Maria Vincenzia began. 'It was Teodora, wasn't it?'

'Why did you do it?' the abbess demanded.

'I don't know what you mean,' the novice replied.

'The poison, the wine you tainted for the visitor. He may not survive.'

'I don't have to answer that,' Maria Vincenzia announced. 'I shall be judged by a higher power than you.' She dismissed Giulia with a glance. 'Than either of you.'

'True,' the abbess agreed. 'But until that day comes you do answer to me, and to the rest of this convent. We shall judge what you did. Go to my *officio* and wait there.'

The novice stalked away, chin held high. Giulia had never seen such entitlement in a nun, let alone a novice. In her experience only men believed themselves so beyond reproach.

'I'm certain that one was responsible for some of what happened to Galeri,' the abbess said, 'but I still can't believe she killed him.

As arrogant as Maria Vincenzia is, even she would feel remorse for murder – wouldn't she?'

The apothecary wanted to believe the abbess was right.

But she couldn't be certain.

Aldo was lying in a field, both eyes closed. Warm summer breezes drifted across his face and arms, while the low hum of insects murmured in his ears. He wanted to get up – no, needed to get up – but was too heavy to rise from the ground. Why not lie here a little while longer? Why not rest and sleep and be at peace for once?

It was tempting. How long since he had last done this, had done nothing?

The warm air became colder. A thick cloud must have slid in front of the sun. Aldo opened his eyes, expecting to be on a hill-side, perhaps with the Arno meandering through the valley below, its lazy bends and curves sliding west towards Pisa . . .

Instead he was in a garden, long grass around him, wild flowers bowing and bending before the breeze. To the left Aldo could see trees laden with ripe fruit. To the right hung a washing line in the air, pure white shifts and smocks flapping and snapping.

Aldo sat up. He was in a small courtyard, surrounded by towering stone walls.

'Thirsty?' a woman's voice asked from behind him.

He was parched, his throat dry and sore. 'Yes,' he replied, croaking out the word.

A hand reached over his shoulder, offering a cup. Aldo took it, and red wine poured into the cup from above. Aldo twisted round to see who was there, but shadows hid her face. She kept pouring, wine overflowing the cup, running across his hand.

Aldo wanted her to stop but couldn't seem to speak, his mouth too dry. The grass sunk into the ground, replaced by a rising tide of red wine. No, not wine – blood. It caught the hems of the clothes hanging from the line, soaking them a vivid scarlet.

Hands pulled Aldo down into the blood, grasping his arms and legs, fingernails clawing his tunic and hose. He fought to stay above the rising red, gasping for one last breath of air – then he was falling into scarlet depths. He thrashed against the grabbing hands. A face loomed from the murk – Galeri, grinning and nodding. Aldo closed both eyes, denying this madness. When he looked again, Galeri was gone – Cerchi in his place. Cerchi reached inside Aldo's left boot, pulling out his stiletto. Cerchi stabbed it deep into Aldo's chest –

Aldo screamed.

Isabella's eyes were becoming too heavy to keep them open any longer. She was sure Aldo wouldn't mind, not if she had a short nap. He wasn't going anywhere . . .

Aldo jerked upright on the cot, startling her awake. He gasped in air, hands clawing at his own chest. Most terrifying of all were Aldo's eyes, glaring at her in accusation. 'What?' Isabella asked. 'What is it, what's wrong?' He didn't reply but kept staring, mouth opening and closing without saying any words.

Isabella was about to call for help when Aldo's eyes rolled back into his head. His body collapsed on the cot, arms flopping over each side. She rose from her chair, unsure if he was breathing. Was he even still alive? She had never seen somebody die before, was that how it happened? Isabella edged closer, listening for any sound, any noise.

Aldo's body started to spasm and twitch, his torso bouncing

atop the cot, arms flailing in the air. Isabella shrunk back, not knowing what to do. She twisted round, searching the infirmary for Dea. There was no sign of the servant nun, but Suor Simona was resting on an empty cot, turned away from Aldo. Isabella ran to the infirmarian, shaking her awake.

'Suor Simona, you must come. It's Aldo, he's –' Isabella realized she didn't know what was happening to him. 'Please, you have to help.'

One glance at Aldo and the infirmarian was up, hurrying towards him. Simona pushed Aldo back down onto the cot. 'Get over here,' she commanded Isabella. 'We have to hold him down until this passes so he can't hurt himself.'

Isabella hurried to help Simona, but by the time she got there, whatever had taken hold of Aldo was gone. His body ceased fighting against the infirmarian, slumping into the sweat-soaked mattress. Simona released him, caution in her face. 'Is he better?' Isabella asked.

'He is in our Lord's hands now,' Simona replied. 'Let us pray for his safe return.' As she spoke Aldo rolled onto one side, both legs folding up into his torso. He was shivering, hands clenched into fists under his chin.

Aldo was on his knees, a cold stone floor beneath him. The blood was gone, Cerchi was gone, the stiletto – Aldo's hands clutched his chest, but found no blade. He had been captured by some sinister *incubo*; it was tormenting him with impossible things . . .

Shoes clip-clopped towards him. He was kneeling in the convent cloister. A sickle moon threw blue light across the nearby grass, turning the lavender grey. Aldo expected to see a nun approaching. Instead, it was Isabella, solemn in her pale dress. As she got nearer, he realized it was Teresa, not Isabella. Cares and worries ravaged her face, aging her. The steady sound of her shoes slowed, becoming the stab of a walking stick as it struck the stone floor. Teresa's kind face curdled, sagging and souring, becoming another he knew all too well.

Lucrezia.

She stopped short of him, leaning on her stick. 'You are not fit to use my husband's name,' she hissed. 'You were a mistake. A moment with some *puttano* slave, up an alleyway while a bonfire burned the vanities of this city.'

'You're not real,' Aldo whispered.

'*Bastardo*,' Lucrezia spat before stamping away. 'They should have burned you when you fell out of your mother. It would have spared your father from dying of shame . . .'

A weapon slid across the stone, stopping in front of Aldo. It was his stiletto, fresh blood glistening on the blade. 'Is that what you used?' Aldo knew that voice.

'Carlo—'

'Don't use the name my mama gave me,' Strocchi snarled. Angry. Righteous. Betrayed. 'Answer me. Is that what you used to murder Cerchi?'

'I didn't have any choice –'

He loomed over Aldo, kicking the stiletto closer. 'For once, tell me the truth.'

'Yes.' Aldo closed a hand round the stiletto. 'And I'd do it again.'

The constable backed away, out of Aldo's reach. He retreated into the cloister wall, the stone closing around him. Like water claiming a corpse . . .

# Chapter Twenty-nine

Strocchi rolled from the bed. He was tired of staring at the ceiling, and exhausted by watching the first signs of morning creep through the shutters at the far end of the room. Tomasia turned over as he pulled on a tunic. 'Found another woman, have you? Better not be Signora Pesante from downstairs.' Their land-lady was as wide as she was tall, with a face that scared passing children. Normally mention of her would make Strocchi smile, but not this morning.

'Can't sleep,' he replied, slumping on a chair. 'Thought I'd let you rest.'

'Carlo, please. If you're awake, I'm awake – and you've been awake all night.'

She was right, as ever. Strocchi had turned over and over, but the questions in his head wouldn't lie still. 'Sorry.'

Tomasia pulled herself to a sitting position, rubbing her eyes. 'You're still deciding what to do about Cerchi and Aldo and Bindi.'

'No matter what I do, someone will suffer.'

'Who will suffer if you don't tell Bindi what you know?'

'I don't know anything. I suspect – but I don't know. It might be easier if I did.'

'You're not answering my question, Carlo. Who would suffer?'

He shrugged. 'I'm not sure anyone would. But –'

'But?'

'A man was killed. Doesn't that deserve justice?'

'So, you go to the Podestà, you make a *denunzia* against Aldo for what you think he might have done. You hand that to Bindi – then what? What purpose does it serve, beyond being a salve for your wounded sense of morality?'

Strocchi was stung by her words. 'Is that truly what you think of me?'

'No, of course not. But you've spent the whole night agonizing over this, and you are no closer to knowing your own mind. I'm trying to make you see that.' She swung her legs off the bed. 'Are you sure it is Cerchi's killing that is disturbing you most?'

'It is,' Strocchi replied. He had chosen to set aside what Cerchi had said about Aldo, the kind of man he was. That could wait for another time. Perhaps it was cowardice to ignore such a thing, but there were more urgent concerns for today. 'Cerchi was murdered, that's what matters. I know he was extorting coin from the man he met on Ponte Vecchio – a man who may well have been Aldo. What Fideli heard, what Benedetto told me, those are enough to make Bindi continue the investigation.'

'I thought you wanted justice,' Tomasia said.

She had an ability to find the weaknesses in any argument. It was infuriating at times – but it was also one of the many qualities Strocchi loved about her. Tomasia would make an excellent officer, if the court ever allowed women such roles.

'There won't be any justice if the investigation ends today,' Strocchi said.

'Not for Cerchi, but you've told me often how much a *bastardo* he was. How he bullied people, even drove one man to his death. You told me nobody mourns that man. Will denouncing Aldo bring Cerchi back? Will it make the city safer, or a more just place?'

Strocchi knew she was right, but murder was still murder. 'If a life is wrongly taken, there should be consequences.'

'There should be, but that's not always the case. Not in this city.' She came over to him. 'What if Aldo killed Cerchi to defend himself, or others? Would that be justifiable?'

'It would depend on the circumstances, but – yes.'

'Then how can you accuse Aldo when you don't know all the circumstances? Doesn't Aldo deserve a chance to explain what happened?'

Strocchi could only nod. 'But the *segretario* is expecting me early this morning.'

Tomasia gave him a hug. 'Then it's simple: find a way to delay the *segretario* until you can talk to Aldo.'

'Bindi won't tolerate that.'

'Or share what you know with Bindi, and let him determine what happens next.'

Neither appealed to Strocchi. 'Aren't there any other choices?'

'Yes.' She kissed him, her tongue slipping between his lips. 'Come back to bed.'


The prioress stared at the small window high up in her sister's cell. The sky was brightening at last, signalling the end of a long night's vigil. But the prioress knew there were many such nights ahead. Violante was asleep, bandages covering the cuts to her hands left by the knife. Other bindings ensured she could not leave the narrow cot. The prioress hated to see her sister tied down, but for now it was better to be safe. Better for everyone.

Violante stirred, her eyes opening.

'Shhh,' the prioress whispered, kneeling by the cot. 'You're in your cell.'

Violante tried to rise but the restraints held her down. Tears brimmed in her eyes before sliding down her face. 'So it was true. I didn't dream that—'

'No.' The prioress rested a hand on her sister's brow. 'But you have nothing to fear, not anymore. I'm here, and I will not leave you again.'

Violante turned her face to the wall. 'You've said that before.'

'I'm sorry,' the prioress said. For years – too many years – she had broken promises to Violante. Ambition and pride and all her other sins had tempted her with the chance to become Abbess. Violante was the one who suffered. She was the one who had been neglected and forgotten. She was the one whose cries for help went unheard.

And this was the cost of that neglect. Locked away in a cell. Tied to a bed. Forever to be known as the nun who cut open a man's face when all Violante had wanted was love and a sanctuary from the world. Now she would always be judged, wherever she went.

The prioress blamed herself for all of that.

Penance must be paid.

She clasped her hands together. 'Lord, hear my prayer. I know my sister can never forget what I have done, that she may never forgive me my trespasses. But I pray one day to earn her love again. I pray to be worthy of that love.'

There was a long silence before Violante spoke. 'Did you mean that?'

'Yes.' The prioress closed her eyes. 'I have deceived you many times, and myself even more. But you know I would never lie to our Lord.'

Violante turned back from the wall. 'I do.'

'This convent will soon be dissolved. When that happens, I will see that we move to another outside the city. An enclosed house, secluded and safe. A place where you will be cared for, where you can be happy. No more being locked away. I want you to have the sun on your face.' The prioress paused. 'More than anything, I want to see you smile again.'

Aldo opened his eyes, not certain if he was awake. Dark shapes were looming over him, whispering to one another. He tried to speak but his throat was too raw. Something had clawed its way up from his belly to his mouth, emptying him out, leaving nothing but pain. A dull throbbing assaulted his head, forcing both eyes shut again.

'He's awake!' The voice was Isabella, Teresa's daughter. But why was she –?

The convent. The dead body, covered in wine. No, not wine – blood.

Aldo's belly rebelled. He lunged over the side of the bed as dry retching threatened to unman him, spasm after spasm. Finally, mercifully, the urge to empty himself ebbed away. He slumped back on the narrow cot, exhausted. *Palle*, what had he been drinking?

'You were poisoned,' Suor Giulia said. 'We didn't know how much you drank, weren't sure you would survive. Your body purged most of it. That probably saved you.'

'And I prayed for you,' Isabella said. 'All night. Well, most of the night.'

Aldo licked his lips. He was thirsty, but couldn't get the words out. Suor Simona dabbed his lips with a wet cloth, squeezing a few drops in his mouth. He swallowed. 'More,' he rasped. She repeated the action. 'Thank you,' he eventually said.

The infirmarian leaned back. 'Keep giving him water. Small sips at first. Then let him rest. I have other patients that need me.' She gave Aldo's left arm a brisk squeeze. 'It seems you will be with us a while longer. Our Lord must have decided it wasn't yet your time.'

The abbess took her place, bringing a cup of water. She slipped a hand behind Aldo's head, raising him a little so he could drink. 'Announcing you knew who killed Galeri so the whole convent would hear almost got you killed as well.'

He sipped the water. 'The poison – who was it?'

The abbess pulled away. 'Isabella, don't you have duties elsewhere?'

'No.' Isabella shrugged, smiling at both of them. 'I'm just visiting. Besides, I want to hear this. I could have drunk that wine too.'

'Let her stay,' Aldo whispered.

Giulia looked around to see if anyone else was within hearing. 'It's safe.'

The abbess pulled a chair closer and sat by Aldo. 'Maria Vincenzia put the poison in the wine. We caught her in the *latrina*, getting rid of the missing aconitum.'

Aldo pushed past the clouds in his recollection. Maria Vincenzia, she was the sharp-faced novice who had been so evasive when questioned about the finding of Galeri's body. Yes, she had enough self-righteous anger to justify tainting the wine. But had she also poisoned Galeri? It was possible. She was out of her bed that night, saying matins and lauds with Maria Celestia. But Aldo couldn't see a reason for her killing the visitor, let alone stabbing him and drenching the body with fresh blood.

'Did she say why?' he asked.

'No,' Giulia replied, her voice a low murmur. 'Maria Vincenzia refuses all our questions. She answers to a higher power than us, apparently.'

Aldo sipped more water. It wasn't much, but the tightness in his temples was easing, as was the rawness of his throat. 'And the visitation? Testardo's report?'

The abbess shook her head. 'It's still early, but I doubt his verdict will take long.' She looked out of the infirmary door to the courtyard. Morning sun was already warming the lavender, Aldo could smell it in the distance.

'I need to rest,' he said.

The abbess put the cup down by his bedside before leading the others away.

'Call if you need anything,' Isabella said, giving a cheery wave.

Aldo smiled at her before closing his eyes. He hadn't wanted to lie to the abbess, but he did not need to rest. More than anything, he needed to think.


Bindi paused two thirds of the way up the wide stone staircase from the Podestà courtyard. Each day the steps seemed to take longer. If the *segretario* didn't know better, he might believe new steps were being added each night. Bindi resumed his climb, gasping by the time he reached the top. His sour mood was not helped by Strocchi pacing the *loggia* that overlooked the courtyard. The constable was too eager, too eager by far.

'Why are you here?' Bindi asked, waddling towards his *officio*.

'You said I should report to you first thing,' Strocchi replied, his brow furrowing.

'Did I?' It stirred a memory, but the *segretario* was not going to admit that. 'The business of the Otto extends beyond you. The magistrates have a session to complete during Holy Week, and precious few hours in which to achieve that.'

'Yes, sir. But you did say—'

'Enough!' Bindi cut in. 'Let me reach my desk and then you may knock at my door.' Pushing past the constable, Bindi went into his *officio*. He stumped to his desk, easing himself into the sturdy chair behind it. *Denunzie* were piled high in front of him. He had read half but the rest still awaited. Whatever Strocchi wanted, it had best be swift.

There was a knock at the door. 'Come!'

Strocchi entered, closing the door before approaching.

'Well? What is so urgent it takes precedence over the workings of the court?'

'Pardon me *segretario*,' the constable said, clutching his cap in both hands, 'but you told me to report my progress in discovering who killed Meo Cerchi.'

Bindi nodded. 'And?'

'I have found new evidence. A witness who heard Cerchi arguing with another man on Ponte Vecchio after curfew on January the eleventh.'

'And who was this other man?'

Strocchi hesitated. 'I'm still gathering evidence about that—'

A new knock at the door interrupted Strocchi. The *segretario* sighed. 'Yes, who is it?' he called. Another constable, Benedetto, opened the door.

'Sorry to interrupt, but—' He stopped, noticing Strocchi. 'Should I come back?'

'No,' Bindi replied, making no effort to hide his displeasure. 'If there is anyone else outside, please, tell them to join us as well.'

Benedetto looked behind himself. 'No, sir, I'm on my own.'

'What do you want?' Bindi demanded.

The constable stumbled in, the door still open behind him. 'A message for you, sent by the Abbess of Santa Maria Magdalena.'

'Very well, hand over the message,' the *segretario* said, snapping his fingers.

'Sorry, it was a messenger,' Benedetto replied, 'not a written message. The boy said Aldo has been poisoned and is close to death.'

Strocchi gasped, making the sign of the cross.

'Close to death, you said – so Aldo is still alive?' Bindi asked.

The constable's mouth gaped but no words emerged.

'You didn't think to ask that, did you?'

Benedetto shook his head.

And the fool wondered why he was fit only to stand guard. 'Very well, return to your duties.' Bindi waved a hand at Benedetto. 'Go!'

Once the constable had departed, the *segretario* turned his attention back to Strocchi. 'I believe you were about to tell me something?'

'Sorry, I'm . . .' Strocchi's words stumbled to a halt. 'That message about Aldo –'

'Never mind him,' Bindi replied. 'What were you about to tell me? Spit it out!'

'Yes, sir. I – I was gathering evidence about the man on Ponte Vecchio the night Cerchi disappeared. I believe he may be the person responsible for stabbing Cerchi.'

'And?' Bindi asked. Strocchi hesitated. 'Are you summoning up the courage to name this other man, or to admit you don't know who he was?'

'I – I don't have conclusive evidence yet. Sir.'

Bindi bore limited patience with constables, and most of that had been expended on Benedetto. 'Then this matter is at an end.

Bring me a *denunzia* against a named suspect and I may reopen the investigation. But the Otto has endured the last two months without Cerchi, so I'm sure it can survive without replacing him. You may go.'

# Chapter Thirty

Aldo closed his eyes, letting the sounds and smells of the infirmary recede. Since coming to the convent, moments alone had been few, and time to consider the case even rarer. Being poisoned was not the usual solution, but it offered a chance to reflect. Once Santa Maria Magdalena was dissolved, its nuns would be scattered to convents across the city and beyond. Those responsible for Galeri's death had to be uncovered today, before it was too late.

Stabbing the corpse and covering it with fresh blood had been intended to disguise how and when Galeri died, Aldo believed, and presumably to protect those responsible. The method was flawed, but still achieved some of those aims. To understand what had occurred, Aldo knew he must re-examine all the events of recent days, starting with Galeri standing outside the convent on Palm Sunday after dark. What had happened next?

Galeri had come with a singular purpose: stealing what Ruggerio and his brethren were storing inside the locked cabinet in the abbess's *officio*. The intruder brought one of his own knives to open the cabinet door, never thinking that same blade would be used to stab his dead body dozens of times that same night.

Aldo berated himself for leaping ahead. Better to follow Galeri's journey step by step. Sift through the possibilities, noting the potential pathways.

Someone used Paulina's missing key to let Galeri inside the convent through the back gates. Not one of the boarders, they were all asleep in a single dormitory that nobody left during the night. That meant it must have been a chapter nun, a novice, or one of the servant nuns. Aldo was certain Galeri had persuaded one of the women to admit him, or coerced her into doing so. Suor Rigarda had confessed that Galeri tried to extort her help – did he succeed? Perhaps not with her, but with someone else?

The abbess had spoken of a faction within the convent that wished for its enclosure, while others among the nuns – including her – were eager to see Santa Maria Magdalena remain open, a place that welcomed the surrounding community. Galeri was part of the diocesan visitation. He could have offered to influence the outcome, promising to fulfil the hopes of whichever nun or novice agreed to admit him.

Once inside, Galeri went to the abbess's *officio*. It was close enough to the back gates that he could expect to come and go without being seen by anyone else. But the lock on the cabinet had resisted Galeri and his blade. At some stage in his attempt a corner of one document slid out beneath the locked door. Galeri pulled at the visible document but succeeded only in tearing away a corner. He had slipped that scrap of parchment into his tunic where it stuck to his skin.

All of this matched the evidence, but then what? If Galeri had left the convent after that, he would still be alive. But he chose to linger. Why? He would have been frustrated by the lock that would not give way. Judging by what Suor Giulia had said of her former husband, Galeri was not a man to accept disappointments well. Did he decide to take that out on whoever had let him into the convent? She was probably keeping watch outside the *officio*, praying Galeri would find what he wanted and leave.

But he wanted more. No, he demanded it.

There was a reason why Galeri had been found naked, after all.

Unable to get what he craved from inside the cabinet, Galeri demanded something else from the woman who had let him in: her body. Aldo knew this was pure speculation, but it was still credible. Galeri was a gambler, a drunk, and violent towards women. It was all too believable his anger could turn into a need to exert his dominance. Sexual coercion was as much about control – the claiming of power, the taking of dignity – as about sating lust.

How did the nun or novice respond? That depended on who let him in. She would have had little choice about his demands. All Galeri need do was start shouting and other nuns would come running. Yes, he would face questions and accusations, but he could still leave. The woman who had let him in was the one who would take all the blame. She would have to live with gossip and whispers for the rest of her life. Galeri had all the power while she would be left to stand alone – accused, disgraced, her vows in question.

Where would she take Galeri? The laundry was a clear choice. There were plenty of clean bed linens there, and it was close to the back gates. Galeri could have demanded she fetch wine, or perhaps she offered to bring him a cup. Faced with satisfying this stranger, Aldo would have wanted a drink too. That must have been when the idea of poisoning arose.

There were two explanations for using the aconitum: murder, or a terrible accident.

If Galeri had demanded intimacy, that would have been more than enough motive to kill him. But if he forced himself on her, when did the poisoning happen? Aldo knew how fast aconitum affected the body. A man like Galeri would not stay to drink wine after forcing himself on a nun. No, he must have been poisoned before he could sate his anger.

Putting poison in Galeri's wine showed intent. But killing a man involved more than ending his life. It also required dealing with the consequences of that. It meant disposing of his remains – never an easy task, let alone inside a convent after dark. It also meant facing guilt and remorse for ending a life. Were any of the nuns or novices capable of that? Some had revealed a ruthless streak, but that was very different from committing murder.

The amount of poison Galeri swallowed was enough to kill him, but murder might not have been the intention. The apothecary had mentioned using small amounts of aconitum as part of a sleep remedy. Whoever put the aconitum in Galeri's cup could have hoped it would save her from Galeri's unwanted attentions, creating the opportunity to get him out of the convent unseen. But the plan had gone wrong – very wrong. She knew a little about the poison, but not enough to choose the correct dosage.

Yes, an accidental death made more sense than murder. A sleeping body was easier to move than a corpse, and created fewer problems. Had Galeri been left slumbering outside the convent gates, he would have woken in the morning with little recourse against whoever drugged him. But ending his life had set in motion events that would likely see the convent dissolved, whether or not the woman responsible for Galeri's death faced justice.

Aldo nodded. Accept that the killing had been accidental and determining the person responsible became much easier. Deducing what happened next – and, more importantly, who was present for it – was another matter . . .

Strocchi left the Podestà, pausing at the gates to confirm the name of the convent that had sent the message about Aldo. Striding north, he wasn't sure whether to be relieved or angry. He had come so close to naming Aldo, but the interruption by Benedetto put a stop to that. There was no value in accusing Aldo if poison had claimed him. It was a relief to have the choice taken away, a relief not to accuse a man who had been such a help.

But Strocchi was angry too, there was no denying that. His chance of promotion was gone, leaving frustration and a sense he had failed. Yet something else was responsible for his ill mood: betrayal. He had trusted Aldo, admired him, even wanted to be like him in some ways. Yet it seemed the officer had lied and deceived and— Enough of that. Strocchi scolded himself for being so self-obsessed. His wounded pride was not enough of a reason to be angry. Cerchi was dead, and it seemed whoever stabbed him – Aldo, or somebody else – would pay no price for that. Hateful as Cerchi had been, an unlawful killing deserved to be investigated and those responsible brought to answer for their actions. That was the law. That was justice.

Rounding the Duomo, Strocchi continued his journey north, all the while deciding what to say to Aldo should they have the chance to speak. The officer was far from a fool. If he had killed Cerchi, Aldo would never simply admit that. He was too experienced, too shrewd to make an unplanned confession.

Strocchi kept recalling the conversation they'd had in Zoppo's tavern. Aldo did not respond at first when he heard that Cerchi has been found. Aldo claimed he was thinking about something else. Looking back, Aldo's next words were curious.

*'Where is he?'*

Had Aldo thought Cerchi was still alive? If he stabbed Cerchi and pushed him from the bridge, wouldn't Aldo have known whether Cerchi was dead? And yet, when Strocchi spoke of finding what was left of Cerchi, Aldo still asked for confirmation.

*'He's dead?'*

That had been the question of a man who did not already know the answer. If Aldo was the one who stabbed Cerchi, he wasn't certain the blow had been fatal. And if Aldo wasn't responsible for his rival's death . . . The constable decided to be relieved. There hadn't been enough proof to denounce. To get that, he would need to talk with Aldo.

When Strocchi found the dirt alley leading to the convent, he also found a notice nailed to the entrance door announcing Santa Maria Magdalena was under order of enclosure from the Archbishop of Florence. Strocchi knocked but got no reply. There would be no conversation with Aldo while he remained inside the convent. For now, the truth about what happened to Cerchi and Aldo's part in that, if any, would have to wait.

Aldo woke to find Suor Giulia at the end of his bed, studying him. 'You're looking better,' she said. 'You have more colour in your face.'

'I'm feeling better,' he replied, and meant it. The tightness in his head was gone, the unrest in his belly receding. Aldo pushed himself up into a sitting position. For a moment the infirmary swirled around him, but that soon ceased. Yes, he was improving.

'Good,' the nun said. 'Bad enough someone took aconitum without my realizing. If Maria Vincenzia had used it to silence you for good . . .'

'I'm grateful she didn't know how much to use.' Aldo beckoned Giulia closer. She brought a chair to the bedside and sat close to him. 'Who would?' he asked.

Giulia smiled. 'You must be better if you're asking that.' Her eyes narrowed. 'I would. Possibly Suor Catarina, though it is some

time since she was my apprentice. I doubt she would remember
enough to be certain.'

'How long did Catarina work with you?'

'A winter and a spring, but that was some years ago. She found
the work too dull. Giulia smiled. 'I suspect she prefers to be among
those who enjoy talking and debate.'

'Have you had other apprentices?'

'Suor Andriana, though not for long. It was agreed her gifts
lay elsewhere. And she leads the laundry well as our draper. The
servant nun Suor Rigarda was my last apprentice before Maria
Teodora. Unfortunately, she found it overwhelming. She struggles
with her letters, so her note-taking was far from reliable.'

Aldo listened carefully. It seemed each of the women mentioned
would know enough to find aconitum and be aware of its uses.
'What about Maria Teodora?'

'She's been with me since the beginning of Lent, but it suits
her ill. I doubt she knows which of my tools the pestle is yet.'
Giulia arched an eyebrow at Aldo. 'Why do you ask?'

Aldo wanted to trust the apothecary. If she was the one who
had poisoned Galeri, it would have been intentional. Giulia knew
poisons better than anyone in the convent, she was would not have
made any mistake with the aconitum. And she had been Galeri's
wife at one time. Her account of their marriage, his violence – all
of that was clear proof of a motive to see him dead. But she had
volunteered that information when a lie could have gone unnoticed.
If Giulia murdered Galeri, she certainly would have concealed her
past with him.

'When your husband was taking out his frustrations on you
– when you were still together – why didn't you fight back?' Aldo
asked. Giulia sank back in the chair before murmuring a reply.
Her words were so quiet Aldo didn't hear them. 'Sorry?'

'What if I failed?' the nun said. 'There were times when he was too drunk or too tired to defend himself. There were times when I wanted to kill him, when I wanted him dead. But what if I tried and failed? I knew what he would do to me. I knew how much he would make me suffer. Fear kept me prisoner for so long. Men like Galeri crush you, little by little. They strip away all the strength you have, all the things that make you smile or hope. Eventually, there is nothing left. They break you, and then complain that you are broken . . .'

Giulia straightened her back, glaring at Aldo. 'And this is what men like you never understand. You are raised to fight back, to use your fists as weapons to solve your problems. Women – girls – we learn to smile instead of showing what we feel. We learn how to endure pain and humiliation when it seems our suffering will never end, and how to agree with those that hurt you. Most of us don't have your strength. We learn to do what we must to stay alive. We learn how to protect ourselves, and each other. How to run.'

Aldo recalled the first year he spent as a boy on the streets of Florence, how often he had been hurt by others. But he kept that to himself.

'Women and girls have to use things other than our fists to defend ourselves,' Giulia said. 'Why do you think this convent was where I found help in the city? The previous abbess made it a sanctuary for women like me. Most left once they had recovered, but I found a new home here. Yet the diocese called that abbess a troublemaker because she refused to turn away those women in need, the wives of powerful men.' She gestured around her. 'Women are stronger together here, and safer. Here we help each other.'

'You help each other –' Aldo nodded. Of course. That was it. That was what had happened after Galeri had been poisoned and died.

'You never answered my question,' Giulia said. 'Why do you want to know about the nuns and novices who used to assist me?'

'Because I suspect one of them killed Galeri,' he replied. 'I'm not sure the person who caused his death meant that to happen. It could well have been accidental. He was poisoned by someone who knew enough to find aconitum in your workshop, and that it could be used in a sleeping remedy – but she didn't know enough to get the proportions right. I'll have to question each of your apprentices to know who was responsible.'

'Maria Vincenzia poisoned you. Do you think that she . . .?'

'Killed Galeri? No. I believe that was someone else.'

Isabella approached them. She had been working with Suor Dea at the other end of the infirmary. Aldo had seen her keeping watch on him, and doing her best to hide it. 'Sorry for interrupting,' Isabella said, 'but someone wishes to speak with you.'

'With me?' Aldo asked.

'With both of you,' she replied. One of the patients had risen from their cot and was shuffling along the infirmary towards them: Maria Celestia. The bandages on her hands still showed red stains across both palms, but she looked much recovered from the previous day.

'Bring her closer,' Aldo said. It was time to get some answers.

# Chapter Thirty-one

Giulia rose from the chair so Maria Celestia could sit by Aldo's bed. The novice was pale, her hands trembling. Giulia ushered Isabella away, explaining Maria Celestia would be freer to speak without an audience. Once Isabella was back helping Dea, Giulia returned to Aldo's bedside.

'I will tell Father Visconti this,' Maria Celestia began, 'when I confess my sins and ask for God's forgiveness, but I wanted you to hear it first. I need to tell you, Signor Aldo, because I have heard you may be able to help set right some of the wrongs I have done. Suor Giulia, you warned me months ago to be careful of Maria Vincenzia. You said her influence was leading me to do things that were questionable, and I—'

'You dismissed my concerns.' Giulia recalled the conversation well. Maria Celestia's response had been so disdainful, it was apparent she was a lost cause. Taking Maria Teodora as an apprentice was an attempt to weaken Maria Vincenzia's malign influence.

Maria Celestia nodded. 'I hope you can forgive my words that day. You were striving to make me see the truth. But I was blinded by someone I believed was a friend.'

'Maria Vincenzia,' Aldo murmured.

'Yes.'

'You both rose in the early hours between Palm Sunday and

Monday morning to say matins and lauds in the chapter house, yes?'

Maria Celestia nodded, clasping her hands together. 'We said matins, and all was well. The convent was quiet. We were returning to our dormitory when Maria Vincenzia noticed she had left her breviary behind. She went back while I went to my bed. Later, I'm not sure when, she woke me. I thought it was time to say lauds, and followed her downstairs. But instead of going to the chapter house, she took me to the scriptorium . . .'

Giulia expected Aldo to prompt the novice, but he stayed silent. It had the same effect, but let Maria Celestia take her time and find her own words.

'The man – his body –' She stumbled to a halt, bandaged hands rubbing together. 'I have never seen a naked man. It was . . . not his body, but the wounds . . .'

Giulia glanced at Aldo. So the stabbing of Galeri had already happened when Maria Vincenzia took the other novice to the scriptorium. If that was true – and the confession seemed heartfelt – then Maria Celestia was not part of the attack on Galeri's corpse. Only in what followed.

'I wanted to fetch one of the sisters, but Maria Vincenzia stopped me. I asked her who the dead man was, who had done this to him. She wouldn't say.'

To Giulia it was obvious Maria Vincenzia had been protecting someone in the convent, going to extraordinary lengths to shield them. But who was it?

'I wanted nothing to do with it,' Maria Celestia continued. 'Maria Vincenzia said she would wake the abbess, tell her I had let that man into the convent and killed him. I knew once Maria Vincenzia decides on a path, she doesn't let anyone stop her.'

Aldo nodded. 'What did she make you do?'

'We said lauds, even though that poor man was still in the scriptorium. After, Maria Vincenzia said it would take a miracle to solve our problem – and I had to provide it.'

Giulia couldn't stay silent. 'She made you cut your own hands open?'

Maria Celestia nodded. 'I had to use the man's knife. But the blade edge was blunt, so I had to do it again and again . . .' The novice stared down at her bandaged palms. 'She told me to drip my blood over his body, to make it seem as though he had just died. But my hand didn't bleed enough for her, so Maria Vincenzia cut the other one. She kept saying our saviour Jesus Christ suffered far worse. I should be grateful to know his pain. It was a test of my faith . . .'

Giulia realized her own fists were clenched so tight the nails were almost piercing the skin. The way Maria Vincenzia had used her fellow novice . . . The Gospels urged forgiveness. They must find it in their hearts to forgive Maria Vincenzia. But Giulia would not forget.

'Even then, my blood was not enough,' Maria Celestia continued. 'Maria Vincenzia talked about patients at the infirmary being bled. She told me to go to the infirmary and bring back a bowl of blood. I couldn't. I was too weak. I think she went instead.'

'She poured all that blood over the body,' Aldo said.

'Yes.'

'It was your task to prepare the scriptorium each day for the nuns who worked there. Maria Vincenzia made you stay there, with the body, until morning?'

The novice nodded. 'I was to wait until I heard others passing on their way to the refectory, and then start screaming. But I lost my senses for a time because of the cuts to my hands and all the bleeding, I suppose. I woke much later than Maria Vincenzia had wanted. My hands . . .' she held them out, scarlet spots across the palms – 'they hurt so much.'

'It must have been Maria Vincenzia's bloodied habit that was found in the laundry,' Giulia said. 'She hid it there, putting on clean garments to hide what she'd done.'

Aldo smiled at Maria Celestia. 'You have been very brave. I doubt you will see Maria Vincenzia again, not after this. But if you should, know you did the right thing confessing.'

'Admit your sins to Father Visconti,' Giulia said, 'and God will forgive you.'

The novice managed a weak smile, but her doubts were still apparent.

'I have one more question,' Aldo said. 'Did Maria Vincenzia say why she didn't try to move the body out through the back gates? The two of you could have managed that if you used the convent's hand cart. Why pretend to discover it instead?'

'I asked her,' Maria Celestia replied, 'but she just cut deeper into my hand.'

After guiding the novice back to her cot, Giulia returned to find Aldo struggling to rise from the mattress. He was still in tunic and hose, but his boots were under the cot. 'Where are you going?' she asked, catching hold of an arm to support him.

'Outside,' he said. 'I want to sit in the sun.'

She knew better than to argue with such a stubborn man.


Aldo sank onto a stone bench in the cloisters. Insects were already buzzing between the lavender bushes that lined the courtyard, its air filling with that distinctive aroma. Once he was settled, Suor Giulia sat beside him. 'I thought these did not bloom until later in the spring,' Aldo said, running his hands across the first few purple flowers.

'Our lavender comes out early,' Giulia replied. 'Suor Benedicta takes pride in how early it blooms. She calls the lavender our little miracle. This year it's especially early, perhaps because the winter was so mild . . .' The apothecary lowered her voice so she would not be overheard by any nuns nearby. 'Did Maria Celestia say what you expected?'

'Yes. I had hoped for more, but –' Best to be grateful the novice's guilt had driven her to confess. 'From what you said, I would waste my time questioning Maria Vincenzia.'

'She is determined to keep her secrets,' Giulia agreed.

Aldo nodded. The more he knew about what happened the night Galeri died, the more he believed the death was unintentional. Murderous women were rare in his experience, let alone inside a convent. But a tragic accident – that was far more credible.

'I believe I know how Galeri died,' Aldo said. 'And now we both know his corpse got covered in fresh blood long after he had grown cold. It is the time between those events that eludes me. Why stab a dead man so many times?' He twisted his head to look at Giulia. 'You know the women here. Would one of them take a knife to a dead body like that?'

She did not respond at first, her gaze moving around the courtyard, watching the other nuns strolling through the cloister or praying. 'If Bernardo had still been alive, I would say no – none of those in the convent could do that.'

'But if he was already dead?'

'It's possible.' Before Aldo could ask, she held up a hand. 'But I will not accuse anyone, not without proof.' Giulia rose. 'I have duties to perform. Will you be well here?'

'If I get worse, I can always call to Isabella.' He gestured to the infirmary door where his step-niece was watching them.

Satisfied, the apothecary departed. As Aldo watched her go, a wave of nausea swept over him. He lay down in the sun, staring at the cloudless *azzurri* overhead. When this was over, he would have to face Strocchi. Perhaps the constable had found no proof for who killed Cerchi. But Strocchi had a dogged resilience. If anyone at the Otto could uncover the truth, it was him. Aldo shook his head. There was nothing to be done about Strocchi. Better to solve this case, rather than waste time on problems elsewhere. He closed his eyes, pushing himself back to the night of Palm Sunday . . .

Galeri was dying or dead, a cup of poisoned wine at his side. Was the woman who poisoned him the same one that stabbed him over and over again? Possibly, but experience told Aldo the answer was no. Galeri was already dead, how would stabbing him benefit the poisoner? It might sate their anger, but a few plunges of the blade would have been enough. Twenty-seven different wounds. That was hatred.

Besides, if stabbing the body was meant to disguise the fact that Galeri had been poisoned, it made sense that the woman responsible was someone else. The poisoner needed to be in bed to prove her innocence. Had she sought help after realizing what she had done? Or had someone stumbled on the dead man and his killer, and offered to help hide what had happened?

The answer to that was less important. It was the deed itself which mattered.

If Galeri was poisoned anywhere but in the scriptorium, his body had to be moved there. Shifting Galeri was a risk, even after dark. Giulia had said she came down to the lower level during the night to tend nutmeg oil in her workshop. Could she be the one who had stabbed him? Giulia certainly had reason to hate Galeri. Attacking the dead man would have been a chance to have her revenge. When Giulia said she had not killed Galeri, it seemed an honest answer – but she was never asked about the stabbing. If asked, what would she say?

Aldo would not blame her if that was what happened.

After all, he had done worse.

Who else bore enough hatred in her heart to stab the dead man so many times? The teaching nun Suor Catarina would be a suspect, but she had been asleep in a dormitory that night from which nobody had come or gone. Then there were the nuns who had private cells, meaning they could go downstairs without disturbing others. Aldo did not believe the listening nun Suor Benedicta had been involved, nor the troubled Suor Violante. He had long discounted the abbess as a potential suspect and seen nothing to change his mind about her.

But some of those in private cells remained suspects. The convent's almoner Suor Paulina was one of them, as was the timid draper Suor Andriana. And the sour-faced sacrist Suor Fiametta also remained on Aldo's mind. She had a zealotry that could be dangerous in the wrong circumstances, an absoluteness of belief that could lead her astray . . .

To gain entry to the convent after dark, Galeri probably had made promises that he had no intention of keeping, such as influencing the monsignor's final report. If Galeri told his poisoner that had been a lie, it might well be motive enough to desecrate Galeri's corpse. A nun or novice who craved enclosure for the convent would know dissolution was now likely. If she was against enclosure, the woman holding the blade would know his death had doomed those hopes. Either way, she had reason to hate Galeri . . .

Opening both eyes, Aldo pulled himself upright. He was better, but still lacked all his strength. The poisoning had kept him inside the convent, but his recovery would soon put an end to that. He had a few hours at most before the abbess must oblige him to leave. For the truth to come out, he needed to question Suor Giulia's former apprentices, and hope that guilt would persuade them to name the hand holding the blade used on Galeri. This required the blessing of the abbess.

Aldo rose from the bench, but his legs threatened to give way. Isabella rushed from the infirmary door. 'Are you unwell again?'

'It will pass,' he replied. 'Hopefully. But I need you to bring the abbess here. She is probably going to be in her *officio*. Tell her it is important.'

The abbess listened to Aldo's explanation of what had happened after dark on Palm Sunday. It was porous as a muslin cloth but made sense of events. He suggested questioning Giulia's former helpers. If nothing came of that, he would leave. But if the truth emerged, the abbess could summon Testardo back to hear it.

She could not help wondering if this was what it was like to make a deal with a *diavolo*. Aldo's offer seemed genuine. He acknowledged that identifying whoever killed Galeri was unlikely to save Santa Maria Magdalena from dissolution. But wasn't it better to know who had committed the darkest of sins? Shouldn't they face the consequences of their actions, rather than all those inside the convent bearing that stain? Perhaps a *diavolo* was this persuasive, but it didn't matter. Better the truth be known, if possible.

The abbess suggested they talk to Giulia's former apprentices in the chapel. Few would be willing to deceive there. Aldo smiled when she said that. 'It's a pity the Otto does not have female officers. You have a talent that the court is lacking.'

Aldo chose to question Suor Rigarda first, asking Isabella to bring the servant nun from the kitchen without explanation. 'You get more honest answers if a suspect has less time to prepare,' he said. When Rigarda arrived, the abbess told her to sit on a pew at the front of the chapel, facing a large wooden carving of Jesus on the cross. If that did not shame her into speaking the truth, there was no hope for the young woman's soul.

The abbess watched Rigarda while Aldo asked his questions. Yes, Signor Galeri had sought to coerce the servant nun into admitting him to the convent after curfew on Palm Sunday. No, she had not done so. Instead, she had come to the chapel and confessed her sins to Father Visconti, praying for forgiveness. Rigarda claimed to know nothing more.

'I understand you were apprentice to Suor Giulia,' Aldo said.

Rigarda nodded. 'But not for long. My gifts lay elsewhere.'

'What do you know about aconitum?'

She frowned, turning to the abbess. 'Was he one of the arch-angels?'

'No,' the abbess replied.

'Tell us about Suor Piera,' Aldo said. 'She's a patient at the infirmary?'

Rigarda smiled. 'Yes. Piera is the oldest sister in the convent. She is always very kind, but has been unwell and feverish.'

'How is that being treated?'

'The doctor said she must be bled. Suor Simona objected, but he would not listen.'

Aldo moved closer. 'Was she bled on Sunday night?'

Rigarda nodded, crimson creeping across her cherubic face.

'And what happened to the bowl with the blood in it?'

She shook her head, tears brimming in both eyes.

'What happened to the blood?'

Rigarda broke down sobbing. The abbess went to the servant nun, sitting beside her, rubbing a hand on her back. 'It's all right. We know how this has been troubling you.'

It still took a while before the answer came. Rigarda left the infirmary on Sunday night to visit the kitchen, needing something to keep her going until morning. When she emerged, Maria Vincenzia was waiting. The novice bullied Rigarda into putting a bowl of blood by the infirmary door, swearing her to secrecy. The servant nun had wanted to speak up about this sooner, but had been too afraid.

Once the servant nun had recovered, the abbess led her outside where Isabella was waiting. 'Take Rigarda to her dormitory,' the abbess said, 'she needs to rest.'

Isabella nodded, leading the novice away.

The abbess returned to the chapel where Aldo was staring at the carving of Jesus on the cross. 'She was telling the truth,' he said.

'Yes. Rigarda is from a small country village. She knows little of Florentine ways, unlike Maria Vincenzia.' The abbess considered asking Aldo about his own faith but held her tongue. He was determined to do what he could for the convent. That was more than enough.

'Who do you wish to question next?'

# Chapter Thirty-two

Aldo had seen how Testardo's abrasive approach angered Suor Catarina, so he chose to be less confrontational. But the teaching nun was already resistant when she strode into the chapel. 'Abbess, why am I here? I answered all the visitation's questions yesterday.'

The abbess did her best to soothe Catarina. 'Signor Aldo is departing the convent by sext, if not sooner. He simply needs to resolve a few matters for the archbishop.'

'Can you say when teaching will start again? I have boarders with nothing to do, young woman eager to learn and who are being kept from that.'

'I expect we will have an answer for you soon.' The abbess guided Catarina to a pew before nodding to Aldo, a warning in her eyes. This would not be easy.

'Suor Catarina,' Aldo began, bowing his head to the nun before sitting on the same pew at a respectful distance. 'I wish to apologize for Monsignor Testardo's conduct yesterday. Accusing you of murder was unforgiveable.'

'I would never take a life,' Catarina replied, 'as I told the monsignor yesterday. But I thank you for those words.'

'You told us that you sleep in the dormitory above the refectory.'

'Yes. My bed is in the far corner. The prioress sleeps closest to the door.'

'And I recall being told the dormitory doors tend to creak,' Aldo said.

'They do. Whenever myself or one of my sisters in God leaves the room, the noise will wake someone.' The hint of a smile appeared on Catarina's face. 'Andriana suggested we put a little olive oil on the doors to make them quieter.'

Aldo smiled. 'Suor Andriana has a good heart.'

'She does.'

He rose from the pew. 'Thank you for your time, Suor Catarina.'

She frowned, looking from him to the abbess. 'I may go?'

'Yes,' the abbess replied, stepping aside so Catarina could leave. Once she was out of hearing, the abbess shook her head. 'I do not understand what was achieved by that.'

'Suor Catarina proved it was impossible for her to leave that particular dormitory after dark,' Aldo said. 'Tell me, is she close with Suor Andriana?'

'Yes. I encouraged younger nuns to seek positions of respon-sibility as openings arose. That caused some dissent. Catarina and Suor Fiametta both defended Andriana from the whispers of older nuns. But I still believe this convent needs—' She stopped herself.

'Fresh blood,' Aldo said.

'An unfortunate choice of words.'

'Indeed.' He had not paid Fiametta much attention, but she was another potential suspect for the stabbing of Galeri, if not his poisoning. She had a private cell, so could come and go at night without waking others. 'Does Suor Fiametta wish the convent to stay open to the community, or would she prefer enclosure?'

'Fiametta believes in enclosure, fiercely so. God help us if she ever became abbess.'

'Why do you say that?' Aldo asked.

The abbess shook her head. 'I shouldn't have spoken that way of another nun.'

'But you did. So?'

'Fiametta is a stickler who believes she is right with absolute certainty, even more than the prioress. Any convent with her in charge would be a place without laughter or hope.'

Aldo nodded. Yes, Suor Fiametta was definitely worthy of further thought.

Isabella appeared at the chapel door. 'Suor Andriana is here.'

'Bring her in,' the abbess said.

Andriana was as timid as Aldo remembered, her shoulders hunched forwards, gaze fixed on the stone floor. The abbess led her to a pew. 'I believe you already know Signor Aldo?'

A quick nod.

'He wishes to ask about what happened on Sunday night.'

Aldo brought a plain wooden chair to the pew, sitting opposite Andriana. In the past he had noticed those who struggled to hear found it easier if they could see the face of those speaking. 'We first met on the morning of Palm Sunday,' he began. 'The abbess was showing me the convent, and you were hurrying from the laundry. Do you recall that?'

She nodded.

'You said you were not feeling well. I could not help noticing how worried you seemed.' Aldo studied the nun's hands and face. She appeared even more fearful now, making herself as small as possible. Andriana was ready to talk, to admit whatever she had done. The challenge was finding the words to let her confess. 'When Monsignor Testardo questioned you about what happened, you said you spent the night in your cell. You told him you went to the *latrina* once. Is that right?'

Andriana did not respond to his question.

'Did you leave your cell for any other reason that night?'

Still she did not reply.

'Suor Andriana?'

After a long silence, the nun lifted her face to stare at the carving of Jesus Christ on the cross. A single word full of regret slipped from her lips in a husky whisper: 'Yes.'

Aldo noticed the abbess stiffen at his right but he kept both eyes fixed on Andriana. 'When Galeri first came to the convent with the visitation, did he come into the laundry?'

'Yes.'

'Were there were others present, or was he on his own?'

'The visitors came to the laundry in pairs,' Andriana whispered, her words so quiet Aldo had to lean closer to hear them. 'But Signor Galeri returned later, saying he had left a glove behind. We searched for it, but found no glove. He was lying, I know that now.'

'What did he really want?'

'He asked me about the convent, how I felt about it being open to the community and what would happen if it was enclosed. I told him the convent does a lot of good, and closing our doors would be a step backwards.' Andriana glanced at the abbess. 'I believe we have a duty to pray and reflect, but we also have a calling to spread God's word through our work.'

'Did Galeri say you were wrong?' Aldo asked.

'No,' Andriana replied. 'He told me the monsignor was searching for reasons to close the convent. But there was a way to change that.'

'Galeri offered to intercede.'

'Yes.'

'If you did something for him.'

Andriana nodded, tears brimming in her eyes.

It took time and patience, but she revealed what had happened on Palm Sunday. How she borrowed Suor Paulina's key, and let

Galeri inside after curfew. He went into the abbess's *officio* while Andriana kept watch, but Galeri was not satisfied by what he found there. He wanted more. He wanted her. When the younger nun described how Galeri threatened to disgrace her unless she satisfied his lust, the abbess moved closer to Andriana and put an arm round her shoulders.

'I wish I had known sooner,' the abbess said.

'I could not tell you,' Andriana whispered. 'I could not even tell our confessor . . .'

'You shall. When these questions are answered, you must admit your sins to God and pray for his forgiveness. Redemption is given to those who seek it with an open heart.'

Aldo listened as Andriana continued her story. Galeri had coerced and cajoled her, bullying the nun into submitting. She made a bed of blankets and sheets on the laundry floor, but her trembling hands made it difficult. Galeri leered at her, removing his boots. He mentioned all the nuns asleep in their beds above them. That had given Andriana the idea to make a sleeping draught. Having seen Giulia mix them while she had been her apprentice, Andriana believed she could do the same. Galeri was delighted when she offered to fetch wine . . .

'He said I was warming up at last,' she recalled, shuddering.

Andriana took two cups of wine from the kitchen to Giulia's workshop, but struggled to remember the jar holding the right ingredient. Not knowing which cup Galeri would take, she mixed powders in both. She almost dropped them when she returned to the laundry.

'He was . . . naked. Lying there, so proud of himself, so . . .' Andriana closed both eyes.

Aldo waited, letting her gather the courage to continue.

Andriana had given Galeri a cup of wine. She feared he might only sip, that what was dissolved in it would have no effect. Instead, Galeri gulped the wine down in a single swallow, gesturing for her to come closer. Before she could, the poison had its effect. Aldo didn't listen to her description. He knew how it felt to swallow aconitum.

The nun went for help. She ran halfway to the infirmary before changing her mind. Suor Simona could never understand. Instead, Andriana went upstairs to find someone who would do what was necessary. But when the two of them returned to the laundry, Galeri was already dead.

'I never meant for him to die,' Andriana sobbed. 'I only wanted him to sleep. Then I could have put him outside the back gates and locked them again. But he – he –'

Her guilty account was convincing. Galeri's death had been accidental. Avarice and lust had been his undoing. What had happened to Galeri's corpse, that was another matter.

'Why did you move his body to the scriptorium?' Aldo asked.

'I didn't,' Andriana said. 'I couldn't look at him any longer, it was too much for me. I went back to my cell and prayed until dawn, asking our Lord for forgiveness.'

'And then?'

'The next morning, I went to the laundry, fearful of what I would find. But his clothes, all the mess he had made, was gone. The blankets and sheets were where they belonged. It was as if nothing had happened. For a few moments I almost believed it had been some terrible dream. Then I heard Maria Celestia screaming.'

Aldo rose from his chair. There was only one question left to ask.

'Suor Andriana, who did you go to for help that night?'

* * *

The abbess closed a hand round her wooden cross as Aldo led Andriana from the chapel. The name she had whispered – could something be both inevitable and still surprising? No. The abbess shook her head. It wasn't a surprise when Andriana said who she had gone to for help. Instead what the abbess felt most of all was sadness.

Aldo returned. 'What do you wish to do?'

'Do?'

'The convent stands on holy ground, so this is a Church matter. The archbishop will decide what happens to Santa Maria Magdalena, but for now you still lead here.'

'We need to notify the archbishop, and Monsignor Testardo.'

Aldo nodded. 'Can you send someone with a message while the convent is enclosed?'

'Not one of us, but we can send a messenger. That's how I informed the *segretario* of the Otto about your poisoning.' A frown darkened Aldo face. 'You disapprove?'

'No, that was necessary,' Aldo replied. 'But Bindi did not agree with my secondment to the visitation. He will be eager to express his disapproval when I return. The *segretario* takes considerable joy from the pettiest of victories.'

The abbess recognized that trait amongst several of her sisters in God, but kept it to herself. A chapel was no place for her to make such uncharitable observations.

'Notifying the archbishop and Testardo will satisfy the diocese,' Aldo said. 'What do you wish to do about those inside the convent?'

'I doubt we will be together much longer, and they deserve to know why. I want everyone to hear the truth at the same time, where possible. I will call a chapter-house conclave – nuns, novices, the boarding girls. Then those who have sinned can ask for the forgiveness of the convent, if they wish. Let the truth be known. Let light shine upon it.'

'Good,' Aldo agreed. 'Then I shall withdraw and—'

'No,' the abbess said. 'I wish you to be present. It is unconventional to have a man of the laity at such a gathering, but I want you there when those responsible are revealed. Andriana will be no trouble, but the others –'

'Very well. Then I suggest the messenger you send requests that Testardo return to the convent. There was no murder here, so this is not a matter for the Otto anymore, if it ever was. But as leader of the visitation the monsignor should take responsibility for dealing with those who have broken the Church's laws. For those who have sinned.'

That made sense. The abbess would not enjoy Testardo's triumph at being proved right, but her discomfort was of no importance. If she had been a better leader, perhaps all this might have been avoided. But it was foolish to believe she might have prevented Galeri's death. Pride was too often her sin. The convent's dissolution and the knowledge that it could have been avoided – that would be her penance.

The prioress had been waiting for the knock on the cell door. There would be consequences for what Violante did, it was only a question of when. But the messenger was not who the prioress was expecting. 'Do I know you?' she asked the girl in the corridor.

'My name is Isabella Goudi,' the girl replied. 'I do not think we have met.'

The prioress recalled mention of a merchant's daughter who came to the convent claiming an interest in holy vows. Whispers in the refectory said she was actually seeking escape from an unwanted marriage. A week ago that would have outraged the prioress. Now she had greater concerns. 'Why have you chosen to disturb us?'

'The abbess asked me to knock on every door in the convent. She is summoning all those who are able to come to the chapter house for a conclave.'

'When?'

'This morning, before sext.'

'Very well. Tell the abbess I have received her summons. You may go. I'm sure you have many other doors to visit.'

The prioress withdrew into her sister's cell. Violante was kneeling by the bed, hands clasped together in prayer. The two of them had spent the night like that, seeking forgiveness and guidance. Violante paused her supplications. 'Who was it?'

The prioress repeated the message, readying herself to offer reassurance.

'I believe we should go to the chapter house,' Violante said.

'Are you sure?'

'Yes.' Violante rose from the floor, folding her rosary beads in one hand. 'I have made my peace with our Lord about what I did. If I can redeem myself in the eyes of God, I can certainly face the other nuns.'

The prioress nodded. It was so long since she had seen such clarity in her sister.

The two sisters embraced.

Giulia was busy in her workshop when Isabella came to announce the conclave. She offered no explanation beyond saying it was about the convent's future. To Giulia, that future was clear. The only surprise was the archbishop had taken so long to order dissolution. But when she went to the chapter house, no clerics were present, no outsiders other than Aldo. He seemed to be recovering, but was still pale and leaning on a chair.

His presence did not go unnoticed by the other nuns, novices and the boarding girls as they crowded the benches either side of the narrow chamber. The chapter house was soon full, but those on the courtyard side made room when the prioress entered, bringing Violante with her. That sent a fresh surge of whispers through those assembled. Everyone had heard some version of what Violante had done. Secrets did not remain so long inside these walls.

Suor Simona was among the last to arrive. The infirmarian helped the convent's oldest nun, Suor Piera, into the chapter house. Maria Celestia followed them, bringing a chair onto which Piera sank with a smile. The abbess hurried over to them.

'Suor Piera, you did not need to come. You should be resting.'

The elderly nun waved away such concerns. 'I've been part of this community since the day Santa Maria Magdalena opened its doors, and a nun longer than you have been alive. If we are no longer to be one house, I wish to be here for that announcement.'

'I urged her not to come,' Simona said. 'In the strongest terms.'

'But I did not listen,' Piera replied. 'I can be quite hard of hearing, when I wish.'

Giulia hid a smile. Hopefully, she would be equally mischievous in her final years.

'Suor Dea has remained behind to care for those still bed-bound,' Simona said.

Giulia nodded to the abbess as she passed, but got no response in return. The abbess strode back to her usual position at one end of the chapter house, facing all those gathered for the conclave. 'Let us pray,' the abbess said, her voice raised so everyone could hear. Silence fell as heads bowed. Giulia crossed herself, preparing for what was to come.

# Chapter Thirty-three

✤

*A*ldo watched the nuns, novices and boarders praying. The abbess showed her authority, calling their attention back to her. 'Sisters in God,' she began, 'two days ago I gathered you here to share an uneasy truth. I told you the body of a dead man had been found in the scriptorium, that he had been killed inside our convent on Sunday night. This was all true. But I also said he had been murdered and in that I was mistaken. He died as a result of decisions made by one among us, but her intention was not murder. The death of Bernardo Galeri was a terrible accident.'

That provoked whispers and mutterings. The abbess waited for the sound to die away before continuing, palms held out to hush the conclave.

'I know you all have questions. I have more answers now than I did two days ago. If you let me finish, and let others speak as I call on them, your questions will be answered. So I ask you to be patient, and listen.' She gestured to Aldo. 'This man is Cesare Aldo, an officer of the Otto di Guardia e Balia. He came here as part of a visitation sent by the archbishop to determine what happened. I ask him now to share his findings.'

Aldo had expected the abbess to describe the events. Now he understood why she had asked him to attend. Better that what must be said came from him. None of those present could accuse him of complicity, or suggest he favoured one faction in the convent over another.

'Thank you, abbess.' Mustering his strength, Aldo came forward to address the conclave. 'First of all, I wish to say Bernardo Galeri did not live a good life. He was a liar, a gambler, a bully, a thief, an extortionist, and a serpent. It does not make his death less regrettable, but he was not a man of God. When Galeri came to this convent as part of a diocesan visitation, it was a ruse he devised to steal documents locked in your abbess's *officio*. He failed, but was determined to try again. To that end he threatened some of you, lied to others, and duped one credulous soul into helping him.'

Without naming her, Aldo recounted how Andriana had let Galeri in through the back gates after dark on Sunday. How Galeri plotted to take her virtue after failing to steal what he wanted from the convent. Aldo described how she unwittingly poisoned Galeri. Several nuns made the sign of the cross, others shook their heads, and one wept. Aldo went to the weeping nun, sitting at the end of a bench near the abbess. 'That's what happened, isn't it?'

Andriana nodded. The nuns closest to her drew back in dismay. 'I never meant to hurt him,' she said between sobs. 'I only wanted to make him drowsy. I thought if I made him sleep, I could get him out of the convent.'

'Before Galeri returned that night, you had doubts about him, didn't you?'

'Y-yes.'

'You feared he might not be worthy of your trust.'

She nodded again.

'So you asked another nun to stay in your cell while you waited for him to arrive.'

'We prayed together,' Andriana said. 'She helped me get the key to the back gates after Suor Paulina fell asleep.' Andriana held up the key. Whispers spread around the chapter house again but fell silent when the abbess cleared her throat.

'What happened when you realized Galeri had died?' Aldo asked.

'I wasn't sure what to do. I went back to my cell and told my friend everything that had happened. I begged for her help.'

Suor Benedicta had been correct. There were two voices in the hallway outside the private cells that night – Andriana and the woman who was waiting in her cell.

'And what did the other nun do?'

'She promised to help. She promised nobody would ever know.'

'But that wasn't the truth, was it?'

Andriana shook her head.

Aldo thanked the sobbing nun for her courage before facing the conclave once more. 'Just as Galeri duped Suor Andriana, so was she also betrayed by someone she trusted. The nun who had kept vigil with Suor Andriana went down to where Galeri's body lay among the blankets and sheets. She hid his clothes behind a pile of laundry, before using the hand cart from beside the back gates to move his body to the scriptorium. A corpse in the laundry would be discovered too early, but a corpse in the scriptorium would only be found when the room was opened later in the morning. The nun who moved Galeri's corpse wanted to shield Suor Andriana from any blame for his death.

'The problem was only a few women in the convent knew about the poison in the apothecary's workshop – Suor Giulia, and her three past apprentices – Suor Rigarda, Suor Catarina, and Suor Andriana. If it was obvious that Galeri had been poisoned, suspicion would fall on them. To protect Suor Andriana, a new reason for Galeri's death had to be created. By chance, it was Galeri himself who provided the solution.

'He had brought a knife with him, hoping it would open the cabinet in the abbess's *officio*. Instead, it was used to stab him. One or two wounds would have been enough, but the woman holding the blade vented all her anger, all her frustration, on Galeri's corpse, stabbing him again and again. He had tried to violate Suor Andriana, so perhaps it seemed just to violate Galeri with his own blade so many times. Or perhaps the woman who stabbed the corpse hoped such a frenzied attack might cast suspicion on another person in the convent.'

Aldo crossed the floor to the prioress and her sister. 'Some of you know the troubles Suor Violante has faced since coming to Santa Maria Magdalena. Yet she has never raised a hand to anyone else, never hurt anyone but herself. The one exception to that was yesterday. Galeri's knife was pushed under her cell door, a crude attempt to implicate Suor Violante in his killing. Later, a member of the visitation forced his way into her cell without cause or warning. She was frightened and defended herself, as anyone would. Suor Violante is not a violent person, and I do not believe she is a danger to others. Had she been left in peace, Signor Cortese would not have suffered the injuries he did. Suor Violante is innocent of having any part in what happened to Bernardo Galeri – of that, I am certain.'

The prioress mouthed her thanks to him.

Aldo turned back to the conclave. 'When the woman stabbing Galeri stopped, she discovered a problem: dead men do not bleed. No matter how many times he was stabbed, no blood came from his wounds. To make a knife attack look like the cause of death, there must be blood. That was how two novices became a part of this *strategia*.

'By now it was time for matins. Maria Celestia and Maria Vincenzia rose from their beds and came here to the chapter house.' He pointed to the bench opposite where Maria Vincenzia was scowling. 'Maria Vincenzia was approached first. I believe she readily agreed, and bullied Maria Celestia into helping. Maria Vincenzia made the other novice cut her own hands so they bled on the dead man's corpse. When that wasn't enough, Maria Vincenzia cut Maria Celestia's other hand, but still wasn't satisfied. So Maria Vincenzia coerced a servant nun working at the infirmary that night to fetch fresh blood from there. It was poured over Galeri's body as the convent awoke. Maria Vincenzia took her blood-stained habit to the laundry, hiding it with Galeri's clothes and taking a clean habit for herself. Finally, when the time was right, Maria Celestia burst from the scriptorium, screaming about murder.'

Maria Vincenzia leapt from the bench, face crimson with rage. 'You're lying!' she shouted. 'You have no proof of any of this!'

'Yes, he does,' a quiet voice responded from the far end of the chapter house. Maria Celestia stepped forward, unwrapping her hands to show those gathered the deep cuts on each palm. 'I told Signor Aldo what you did, and what you made me do. How you planned to spread rumours about the cuts to my hands being stigmata. How you used Suor Rigarda and Maria Teodora. How you had all of us do your bidding. Why, Maria Vincenzia? Why?'

'Yes,' Aldo echoed, 'tell us. Tell everyone why you poured blood over a dead man's corpse. Why you made another novice push that knife under Suor Violante's door. Why you poisoned a jug of wine and used it in a crude attempt to silence me after I loudly announced I knew who had killed Galeri. Why did you do all of this, Maria Vincenzia? Why?'

The red-faced novice lunged at him, fists flailing at the air. Aldo caught her wrists before she could strike him. She lashed out with her feet instead, kicking at him. Using the last of his strength, Aldo pushed her away. She tumbled to the floor, sprawling in front of the conclave. Maria Vincenzia whirled round, ready to—

'Enough!' The prioress rose, pointing at the novice. 'You will cease this behaviour before you cause any more harm to yourself or this convent. Is that understood?'

Maria Vincenzia glared, panting like a cornered animal.

The prioress strode to her, looming over the novice. 'Is that understood?'

There was nothing but silence. Aldo could see almost every eye in the chapter house was fixed on Maria Vincenzia. Almost. One amongst them was staring at the floor. She knew what was coming. She knew the accusations were not yet at an end.

'Yes,' Maria Vincenzia spat. 'I understand.'

'Good.' The prioress returned to her bench. 'Now, answer the questions. Truthfully.'

The novice gave the most grudging of nods.

'Thank you, prioress,' Aldo said. 'Now, Maria Vincenzia, if my account of what happened on the night of Palm Sunday is so wrong, please – tell us what did occur.'

She rose from the floor, brushing dust from her habit, trying to reclaim her dignity. 'Maria Celestia and I did come here to say matins. As we were returning to the dormitory, I realized I had forgotten my breviary. When I came back, I heard a noise from the scriptorium. I went in, and found one of the sisters with Signor Galeri's dead body. She said he had tricked his way into the convent and attacked her. She asked my help.'

'What were you asked to do?'

'She said if fresh blood was poured over the body as morning approached, those who came to investigate would mistake that blood for his. It would seem as if he had died not long before morning, while she was elsewhere.'

'You wanted to protect her,' Aldo said.

Maria Vincenzia nodded. 'I should not have involved Maria Celestia. That was a mistake. The blood from the infirmary would have been enough.'

'What about the knife, and the poison?'

'The sister found me again on Monday night and gave me the knife to hide. She said I should put it under Suor Violante's door if the visitation was getting close to finding it. And she told me where to find the poison.' The novice glared at Aldo. 'It was my idea to use that on you. I believed you were going to arrest her. You had to be silenced.'

Aldo nodded. That was what had passed between the novice and the chapter nun in the conversation Isabella overheard on Monday night.

The abbess rose from her seat. 'Then we can count ourselves fortunate you did not succeed. Not just because it saved a life, but because it also saved your immortal soul. If that wine had killed Aldo, you would have been beyond redemption.'

'We have heard what happened,' Aldo said, leaning on a chair for support, 'but you have not told us why. What drove you to such desperate acts, and who persuaded you to do such things?'

'I did not need persuading,' Maria Vincenzia replied, her chin held high. 'I believed I was saving the convent. I still do.'

'How?' the abbess demanded. 'How was all of this saving the convent?'

'For too long Santa Maria Magdalena has squandered its energies helping those who will not help themselves,' the novice said. 'This convent – all convents – would serve our Lord far better if we were enclosed, if we devoted ourselves to prayer and contemplation. If we followed the true path of our Lord, we would know the majesty of his glory.'

'Blood and poison and bullying, are those the stations of the cross on your true path?' Aldo asked.

Maria Vincenzia shook her head. 'You do not understand. But others here do.' She looked around the chapter house, searching for approval. Aldo followed the novice's gaze, but the faces staring back were ashen or shocked. Maria Vincenzia went to the prioress. 'You agree with me, don't you, sister? You are always saying the convent should be enclosed.'

'That is what I have long believed,' the prioress replied. 'But I could never condone what you have done. This convent faces dissolution. How does that serve the greater glory of God?' The prioress took Violante's hands in her own. 'And I could never forget what you did to my sister, even if I must forgive you for your trespasses.'

The novice staggered backwards as if slapped. 'But I thought – she said that you –'

Aldo called to her. 'Who was it? Who was the chapter nun that duped you? Who was the woman who lied to you, and used you the way you used all the others? Who was the one that slipped the blade into your hand, and put thoughts of poison in your head? Who was it that let you do all these things while her hands remained clean?'

Maria Vincenzia stopped, staring at Aldo as if seeing him for the first time.

'Who was it?'

She looked round, searching the faces of those gathered. The novice pointed at one of them. 'It was her.' Aldo followed the finger, seeing who it was she had picked out.

The convent's teaching nun, Suor Catarina.

# Chapter Thirty-four

❧

*A*ldo was grateful he had persuaded Isabella to remain at the infirmary helping Dea with patients. He knew how much she admired Catarina. Isabella would still be shocked when she heard, but there were better ways to discover those who help others can be flawed or broken.

It was a lesson Strocchi could soon be learning, if he had not done so already.

To her credit Catarina did not deny her part in what had happened. She rose at the abbess's invitation, coming forward to address the conclave. Aldo retreated to lean against a wall. He already knew the truth, had done since Andriana had sobbed out her confession in the chapel. But the convent needed to hear it from Catarina.

'I do not weep for Bernardo Galeri,' she began. 'What Signor Aldo has said about the dead man was all true. Galeri came to this convent as part of a visitation from the diocese, but used that to advance his own sinful purposes. He came to steal, and stayed to leer at the girls I teach. When I objected to Monsignor Testardo, nothing was done. Even here, inside our own convent, we are not safe from such men.

'Andriana told me of her unwise alliance with Galeri when we broke bread in the refectory on Palm Sunday. I stayed in her cell that night, rather than sleep in the dormitory.'

Aldo had confirmed this with the prioress whose bed was by the door of the dormitory where Catarina usually slept. When Testardo had questioned the prioress, she had been truthful in saying nobody left the dormitory that night and was about to tell him and Aldo that Catarina had spent the night elsewhere. But the monsignor's questions and his sneering attitude so angered the prioress that she kept it to herself. In his haste to conclude matters Testardo had missed a vital clue. Aldo knew he was equally culpable. Catarina had been so convincing when she denied killing Galeri – not a surprise, since it was the truth – that Aldo had not noticed her sin of omission about where she spent the night of Palm Sunday. A simple oversight, but one that had nearly cost him his life.

'I urged Andriana not to let Galeri into the convent,' Catarina said, 'but she believed his sly words and false reassurances. Her only folly is to see the good in those who can never be as pure of heart as her. That she must bear the cross of what happened . . .' Aldo noticed the nun's fists clenching at her sides. It was anger that had been her undoing. 'I blame myself for what took place that night, and in the days since. But Andriana was adamant, so I helped her. I went to Suor Paulina's cell and took the key for the back gates when she snored.'

Catarina clasped her hands together. 'When Andriana returned from meeting Galeri, I knew something terrible had happened. She showed me his body, told me what he had wanted her to do . . . His death was an accident, but I knew few would believe that if he was found there. I promised Andriana I would protect her. In that, as in many things, I failed. I knew we could not simply leave his body outside the back gates.'

She told the conclave about tidying the laundry, moving the body to the scriptorium, using Galeri's own knife to stab him. 'I lost myself,' she said, explaining why there were so many wounds. 'And then Maria Vincenzia came in. I knew how passionately she believed the convent should be enclosed. She would do almost anything to achieve that. I told Maria Vincenzia what she wanted to hear so she would do my bidding. Another of my failures . . .' Catarina shook her head. 'The fault is mine, and mine alone. I sought to protect one of my sisters in God, and in doing so I have sinned against our Lord and all of you. I shall confess all my transgressions, and let the judgement of others determine my future.'

Catarina's last words were to the abbess. 'I pray you may forgive me one day.'

Aldo led Catarina to the chapel where Father Visconti was waiting to hear her confession, as the abbess had arranged. Aldo went back to the cloister, slumping on a bench by a lavender bed. He inhaled, the plant's distinctive scent filling his nostrils. Would that aroma always bring him back to this place? Perhaps. But he carried worse memories.

Isabella came hurrying along the cloister. 'Is it true?' Word of what was revealed in the chapter house had reached the infirmary, it seemed.

'About Suor Catarina? I'm afraid so.'

'What will happen to her?'

'That is for the Church to decide,' Aldo replied. The same was true of Suor Violante after what she had done to Cortese, and of Suor Andriana for poisoning Galeri. Across the courtyard Monsignor Testardo was demanding entry, pushing his way past

Suor Benedicta, 'All of those involved must face the judgement of the diocese, as will the whole convent.'

Isabella sank down onto the bench beside him. 'That means I can't stay here, doesn't it?'

'Not in this convent, no. But if you wish to remain among nuns . . .'

Testardo was stalking towards Aldo.

Isabella laughed. 'Me, become a novice? I don't think so.'

'Then I shall take you home when I leave. Your parents will be relieved to see you.'

'Aldo!' Testardo snapped as he reached them, brandishing a scroll of parchment. 'What is the meaning of this? I was about to give my report on Galeri's murder when I was summoned back here. How did you get back inside this convent?'

'I never left,' Aldo replied, rising from the bench with Isabella's help. 'And there was no murder. Galeri was poisoned, as I told you yesterday, but his death was accidental.'

The monsignor snorted his disbelief. 'Do you have any proof of that?'

'Those responsible have already confessed their sins to the entire convent. Every nun, novice and boarder will be able to tell you what happened.' Aldo led Isabella away. 'I suggest you start by asking the abbess. She can confirm everything.'

Suor Giulia retreated to her workshop after the conclave concluded. She had little wish to engage in the gossip that would fill the convent for the rest of the day. Everyone had heard the words of Andriana, Catarina and Maria Vincenzia. Further talk would change nothing. The days of the convent were few. Better to spend those preparing for what was to come.

But she had not been in her workshop long when the prioress knocked at the door. 'I need you to come with me,' she said, offering no further explanation. Giulia followed her into the abbess's *officio*. The abbess was sifting papers at her desk, but Giulia could see no enthusiasm in the effort. 'I wish to apologize,' the prioress said. 'Since the day you became abbess, I have done little to support you and much to undermine you. Pride would not let me accept a younger woman as abbess, and my vanity made me believe the convent deserved better.'

Giulia struggled to keep the surprise from her face. In the many years she had known the prioress, there had never been such humility in the woman.

'Judging by the past few days,' the abbess said, 'I cannot help but wonder if things would have been different with you as our leader.'

The prioress shook her head. 'Things would have been worse. I am too stubborn to accept the wisdom of others. Suor Giulia came to me more than once, warning there was a serpent among our novices – but I did not listen. So, I am stepping aside, and I suggest you make Giulia prioress for however long we have left here. If she is willing, of course.'

Giulia failed to hide her surprise. 'I . . . I don't know what to say.'

'Then I will take that as an acceptance,' the abbess said before turning to the prioress. 'Our dissolution will be ordered before Holy Week ends. What will you do then?'

'I have promised Violante we will find a new convent, a fresh start for both of us. She will face punishment from the diocese for what happened with Signor Cortese, but I have a few allies among the archbishop's clerics who may be able to help us. A convent outside the city would be for the best, somewhere Violante can know peace and contentment.'

That sounded inviting to Giulia. But before she could wish the prioress and her sister well, a fist bludgeoned the *officio* door. 'Abbess, it is Monsignor Testardo.'

'Enter,' the abbess called.

Testardo strode inside. 'Is what Aldo told me true?'

'One moment please, monsignor.' The abbess smiled at Giulia and the prioress. 'Thank you both for all you have done. It seems I will be occupied with other matters for quite some time, but I hope to see you later in the refectory.'

Giulia bowed to the monsignor on her way out, getting a curt nod in return. It was a long time since she had been so grateful to escape a man's anger.

Aldo escorted Isabella back to Palazzo Fioravanti as the sun reached its peak over the city. After the quiet solemnity of the convent, the bustle of Florence was an assault on the ears, the eyes and the nostrils. The closer he and Isabella got to the Duomo, the more crowded the streets became. Horse-drawn carts rumbled through the crowds, while hawkers did their best to interest passing servants. The ripe aroma of piss wafted from channels in the centre of each street, while body odour and flies crowded the air.

It was a relief to escape along back streets and side alleys. Isabella kept stopping to look around herself, as if seeing everything for the first time. 'I don't often get to walk,' she explained. 'Certainly not without Mama or my maid for company. Even when we go to church, I have to ride in our bumpy old carriage with *Nonna*.'

When they reached the palazzo, Aldo told Isabella to go in alone. He bore no wish to encounter Lucrezia again. Besides, he had done what Teresa had asked, bringing her daughter home from the convent. It took two days, far longer than he had expected, but she was safely returned. Isabella seemed disappointed when he refused to accompany her inside. She embraced him, promising to write letters. 'Where should I have Nucca deliver them?'

'The Palazzo del Podestà,' Aldo replied. It was as good a place as any to find him, though he might not be an officer much longer. Not if Strocchi had discovered the truth.

Isabella went inside, and Aldo strolled past Santa Croce to the wide piazza beyond it. The day and a half inside the convent had almost been the death of him. But it had also been a respite. There were times inside Santa Maria Magdalena when Aldo had forgotten what was waiting. But as he crossed the piazza, the prospect of returning to the Podestà loomed ahead.

'Cesare!' He looked back and saw Teresa running towards him, one hand holding the hem of her gown to keep it out of the dust and dirt and worse. She stopped several paces short of him. 'You didn't come in.'

'No. Not after last time.'

She grimaced. 'I'm sorry for what Mama said to you.'

'It doesn't matter,' Aldo said. 'I stopped caring what that old *strega* thought of me a long time ago. She can drown in her own venom. It would be a just end for her.'

'I still wanted to thank you. For bringing Isabella back to us.'

'She has a good heart. She reminds me of someone else when they were her age.'

Teresa smiled. 'I have persuaded Mama to delay the wedding.'

'Isabella will be pleased, Aldo said. 'Now I must report to the Podestà, otherwise the *segretario* will think I have died.'

'You almost did.' Teresa forced a smile. 'Isabella told me what happened.'

Aldo's gaze slid past her to Palazzo Fioravanti in the distance.

'You cannot see poison when it is hidden in a cup, or in a place.' He bowed his head to Teresa before striding away.

'Will we . . . see you again?' she called.

'When the old *cagna* is dead. Not before.'

Strocchi spent his morning investigating a *denunzia* made by an angry landlady who claimed her tenant must be torturing people, so long were the cries coming from above her. In fact, the tenant was entertaining a boisterous and very loud young woman. Strocchi suggested they try being quieter or meeting elsewhere before leaving them to their pleasures.

The constable strode back to the Podestà, frustrated at wasting his time. Was this the way things would be while he remained a constable? Perhaps he should join another court. The city had dozens of them, and most needed good men. While Bindi remained in charge it seemed there were few prospects at the Otto. If Tomasia did have a baby, then coin would be much tighter for them, and constables had few opportunities to earn extra *giuli*.

He was still worrying what to do as he neared the Podestà gates. A familiar figure was approaching from the other direction: Aldo. The officer seemed more tired than usual, grey stubble across the chin adding years to his appearance. In that moment, Strocchi knew. Aldo had killed Cerchi. There was no proof, there never would be unless Aldo confessed.

But Strocchi knew. He knew.

Aldo noticed the constable and smiled, but there was a wariness behind his eyes. 'How goes the investigation?'

Strocchi paused, unsure how to reply. Should he say Bindi had closed the case? Aldo would hear that soon enough. 'I could not find enough proof to satisfy the *segretario*.'

'And what about naming a replacement for Cerchi?'

'No new officer has been named, nor does it seem any will be.'

'I'm sorry to hear that,' Aldo said, resting a hand on the constable's right shoulder. Strocchi flinched, unable to stop himself. Aldo stepped back, a shadow passing over his face. 'Well, shall we go inside?'

They strolled into the courtyard side by side, Strocchi aware of the distance between them. 'Despite what the *segretario* has decided, I believe I know who Cerchi met that night.'

'You do?'

'Yes.' Strocchi stopped by the stone staircase. 'I need your advice on what to do next.'

'Of course,' Aldo said, his face a blank mask. 'I suspect I will be busy much of the day. I could buy you a cup of wine at Zoppo's later, if you are feeling brave?'

Strocchi recalled his last visit there. 'I'm not sure he will welcome me back so soon.'

'Aldo!' The name echoed around the courtyard, bellowed from above by Bindi, standing in the *loggia*. 'You have some explaining to do. Get up here. Now!'

'Yes, *segretario*,' Aldo replied before smiling at the constable. 'Seems I am needed.'

'Ponte Vecchio,' Strocchi blurted. 'That's where I'll meet you. Tonight, at sunset.'

Aldo arched an eyebrow at him. 'Are you sure that's what you want?'

No, Strocchi wasn't sure. He didn't know why he had made the suggestion. But he couldn't hide away from the truth any longer. He had to know. 'Yes.'

'Very well.' Aldo strode away up the stone stairs.

Strocchi swallowed hard. What had he done?

## Chapter Thirty-five

*I* n his *officio* Bindi summoned Aldo forward with a single finger, pointing at the floor where the officer should stand. 'I had a message to say you'd been poisoned.'

'I survived,' Aldo replied.

'You seem to have a talent for making people want to kill you,' Bindi observed.

'Serving the Otto can be . . . challenging.'

'You could always serve another court. Perhaps the Office of Decency? Bearing in mind where you live, I would have thought you had an . . . intimate knowledge of such things.' It did not help the reputation of the court to have one of its officers call such a place home. Bindi hoped his comment might unsettle. Instead, it provoked a smile.

'I am happy where I am,' Aldo replied.

'So be it. I will hear your report now.'

'*Segretario?*'

Did Aldo not understand, or was he being wilfully obtuse? Bindi had few illusions about how cunning a creature stood in front of him. 'I wish to know what occurred at the convent. When an officer is seconded to another authority, either within the city or outside its walls, I am entitled to know the substance and outcome of those duties, in case they should have any bearing on or relevance to the deliberations of the Otto.'

Aldo gave a summary of what had occurred inside Santa Maria Magdalena in recent days. Little was relevant to the court – an accidental death by poisoning, the desecration of a body, another poisoning attempt – but Bindi enjoyed asking Aldo needless questions and interrupting him as often as possible.

When the tale was told, Bindi let himself smile. The court had been fortunate to escape involvement with such a tangled web of deceit. 'It sounds as if Monsignor Testardo will have a difficult time explaining all that to the archbishop.' The *segretario* had met Testardo a few times, and found him to be both officious and self-righteous.

'Indeed,' Aldo agreed.

'What will become of the nuns responsible for these incidents?'

'That is a matter for the Church to decide—'

'I'm quite aware of that,' Bindi snapped before he could stop himself. No matter the disparity in their positions or the frequency of their meetings, Aldo continued to be a stone in the shoe – irritating, irksome and persistent. 'I was merely asking for your assessment of what actions shall be taken.'

Aldo pursed his lips before replying. 'The convent faces dissolution, but the abbess may still have an opportunity to influence where her nuns are sent. If wise – and I do not believe her to be any kind of fool – the abbess will ensure the novice Maria Vincenzia is kept from taking her vows until she shows true remorse. The others know what they did was wrong, and are seeking redemption. But Maria Vincenzia . . . those who believe the absolute correctness of their decisions are always the most dangerous.'

Bindi sent Aldo away, but those final words festered afterwards. The *segretario* believed in the absolute correctness of his choices. Or had Aldo been talking about himself?

* * *

The abbess spent an unhappy hour explaining all that had happened to Monsignor Testardo. He insisted on confirming events with the prioress, and speaking to both Suor Andriana and Suor Catarina, before finally accepting what he had been told.

'I shall alter my report to reflect this new information,' Testardo said, 'but certain fundamental truths remain. A diocesan visitor died within these walls due to the actions of one of your sisters in God. His body was defiled, and two novices attempted to conceal aspects of that. When they failed, one sought to kill another visitor by poisoning him.'

The monsignor's interpretation was partial, but the abbess held her tongue. Men such as Testardo did not respond well to being corrected, let alone by a woman.

'I shall still be recommending this convent be dissolved,' he continued. 'There has been a fundamental failure of leadership here. The fact that someone responsible for teaching the daughters of this city's most important families could be part of this . . .' Testardo shook his head. 'I will urge the archbishop to act with every haste. Holy Week must not be further disrupted by what has happened here, by what your nuns have done.'

The abbess escorted him from the convent, bowing respectfully as he departed. In any other circumstance his supercilious sneering would have enraged her, but she did not have the luxury of such anger. There was no denying what was to come, no bargain to be struck. All that remained was sadness and acceptance.

She took a slow walk around the cloister, enjoying the scent of Suor Benedicta's early lavender as it blossomed in the warm after-noon sunshine. She would miss this place, the quiet hum of prayer, the texture of the wooden benches and doors, the way the bells of the church echoed round the courtyard. She would miss the company of women she knew and loved as sisters in God. Some she would see again, others would be cast to the wind, sent to convents far beyond the walls of Florence. She might well be one of them, banished from the city for her failures. But before that happened, she would write a letter recommending Maria Vincenzia be refused the chance to take her final vows.

Perhaps attention would be paid to such a letter, perhaps not. The novice's *famiglia* gave many generous donations to the Church, and to the archbishop in particular – Maria Vincenzia had made certain everyone knew about that. It was her sense of entitlement that made the novice so dangerous. Let her never become a leader of women.

The abbess knew her own time in a position of authority was over. But perhaps the good that had been done at Santa Maria Magdalena would live on in the community, and in most of those who had lived within its walls. That was still worth believing in, wasn't it?

Aldo went from the Podestà to the *bordello* for a rest, and a fresh tunic and hose. Better to banish the scent of lavender from his nostrils before going to Palazzo Ruggerio, just as it was wiser to set aside thinking about the meeting to come with Strocchi. Aldo needed to gather what strength he had left after the poisoning. He would need all of it in the hours still ahead. There could be no distractions when facing a venomous creature like the silk merchant in his own home, and no signs of weakness could be shown.

Ruggerio beamed as Aldo was ushered in. 'Welcome back.' The merchant rose from behind the impressive desk, emerald robe fluttering as he strolled to a side table. 'May I offer you a drink?' he asked, pouring wine into a golden goblet.

'No, thank you,' Aldo replied, grimacing.

Ruggerio nodded. 'Yes, I heard about that unfortunate incident.'

How did the merchant know? Nobody outside the convent had been told, except . . . The abbess had sent Bindi word. It was foolish to believe Ruggerio did not have at least one man within the Podestà ready to report anything of value to the merchant.

Aldo forced a smile. 'It seems I am not easy to get rid of.'

'True. But we all have our . . . vulnerabilities.'

Aldo had not come to indulge his host's fondness for intrigue. 'Do you need me to recount what happened inside the convent?'

'No.' Ruggerio returned to his high-backed gold chair, goblet of wine in hand. 'I have already heard from certain sympathetic individuals within the archbishop's residence what Testardo reported. Quite a tangled web seems to have been spun inside my dear sister's convent. No, I prefer to hear about the items my brethren placed at the convent for safekeeping.' He leaned forward. 'Tell me, Cesare, are they secure? Are they safe?'

Aldo bristled at hearing the name his father had given him come from those thin lips. 'I have seen them,' he said. 'I know where they are, and I know what has happened to them.'

'Where—'

'But before I share that with you, I have questions of my own.'

Ruggerio sank back in his chair, sipping the wine. The silence between them stretched and grew, like a serpent uncoiling in the late afternoon sun. But Aldo held the merchant's glare without flinching, well used to such *stratagemmi*. 'Very well,' Ruggerio eventually said. 'Ask your questions.'

'When last I visited, you admitted Galeri had been a member of your confraternity. You indicated he bought his way in, but was unable to sustain the level of donations expected because his fabric-dying workshop went out of business. Galeri misspent his funds on gambling, whoring – the usual tawdry vices, I believe you said.'

'I thought you were asking me questions, not repeating my words back to me.'

Aldo smiled. 'I've been to Galeri's workshop, and I've seen where he lived. Your men did a thorough job with their ransacking, you'll be pleased to hear. Such a pity they could not find what they were looking for . . .'

'I don't know what you mean—'

'Yes, you do,' Aldo cut in. 'There is no possibility Galeri ever had enough coin to join the confraternity. His business had been close to collapse for years. No. I believe someone paid on Galeri's behalf so he could become one of your brethren. And I'm certain that same person vouched for Galeri's good character. After all, a respected confraternity would never allow a stranger to join its membership without the correct assurances.'

Ruggerio's face soured but he did not reply.

'I will take your silence as agreement,' Aldo said, moving closer to the desk. 'And if I were to enquire further, no doubt I would find your name among those to whom Galeri owed coin before he joined the confraternity.'

'He owed money to a great many merchants—'

'So you offered Galeri a way out. An opportunity to clear his debts, to escape the noose into which he had placed his own neck. Your sister, the Abbess of Santa Maria Magdalena, had become unhelpful. Perhaps she refused to allow you access to what was stored in her *officio*. It was fascinating to see the papers in that locked cabinet, to discover what they revealed. Galeri was drawn to one in particular, a warrant of authority written by Savonarola for his youthful acolytes.'

'Ask your question or leave,' Ruggerio warned. The fact that he had not contradicted Aldo's speculations helped confirm them.

'All in good time.' Aldo smiled. 'Perhaps I will have some wine. No, don't get up. I'll pour my own.' He strolled to the side table, filling a goblet as he spoke. 'I wasn't alive when Florence fell under Savonarola's influence, but I've heard the stories. How fear of damnation drove people to worship a monk with a gift for sermons. How angry mobs gathered to do his bidding. How young men roamed the streets, beating at the doors of God-fearing citizens, demanding they surrender their vanities for the bonfire – books and paintings, musical instruments and the finest clothes, manuscripts for songs about anything other than God. A collective madness gripped the city, and terrible crimes committed in Savonarola's name went unpunished.' Aldo sipped the wine. 'Hmm, very good.' He approached the desk. 'You must have been fourteen or fifteen when all of this was happening, as would the others who now lead your brethren. The perfect age to become acolytes of Savonarola, his *piagnoni*.'

'Enough,' Ruggerio hissed.

'That doesn't explain why you – sorry, why members of the confraternity – have kept Savonarola's warrant of authority safely locked away all this time. Most people who have done terrible things would destroy any evidence of their part in it. But you and your fellow *piagnoni* did not do that, I wonder why? Perhaps those named on that warrant of authority still believe in the mad monk's teachings. Or perhaps there is another reason, something that has bound them together ever since. So instead of burning the evidence they chose to keep it safe, locked away where none of them could get at it, knowing that if any one of them sought to use that knowledge all of them would be destroyed. An unholy pact, but one that became the basis for your confraternity. One that turned you and your brethren into a powerful faction within this city. But then something changed.'

Aldo put the goblet down on Ruggerio's desk. It was fine wine, but tasted sour on the tongue. 'You paid for Galeri to join the confraternity, vouching for his good character so he became one of the visitors Testardo took inside the convent. When that attempt to retrieve the documents failed, you gave Galeri coin to hire a burglar adept at climbing to steal inside after dark. Still Galeri could not deliver what you craved, and a report reached the confraternity about an intruder trying to get into the convent after dark. You offered to use your influence with the Otto to have this report investigated, reassuring your brethren. But you also sent Galeri in by himself, after dark on Palm Sunday. He failed a third time, and this time his lust got him killed. No wonder you so willingly agreed to have me take his place in the second visitation. You needed someone to tidy your mess.'

Ruggerio rose from his chair, calling for servants to escort Aldo out.

'I still want answers,' Aldo said, raising his voice to be heard over the merchant's shouting. 'Why the sudden urgency? Those documents have been safely kept at the convent for years. Why the need to reclaim them now? Did you fear what Testardo's visitation might find? Or was there another reason? The abbess told me about a thief who stole into the convent months ago, a thief who claimed they were searching for treasures. Did you hear about this and realize there were others trying to get their hands on what was in that cabinet?'

Servants burst into the *officio*, followed by two guards. 'My guest is leaving,' Ruggerio told them. 'Please ensure he does so. Now.'

'Someone else knows what you did,' Aldo said as the guards grabbed his arms. 'Someone who isn't part of your cosy confraternity.

Someone who can't be bought for a pouchful of coin like Galeri. Someone who makes you afraid.'

'Get him out of here,' Ruggerio snarled.

'I look forward to being there when they show you justice,' Aldo called as he was dragged from the *officio*. 'Consequences catch up with us all one day.'

## Chapter Thirty-six

Strocchi strode up the stones of Ponte Vecchio as the warm spring afternoon was fading. He hadn't known what to do with himself while waiting to meet Aldo. A trip home to see Tomasia proved fruitless. He had forgotten that she was working late. He considered leaving a note explaining where he had gone and why, in case his worst fears became the truth. If Aldo had murdered Cerchi to protect himself, what would he do to someone who discovered that? But the right words escaped the constable. He would have to trust his beliefs. Aldo was capable of killing, but did not take a life without reason. They had a friendship of sorts.

That should be enough protection – shouldn't it?

Now, as Strocchi reached the crest of the bridge, he wasn't so sure. Aldo could be utterly ruthless when it was necessary, doing whatever he must. That was how he had stayed alive in Le Stinche, a prison holding many inmates who had been sent there by him. Plenty did their best to kill him, but Aldo had walked back out, bruised and battered but still alive.

Confronting him, accusing him, threatening him – all were inviting a closer look at Aldo's stiletto. Whatever else happened, the constable knew he must not make Aldo believe there was no alternative to leaving the bridge without bloodshed.

Ponte Vecchio was near empty. All the stalls had shut for the day, servants and traders gone home for a meal and wine and sleep. The closer it got to curfew, the fewer people were left. Strocchi leaned against a stone parapet, looking down the Arno towards the setting sun. A cool breeze was blowing along the river. But it was not cold enough to explain his shivering.

'Beautiful, isn't it?' Aldo stopped beside Strocchi, the setting sun warming his face. 'There are few better sights than watching a day's end from this bridge.'

'It is impressive,' Strocchi agreed.

They stood in silence, watching the sun slip out of sight, its last rays colouring the distant clouds. By the time twilight was lowering its shroud over the city, they were alone. Nobody else to witness what happened, nobody to hear what was said. Aldo turned away from the river. 'So you believe you know who met Cerchi here the night he died.'

'Yes.'

'How?'

Strocchi hesitated, choosing his words with care. He did not want to accuse Aldo outright of murder or of his other alleged sin. 'A witness heard them talking. It seems Cerchi was extorting coin. He said from that night on the other man would be his whore. The witness heard a sound that could have been Cerchi getting stabbed. Then something fall into the river.'

Aldo nodded. 'That matches what you told me at Zoppo's tavern. But it doesn't explain how you know who was here that night.'

'Cerchi mentioned a name, someone who had unwittingly given Cerchi the means for his *stratagemma*.' Strocchi looked in Aldo's eyes. 'That person doesn't know any of this. All they recall is Cerchi getting them drunk, and asking a lot of questions about another officer with the Otto.' Aldo remained impassive. 'Questions about you.'

Still Aldo did not respond.

Strocchi was finding it difficult to swallow, his mouth dry. 'I made my final report to Bindi this morning. Told him there wasn't enough evidence to prove who was here the night Cerchi was killed. The case is closed. It's over.'

Aldo nodded. 'But you still have questions.'

'Yes.'

'And you want my advice before deciding what to do next.'

'Yes.'

To Strocchi's surprise, Aldo laughed. He continued laughing, shaking his head. 'Forgive me,' he said, holding up a hand. 'I was warning someone earlier that consequences catch up with us all. I should have listened to my own words.'

'I don't understand,' Strocchi said. 'Are you admitting that you ...'

The smile fell from Aldo's face. 'I don't have to explain myself to you.'

'But I need to understand what happened.'

'Why?'

'I'm sorry?'

'Will it make a difference? Did discovering how Cerchi died bring him back? Will proving who killed him undo what was done?'

'No, but—'

Aldo jabbed a finger in Strocchi's chest. 'What makes you think it was murder?'

The constable took a step back. 'I saw his remains, the notch in his ribs where the blade passed between them.'

'You saw what probably killed him.'

'Yes.'

'But what makes you think it was murder?'

'I—I don't understand.'

'No, you don't. And that's the problem.' Aldo strode to the other side of the bridge, putting distance between himself and Strocchi. The constable noticed a weariness in Aldo. Was that from the poisoning he had suffered at the convent or was something else weighing on him? 'Let's say you're right about how Cerchi died. He was stabbed here on Ponte Vecchio. He fell over the parapet and into the Arno. The river swept him away, drowning Cerchi, if he wasn't already dead. What if the person who held the knife was defending themselves, or someone else? What if killing Cerchi saved lives? Would his death still be murder?'

'I . . .' Strocchi shrugged. 'Tomasia asked me much the same thing.'

'And what did you tell her?'

'That it would depend.'

'On what?'

'The circumstances.'

'So if the man with the blade feared that his life was in immediate danger, stabbing Cerchi would have been justified?' Aldo reached down to his left boot. 'What if the danger was not immediate, but they knew Cerchi would be responsible for their death, sooner or later? Would that have been justified?'

'I don't . . .'

Pulling out his stiletto, Aldo marched at Strocchi with the blade in front of him, ready for use. 'If I put this to your throat now, if I made you fear for your life, would you be right to kill me?' Strocchi stumbled backwards until he was pressed against the parapet. Still Aldo kept coming closer until the tip of his stiletto was a hair away from Strocchi's neck. 'Well?'

'I don't know,' Strocchi whispered, fear clenching inside him. 'I don't know!'

Aldo stared into Strocchi's eyes, keeping the knife at his neck.

'That's the problem,' Aldo said at last. 'You don't know the whole truth of what happened that night. You may have discovered some of it, but not enough to determine what justice, true justice, would be.' He stepped back, returning the stiletto to his boot.

Strocchi pressed a hand to his throat where the blade had been. For a moment he had feared what Aldo might do, had imagined what it would be like if the tip pierced skin. 'Tomasia tells me I am too innocent for the Otto, too credulous. That I believe too easily.'

'She's right,' Aldo said. 'You believe what you have been taught. That there is good and evil, and nothing between them. That there is only one way to love and be loved. But this is Florence. This city knows all kinds of love and sin. Justice can be bought and sold here, if you have enough coin. You witnessed what happened with Corsini and Ruggerio. One died, the other ordered it, and the law was set aside because of Ruggerio's power and influence. Your folly is to believe there is only one truth to any crime.'

'What you describe as folly I call principles,' Strocchi said.

'Perhaps, but they have little place in this city. Have you not grasped that yet?'

'Cerchi was murdered—'

'Cerchi was killed,' Aldo cut in. 'You are the only one calling it murder.'

Strocchi didn't have an answer to that.

'Is the world a worse place without Cerchi?' Aldo asked.

'We do not kill people to make the world a better place,' Strocchi insisted.

'If Cerchi were here he would not hesitate to do exactly that.

He used and abused his position with the Otto. He drove at least one man to death. You talk about justice, yet did Cerchi seek justice for the murder of Corsini? No. All he saw was an opportunity, a chance to fill his pouch with coin.' Aldo raised his chin. 'I cannot – I will not – regret Cerchi's death. You must decide what you do now. I have no advice to give you. None.'

Strocchi realized he and Aldo would never agree on this, or the other matter they had been discussing without ever saying so out loud. They were further apart than the banks of the Arno, with no means to span the gap. 'Very well,' he said. 'But I cannot – I will not – work alongside a man who finds nothing to regret in what happened here.'

'Meaning what?'

'One of us must leave.'

'Leave?'

'The Otto. Or the city. Something must change, Aldo. I know too much now, and I cannot continue with things the way they are.' Strocchi raised his hands, hoping to make some argument that would convince Aldo, but could not find the words. 'It's what you said earlier. These are the consequences of what happened.'

Aldo's glare softened. 'Consequences catch up with us all one day.'

'Yes.'

Strocchi looked around. Night was falling across the city. While they talked the buildings either side of the river had become black shapes against the blue of the darkening sky, lights from lanterns peeking through shutters. Tomasia would be home by now, preparing food and wondering where he was. 'I'm going to be a father,' he blurted.

'You are?' There was enough moonlight for Strocchi to see the surprise in Aldo's face. 'Tomasia is with child?'

'She thinks so. I didn't mean to tell anyone until she was sure, but –'

Aldo smiled at him. 'You will make a good father, Carlo, with her at your side. Especially when you learn that certainty is never so certain as you first believed.'

'If I am half the man my own papa was, that would be good enough.'

Aldo's smile faded in the darkness. 'So . . . one of us will go.'

'It seems . . . necessary.'

'So be it.' Aldo strolled away, heading south towards Oltrarno. He paused, looking back over one shoulder. 'Give my best to Tomasia.' Then he disappeared into the shadows.

Saul was closing his front door as Aldo strode along via dei Giudei. Hard to believe it was only two nights since they had parted company here, not after all that had happened since . . . Two days, two nights, and a lifetime in between. But the doctor's smile was still the same warm welcome when he saw Aldo approaching.

'You're back,' Saul said, his eyes twinkling in the light that spilled from his doorway. 'Do you require more medical advice?'

'Not this time,' Aldo said. 'There are things you need to know about me. About why I stayed away so long. About things I've done. To protect myself, and you.'

Saul put a hand to his skullcap. 'In case you hadn't noticed, I'm not a priest.'

'And I'm not asking for absolution. But I still need you to know the truth.'

'We all have our secrets, Cesare.'

'Yes, but—'

'Whatever you need to say, whatever you believe I should know

– we can talk about it later.' Saul stepped aside, gesturing for Aldo to go in. 'We've waited long enough.'

Aldo swallowed hard before stepping across the threshold. Saul closed the door behind them, shutting out the world.

# Historical Note

*The Darkest Sin* is a work of fiction, but some aspects and certain characters in the story are based on real incidents and people. Andrea Buondelmonti was the Archbishop of Florence from 1532 until his death ten years later. By many accounts he was a venal and grasping man, which informed his portrayal in these pages. The character of Suor Violante was inspired by an incident recounted in the letters of Sister Maria Celeste to her father Galileo Galilei, as translated by Dava Sobel in the excellent volume *To Father*.

The convent of Santa Maria Magdalena and its nuns are my own creation, but there were numerous convents clustered along via San Gallo in this period. Estimates vary but it is believed that one in twenty Florentine women were nuns, and some believe far more were living in convents at this time. My portrayal of convent life is based on factual accounts of Florentine convents from the fifteenth, sixteenth and seventeenth centuries. Sobel's book was one of these, alongside *Nuns' Chronicles and Convent Culture* by K. J. P. Lowe, *Sisters in Arms* by Jo Ann Kay McNamara, *Nuns and Nunneries in Renaissance Florence* by Sharon T. Strocchia, and *Nuns: A History of Convent Life* by Silvia Evangelisti. This novel owes a debt to those texts, and many others too numerous to name here. Any mistakes or historical inaccuracies in how *The Darkest Sin* portrays convent life during this period are mine alone.

The enclosure of convents was a matter of considerable debate in this period, both inside and outside their walls. In some convents the nuns were united against attempts by the Church authorities to enforce enclosure. For example, there is a wonderful account of nuns climbing on the roof of their convent and hurling tiles at male clerics to stop them imposing such an order. But the issue also fiercely divided many convents, as portrayed in these pages. In Florence, Duke Cosimo de' Medici ordered a census of the city's nuns during the 1540s and interfered with the convent system during that decade and the next. His actions were a forerunner of what was to come with the enclosure of convents being mandated by Church decree later in the sixteenth century.

# Acknowledgements

*I* am indebted to everyone at Pan Macmillan for making *The Darkest Sin* look so splendid and read so well. Special thanks to editor Alex Saunders, cover designer Neil Lang, publicity director Philippa McEwan and to publisher Jeremy Trevathan for believing in Cesare Aldo.

Numerous friends have helped make this novel happen, too many to name here. But special thanks go to fellow writers Nell Pattison and Liz King, and to my colleagues El Lam and Daniel Shand on the creative writing programme at Edinburgh Napier University; their support and reassurances made a world of difference during the writing process.

I am blessed to be represented by the wonderful literary agent Jenny Brown, whose enthusiasm and effervescence lifts up so many writers.

But most of all I must thank my better half, who survived me writing this book during lockdown. Saints could learn from such patience and support. Thank you!

Read on for an extract from book three
in the Cesare Aldo series . . .

# Ritual of Fire

## BY D. V. BISHOP

# Chapter One

***

Thursday, May 23rd 1538

Cesare Aldo could still smell flesh burning, even from this distance.

In Florence it would have been one scent among many, easily missed in the city's overwhelming assault of stenches and sounds and sights. But here in the Tuscan countryside there was time to inhale unexpected aromas, to deduce where they were coming from, and to follow an acrid odour across a hillside to its source.

Even in the meagre light of a sickle moon, Aldo had not struggled to find his quarry. Few people roasted meat over an outdoor fire this long after midnight, not unless they were fools or banditi. Looking down on the inept cook hunched in the hollow of a rocky slope, Aldo knew this was no bandit. Any doubts about their foolishness were banished when the stolen capon fell into the fire, prompting a string of curses. The panicked thief failed to retrieve the bird but almost set his sleeve alight. More curses filled the air.

Aldo had seen and heard and smelled enough. Pulling the stiletto from his boot, he chose a careful path down the hillside, avoiding fallen branches and tinder-dry twigs that would signal his approach. His quarry was too busy pushing the charred capon out of the fire with a stick to notice until Aldo stepped into the light.

'What are you doing here?' the thief asked.

'I could ask you the same question,' Aldo replied, 'but the answer is at your feet, Lippo.' The thief had been a successful pickpocket in Florence until he was arrested by Aldo and sent to Le Stinche. Repeated rule breaches inside the prison led to Lippo's favoured right arm being cut off as a punishment. 'Things aren't going well, are they?' Aldo asked. 'Reduced to stealing farmyard fowls from peasants in the countryside.'

'I wouldn't take food from peasants,' Lippo protested, jabbing a stick through the charred capon and lifting it in the air. 'This came from that grand villa further up the hill.'

The grand villa belonged to Girolamo Ruggerio, one of the most ruthless merchants in Florence, but Aldo chose not to mention this to Lippo. Not yet. 'I know where the bird came from,' Aldo said, 'but thank you for confessing where you took it from. Saves me having to gather any more evidence.' He pointed his stiletto at the ground in front of Lippo. 'Sit. It won't be sunrise for a few hours, so we'll be waiting here a while.' Lippo scowled but did as he was told. Aldo leaned against the trunk of a stunted olive tree, blade still in hand. The prospect of chasing the thief in the weak moonlight was not appealing.

'Can I at least eat the bird?' Lippo asked.

'If you wish,' Aldo said, 'but most of it is probably still raw. Better to leave it in the embers until the flesh cooks through, otherwise you'll be sick all the way to Florence.'

'You're taking me back? For stealing a capon?'

'For stealing three capons, one barrel of wine, half a sack of millet you abandoned a mile from where you took it, plus that doublet and the boots you're wearing.'

Lippo looked down at his clothes. The doublet was made of black embroidered silk and the boots were of the softest brown leather, while his woollen hose were a patchwork of tears and stains. 'Have you been following me all the way from the city?'

Aldo laughed. 'Far from it. I am the Otto di Balia e Guardia's representative for the lands east of Florence, enforcing laws and hunting criminals for the court. I spent the past two days investigating a supposed dispute between two farmers in a village twenty miles further east of here, after someone sent me a letter claiming the quarrel was about to turn bloody. But when I finally got there, both men denied having any argument, or knowing who sent the letter. I returned to a message from the Otto containing an order for your arrest. It said you were released from Le Stinche after serving your time and went straight back to thieving.'

'I didn't go straight back to thieving,' Lippo protested. 'Well, not the same day.'

'Perhaps. But trying to steal the purse from one of the Otto's own magistrates?'

'It was a mistake,' the thief conceded.

'So was fumbling the job and letting him see you were missing an arm . . .'

'That was shameful.' Lippo stared at his stump. 'Never would have happened before.'

'When I read that you had fled into the dominion, I knew it wouldn't be long before you got into more trouble,' Aldo said. 'So I offered coin for reports of any petty pilfering in this area. You obligingly left a trail of thefts all the way here from Florence.'

'A man's got to eat.'

'Half a sack of millet?'

'That was also a mistake.' Lippo sighed, giving the capon a prod. 'You working in the dominion now? Wondered why I didn't see you at the Palazzo del Podestà last time I got arrested.'

Aldo smiled. 'Consider it fortunate I'm the one who caught you out here.'

'Why? You're taking me back to Le Stinche. I won't last a month in there.'

'I'm surprised you survived a week out here. The Otto has branded you an outlaw. That means any other outlaw can capture or kill you and get their own offences reduced as a reward. That's better than any bounty. Most of them would kill you.'

Lippo shook his head. 'I didn't know.'

'You wouldn't . . . until they found you.' Aldo folded both arms across his chest but made sure the stiletto was still visible in his grasp. Lippo had many flaws, but he was far from lacking in guile. If there seemed any chance of escape, he would take it.

'So,' the thief said, 'why are you out here?'

'It's a long tale . . .'

'If we're going to be here till sunrise it might help to pass the time.'

'It's a long tale,' Aldo repeated, 'but not one I care to share with you.'

'Fair enough,' Lippo said, holding up his one hand in surrender. 'I understand, I do. Leaving the city that you love, it tears at a man. Makes him feel—'

'You can be silent, or I can make you silent.' Aldo stood upright, unfolding his arms so the stiletto caught the firelight. Lippo opened his mouth to speak, but closed it again.

A wise choice.

*You wait. Everything is prepared, everything is ready. The cart is lined with tinder, oil poured over it to be sure the dry hay and twigs burn fast. The gibbet you nailed to the cart is sturdy, strong enough for the weight of two men. You have several flints to start the fire, should one of them fail. You have more dry hay and discarded paper to catch the spark.*

*You wait. It will be time soon enough.*

*You know the patrols that wander the streets of Florence during curfew, the long hours between sunset and sunrise. The men seem lazy and witless, wandering the same circuit through the murky gloom each night. They pass once as the bells chime for the end of the day, a second time near midnight, and a third as the first hints of sunrise lighten the sky.*

*You wait. Your fingers itch.*

*Luring your target here was simple. You delivered the letter a day ago, along with a full pouch of coin and the promise of secrets. One was true currency, but secrets are always more valuable in this city. The target came willingly, without guard or escort. Greed and his lust for knowledge were too potent a snare. One blow of the cudgel took his senses. Another ensured he stayed silent while you bound him to the gibbet.*

*You wait. Your mouth is dry.*

*You know the target's name but do not speak it. Not when you tied the gag across his mouth. Not when you accused him, the words hissed in his face. He shook his head, offering nothing but denials. You cut away his clothes and shaved his scalp while he raged at you, anger causing cuts to his scalp. When you said what was to come he whimpered, begging for a way out. He offered names, and you took them. As the night passed you told him it had become May 23rd, and he wept.*

*You wait.*

*You wait.*

*Now, at long last, it is time. You go to him, struggling not to breathe in the foulness that has fled his body. You lift his chin and stare in his eyes one last time. He seems to search your gaze for hope; you offer nothing but righteous resolve. He screams into the gag, and you silence him with the cudgel.*

*You peer outside the stable. There are no lights at any windows overlooking the narrow alley. You move the cart through the doors, grateful for the sacks you tied round its wheels to hide their noise. Pushing the cart with the target bound to the gibbet is not easy, but you will not fail. You made a vow.*

*You reach the end of the alley when it meets Piazza della Signoria, the most important square in all of Florence. This is where citizens gather to celebrate and protest. This is where the people come when they want to change the way things are in their city. This is where it happened all those years ago. This is where it must happen again.*

*You smile. The piazza is empty.*

*You push the cart into the centre of square, ignoring the looming silhouette of the Palazzo della Signoria, a symbol of the power held by so few over so many in Florence. No doubt those few will judge what you do here, while others may applaud. No matter.*

*You strike the flint, sending sparks into the dried hay and paper and tinder.*

*The sparks catch to become a flame, and the flame becomes a fire.*

*You stay until tongues of heat are licking the target's skin.*

Carlo Strocchi couldn't remember what it was to sleep for a whole night. As a boy he had slumbered like a stone, or so his mama always said, a sleep so deep nothing could wake him. When he came to Florence the sounds of the city at night were different from the small Tuscan village where he had grown up, but Strocchi still found little difficulty in sleeping until dawn. After Tomasia came into his life he had slept less, but that was because of their hunger for each other. His sound sleep returned when Tomasia was with child.

But Strocchi doubted he had known two hours of sleep side by side with Tomasia since Bianca was born. She was a beautiful bambina, six months old now. Leaving her tore a hole in his heart each morning, but coming home at night filled his heart again. Strocchi loved everything about his daughter. But she did not, could not – would not – sleep through the night. Was that unusual? Strocchi had been an only child himself and knew little about infants. In the months leading to Bianca's birth he had known so much fear. The prospect of becoming a father was what it must be like to stand before the sea, waiting for the tide to come in.

Now all he knew was exhaustion.

How could a soul be so tired, so weary? Tomasia tended to Bianca most nights, but Strocchi did what he could to help. He hummed the lullabies Mama had long ago sung to him, rocking Bianca in his arms until she drifted back to sleep. Yet no sooner was she nestled in her cot than she would wake again, often as Strocchi was returning to bed.

How did other parents cope? How did they keep going?

If nights were bad, the days were worse. He would stumble to the Podestà, struggling to stay awake while Bindi complained about whatever was vexing him that morning. The segretario seemed even more disagreeable now Strocchi was close to becoming an officer. As a constable he had been spared much of Bindi's wrath. Not anymore.

Once Bindi's tempests had finally blown themselves out, Strocchi faced long hours of patrols and questions and lies. Then he staggered back to the narrow rented room in the city's western quarter. A single smile from Bianca could lift his mood when he got home, but the restlessness of her nights made Strocchi weary to his bones.

Tomasia finished feeding Bianca and put her down in the cot before coming back to bed. Strocchi rolled over, nuzzling himself into her back and buttocks, sharing his warmth with her. Even when he was this exhausted his cazzo still twitched at Tomasia's closeness, enjoying her presence. She reached back to slap him away. 'Not now, Carlo. It's too hot.'

Summer had come early this year, and the nights were already sweltering. He didn't blame Tomasia; the instinct was more reflex than lust. It had taken them a while to find a way back together after the birth, and their mutual weariness did not help. But being close to Tomasia always comforted Strocchi, soothing away his cares as sleep wrapped itself—

'Is it here?'

Strocchi jolted awake. Someone was shouting outside. But it was still dark, which meant it was still curfew. Only those with authorization were permitted on the streets at night, and few had that other than the Otto's night patrols. No, please don't let it be—

Before Strocchi could finish his silent prayer, heavy feet were stamping up the stairs. A fist beat at the door. 'Strocchi, you there?' someone called from the landing.

That woke Bianca. She was crying by the time Strocchi got up. He lifted her from the cot and handed Tomasia the baby before stalking to the door, muttering dark curses all the way. Strocchi opened the door to see which fools had come calling. It was Benedetto, a fellow constable banished to night patrols by Bindi, along with another idiota whose name Strocchi couldn't recall. Manuffi, perhaps, or Maruffi? It didn't matter.

'What do you want?' Strocchi kept his voice a terse whisper, the sound of Bianca's cries behind him a dagger in his ears.

'There's a fire,' Benedetto replied, 'at Piazza della Signoria.'

'Why wake my family and probably everyone in the street to announce that?'

The other constable – Manuffi, that was his name – attempted an ingratiating smile. 'The segretario always says if we see something on night patrol, something that won't wait until sunrise, we should find an officer and tell them.'

'I'm not an officer,' Strocchi said. 'Not yet.'

'But we knew where you live.' Manuffi pointed at Benedetto. 'Well, he did.'

'What kind of fire?' Strocchi stepped out onto the landing, closing the door behind him. With luck, whatever had happened would be some foolhardy prank by drunks lurching home long after curfew. But the grim edge to Benedetto's features said otherwise, as did the heavy pall of woodsmoke seeping from the constables' tunics.

'A cart, set ablaze in the piazza,' Benedetto said. 'There was a gibbet nailed to it.'

'A gibbet?' Strocchi wasn't sure he had heard right.

'Like a gallows,' Manuffi added, 'for hanging someone.'

'I know what a gibbet is,' Strocchi hissed. There was more than woodsmoke clinging to the pair; another odour tainted them: roasted meat. Strocchi's belly rebelled at what that meant but he still had to ask. 'Was there a body on the gibbet?'

Benedetto nodded, his eyes cast down.

'Santo Spirito,' Strocchi said, making the sign of the cross. Who would burn a body in this way, and in such a place? What madman would choose to— No. There would be time for questions later. 'Is the cart still burning?'

'Yes,' Manuffi replied. 'At least, it was.'

'Who did you leave there?'

'Leave there?'

'Is one of the other patrols at the piazza?' Neither of the pair responded. Strocchi shook his head. The fools had not realized one of them should remain with the cart while the other came to fetch him. Such stupidity was little surprise from Manuffi, but Benedetto should have known better. 'Return to the piazza, both of you. Nobody else is allowed near the cart, understand me? Nobody. I will be there as quick as I can. Go.' Still the pair remained where they were. 'Go!'

Strocchi went back into his home as the constables thundered downstairs, the faint smell of sour milk comforting after the stench that had clung to Benedetto and Manuffi. Tomasia was sitting up in bed, nursing Bianca. 'I washed your hose and tunic. They're hanging over the chair, should be dry by now in this heat.' Strocchi nodded his thanks, already pulling off his nightshirt. 'How long will you be?' she asked.

'I don't know. Hours, if what they said is true.'

Tomasia grimaced. 'I heard.'

'The whole building probably heard.' Strocchi pulled on his hose, shivering despite the warmth in the air. 'Burning a body in Piazza della Signoria? It's madness. The whole city will know about this within hours.'

'That's probably why the piazza was chosen. Whoever did this, they want everyone to know. They want the attention.'

After shrugging on his tunic, Strocchi leaned over the bed to kiss Tomasia and Bianca. 'I'll be back when I can.' He strode from the room. There was nothing to fault in Tomasia's reasoning. But it asked a more troubling question: if burning a body in the piazza was a stratagemma to get attention, what would those responsible do next?